Saga of the Dead Men Walking

Snowflakes in Summer

Book I of the Snowflakes Series
The Battles of Coldstone's Summit

Joshua E. B. Smith

CONTENTS

Acknowledgments

Prologue   1

I   A Chill in the Air   8

II   Snowfall   13

III   A Winter's Wind   30

IV   Tip of the Iceberg   42

V   Dead Cold   48

VI   Frost's Bite   69

VII   Hailstorm   103

VIII Rimes Awakening   140

IX   Warm Welcome   155

X   Lost in the Frost   167

XI   Glacier's Peak   180

XII   Blizzard of Truths   206

XIII Avalanche of the Dead   242

      Compendium of the Damned, the Divine,   257
      and All Things In-Between

      The Saga of the Dead Men Walking   267

      Welcome to a World...   269

ACKNOWLEDGMENTS

If you're reading this, you're reading what I should probably (but won't, for legal headache reasons), a "second edition." What's the difference?

About four long years of self-taught education.

Seriously, that's the difference. Learning better ways to format a document, better ways to design covers, better ways to engage in the dreaded concept of 'write to market,' and better ways to edit.

I want to say better ways to advertise but of all the things I am, a marketing genius I am not. (So if you bought this after reading an advertisement – You. Are. Awesome.) Or it's entirely possible you've 'updated' the book on Amazon and picked up a more recent e-book variant.

Either way.

Snowflakes is still my baby, four years later. This is the start for me of a lot of things, good and bad; hundreds upon thousands of hours invested into the series, thousands of dollars sunk into publishing, time, effort, energy, frustration, tears, drinking, sobriety – so many emotions, so little time.

Biggest difference:
I added a bit to the prologue. Weirdly – and this may seem out of the way if you are just picking this up for the first time – I was told that starting with the flowery high-fantasy setting made it sound like it was a romance, and not a grimdark fantasy series. So, A Change Has Been Made(tm).

I promise, even with the Order of Love the first and foremost focus on the story, that isn't the case.

With that said, SFIS starts a brutal series of blood, guts, tears and gore. I honestly mean it when I say, from the bottom of my heart, that I hope you enjoy.

~Joshua E. B. Smith
Author, the Saga of the Dead Men Walking

PROLOGUE

I have known Akaran since he first was brought to the Order.
Even then, others in our ranks believed him to be unsuitable.
Unreliable. Undisciplined. Unstable.
Yet, it was not our decision to make.
We were told to accept him, and thus we did.

He survived the training. Excelled in some exercises.
Failed others, with some degree of flair.
His approach was cocky, violent, and frequently terrifying for
all those involved. But he still survived every situation we placed him in,
and always on his own. He flinched but he fought,
the one often leading to the other.

Eventually, he reached the pinnacle of his lessons.
There was no more we thought we could teach him.
Every exorcist has one final trial, a task,
a simple quest to be undertaken on their own.
Once completed, they are sent into the world to bring the warmth
of the Goddess of Love to those things that are Her anathema.

There was... a simple disturbance.
A haunting. A simple haunting.
It was just... there was snow. It was just ice, and snow.

We knew there was a wraith.
A wraith that made and was made of ice and snow.
That is what it was, that is what we could sense from afar.
Please do understand, please let me speak it again:

*That **is** what it **was** and we sensed **that** from afar.*

All these years later? Through the battles and through the Crusades?
Even after Civa? And Agromah? Even after Draedach, Roschell, and
Zordak?
I still don't understand how he could have made such a 'simple haunting'
so complex, so disastrous, so brutal, and so caked in frozen blood. So
much blood.

Snowflakes in Summer

I do not know how he did it.

*And **I** was **there**.*

~Sir Steelhom
Office of Oversight
Order of Love

The only sound came from the steady 'drip, drip' of rancid blood onto the old stone floor.

The audience looked down at the mess in numb, mortified silence as their stand-in proctor shook the bloody mass on his fingers free. The chunks joined the steaming body at his feet. It wasn't the first execution of the day, or even the hour. It was more of a mercy killing than a passing of judgment, though that didn't make it easier to stomach. The smell alone made it difficult.

It was one thing to kill someone. They didn't have much of an odor at first. Maybe an iron odor if there was enough of it. Shit and piss, maybe. Certain gut wounds or a rough disembowelment would stink up a room in a hurry.

But their guest-proctor hadn't killed just *someone*.

The rotting, putrid corpse shifted as it slowly disintegrated from the inside out. Little blue flames coursed up through the back of its torso and out of its decaying ribs. "There's no end to the ranks of the dead," their proctor intoned as he walked across the floor, "and no end to the sheer volume of depravity that spreads out of the Abyss. The ones we want you to reflect on today are the ones that look like us."

He wiped his hand on the side of his smock and approached the third corpse chained upright on an old post sunk into the ground. "They look like us because they used to be us."

A few startled sounds erupted from the audience as they looked down into the training pit. The amphitheater was indoors, though buried half-underground with a single set of steps leading outside and a slightly arched roof overhead that was open to the elements. When the Order needed to, they could close the arches off with shutters – just in case they needed to act in the dark.

You could smell the ocean breeze outside, and there were vents along the lower walls where seawater would rush in every high tide and help scrub away the day's training. That breeze was the only thing that kept some of the students from throwing up. That, and the knowledge that if they did, they'd be responsible for cleaning up the pit when their proctor was finished.

"Most of the monsters in this world – the *real* monsters, not the preternatural creatures – are stupid. They're echos of the past. Or they're the result of wild magics run amok. Or they're the result of necromancy," the one-eyed priest said with a slow nod at a pale-faced man standing nearby. "But sometimes, they're souls. Souls like the ones we have. Souls that should be elsewhere, but aren't."

"But once a person dies, don't the Gods judge their souls and send them to the Abyss? How can they get out?" one of the students asked from the upper gallery.

"Well, for one, not all souls go to the Abyss, for which we should be grateful," he answered with a grin that made his goatee bob. "For another, we don't know why the Gods let some souls free. We assume the Fallen permit it to sow discord in the ranks of the world, but others? Or how any of them get past the Warden of the Pit?" he shook his head and shrugged. "Not even the First Exorcist knew that. What we know is that sometimes, they do," he said as he laid his hand on the shackled corpse.

The corpse twitched. Then it flinched, groaned, and twisted. His touch woke it up from the slumber it had been placed in. It struggled against its chains and tried to pull away from the post it had been fastened to. The abomination looked up at the students with long-empty eyes and a jaw that was only held up by a few last strips of muscle and flesh that hadn't given up yet.

"There are two types you'll encounter in the wild more than anything else," he began as he pulled a stained steel hammer out of it's sheath on his hip. "*Arins*. Wraiths – spirits of the dead, or residual magics taken form. Some arins can take over a corpse and animate it – again, how? Well, I'm not much older than the rest of you. Ask him," he said as he pointed up at a fully-armored priest standing by the door, "but get ready for a *long* lesson."

The older, gray-haired man cleared his throat and his eyes flashed with mirth – among other things. "I only give long lessons so that you can have a long life."

"I didn't think we got to live long lives," his student – and their stand-in – said with a laugh that wasn't really all that joyful, "and this thing lead too much of one. This is a *corpusal*. Most people know them as the common name — zombies, walking corpses, whatever. *We* know differently. *We* know differently because not every corpusal is alike. Some are just like this sad creature; broken, beaten, decayed, and more dangerous to itself than anyone else. Still dangerous, but not always."

He hefted his hammer and drove it hard into the side of its head. The skull crumbled and gore showered his face and the upper part of his tunic. The monstrosity stopped moving and slumped forward as he pulled the chunk of steel free from its skull.

"Take their heads. Magic tends to focus on the skull. We know that the gunk inside a head makes bodies act like bodies. Break that, and the rest of the body stops moving until it can be burned later. *Usually.*"

He let the word hang in the air while gore dripped onto the floor at his feet and the real proctors excused the class. When the last few students made their way out of the training pit, the one he had called out to made his way down to join the stand-in. "Well, Akaran, that went well."

"Speak for yourself," the pale-skinned, older man beside him wheezed. "Do you know what it takes to put these back together?"

"I'm sure the Holy General might be willing to take time off for good behavior," the proctor replied with a sneer and a dirty look. "Or your head, one or the other."

The one-eyed priest coughed into his glove. "Be kind, Brother Steelhom. What was it you told me? Sometimes to clean the sewer, one must befriend the rats."

The necromancer gave them a ghastly look as his lower lip quivered, but he shut up and went to work unhooking the corpses from their chains.

"Rats aside," the older priest retorted, "thank you for providing this lesson. I know it wasn't what you wanted to do today."

"No, I wanted to go put some time in on the sparring grounds. Why did you send me down here into the meat grinder?"

"We do not call this room the 'meat grinder,' my boy."

Akaran shrugged and wiped a bit of brain matter off of his shoulder. "No, *you* don't. Everyone else does. My point stands."

The proctor let the remark slide. "Another test. Most places that the Order goes, the average Queen's citizen can't tell their asses from a hole in the ground — let alone the difference between a wraith and a ghost."

"One is the sentient, or semi-sentient, soul — or dark energy, wild magic, or the like that's manifested as a conscious being," Akaran recited, "the other is remnant of someone that's passed over. Acts more like an echo, or fixates on someone that's wronged them in the past. Neither are all *that* dangerous unless they've been... *enhanced.*"

"Yes, exactly. The ability to explain that is important. You won't convince people to do as you tell them if you cannot give them reason to believe you – no matter how loud you yell about the authority you possess," the Steelhom answered earnestly. "Which brings me to why I am here."

Akaran stopped his futile attempt to clean off his tabard and frowned. "I don't like the sound of this. I'm not going to spend the night stretched out along the beach, am I?"

"Not if the Sisters have their way about it," he replied as he gestured past the open roof and toward a massive tower that wasn't that far off in the distance.

"The Sisters? What do they want?"

"You," Steelhom replied as he looked up and out of the pit with his perfectly pale, iris-free eyes. Years of magic had discolored his irises entirely, and while it hadn't left him blind, the haunting empty look in his eyes was unnerving at best.. "My understanding is that they've had your name on their lips all day. The wind is whispering, Akaran, and they've been listening to it all day."

His student took a deep breath, nodded his head, and preemptively went to go pack.

The view from the top of the Temple of Love was one that very few people would ever see. The highest point of Southern Dawnfire, the tower even eclipsed the Queen's own loft (a fact that the royal only tolerated because the distance between the two was so great she didn't have to see it). It was one of the two largest towers in the known world – contested only by the Citadel of Civa Prime. It was said that from the top of the domed tower, you could feel the warmth of the Goddess's very breath on your skin. That you could see the ripple of Her beauty if you looked out to the ocean.

There was so much of it and about it that was shrouded in so much mystery and mysticism, any story could have been true and none would have been the wiser. Stories of how the room was built of the purest white marble (it wasn't). Or how the top of the dome was open to the sky so one could look and see the moons and the smell fresh air from the sea (that was silly; it was on a coastline, and it rained there as much as it did anywhere else – probably more – so if it was open to the sky all the time the entire tower would have flooded out decades ago).

The stories would speak of the glory of the Sisters of Love, the ladies tasked to hear the words and whispers on the wind from the Goddess, so in-tune were they with Her desires. The stories would say that no mere woman could match them for their grace and their poise. Hushed whispers stolen between scribes and pages would awe at rumors of their beauty, for if they were chosen by the Goddess Herself, they must be of angelic stature.

But in truth, Love takes many forms and knows no one shape or size. It was not the beauty of the Sisters that made them instruments of Her will. Nor was it their elegance or radiance.

There were many stories. Stories of women draped over silken pillows, lost in a hazy fog of incense and heady herbal concoctions as they sipped the finest of wines from gold and silver goblets. Stories of the most resplendent of sheer silken robes that adorned their skin, or in the minds of many, a marked lack thereof.

The stories that were the most important were not the ones of wishes and daydreamed hopes. The stories that were of true importance began with a whisper in the wind. They began with a voice that only the Sisters were (falsely) believed to hear. Words spoken to them, things so far off in the distance that nobody else could manage to tell were even there.

Those stories, and one of the greatest of their stories, began on a summer eve with a few wisps of clouds that hung high in the sky. It was the first time, but not the last time, that the Sisters of Love would find themselves surprised by the chaos that stirred within the Order. It was in the halls below them, on the beaches they could see. It was chaos that lived with them and was trained by them by divine edict.

It started with a whisper.

Two of the Sisters heard it and understood it. They listened to it even as a girl – a small, blonde thing, barely a waif, barely a girl – rushed from the Capitol bearing a message from an outpost far away from any place near a beach. Or near warmth. Or near any of the other places that the up-and-coming priests or paladins or scribes or healers would have enjoyed being sent to. The least of those was the agent of love-condoned madness in their ranks soon to be tasked to deal with this... disturbance.

They knew the message before Daniella could even get close to the tower (they even knew her name, so detailed was the whisper that flitted into their ears) and they knew who was to be sent to deal with a single, simple problem (oh were they ever wrong about *that*). They scried for as much as they could and they determined that the threat was real, but minor (even clairvoyants could have bad days). A small darkness had taken the gaze of the Lady, and She wished it brought into the light of day.

They had an edict crafted before word could reach them, leaving all to wonder more and more about what powers they truly had. When did they know of disaster? Did they really speak to the Goddess, did they possess some kind of future sight? Those were stories they would never tell.

Their part in the story had now been played. Content with that, they returned to their diversions as they looked out to the beach and down to Her followers milling below. They stood with smiles, and stood in the sheerest of silk robes, while sipping the finest of wines from little gold and silver goblets.

Not all of the stories about them were wrong.

I. A CHILL IN THE AIR

The town of Toniki had a serious problem; a problem old, a problem odd, and a problem, well, quite cold. It seemed that despite the best efforts of nature to let rain fall on this sad little place in the mountains when and as it should, the only thing that landed upon the hundred-and-a-half heads of the merry men and women of this lovely local town were snowflakes. This was hardly appropriate.

Now, to be honest, the heat of the sun didn't often fall upon the lovely people of this lovely village; no, they had the luxury of enjoying about four months worth of lukewarm temperatures and rain before the icy grip of winter reached down from the skies and strangled their village with snowdrifts and blizzards and icicles for good measure. It was neither an easy life nor a fun one. But it was a life, and it was theirs.

But now, it seemed, even those few months of rain had been stolen from the village – and they were getting quite upset about it. While most of them considered the Goddess of Ice to be a frigid bitch, She wasn't normally known to be excessively cruel. Winter happens, and in the mountains, it never tends to be pleasant.

Still, you see, without the rains the herbal remedies that they made from the plants that grew in the surrounding passes and valleys couldn't be brewed. With the roof of the local mine collapsed from the weight of the snow and ice above it? And the larger of the highways ruined from an avalanche, leading travel to and from Toniki to take days longer than it should? Without those, the town had little to trade. In the eyes of the Kingdom, it made the entire area just about worthless to everyone on the outside.

Just as unfortunate, it also placed undue (and unwelcome) need to rely on healers and priests from the Orders of Light or the charlatans that posed as them. Up to this point the need for such aid was at a minimum. What needed to be done could be managed by the dwindling stores of the village alchemist while critical care could be granted by an outpost of the Queen's Army at the bottom of the mountain. It was an inelegant solution for an inelegant time.

The weather was not their immediate worry, depressing as it was (and really, it should've been – as signs went, unceasing winter was a big one). Their immediate worry began when they started to hear the howling. True, there were wolves in the woods. The path to the upper mountains and outside of the borders of Dawnfire were fraught with wildlife that was not always so welcoming to people. Or as a bevy of bears, wolves, and the occasional mountain troll called them: dinner.

So the howling, when it started, was also at first ignored.

Before long, the howls were joined by the discovery of wildlife mangled into unrecognizable chunks. Worse still, those chunks did not appear to have been mangled by anything native. Not totally oblivious to this threat, they made a choice that they'd soon regret.

Hunting parties were sent to find the beasts and kill them before they threatened the peaceful people of the village. Sending them out wasn't a bad idea. It was perfectly reasonable and by no means a foolish choice based on the information they had available.

At first, the parties found nothing. Then they found tracks that looked like very large wolves. Later, they came back with tales of larger creatures ripped to bits which gave them cause for slightly more concern.

After a while, they simply quit coming back home.

They lost four people before they stopped volunteering to try and resolve it on their own. As questionable luck would have it, there was one person who might have been able to help if they just asked. Their main concern was not if he could help – they had a markedly high level of respect for the man – but if they could puzzle through the chaos on their own without having to rely on him. Magic always has a cost and his was no different; most of the village was happy to pay any price they could for his aid. But the elders weren't, so they waited.

There was a wizard that long ago had taken roost in a cottage a day away in a march that would take them deeper into the woods and further up the mountain. He wasn't well-liked but he had his uses. Respected, yes, but not well-liked. Unfortunately, he wasn't really the wizard that they thought he was and he had his own issues with the village.

That wasn't to say that the elders and the wizard weren't on slightly amicable terms. They traded on a regular basis: his skills with magework and magicraft in exchange for food and clothes and tools. All in all, no different than anywhere else. Still, his abilities were strictly and passionately involved in his "work," and even if he could have done much about a pair of supposed "wolves," it was anyone's guess as to if he would. Eventually though, they had to cave and find out.

Continuing their impressive run of foul luck, nobody could get close enough to his house to find out what or if he could do to help. A feeling of absolute dread filled them every time they got too close. Eventually, two brave adventurers dared to risk the trek and press forward against that feeling of doom and gloom.

One of them never came back. The other one ran and made it back home with fresh piss freezing in his leggings. He never spoke a word of it after; he never spoke again as far as anyone in the village knew. They found him missing from his home the next day, with all of his belongings packed up and his horse long gone.

About this time they finally started to show some inkling of sense and realized that the wizard hadn't come to see them in nearly a year. People began to wonder if he had turned against them, or if the source of the howling had made him vanish the same way their trappers and woodsmen had. Sure, he came to help by divining small springs or to make the odd bit of medicine with the town alchemist – a middle-aged, round-bellied woman who was more than happy to share the duties of managing the town with her brother, a butcher named Ronlin.

Aside from simple spells and a slight knowledge of medicinal works? That was all that most people really knew about him. There was a *lot* more to his story than that but most of the people were either not privy to it or didn't remember some of the older rumors that, back in the day, had entertained the village spinsters with gossip that went on for years.

With their numbers dwindling – people moving away from the village to find safety in the foothills, or leaving the province entirely to go someplace markedly warmer – Ronlin, in a fit of pure desperation, sent a missive to the army outpost a few days away at the base of the mountain. In response, seven soldiers were dispatched to tame the wilderness and wilds. You simply couldn't have terrified citizens going missing under the Queen's all-encompassing benevolence.

That would just be... unheard of.

And missing villagers? That kind of thing sets a bad precedent. It would just look *awful*. It couldn't be done. The garrison commander knew this and embodied it in all of his actions and his cherished duties. He hand-picked those seven men and bravely sent them into the ever so increasingly cold wilds to the north while he relaxed in the arms of his wife as far away from the cold as he could.

They were armed to the teeth.

They were not adequately prepared to defend against teeth, but they were armed to them.

Even in hindsight, the decision to call for them was the best one. Under normal circumstances they would have come and vanquished the beast(s). After, they would help banish the threat the stores of mead posed in the village tavern. They might have even mounted a daring endeavor to battle through the hazards posed by the village daughters and their hopefully wanton ways. That was the way the world was supposed to work. Even if there were questions as to if the mounting would be willing or not, it was the way the world was supposed to work.

The world disagreed.

The world was not supposed to spit three of the soldiers back. Nor was it supposed to leave two of them covered in festering scratches and drool that was paradoxically both frozen solid and so hot that it was steaming. It wasn't supposed to have one fall over dead within an hour of their return. It wasn't supposed to send the third into a catatonic state not much longer than that.

It really wasn't supposed to leave the healthiest of them so terrified that he begged them to call for aid from (almost) any of the priesthoods that comprised the Orders of Light. That was *not* something that the army on this side of the kingdom wished to do. Ever. True, the Orders had their uses – but this close to the border? No. Just, simply, no.

In the town of Toniki, what started as a few snowflakes and a disconcerting howl was now something that made them debate doing the unfathomable. Most felt that while the Gods were still to be trusted the people that worked for them scarcely were. Did they have a choice? If the army was of no use, if the bravest of the townsmen were unable to head north to find aid? Did they have to reach to the capitol of the Kingdom and call for aid?

Was there a choice?

After a lengthy – and (ironically) heated – debate, Ronlin sent his fastest rider down the mountain to rush back to the local army outpost and plead for help from the Orders of Light. *That* particular conversation didn't go over much better with the military than it had with the rest of the village. There were still protocols to be observed, regardless if they liked the thought of it or not.

They didn't like the loss of their brothers-in-arms, either. The military was not as obstinate as the men of the village and if the garrison's patrol couldn't handle it, there was no real shame in reaching out to those that could. Luckily for them, there was already a whisper in the wind that raced across the land faster than any of their missives could have hoped for.

Still. There was hope that someone from one of the Orders would be dispatched to solve the problem quickly and aggressively. A Knight of Purity, mayhaps, with a crystalline blade and righteous fury to banish the evils of the land? Or from the Kingdom's divine matron, the Goddess of Destruction? The army *unquestionably* cheered for their priests when they arrived. It could have even been a Steward of Blizzards from the Order of Ice (they were a strangely haughty bunch) for all they cared.

That would have fit perfectly for the situation at hand. Someone else thought so too.

Not that it did any good, but someone else thought so too.

The Order of Love was not the Order they expected to get. This was the kind of situation that they took seriously. Very, very seriously. Their reaction time to respond to an *issue* like this one was, as the Sisters were demonstrating on the other side of the Kingdom, borderline instantaneous.

On the upside, they did have their own way of sending someone somewhere urgently and their agent arrived faster than anyone elses's would have. The method wasn't necessarily fun or even comfortable. Or cheap. Though it worked. That was about all you could say about it.

This time was no different. When their representative hit the ground running, he actually did hit the ground. Upon receiving a face full slushy mud upon his deposit a few miles between Toniki and the outpost, their exorcist had to sit up and wonder something aloud. He started with profanity (it was well within his nature, even if it wasn't approved off by his superiors); words best not said in polite company nor ever to be recorded by any scribe. The point was made without hearing most of it though there was one poignant line within his expression of aggravation.

"Goddess, who in the fisking Heavens did I piss off to make You send me *here*?" The undignified arrival, and that statement, set the tone for his task.

II. SNOWFALL

The village had seen better days. Many of the houses were abandoned and dilapidated, while the village square had been reduced to a slushy mess of chilled mud and chunks of rock. There were a few animals loitering in the village – but just a few. Stalls that looked like they could accommodate a dozen horses at a time barely had four (he couldn't tell if the fourth was alive or dead and just propped up against the wall). With more than two-thirds of the settlement gone and the remaining third huddled together to try and find security and comfort against whatever it was outside, he did not have the most comforting of welcomes.

The people themselves weren't much warmer in their greetings. The first person he saw made such a commotion that half of the menfolk left in the town crept out of their hovels and demanded to know who he was and what he was doing there. He didn't even have to wonder if they would be warm to his arrival.

They weren't. At first they disbelieved him. It wasn't until after he showed them the emblem of the Order of Love hanging from his neck that their resistance started to crumble. He knew that there was reluctance in these parts towards priests as a whole, although you would have thought that at this point they would be at least willing to pretend to be happy to see him.

Their second response was to continue to cautiously question his intentions. Still, try as hard as he could, he really couldn't blame them all that much. He'd be nervous, too. It didn't help him feel better about any of this. Of course, *his* comfort wasn't important.

It wasn't until he took the heavy gray deer-hide cloak off of his shoulders that they really believed him (sigil be damned, apparently). He wore a thin chainmail tunic that went from his neck to several inches below his waist, and under that, a brown leather jerkin laced with wool under it. His legs were covered in much the same, though bound with some extra chunks of fur to keep the winter chill from ruining him totally. He didn't even care that he was sweating under the pile of clothes; it was better than taking a chill.

Over all of that, he had a white tabard with an image of two entwined lovers burned into the center. As uniforms went it was practical, even if not the most fashionable. Still, it got the job done, and it did help the Order stand out like a sore thumb in the midst of the garish outfits that the Dawnfire quartermasters leaned towards outfitting the army in.

Then again, maybe it was his age. Maybe it was because he introduced himself as a man that had completed his tutelage a month before. Or maybe it was because how proud he was over his freshly-minted sigil. It could have been any of those things, or maybe it was all of those things. Or maybe it was just because they didn't trust him, or if not him, the Order of Love as a whole.

Simply, even with their pleas to aid them, the locals just weren't all that comfortable with one of his ilk in their town. After they finally believed that he was whom he said he was, only two people were kind enough to offer him basic hospitality. That was fine. Rude, but fine. Still, they did have other things pressing on their mind.

Things like the soldier laying in a pile of blankets in small stone hut at the far-outskirts of the edge of the town. His name, they told him, was Lativus, and he didn't look good at all. They had him wrapped up in a swath of bandages that started where the lower half of his right arm should have been, and continued down his side. His face and other arm was covered in lighter scratches and burns that had started to turn into festering sores that simply weren't responding to any treatment that the local alchemist could provide.

Another soldier was with him, a man only slightly older than the wounded warrior. When he saw the priest, the chilly welcome he had been enjoying so far went a little bit colder. "The Army of Dawn requested a priest of one of the Orders of *Light*. Why did they send an *exorcist* of *your* wretched hedonistic temple?"

"Don't know."

"You don't know?"

"I don't know. They told me to come, so I did."

"We've no need for one of your kind. Go back, and tell them to send someone from one of the true Orders of Light. This is a task for a Knight of Pristi, not some low-ranking priest of the Harlot," he said without any attempt to hide his disgust. "If it isn't too late already."

Nope, no chance that the tone for this particular quest was going to improve anytime soon at all. "If someone else is needed, I'll go get them myself. *When* it is determined if I am needed, or not. I have yet to determine that."

The soldier cleared his throat and glared daggers at the exorcist. He looked enough like the wounded boy on the cot to be his brother. His face was covered in a scraggly unkempt black beard that violated at least half of the rules on how the Queen's men should be presented at any given time. Even in a disaster, there were protocols to be followed. Knowing the jerk would have to answer to a superior officer in the army at some point gave the exorcist a little bit of peace as he tolerated the abuse that rolled off of his tongue.

You could see the genuine worry in his eyes and there was a noticeable tremor in his hands. "I don't think that Lativus has that long. Please. Don't make this harder on him than it has to be. Just go, get someone that can help."

Akaran shook his head in response and placed a hand on the shredded soldier's shoulder. "You have no idea what caused this?"

You could see the desperate conflict in the soldier's face. "I... no. I've served as a medic in the Queen's Army for seven years. I've fought on battlefields against man and beast alike. I've never seen something that could ravage and poison a man like this."

"Then how do you know you don't need me?" the exorcist asked, quietly, calmly.

Whatever weakness he had first shown quickly turned back to scorn. "Because there's nothing that a follower of the Harlot can do to save him. I think he's even beyond the reach of the Pantheon above. The only thing a priest can do now is provide him a blessing to take his soul to the Mount, and that is something that your people have no right to offer."

With a shrug, the exorcist continued to run his fingers down the length of the dying man's wounds. "So we'll have to make sure that he doesn't die." The medic tried to make a retort, but he got cut off. "What's your name, soldier?"

"Tornias Morden. Medicinal Aid, attached to the Fifth Ray of Dawn."

"Combat medic?"

There was a short sigh. "Yes, if you must."

Matching the sigh with an equally short nod, Akaran pressed on. "Patron?"

"The Lady of Crystals, the Guardian of the Mount, Protector of the Pantheon."

"Ah. Pristi… Order of Purity." *That explains that*, he directed inwardly. *Snobs.*

Tornias gave a curt nod. "I cast my hand to Her services but I can only pray for Her aid. I've no skill with magic. A follower, nothing more."

That made the youngest man in the room smile. "Well. I do, so maybe we can meet in the middle."

"Your magic has no power against poison borne by beasts, not… not dogs," the medic argued, struggling to contain his sneer, "and I've heard enough stories of the things the Exorcists of Love do to know you've no chance of doing anything to help Lativus at all."

"You've never seen anything like what's happened to your friend, but you know I can't help." The priest drew a deep breath and affixed the medic with an annoyed glare that could have cut through him like a headsman's axe. "I wasn't aware that the army trained the medical corps in the art of foresight."

Shocked, he straightened up and looked like he was ready to punch the exorcist for his gall. "Who in the pits do you think you are to show such rudeness?"

The man from the Order of Love continued to stare at Lativus's bloody wounds out of his one (and only) eye. He wasn't sure what he was looking at, but the longer he did, the less he liked it. "Akaran DeHawk, Exorcist, under the hand of the Goddess of Love, Lady Niasmis."

"Rank?"

"Is it really that important?"

"You're not… no, they wouldn't…?" Tornias jumped out of the chair as he grabbed the boy's wrist. "A neophyte? They didn't just send an *idiot*, they sent a *boy* barely out of his *swaddle-cloths*? How *dare* your masters show this level of disrespect for their betters!"

The exorcist cleared his throat. "We're good at offending just about everyone. For what it's worth, I'm really about to piss you off. Oh am I ever gonna piss you off…"

"Choose your words carefully boy, or you'll pick your teeth up out of the snow."

Akaran pulled his wrist free and slowly slid the glove off of his right hand. He placed two fingers on Lativus's forehead and whispered a soft Word. "**Illuminate**."

The effect was instant but quiet. A ripple of light ran across and over the soldier's body. Wherever it touched a wound, a soft streak of blue light encircled it. Within seconds, a larger pool of light coalesced around an unblemished patch of skin over his stomach. Tornias watched, eyes lit with fury. "What... what are you doing to him? What did you just do?"

"Proven that you're wrong," he spat back. "Back away from him. *Now*." When the medic tried to argue, the exorcist grabbed his tunic and shoved him back and away with one hand. Before one of Dawnfire's finest could take a swing at him, the exorcist had a knife in his hand and pressed to the dying man's gut. "If you interfere, he will die."

Tornias hadn't even seen him pull the bejeweled weapon out of its sheath on his waist. "You *threaten* him? Remove the blade or I will kill you myself!"

"Just a moment." Before the furious medic could do anything, Akaran growled out another Word. "**Purge!**"

This time, the ripple of light was nowhere near as soft. The spell rushed down the short blade and illuminated a series of curves that had been carved into the metal, from hilt to tip. A cloudy white gem in the handle flared with a stunning purple glow that easily illuminated the room.

Nor was the edict met quietly.

A scream filled the room as the spell pulsed into the wounded man – and it didn't come from his mouth. A shadowy, vaguely human shape pushed itself up from his body for barely a second, and just as quickly, burned away to nothing. Akaran stepped back, flipped the blade in his hand, and put it on his belt as quickly as he had drawn it.

On the bed, Lativus took a long deep breath and sighed, still unconscious, but suddenly seemingly at peace. The pain on his face melted away to something far more serene. The next few breaths the wounded warrior took were desperate and deep, but after that, he was calm and then relaxed.

The medic looked back and forth at the two men with his mouth agape. "What was... what did..."

"What was that? What did I do? I did my job. If he can survive the wounds, he'll live. They weren't his biggest problem."

Tornias continued to stare, and edged closer to his friend. Akaran didn't try to stop him. "That doesn't tell me anything..."

He shrugged. "It tells you that the next time you decide to argue with an exorcist about if he can or can't help someone, you may want to *wait* to make sure that he actually can or cannot help with it before acting like I intended to sodomize the man with a goat."

"Insolent little... what did you do to him?"

"Whatever it was that tore him apart was steeped in magic. Utterly foul magic. Thank whoever it was that relayed the message to the Temple because I *really* doubt that he'd have lived to see tomorrow if one of us hadn't been sent." He snorted and crossed his arms. "What in the name of the Goddess did this to your squad?"

The medic ran his hands over his face and looked down at his cleansed companion. "How did you know?"

"I didn't. But you're a medic, and you couldn't manage more than to just bandage his wounds. You're on the edge of the Free Cities of Ameressa, which means that odds favor that either there's a Fellowship-trained alchemist somewhere in this town, or at least, there *was* one, and they probably left enough of their remedies behind that you could have treated him well enough to get him through the worst of the infection. Even if there wasn't, you could. That, or you're a horrible medic that shouldn't wear the badge."

"I treated with what I had and here you come and... what sort of spells did you use? What kind of harm did you do to his soul?"

"Your soul isn't damned just because you had an encounter with one of us," Akaran snapped. He gave the unconscious man one last lingering look before giving another shrug. "If you remove the natural, the supernatural is the only other option."

Tornias looked at him — really *looked* at him — and gave a slow nod as someone opened the door to the outside. "I don't know what to say."

"A 'thank you' would be appropriate about now. Or you can tell me what did this to him. Or both."

"I never saw... not clearly. Wolves, had to be wolves, no dog is that big."

Perplexed, Akaran looked down at Lativus and cocked his head to the side. "Wolves wouldn't do that."

Tornias re-affixed his apparent omnipresent glare back on the priest. "Then you tell me what could have. I don't know how many there were. More than one. Huge. Fast. Tore into us just as the sun set. Their eyes..."

"Their eyes what?"

"Reflected our torchlight. That's the only thing that makes sense. Their eyes reflected the torchlight. Had to be reflections…"

The exorcist opened his mouth to ask another very poignant question before someone else interrupted him. An older gentleman stepped inside and made a scolding sound. "As the priest said, a 'thank you' would be appropriate. Since you can't seem to, I will." He extended a hand towards the exorcist and gave him a respectful nod. "Thank you, Sir Exorcist."

"I'm no sir, friend, but… you're welcome."

With a head of thinning gray hair and streaks of it through a short beard down his cheeks and neck, the newcomer introduced himself. "My name is Ronlin, and I speak for the township. I watched you work through the window. Didn't wish to disturb, son, but I'll say it again. Thank you for saving his life. I pray it is not too late for the rest of us."

"It's why I'm here. At least, a little bit of why. I think."

"And now to make a lot of why. Is it within hope that you would know what hurt him so and killed the others?"

A different voice from outside the home spoke up to interrupt everyone (mostly just because she could). "How about *all* of you shut your mouths so the man can actually get some peace? Or do you intend to wake him up with your constant yammering?" The source of the voice peeked her head into the room and gave a scowl that easily trumped anything that the entirety of the township had shown the exorcist so far. "*Now.*"

Ronlin grimaced. "Exorcist, please excuse my sister. She is… abrupt."

"She's also right," Akaran reluctantly conceded. "He needs rest, and I need something to eat, drink. Something hot enough to warm my body or ale strong enough that I won't care. Is there someplace I can store my gear, and find a meal?"

"If I tell you where, will you let the man sleep?" She was short, plump woman with dark hair, and that look on her face could have stopped an army in its tracks.

The elder mouthed a "*Best to do as she says,*" to the exorcist, and quickly turned around. "Yes, yes, of course. Let's get the boy to his room and then we can discuss our nightmare further." With that, he was out the door with his sister in tow before the exorcist could get a word in edgewise.

As he was leaving though, the medic stopped him with a remark of his own. "That *is* the alchemist."

There was a growling huff of irritation from outside. "Yes, and I'll be right back in there to look at whatever mess you two jackasses left him in. Don't trust either of you fools to know the difference between a bandage and a bone saw."

Oh, Goddess, she's going to be a delight to work with, Akaran groaned to himself. *Here's hoping I don't have to.* "I'd expect nothing less, lady."

Tornias smirked. "I don't imagine you would, would you." The exorcist was going to leave it at that and pray he'd never have to deal with the medic again, but then the man said something else that helped mellow out the evening, even if just a little. "If he awakens, I'll let him know you saved his life."

That was the best that he was going to get, and he knew it.

Akaran took it with a smile and nod, and left to hopefully find something remotely resembling ale. However, well... he was about to find a whole lot more than just ale. And to his eventual chagrin, almost none of it would be good. He just didn't know it yet.

It wasn't a total loss, at least. There was ale, and there was food. It helped.

A quarter-candlemark later, and he revised his opinion of how much the meal actually helped. Still, it came with a hot fire burning in the middle of the room and something he was going to call a boar slowly roasting on a spit over it. It didn't quite taste like a pig, though it didn't taste awful. It was warm enough and was somewhat filling, so he wasn't gonna press the subject. There was plenty of room to doubt the ale, too.

Plenty of room. Oh is there ever plenty of room.

It took Ronlin about an hour to explain everything that had happened up to the point where Akaran stepped foot in town. He did talk about the unseasonable cold, and how it had gone on for a lot longer than it should have. As miserable as it had made life in the village, he assumed that it would be something that would pass when the mountain grew tired of the chill.

There was talk about the wizard that occasionally frequented the village. Akaran's interest went there right away. He peppered the elder with questions about him: What was his name? Where was he from? Was he registered with the Granalchi Academy? What branch of magic did he study and practice? How powerful was he, what could he do? Did he ever show any ability to command beasts, or commune with supernatural creatures that could do the village harm?

Ronlin had few answers. To the best of his knowledge, he never had control over any kind of animal, and he had never done the village harm. He had moved to Toniki decades ago but had been exiled for sins that Ronlin's father had never felt inclined to share. Being a wizard, he did what wizards naturally do – followed the letter of the law, if not the spirit.

While he did leave he didn't go far. It was several years after the death of Ronlin's father that he eventually made a return to the town. For whatever reason he never quite seemed the same; there was an aura of mistrust about him aimed at everyone near him. Over the years he occasionally interacted with the villagers and provided some basic aid; nothing more than that.

Outside of that, all he could do was give the man's name. "He called himself Usaic Olemir, and he never spoke of any kind of 'academy.'" The elder gave him a puzzled look. "The man's never given me cause to worry of his intentions."

"But you don't know why your father banished him?"

"Well, no, but..."

The exorcist tried not to show the villager his frustration and bit back a sigh. *A rogue wizard? A possibility. No idea on power or school of study? Could be anything from a necromancer to a combat mage to an elementalist, summoner, or even a deceiver. Not good. If he's turned against the town... well, he wouldn't be the first mage to go mad. Depending on what he's been playing with, he may not even know it if he has. Finding him is going to be key.* "Where does he live?"

"He... to be truthful, all I know is that he has a cabin to the north. I believe it's by Teboria Lake."

"Tornias thinks that his men were attacked by some kind of hound, or wolf. Have you had problems with things like that before? What were the soldiers after, specifically? A general patrol to hunt for the monsters out there, or did they seem to have an idea of where to look?"

"They were headed towards Usaic's cabin, I'm afraid. It was their third trip out after arriving. They didn't find anything before that."

"Suddenly they head to the cabin and end up dead? Oh now that *can't* be coincidence. So, Tornias said it was a pair of large wolves. Ever been harassed by an unusual pack of them before?"

"No more than what any other village would. We hunt, they hunt. It's as nature intended."

21

Chewing on that thought, the boy tried to figure out what else it could be. "What manner of beasts makes its home in these parts?"

The elder worked the thought around his head for a few moments and shrugged his shoulders. "Wolves, of course. Bears. It's rare to see a wild dog although it is possible a pack may have wandered up from the foothills... I can't think of a reason why our trappers wouldn't have been able to kill them. Or even those soldiers. I can't think of anything much else with fangs and claws and desire to use them."

"Nothing preternatural?"

"Preternatural?"

Akaran paused long enough to figure out the best way to explain what his instructors had bashed into his head over the years. "A creature born with magic that occurs naturally in the world. Something that... some creatures out in the wilds have their own abilities that fly in the face of the Laws of Normality. Simply, they exist because they exist."

"I still don't know what you..."

The exorcist took a short breath and expounded on it. "Sand-skimmers in Sycio can swim through the dunes without disturbing a golden grain. Lastratas fly in the skies about the Midlands, without a single wing on their serpentine bodies. Caveriks ignite their prey before gorging themselves on the ash."

"Oh, I see." He didn't, but he was willing to lie about it. "No, no, we've nothing like that at all."

"Then it may just be a pack of rabid dogs," the boy offered, for no reason other than to just assuage Ronlin's fears. It was as much of a lie as a lie ever could be.

*That poison left behind. That corruption. There's no dog in the world that can do that. It **has** to be something preternatural on the darker end of the spectrum or... it could be something natural that was exposed to Abyssian magic, ending up as one of the Defiled. Either way, I won't be getting much more about the monsters from him.*

Akaran's assumption was right: he wouldn't. The rest of what Ronlin could say about the animals in the area was scant and largely unhelpful. He was able to tell him where they had buried the remnants of the soldiers that had tried to help, and where they had disposed of the ruined bodies of the woodland creatures they had discovered.

He also gave him directions to where the patrol had been massacred. Tornias had told him so he could warn the rest of the villagers away from it. Ronlin felt that the exorcist would be better off having the information himself just in case he'd need to see where and what had happened.

He would. He wouldn't like what he found. But, he would.

When he finished, it was too late to go back into the cold. The morning would be different – some things are best left to deal with in the light. Just because he could purge the taint from the attack from one man didn't mean that he could deal with the things that had taken out a full patrol and some of the locals in the middle of the night. Since the creatures had stayed outside of the village grounds he wrote off the thought that the people were in immediate danger overnight.

It was not the first time the novice exorcist would be wrong.

Content with Akaran's confidence, Ronlin left the inn not long after they finished their talk. He failed to realize that the exorcist's bravado was borderline entirely false. Not only did he have no idea what was out there, he had doubts that he'd be able to dispose of it on his own. It *did* eat some of Dawnfire's finest, after all. He may have been able to lie to the elder about his confidence (or lack thereof) but he couldn't lie to himself.

On the other hand, there was one thing that helped him console his nerves.

Literally, she was on his hand.

Much to the innkeeper's chagrin, the young man had drawn the eye (and soon after the body) of his wife. In Akaran's defense he didn't have much say in the matter – granted, he didn't try all that hard to protest the situation. She landed on his lap the exact moment that the village elder left to go home.

She seemed to be utterly fascinated with his eyepatch and was the first person to like the sigil he wore. He was simply thrilled that the woman was helping him warm up. The fact that she was voluptuous was a bonus. Happiness was being had by most (except for her cuckolded husband, who really didn't approve of the situation), but it was being had by the two almost-lovers.

A nagging voice in his ear told him that he should have politely excused himself. He ignored it for two simple reasons: this far away from the capitol, who really cared about being civil? She apparently didn't. Also, well... it was hard to say 'no' when nobody had ever said 'yes' before.

But happiness was not being had by the woman that began to cry with a sorrowful (yet breathtakingly beautiful) wail outside of the inn – and her cries were nearly loud enough to wake the dead. Ironically, *that* would have solved some of their problems. Of course, they couldn't be that lucky. Such as it was the young exorcist was 'inspired and compelled' (words synonymous 'with being kicked out of the inn to do his damn job') to go out into the cold.

He had no idea why the innkeeper thought it was his problem. It didn't sound like the terrible growling that had been plaguing the area so far. A woman's mournful voice echoing through Toniki? Heaven forbid that these uncivilized settlers on the edge of the Kingdom wouldn't know a good thing when they heard it.

He suspected other motives behind his expulsion. He was right, but, he endeavored to hurry up regardless. Being in the cold and being away from the lovely lady Rmaci didn't make him any happier at all. His haste to return would be rewarded with a punishment in very short order.

Despite his best efforts, he couldn't understand a single word that lazily spun through the air. Her verse was melodic, it was soft, but the way it filled the beleaguered township made something in his heart feel like it had just lost the world. It really was beautiful. It flowed along the blustering winds like it belonged there; a beautiful poignant tune that coaxed a tear from his eye as he listened to it and looked at her.

When he caught up to girl, she was aimlessly strolling through the village. Her sad cries rolled freely from pale pink lips. Those lips adorned an equally pale face with eyes of the softest crystal blue. She walked with a gnarled wooden staff with a small white crystal upon it; the gem glowed just enough to help to light her way.

Her hair danced in the wind without a care. Long brown locks mixed with snow-white strands licked at her cheeks and neck, unfettered, free, and untamed. She was a few inches shorter than him, but from what he could see, she had the build of a woman that had been half-starved. There was an otherworldly, ethereal quality to her movements. She looked more like she was gliding or swimming through the air more than she did walking across the ground.

What she wore was impossibly careless. She had a thin wool coat draped over her shoulders, held closed by an odd clasp that looked like a pair of inverted blue "V's" on an amber oval with a silvery shine just below her throat. She hadn't bothered to wear gloves and the brown, threadbare wool and linen dress under her cloak? It barely looked like it would be enough to stop a warm rain, let alone the cruel chill in the air. At least she had on boots – tall leather ones that disappeared under her dress.

It was so cold under the starless sky that the first words out of his mouth weren't to express his quiet admiration for her eyes or the ache in his heart that her haunting song left in its passage. The wind was vicious as well. It whipped snow and ice into every crack of every building, hut, and abode in the village. No, what he said was something far less polite but equally as heartfelt.

"Lady! Have you lost your mind? Come inside before you freeze!"

It wasn't the most eloquent of requests but it didn't come from the most eloquent of men, so he had an excuse. It did, at least, serve to gain the attention of the grief-wracked young maiden. "I am lonely. So tired. So tired," she pined. She looked at him with eyes full of tears. "Will you help me?"

With every thought of the eager woman in the inn banished from his mind in a sudden rush of 'chivalry,' the exorcist trudged through the snow and took her by the hand. "My name is Akaran. I'll help you with what I can. But not out here."

"But it is so beautiful out here," she sighed. "So pristine; so pure! A faint shadow of home but so close to home even so far away!"

"So right bloody cold," he snapped. "You may not have bits on your body that don't object to this weather, but I surely as all do." His grip tightened ever so slightly and the girl relented. "What are you doing out here? You can sing inside, can't you?"

"I could, but why?" She didn't offer anything else to say until they reached the door to the inn. "I am lonely, so tired. Too much to do. Must we go inside? I've far too much to do."

He looked her up and down before unleashing a deep sigh that turned to fog before his eye. "Girl, you're practically frostbitten – being lonely is the *least* of your concerns. If you're missing companionship that much I'll see if I can't find you a stable-boy. Or a priest. Or a priest and a barmaid if you both would want."

"Frost doesn't bite. You don't understand," she whined. "My lord has been locked away and I cannot reach him! I am lost without him. Work still to be done to reach him. Much work. You were sent to help, yes? Are you the help that was spoken of? You must help me find a way to rescue him!"

After giving her a look typically reserved for the lame, the inept, or the terminally stupid (he wasn't quite sure which one to peg her as), he gave a quick answer to encourage her to do anything else other than stand outside. "Tomorrow, if the weather permits, I'll aid you. Tonight, you must come inside."

"But if I come inside what help will there be? The help needs to be outside here, not inside there!"

Instead of answering her, the priest turned his back to the girl and walked back to the tavern. Frustrated, she followed, but it wasn't until he stepped inside that she realized he was serious. She gave him a sad, heartbroken stare before she bowed her head and reluctantly followed him inside.

Once within, he steered her towards the smoldering fire in the dining area and sat her down. What he didn't notice was more telling than what he did – while he noticed she looked a fright, covered in snow, with ice nestled in the wrinkles of her clothes, he failed to realize that the closer she got to the flames worse she looked. "Tell me your name."

"Eos'eno," she answered, a slight tremble in her voice. "Must we be so close to the fire?"

"You need to warm up. Much longer out there and you'll end up frozen through and through." Exasperated, he took her hands in his and squeezed them. "Your grief will do you no good if you die of the cold."

She sighed and sank back against the floor after she tucked her legs under her cloak and her hands against her sides. "The chill is not to be feared," she complained. "So much nicer than the flame."

He mistakenly wrote her ramblings off as nothing and accredited her addled thoughts to her body being overwhelmed by frost. His assessment was only partially wrong. Still wrong, mind you, but only partially. "What were you doing out there?"

"Where else would I be?" Perplexed, she looked up at him. "Why waste such a lovely evening?"

"In bed, in front of a fire or some such. That was my plan, at any rate."

"But it really is beautiful, so beautiful out there, out in the open, where it is we belong."

This was obviously going nowhere. "You said you lost someone. Who?"

"My lord, Lord Usaic Olemir, an elementalist of great power. A master of magic." At the mere mention of his name she perked up, as if she was excited to even utter it. But that quickly turned to sunken disappointment and depression. "But he has gone. I must stay. Too much to be done. Must stay behind."

At the other end of the tavern, a few of the patrons stood up from their tables and backed away at the mention of his name. They all looked a bit confused at this new arrival and they thought it odd that she knew the mage. He missed them going on the defensive. He'd regret it.

Suddenly he liked this conversation a great deal less. "The wizard? An elementalist? I was told he was just a dabbler."

"No! Master has great strength! No dabbler. No weak-willed man. A master! My master!"

"What was his specialty?" The answer to that question was becoming uncomfortably apparent. He was inexperienced, sure, but not stupid.

"Akaran, who is this?" The innkeeper's wife had finally found the courage to creep out of her room. The wailing outside had sent her and some of the other villagers scurrying for safety. Curiosity (and lust) had finally won the day versus nerves and a feeling of impending doom.

He started to wave her back to her (and hopefully his) room, but the girl answered before he could. "I am Eos'eno."

"You didn't tell me that someone else came with you," she pouted from above. She hugged herself tightly and looked down from the balcony with confusion in her otherwise dim eyes.

The exorcist looked over at the girl and cocked his head off to his side. "Nobody did... you mean she isn't from here?"

"No, never seen her before. And I know every soul that comes through those doors." She brushed long strands of coal-black hair away from her face as she talked, her fingers clutching at the balcony rail.

He moistened his lips and started to size the waif up. "You're not from around here? Where do you hail from?"

"Hail? No, no hail. Hail is for the fallen. Snow is at home." Eos'eno looked at him and for the first time since he met her, a tiny smile started to form in the crook of her mouth. "Home is cold. Home is of *all* cold. *Tundrala.*"

Names have power. Some more powerful than others. Tundrala was not a city, nor a kingdom, nor a place for anyone with a pulse (and assuredly *not* waifish little girls like this one appeared to be). No. The Upper Elemental Plane of Ice was no place for mortal men or women. It wasn't much of a place for anything but the spawn of the Goddess Istalla Herself.

Either Eos'eno she was delusional, or...

...or blessed be unto the **Goddess**, *they may have sent the wrong person here for this job.*

Her proclamation set in motion a series of events that were inevitable once all the pieces were put together. He (incorrectly) thought it answered the question of who (or what) was the source of the cold. It *did* explain the girl's fear of fire, and gave a second reason for her skin to be so cold to the touch.

It also explained the sudden appearance of the sword in Akaran's hand and the tip of it against her throat. "In the name of the Goddess of Love, speak now and speak truthfully or be banished from this realm," he growled. Surprise covered her face as she scrambled backwards to avoid the point of the blade. "What is your purpose here?"

Her eyes had gone completely wide. "To find the help that was promised to come! To find you! To find the Guardian of Winters!"

"Find me? The guardian of *what*? Help for what?"

"To be reunited with my lord!" she exclaimed. A frozen jet of air and snow from out of nowhere punctuated her exclamation, and it knocked chairs over and extinguished candles. "Are you not my help? I mean no harm! I am here for the people of here! He commanded me!"

"A dying village says otherwise," he growled. "Leave our world on your own, or I'll remove you myself."

She drew herself up to her full height and then some. Her feet left the floor and her hair billowed out. A steady wind started inside the room and ice began to form on tables, counters, and chairs. "I will not leave without my lord and his work! You will not stop me! You are not the help promised to be! Liar in motive and lair in heart!"

Sometimes the wrong answer is worse than no answer at all. Words could have been said, but actions did truly speak louder. He covered the distance between them in three heartbeats but her powers were faster than his athleticism. Eos'eno leveled her staff at his chest and screamed something in her previously-melodic language at him.

It pierced his ears and made him drop his sword as he lifted his hands to protect them. The shout sent a wave of pain stabbing through them and into the back of his skull. The spell that followed? That hurt the rest of him.

Before he could even attempt to pick up his sword, her magic flowed into her staff. A gust of wind flung him into the closest wall. He faintly recalled hearing a shriek from above as the barmaid panicked at the sight of her 'valiant warrior' being flung across the room.

A spear of ice darted out of the staff and pinned him to the wall through the hood of his cloak. Another quarter-inch to the side and his story would have come to an abrupt (and irreversible) end. As it was, the impact of his head against the side of the inn was enough to take him out of commission. When the room quit spinning and the pain in his head shrank from blinding to bearable, he was able to stand up and see

28

that Eos'eno was long gone.

The only thing that marked her passing were icicles dangling from the rafters and a snowdrift in the middle of the floor. A few moments later and the storm outside calmed. He wasn't enough of an optimist to think that she was gone for good – and all thoughts of finding warmth buried deep inside a willing woman were dashed away with her.

When the girl pouted at him and asked why a short time later, the only answer he had didn't satisfy her. "Because I fear tomorrow will not be an easy day."

Finally, he was right about *something*.

III. A WINTER'S WIND

The next day brought a meeting of minds in an impromptu village gathering with the exorcist firmly at the head of the rally. The place was already on the cusp of becoming a ghost town well before last night's excitement – and now? The appearance of the extra-planar woman last night wasn't helping. Two more families had packed up to leave when Ronlin called them to the village square to try to convince them to stay.

Sadly, it wasn't likely that any kind of explanation Akaran could give them would help, either.

Not that he had one to give.

The gathering had most of the village on hand for it. It didn't take him long to pick out some of the people that Ronlin had mentioned last night. Vestranis, the blacksmith, was easy enough to pick out of the crowd. He had enough muscles in his arms and upper chest to look like he could pick up a barn on his own with a frown to match. The thought of somehow ending up on his bad side was one he would do his absolute best to avoid.

Then there was Rmaci, the lovely woman that had entertained him last night. Idly, she ran her fingers through a tangled mess of hair that was as dark as a chunk of coal. Her alabaster skin shone in contrast against it with soft pink lips and eyes tinged with hints of green. He'd be lying to himself if he tried to deny an overwhelming urge to see the rest of her and to feel those lips on his... everywhere.

While that thought warmed his, shall we say, heart, he caught sight of someone else. Beside her, there was Yothargi, her exceedingly ill-amused and ignored husband, the innkeeper of the Rutting Goat. There must have been a horrid story in his life; almost every inch of him was covered in scars. Most of his face and all of his scalp had to have been ravaged by flame. It must have taken a miracle for him to have survived whatever it was that he'd managed to live through.

Standing almost close enough to them to make a man wonder what kind of relationship he had to the unhappily married couple was one of the first people to greet him on his arrival. He was a pudgy, muddy-haired, hunched over woodsman that called himself Moulborke. So far the only impression he had left Akaran was simply 'drunkard.'

His gaze wandered over to the most eligible bachelorette of the village, a girl who went by the name of Mariah-Anne. It was hard not to notice her; she stood half a head taller than anyone else (except for Vestranis) and her blonde hair stood out in the sea of reds and browns. She didn't seem to be comfortable in the throng of agitated townsfolk. With a dismissive wave of her hand, she rolled her eyes in annoyance when she realized that she was now the center of his attention.

He had no idea if she had anything to offer to the discussion or not, but at least it was a (vaguely) friendly face. The others he couldn't really place. Oh, except for the town stable-master. Mowiat's claim to fame wasn't his brawn or beauty (or lack of). He had lost an eye years back, giving the exorcist someone to relate to. He also wasn't really the stable 'master' as he was the 'last remaining stable-boy. Either way, he made a note to visit him later on to see about the kind of mount that Rmaci couldn't provide.

There were a couple of others that he recognized from Ronlin's descriptions last night. Romazalin, the auburn-haired, middle aged farmer (one of two that hadn't yet moved away). She was with her two, quote, "rotten, worthless, and generally stupid children." She was flanked by the brothers Jacobi and Dillan Kalor. Neither of them would win a beauty contest, that was for certain. For that matter, they wouldn't score points on academic pursuits. Whatever their story was, their blank stare all-but ensured it wouldn't be told in the here and now.

All told though, he didn't get a feeling of warmth or welcome from more than two or three of them. He wondered if any of them really realized who he was or what he could do. That thought in mind, he steeled himself for what even he (with all of his inexperience fully in check) could tell was about to be an uphill struggle.

Sadly, he was right. So very right.

Ronlin announced him to the village from a raised platform in the middle of the square. He was welcomed as "Akaran, a priest of one of the Goddess from the Lower Mount of the Divine." That... well, that was just simply insulting, to put it bluntly. The Lower Mount held the divine Gods and Godlings that nobody gave a damn about or who had any measure of demonstrable power.

Even with the Upper Pantheon pissed at Her, Niasmis had more than just a mere 'measure' of power in Her works. She was all-but responsible for the Pantheon to even exist. If Her nature didn't manifest in the hearts of the followers of the Divine? They would have no worshipers, no temples, no glorious edifices, no real power.

Niasmis also had a chip on Her shoulder the size of both of Kora's moons combined in regards to the Abyss and all things in it for the hand that it had had in orchestrating Her downfall. That alone is why so many of Her children turned to the path of holy warriors and exorcists. One, it made them useful to the rest of the world (and thus, marginally tolerated). And two, She got to enjoy watching the pit-born suffer.

Love's a bitch, if you hadn't heard.

This was one of those rare times where someone actually entrusted Akaran to speak in public without a handler nearby. There would be some question later as to if his superiors should have someone on hand to watch his mouth every time he'd be in a position to talk to a crowd. Or to talk in general.

The answer to that question was, is, and always would be a unanimous **yes**.

Akaran cleared his throat as he looked around from the dais and continued to take stock of the locals. "Let's cut the bullshit. I'm here, I know you don't want me here, and I don't really want to be here."

Tendencies to make bad situations worse or not – you couldn't fault him for his honesty.

"Then leave!" somebody from the back shouted.

"No." Try as he might, he couldn't see which of the village women shouted that out. She had to have been a younger lady but there was nobody he could put a face or a name to. "I know that when you sent a request to the local garrison to send aid this town, you expected someone from the Order of Purity. Or a Melian Knight. Or that somehow your plight would cause one of the Queen's Maidens to grace your frozen little border-town with her presence."

A murmur of agreement answered him and was joined by no shortage of nasty glares.

"You didn't get that. You got me. Since we agree that neither you nor I want me to be here my goal is to get this over with as quickly as possible so we can all go back to living our lives without further interruptions."

A *much* louder murmur went up from the assembled rabble. "What makes you think you can do it?"

He gave a shrug you could see from the other side of Toniki. "Because I'm the one they sent."

"That's it? That's all?" The speaker was a younger man in the front row.

Rubbing his hands together, he tried to watch their faces as he answered. "That's it and all. Look. Let me make this as quick as I can: the missive that the army sent back to the capitol declared your plight to be of demonic nature. Maybe it was right or maybe it was wrong. Whatever it was? It was enough to get the attention of the Office of the Holy General."

The reaction was immediate: about a third of the village cringed. The rest of the village *really* cringed. "We just need soldiers. More soldiers. That's all we need," a grizzled man from the back argued.

"The Office disagrees."

While they looked like they wanted to throw piles of horse shit at his face, they were wise enough not to press the matter further. Instead, they decided to attack him directly. "Why would they send a boy to come do it? What makes you think *you* are able to do this? Fisk your whore of a Goddess – what about *you*?" That question came out of the mouth of Yothargi, and every insult carried a mountain of loathing behind them.

It was neither the first time nor the last that the question would be posed. "Because I know better not to question the General, the Sisters, and the authority granted to them by the Queen. They *say*, so I *do*."

"What is it that you think you do?" This time, the inquiring voice belonged to the same woman that had told him to leave just a moment before.

"I make demons bleed."

Then it was Ronlin's sister that snapped up at him. "You? A boy your age makes *demons* bleed? How? Do they chip their fangs when they bite through your thick skull?"

"All the same I'd rather they not; or if they do, the hope is to make them choke on me all the way down." Later, he'd vaguely remember those words (and regret them). "Now, if we can move on? I am an Exorcist of the Order of Love. By rank and title, with the permissions of the Queen herself, I am to be afforded whatever supplies that I deem fit to requisition and I am to receive sworn testimony from anyone I deem fit to question. The sooner you help *me*, the sooner I can send whatever it is that's after the lot of you back into the churning flames of Gormith's gut where it came from."

Those were not the words of comfort that the village cared to hear. However, it stopped the insults long enough for him to get some details from the citizenry. "Speak quickly then boy; the sooner we're rid of you the better," Hirshma snapped.

"What do you folk know of Usaic Olemir?" After a minute went by with no response, he looked back down at the small rabble of unclean, tired, and chilled villagers. "Please. I'm here to help. Let me help."

The village elder was the first one to speak up. "Not much more than what I told you last night. He's a local wizard. More sleight of hand and trick than magic. Nothin' stronger than that, not that he ever showed us."

"The woman that attacked the town last night said he was powerful. You don't think he is?"

"No, not a one of us ever has had reason to." Pensively, the besotted leader repeated another claim he had about the mage. "He lived his life as a hermit. Whatever he did, didn't involve none of us."

Something about the way he said that made the exorcist give pause. "Does *anyone* know why he was kicked out?"

"Not that it's any business of yours, but he and father just didn't get along," Hirshma hurriedly interjected before anyone else could say a word. "Some menfolk just don't like each other. They never saw eye-to-eye on anything."

Akaran believed that less. Her brother moved in to agree with her just a little-too-quickly. "I couldn't tell ya, boy. If you weren't a soldier a miner or a blacksmith, father never really had much use for you. 'Course, could've been any number of other reasons, I suppose, but..."

"He never had much use for you even if you did." That came from the blacksmith. The silvery-haired tradesman spat it out with a snarl on his lips – no love lost there.

Frowning right along with him, the priest tried for a different approach. "Well. That girl... thing... last night said that the mage was no journeyman. I don't know why, but I've got a bad feeling that she wasn't just... I mean, I don't think she was lying."

"I thought she said he was some kinda, no, not a mage? She said he was an elementalist?" the (incredibly unhappy) innkeeper asked from somewhere in the back. "What does that mean?"

A few murmurs started, but nothing that the exorcist didn't stop quickly. "An elementalist is a mage that focuses on the very base building blocks of our world. Things like fire, or air."

"Or ice?" Ronlin asked, rubbing his chin.

Akaran bit his lip and nodded. "Or ice," he answered. "What do you know about the girl?"

He didn't get the response from that question that he was hoping for. The general consensus was that she had never been around the village. Nobody could think of any time when Usaic brought her about whenever he came to town. They couldn't even think of a time when he mentioned her.

That was less than helpful. Still, it cemented the thought that he was probably at the center of the attacks. But... "Does anyone have any thoughts that he might have grown angry with anyone here? Was he ever wrathful, did he ever do anything to threaten anyone?"

Again, the answers were a chorus of "I don't knows" and "not sures" went up from the crowd for a few minutes until Mariah-Anne spoke up. "If he was ever mad at any of us, he never showed it. I know I've not been here as long as most, but I never heard of the man causing harm to nobody. To me, having a wizard living nearby? Didn't seem that bad of an idea."

"Seems like a bad one now," someone grumbled from the back. There was a murmur of support for the speaker.

"You didn't say that when he helped your chilabi berries take root couple years back," Mowiat argued.

"Or when the western bridge pass fell apart, if you forgot about it."

He didn't realize the kind of debate he had started. "He wasn't much help when we asked him if he could help clear that small avalanche before he helped with my berries!"

Akaran tried to clear his throat to get their attention again. It didn't work. Resigned to the shouts, he opted to let the villagers vent a little bit of their anger at each other. *If they keep at it, maybe someone will say something helpful.*

He didn't have to wait too long (which was just as well; the wind had started to pick up anew, leaving his chin to start to freeze under his goatee). "Exorcist? My name's Peoran. Trapper by trade. I don't think they're being all-too-honest about his skills."

If looks could kill, a solid third of the villagers would have murdered the man on the spot. Sizing him up took just a moment; curly auburn hair peeked out from a hide cap that just barely covered his ears. "Howso?"

Peoran shifted a bit where he stood, his broad frame all but screaming 'soldier!' at the top of its lungs. Heavy scars crinkled across his forehead and cheekbone as he spoke. "About five, six some years back, a big fire engulfed half the valley to the west. The smoke smelled... horrid. Like rotting fish and brine. Now, we never figured out the cause of it but Usaic showed up right after I did. Dunno if he ever saw me, but I sure as fisk all saw him."

"I told you that you had to be seeing things," the alchemist interrupted. "Never saw him do anything out of sorts, never saw him do much more than just simple little tricks. Twisting nature around to do stupid, pointless things."

"He did install that fountain by the shrine," yet another villager added. "You know, the one he said was... um... oh, yeah – '*Water that flows by the grace of perpetual ice*.' Ain't that a lot of words for a simple wellspring?"

Patience fraying, the exorcist raised his hand and snapped his fingers (as best as he could through the digit-numbing chill). "Let the trapper talk."

Nodding his thanks, Peoran resumed his story. "Saw him lift his hands like so," he said as he lifted his arms up and outstretched from his side, "and as he did, a wicked as all blizzard sprang up outta nowhere. Could just *feel* something bringing it on. Know it wasn't natural. Put the fire out before it engulfed more than three, four acres."

*Weather manipulation? That is **not** a trick a hedgemage could do. Has to be ranked as at least an upper-level Adept. A cyro-kinetic elementalist? Explains the cold. And he's playing with a creature from Tundrala? Oh he is **so** going to get to have a talk with me.*

"Nobody else has ever believed me about it, but I know what I saw, exorcist. As sure as I do stand here today I do know it."

"That blizzard was a blessing from the Gods," Yothargi grumbled. "Would have turned our homes to ash. Ain't no simple wizard got the strength to halt a blaze that big. Simple wizard. That's all he is."

It was the trapper's turn to cast a dirty look. "You know as well as I do that the Gods don't care about us, never have, never will. Fisk 'em all, but I damn well do know what it was I saw."

Rmaci took the time to agree with – and add to – her husband. "Say what you will about the Gods. Though for all we know, he's the one that started that inferno."

"Naw! He had a healthy respect for the flame," Vestranis countered. "Didn't seem to understand quite how it worked though.

Acted like it was just… completely unnatural. Like it was his enemy. Oh, and he had the oddest request some time back."

The exorcist raised his hand and tried to snap his fingers. They weren't just a little numb by that point. They felt frozen solid. It made it sound like he was hitting a wool rug more than anything else. "Odd request?"

They ignored him. "But he *did* help with Jhen's wellspring! About saved the town when that awful cough cut through us, too. Made sure that Hirshma had all the herbs she could use to brew us up some relief!"

"Yeah well, with everything else going on, maybe he caused *that!*"

"**HEY!**" Akaran shouted, finally, finally, cutting through the din. "What kind of odd request?"

The blacksmith looked at him and rubbed the stubble on his beard. "Weirdest thing. He asked for some tips of the trade for tempering metal with ice some years back and startin' fires in snow, but that was about it. No, not in snow. *With* snow. Making ice burn. Strangest thing. Fire from ice. Thought he had lost his mind."

"And that's why I've *always* said that he's the one that started that inferno," the innkeeper grunted. "Don't know why any of you ever let him come back here after that."

Slowly, the exorcist blinked his eye and tried to make sense of it himself. *Probably did start the fire. But setting ice aflame? They're right; that IS odd as all.* "And he never said why? Did he say anything about it, at all?"

"Just that there were things that fire couldn't melt but it might be enough to crack open some kind of glacier to get something out of it he wanted. Weird stuff, strange things."

That made even less sense. "Well, maybe… Does anyone have any idea what he was working on out there? Why he lived here, and not someplace else? Anyplace else? Ronlin, if your father threw him out, do you know why he stuck around?"

"No boy, not a clue. He never talked about what he did or why. He'd just come help when we needed one thing or another. Never left with anyone, never took anything back to his cottage except for furs, wine. Stuff to live on. Odd though, one thing we never figured out."

"What's that?"

"Well… not too much land here to farm. Just enough for us, enough for our animals. None of our trappers ever saw sign that he was out huntin', less he was really stealthy about it. Not much to grab or gather in the winter months even in the best of times."

Akaran couldn't hide the half-laugh. When the elder gave him a confused look, he tried to pass it off. "You have to forgive me. I've just, well. Never heard of a stealthy wizard. They don't normally live quiet lives."

"Oh," Ronlin said, the mirthfulness completely lost on him. "I suppose if you say so. Can't say that I know too many. Guess you do, you have to."

The innkeeper pushed his way forwards. "So what are you going to do about that girl that tore up my tavern? Stand here and hope she can hear you – and gets bored to death listening to you talk?"

"I'm going to find out what she's doing, and send her on her way."

Off to the side, the blacksmith looked at him like he had grown a second head. "Send her on her way?"

"If she's where she says she's from, she isn't the one that ate the contingent from the garrison. **If**. I don't know if she *is* from where she said she's from, but if she is, she didn't kill those men. Tundrala is far from a welcoming place, but her aura wasn't black."

"And how would you know that?" a familiar, if not still shrill, voice piped up.

He looked over towards the alchemist as she made her way through the crowd. "Her aura is... different. It didn't leave behind the same stench as the thing that poisoned... what was his name? Lativus? What latched onto him was Abyssian. Touch it once and you'll know it for life."

"And how do you know she's not controlling them?"

It was actually a good question. "I don't. Not sure what those things even are. Yet."

"So you don't know if she's telling the truth, you don't know what attacked the men. All you've done so far is get the attention of some magical bitch, dragging the threat right into the middle of our homes."

Ronlin looked over at his sister with his mouth agape. "Hirshma! Watch your tongue. The boy is here to help, can't you see?"

"I can see that he doesn't really know what he's doing. Asking so many questions, dismissing the creature that strolled right into our town instead of going out right now and hunting her down. What good is standing here talking doing?"

Akaran looked at the plump little woman and considered the next words that came out of his mouth very, very, carefully. "Whatever magic has befallen here, whatever thing that girl may be, I can't rid you of it until I know what it is. You've lost enough lives here; I do not wish to add more Uoom's Ledger."

"And yet you invoke the God of Death – whom is it you really serve, hmm?" Hirshma quipped.

"Sister, mind yourself. The boy is doing what he can for right now. You can't go to war without knowing the battlefield. *Makaral, Niorma, Perniel; May the Berserker God and His vanguards give you a mind as sharp as your sword.*"

That was an odd blessing to cite. Makaral wasn't a God brought up by many except soldiers, mercenaries, or gladiators. Ronlin's alignment was worth noting for future reference. The dirty look from his sister wasn't the only response from the crowd that came to it.

"*Guide your mind as you would your heart; rushing into a task is as dangerous as rushing into desire and lust,*" Rmaci added with a smile. He missed Romazalin giving her a strange, befuddled look after she spoke.

For people that claim to hate the Gods, they seem to have a fondness for some of them. He had to give a brief pause and a hard *look* at the innkeeper's wife before the alchemist scoffed at all three of them. *Why is that woman quoting from the Tenants of Love?*

Hirshma dismissed him with a wave of her hand. "That girl came after he used his magic. Magic attracts magic. That is all that it was. Probably came to see if he was worth killing. If the creature decided he wasn't of threat to her, why should we think anything of what he *supposedly* can do?"

This was quickly turning into an argument that he didn't want to be involved in. Frustrated, the young priest offered up another opinion to try and soothe them. "Listen everyone. Your haunt last night seemed a lot more agitated about not being able to find Usaic or to even get near wherever she thinks he is. She hated that more than she hated me. I don't think she'd intentionally hurt anyone that lives here."

"She threw you across a bloody room!" the barkeep's wife shouted.

He shrugged. "I came at her with a sword and threatened to kill her. I would have thrown me too. Then she ran off right after. She could have gutted me and torn apart everyone else in the tavern if she really had wanted."

"You're a forgiving bastard then, aren't ya, holy man? She ain't normal, she ain't natural. That means it's your job to cut her down and scatter her ashes to the wind, isn't it?"

"It means that my job is to discern the best way to bring peace, and to protect the people of the world from anything tainted that may walk on or in it. By whatever means necessary, I promise that I will restore the natural order." He said it with no shortage of pride and cockiness.

The attitude wasn't lost on every single one of the villagers, let alone the alchemist. "Your *best* isn't good enough for these parts, boy. You bend to the land, or the land bends you. Easy enough to see which will happen just by looking at you."

"Hirshma, quiet! We asked for his help! No need to belittle the boy!" the elder snapped.

"Oh, put it to rest Ronlin. I've seen his kind before. Young, fresh, cocksure? Oh, he's barely outta the nest. If he saves us all, why, then he's learned something! If he doesn't come back, then his worthless Order'll know there's a real cause for concern and will send in the troops... be damned all what happens to us until they get here!"

"She's right!" Vestranis thundered. "The Gods don't care about us! Never have!"

"Why would you expect them to if you all hate them so?" Akaran snapped. Glaring, he tried to bring his full attention to the alchemist and forced himself to soften his tone before he addressed her. "Hirshma? I don't mean you and yours any grief. Can we start fresh? How would you like to be addressed? I don't know much about the titles given to your type. Lady? Teacher?"

"My *type?* Like it would matter. I'm no lady and I doubt you give a damn for what the Fellowship of the Alchemetic has deigned to name me. Or do you want to call me by my family name, Kalabranic? No. Don't bother remembering it, you won't be around long enough to care," she spat.

"I'll be here as long as it takes. I can't promise I'll fix it. But I'll find out what it is. I give my word."

"An' if you'd have earned the right to have your word mean anything, I'd believe you."

Her voice was enough to shatter glass. It wasn't doing much more for a slowly growing headache right behind his eye. "What would it take to convince you it did?"

She thought about it for a moment, almost everyone in the crowd looking at her (or looking near her and trying to pretend that they weren't). "Well. I'd suppose you'd have to kill the creatures that are killing us, won't you? But since you're just graspin' at thin air, I'm going to bet that you can't."

"I take it you know where his home is then?"

She rolled her eyes. "Of *course* I know where that damnable blot on the stoneface is. Most of us do. The mountain cried when he built it. Sad little cottage. Loaded with stuff the world doesn't need. He was a fool, practicing magic he knew little about and distorting the elements to his supposed 'needs'."

*The mountain cried? Since when do those that forsake the Gods and delve into the study of worldly crafts hear anything that the land does? Dirt doesn't exactly **talk** to people.* "Can you lead me to it?"

She nodded. "Can, but won't. Not worth my life. If he ain't there, something else has taken it and owns it. Probably that icy whore. Ain't my concern what happens there."

He tried not to let the frustration he was bottling up to creep back into his voice. "You don't talk like someone that only studies the land. You have a passion for it. Are you a druid, by chance? A follower of Nature Herself?" he asked suddenly, cutting off her diatribe.

The elder choked and sputtered, giving the exorcist a terrified look. A few of the more outspoken villagers looked bewildered – but a couple of them, the older ones, looked uncomfortable by the accusation. "Of Kora'thi? Are you *mad*? The Gods have done *nothing* for us. They have *always, **always*** left destruction in their wake. Fisk every single one of them and **damn** the people that cast their lot to them, **you** included."

"Sister!" Ronlin all but shouted. "Restrain yourself – show the boy a measure of respect, please!"

"No. She's right. She obviously has no reason to trust me. I get that. Respect is given when it's earned. I mean to rid you of your grief. The Goddess can only hope that you'll gain some faith in the divine when I do."

Hirshma turned away from him. "Go choke on your *faith*. See what good it does."

Ignoring her, Akaran pressed a little harder. "I'm pretty damn sure that there's more than a waifish woman spitting snow your people and leaving ice in her wake for years. I won't ask again: will you aid me or not?"

"You're *pretty sure*? Did they take half your mind when they took half your sight? What a brilliant determination! Fine. You want me to treat you with respect? Come with me. Now."

It wasn't a request. Her brother tried to silently dissuade him but there was something about her hate that intrigued him. Against all better judgment, he followed. Not long after, he wished he hadn't.

41

IV. TIP OF THE ICEBERG

The graveyard was just outside the western edge of the village. There wasn't much to it – a small plot of land with a cobblestone half-wall that wrapped around it. The hilly nature of the terrain around Toniki gave way to dips and curves throughout to a point where he couldn't see where the southern side of it ended.

Their disinterest in the Gods had made its way inside the hallowed grounds; there were only a few graves marked with any symbols of any of the Pantheon, and those were kept in ill-repair. The sole exception was a raised, two-tiered wrought-iron platform in the north-eastern corner. An iron dome hung over the edifice, held aloft by chains attached to three blackened statues no more than one-and-a-half of a man's average height.

The statues in question belonged to Kora'thi, Solinal, and Pristi – the Goddess of Nature, the God of Peace, and the Goddess of Purity. On second glance, he noticed that just because they were *there*, that didn't mean that anyone was trying to manage any kind of upkeep for them. The statues were covered in dried up vines and dead weeds. The pyre itself looked equally as unloved, and that was not a happy discovery at all.

I don't think it's been used in years. For all of the grief that has befallen these people, why haven't they been putting a torch to the bodies of those that have passed on? Couldn't they find them? Don't they care?

Those questions were answered immediately, albeit with terrible implications.

"You claim to be an exorcist, is that right? One of those 'damn them all' types that has the authority of the Queen to do anything and everything you like?"

"More or less, yes, I am. There's evil in the world. We have to be willing to fight against it." He smiled at her. "That's a lot like you, I think. You're more than a little protective of your people. You could be a great voice for Love in the world."

"And be forced to suckle on the Divine Prostitute's tits? I'll take my chances seeing what the land has in store for me when it's time to put me in the ground."

He shrugged. "Well. Worth a try. And, truly, would it be too much to ask to hold back on the blasphemy? I really *don't* mean you and yours ill, and the attacks upon my Goddess are getting tiresome."

"Oh, they're getting *tiresome*, are they? Well well. Not going to challenge me, not going to recite chapter and verse from whatever holy text you take to bed every night? Not out to spread the word of your Matron?"

"I do," he countered. "For the work that I am tasked with, that word is usually '*begone*.' Doesn't necessarily win converts."

Hirshma grunted. "How wonderful."

This was rapidly turning into an exhausting endeavor. "So. Why have you brought me here?"

"You're the so-called exorcist. Aren't you able to tell me when there's something wrong?" With that, she stepped back – well back – and crossed her arms.

Perplexed, he watched her in silence until he realized that she meant it – she wasn't going to explain herself. Rising to the challenge, he walked into the middle of the graveyard and looked around. Other than the cemetery being slightly overgrown from currently-withered weeds of all shapes and sizes, nothing jumped out at him right away.

Of course, that was probably the point she was trying to make.

He worked quickly and in near-silence, first pulling a small bag free from one of the pouches along his waist before casually tossing it into the snow at his feet. The alchemist couldn't make out what he said next. The spell, however, didn't need him to be loud. The pouch flared with white fire and sank into the ground. As the smoke from it cleared, he turned to her with no humor at all.

"You're short." She growled. He clarified. "Bodies. You're short bodies. The ether here... it reeks. Not the same stench as whatever tried to eat that soldier, but it still reeks."

"So now there's something else? How dreadfully fisking wonderful."

Akaran had to agree with her. This was getting worse by the minute. "How many? Seven? Eight?"

She nodded. "Eight graves were opened."

Dammit. "What happened to them?"

The look on her face was a lot less haughty than it had been in the village square. Her voice didn't sound half as confident, either. "Now that would be the question, wouldn't it? I've done what I could to keep it hidden from the rest. My brother would fall over and die if he knew."

"No wonder nobody mentioned this last night. You are aware of how horribly *bad* this is, yes?"

"It's 'bad,' is it? I had to bring my apprentice out here and cover everything up after I found it. Whatever took 'em... the soil was torn up. Whatever brought these bodies back to life... I don't have any clue, boy, none at all."

"When did this happen? Barely any tracks here to be seen... please tell me it was years ago."

She shifted uncomfortably where she stood. "Six days back. A day or two after those poor bastards from the garrison limped back here."

"Six... almost a week. And you told nobody... why? You didn't bother to send this information along when the soldiers requested assistance?"

"Because I *thought* that the Queen's Army wouldn't take half-measures, not when their own have been threatened. Anyone they could send should be able to put them back where they belong. Then I met you."

If they burned their dead as they should, this wouldn't even be an issue. That pyre looks serviceable enough... or for the sake of the Goddess, a clearing and a couple of torches would suffice. "The risk you've exposed them to -"

"- is no greater than the risk they're already under," she countered, a haughty air to her tone.

"You don't have the right to make that decision."

Huffing, she crossed her arms over her chest. "And you do?"

The exorcist placed his hand on his sigil and stared at her in disbelief. **"Yes. I. Do.** The sooner you get that in your head, the better off we'll all be."

Unrepentant, she resumed her attempts to defend her actions. "They wandered away. They didn't come back here. If they had I would have told everyone. Hid it from them to keep everybody calm and to keep them from running off or going into a worse panic than what we've got now. What good do you think would come from it then if they packed up and ran off?"

"I think it would have helped keep them alive..."

Hirshma stood her ground. "I found a few not far from here. Put five of them back to rest. If I can, anyone can. They're no threat to the village."

"How?" With his lips pursed as he took it all in, he gave the new revelation some thought. Not a lot, but some. "No... don't bother telling me. I need to see where you culled them. That will tell me more."

"Oh they won't be walking no more. I can assure you of that. But there's at least three I just couldn't catch before they got someplace I didn't want to risk going into. Locked them up; they won't be bothering anyone else."

Akaran just blinked in disbelief. "Locked them up? They're the *dead*, not bloody pickpockets!"

"Which is why I brought you here to see this. They deserve to be put back to the ground. Their souls, bless them or damn them, need to go back to wherever they were. Do you want to prove your worth to the village? Then prove it to me."

"To you?! You admit that you left the town at risk because you think you know what's best for everyone! If *anyone* needs to prove themselves, it sure as all *isn't* me!"

The alchemist shook her head. "Oh it isn't? As opposed to what it is you do? No. There's no difference."

There were more differences that he could name than there were stars in the sky. Letting it slide (against a very big urge to tell her as much), he dug down to the meat of the matter. "Well. Bears repeating, I guess. This is bad."

"No, really? I can't imagine that anyone would be upset about their husbands and daughters walking around with their bodies half gone to rot. I think it's a wonderful idea; why, I had hoped you'd be able to find a way to raise more of 'em; we miss them so much. OF COURSE IT'S BAD, you bumbling idiot!"

A growl of his own just an inch away from his voice, he tried to put a stop to her torrent of hostility. "Calm down, friend," he started.

"I am no friend of yours," she snapped.

"Calm down anyways. Let's make a deal."

She raised her chin up and looked him right in his eye. "Go on."

"You wouldn't have brought me here if you didn't think that I could deal with this. All you had to do was ask and I would've done it without an argument. Dead men shouldn't walk anywhere. They're dead.

Animation of the dead is an affront to the Gods. It can't be tolerated."

"An affront to the Gods? What about the affront to *us?*"

As they talked, he knelt back down to the dirt and buried his hand in a pocket of snow. Hirshma watched him but she couldn't tell what he was doing – if anything. What she didn't realize was that the ground vibrated at his touch. Faintly, softly, but it did vibrate. The tremors spread from his fingertips to each grave in turn before the cobblestones around the graveyard gave the barest of shakes and discharged little puffs of snow from their upper edges.

She didn't hear the prayer he made, but he did mutter one below his breath. *"Blessed be, Lady of Love, blessed be. Warm this dirt, warm those long-departed, touch those recent. Let none rise from the grave again."*

A tingle crept over her skin and made the hairs on the top of her head stand up. It wasn't a bad sensation, but it wasn't an entirely comfortable one. "Did you feel...?" Perplexed, she studied his features for a few long heartbeats. "What did you do?"

The grounds freshly sanctified, Akaran stood up and brushed snow and mud off of his knees. "An enchantment. Just to keep things at rest. Nothing more."

"Oh."

"You don't need to lose any more of your deceased."

She agreed with him before she continued on with her demeaning little remarks. "So. As long as you're here you may as well do something useful. We've done nothing to deserve this grief."

"There must be some kind of necromancy is at foot here. That's all it can be. You've said a few things about that mage. Do you think he has the capacity to unleash a disturbance of this magnitude?"

The elderly woman answered with a somewhat short 'no.' "I know the man. He may be eccentric but he's no monster."

"So if he isn't..."

Unimpressed by his line of questioning, she huffed a cloud of steaming air in his general direction. "Then someone else is."

"Yeah. So. If I track these poor bastards down and send them back to the next world, will you show me the way to Usaic's cabin? If he isn't the cause, I'm willing to bet the source has taken up residence there. Or at least, I hope."

He was wrong about that, too. Kind of. He was close enough for the time being. "Maybe. Maybe not. Could be someplace else entirely."

Later, he'd loathe the fact that she was *completely* right about that.

"Will you help me or not?"

She snorted. "Oh, I will. I just wanted to make sure you understand one thing little man – magic has a cost. This land was pure until that rotten bastard came around and started performing his little 'experiments' with the mountain. We never had nothing that vexed the laws of nature 'til that fool started working his trouble near us. He ain't the source. But he sure as all didn't help."

"*Life* has a cost. Our world isn't meant to be free."

"Maybe it is. Maybe it isn't. This price? They're more than what they seem, too – I can tell you that girl is only *part* of the taint festering here, whatever she is."

Akaran disputed that for a brief moment, but it did no good. "I don't know what she is. But I promise you, there is no taint to her."

"She isn't of this world. Means she shouldn't be here. I don't have to be a priest to know that much. I dunno if you can feel it boy, but deep in my bones, I can feel something hungry out there." She gave him one final, searching stare. "And honestly? I ain't in any mood to let it get its fill from my skin."

He had to agree. Before he left, he took the time to say a prayer and place a second spell in the graveyard. It wouldn't do much. It was designed to give him a warning if a critter not of this world entered the area. Just a word of warning, and one strong enough to dissuade minor spirits from entering the area. In theory – and just about any other time – it would be considered a great idea. In practice?

He'd later blame himself for attracting more trouble than it was worth.

V. DEAD COLD

It hadn't taken more than half of an hour to get utterly disgusted by the snow all over again – and he'd been out in it for two hours now, just trying to reach the mine. Making his way to Toniki had been a trial in its own right.

Now? Having to leave the warmth of the townspeople's hate to track down the shambling dead in the icy dandruff of the Gods? Oh no. This wasn't doing *anything* to change his opinion of the freezing little flakes of white shit.

Although... while having to be out in it wasn't fun, the snowfall did help make it easier to track the dead men. Even though their tracks were mostly gone, there was just enough... stuff... littering the ground as he got closer to the mine. *I don't know what those things are, and I am glad I don't know what those things are.*

Most importantly, even without footprints, there were ways to track them down.

The majority of those that could wield magic in the mainstream Orders of Light only learned a few spells; normally just one or two for even the eldest of their ranks. Sometimes it was magic to light their way. Or to conjure fire (for those that followed the Burning Lady north past the mountains), or to force a liar to speak the truth (Pristi absolutely hates a liar).

Some even learned how to cast spells to soothe the suffering (Pristi, Niasmis, and Kora'thi all taught this). There were those that could give sustenance to the hungry or parched (mostly Kora'thi, but the God of Waves had a thing for making water come out of thin air). Almost uniformly though – they did not learn how to use the magics of the

48

Pantheon until they were well versed and experienced in the more mundane matters of faith.

The Order of Love took one look at that requirement, said 'screw that,' and rewrote the book. Among other things, that meant that he had more than just 'one or two' spells at his disposal. Quite a number more than just 'one or two.'

Elders of his Order were always chastised for teaching spells to the lowliest of members. His instructors always made the case that most of the *other* Orders didn't send their members into situations where being killed by things that defy description would be the least of their worries. There were valid points on both sides of the argument. All told, though?

The other Orders could shove it.

His instructors at the Temple had pointed out (more than once) that many things, once risen from the grave or otherwise released from the underworld, well... they tend to have many, many reasons to hide. If you stopped to think about it, there wasn't much strange about the concept. Would *you* be so willing to go back to the pit?

These are souls that have escaped the unceasing madness and swirling storms pain and eternal suffering of the pits. Why would they be in a hurry to announce themselves? Why not wait in the shadows, hide, enjoy living in the world once more? Or spend time hiding for centuries doing nothing more than accumulating power so that when or if they were eventually found, that they would kill those that came to slay them?

For most of the walking damned, they were hunted by anyone with a sword as a matter of self-preservation (or as in regards to those lovely mercenaries from the Hunter's Guild, a matter of income). They weren't welcome by any of the holy or the devout, even if they were not specifically trained to exterminate them. Even the Fallen had no care for the damned that walked freely, if they didn't have an oath of fealty sworn directly to them and only them.

True, that wasn't the case for all manners of escaped souls from the pit, but for most...

The bottom line was that condemned souls and other related monsters had no reason to ever feel safe above ground. Yes, there were the occasional full-fledged Daemons that wanted to explore options of world conquest or wanton destruction and torture of innocents. And there was no denying that there had been creatures of the Abyss that sought to ascend to demigod status. They were (blessedly) rare – but it *was* known to happen.

Mostly? Mostly, they hid. Not entirely, but mostly, they tried to hide.

There was another good reason for that. It was rumored that the Warden of the Abyss did not *approve* of His charges escaping their fate in the afterlife. Supposedly, it left Him quite *irritated* when they were sent back.

That was *not* a reckoning that most of the unholy returned were in a hurry to rush back to.

To that end, learning how to find some of those things is paramount, and thus simple spells were crafted to be used to track creatures of the night. Unfortunately, their range is limited. It was further complicated by the truth that the things that *really* had an intense reason to go to ground tended to find ways to mask their auras.

It was almost like cheating. What good was having the ability to search for foul magic when the worst of the creatures that used it the most could eventually figure out how to cover their own tracks? *If half of the elite of the Abyss ever realized that it was their minions that gave their presence away, we'd never find them.*

While the Sisters at the Temple could track a threat from continents away, the best his magic could do was a couple of miles. Even then, that was pushing it. *At least I'm lucky enough that these corpses don't have a clue how to blend their stench in with the world's ambient energy. I do **not** want to spend any more time than I have to trudging around out here.*

But when it worked... scrying for the undead worked just fine.

He found the abandoned mine just where Hirshma had said he would. It wasn't that far out of town – about an hour in good weather, two in this irritating snow and slush. Normally you'd see a village spring up right next to a shaft like this one, but if the rough marsh around the entrance was any sign of how it looked in the summer, he could see why people were hesitant to put their homes anywhere near here.

There was another clue on the way to the mine that jumped out at him. Someone had been kind enough to ruin a decades-old body and left its remains to rot in the snow. If he hadn't been looking for things of that nature he probably would have overlooked it. Whoever had disposed of it had done a wonderful job of reducing it to little more than ash and a few chunks of bones... a partial skull, a few ribs. Burnt, but it showed obvious signs of decomposition.

Then again, he wasn't looking that hard. It had more to do with the fact that he had stepped into it more than anything else. *That cranky old bat had said she put down five of them. I'm a little surprised she didn't do more to cover it up if she's so afraid that the rest of the village would find out. Wonder if she was in some kind of hurry to get back.*

Probably just fear. Mundanes don't usually like to stick around magic they don't understand. Can't say I'd blame her any.

It was beyond him for why someone would try to build a mine next to a swamp to start with (and equally odd that there was a swamp this far into the mountains). He was hoping it would just be one of those mysteries forever lost in time. He really just needed to give up hope at this point. That particular four-lettered word was only serving to provide him with disappointment after disappointment.

Hirshma wasn't kidding that she had sealed them in. Someone had put in an iron grate at the entrance of the mine to serve as a door. He could see through it but there wasn't much to look at – the excavated cave was pitch black and the opening curved just a few feet in. That wasn't as important as what the alchemist had done to the lock.

Somehow, she had melted it into the stone it was set against. It was completely slagged and sealed tight. Even your average strong-man wouldn't be able to open it unaided. A long-dead, shambling lost piece of rotting corpse? They wouldn't stand a chance at getting free.

For that matter, *he* wasn't going to be able to break through without a war-hammer. Or at least, he'd need one *if* she hadn't been so kind as to give him a key. He fished out a small bag out of one of the pouches hidden under his coat. It was packed full with some kind of ground up rock and fine dust.

He was immensely skeptical of what good it was going to do.

There was another package too, tucked safely away on his equally unhappy ride to the mine. She hadn't bothered to explain (and he wouldn't have been able to understand it even if she had) what the two compounds would do. She did warn him to make sure that under no circumstances, they shouldn't touch together until he was at the door. She didn't say *why*, just that they shouldn't be.

Glowering at the slagged metal and the pouch, he took a minute to quietly vent a little more frustration to himself. *Alchemists. I can see why my instructors never spoke fondly of them. Always trying to show off that they can do things on their own instead of trying to learn to do real magic. Takes them forever to do anything. Egomaniacal twits...*

Her warning firm in his head, he turned to the fill-in stable-master to ask him for help. As luck would have it, Mowiat was one of the few people that was happy to see a priest intervening. He didn't even care *which* priest, as long as *someone* got involved. As luck would also have it, he had a horse that Akaran could use.

There wasn't much to the mare. She was only two years old, which was a plus, but she didn't look like she'd win any races or would be much use carrying a lot of baggage. She had a brown coat with a few white spots along her back, with a scraggly mane and an unkempt tail. Akaran thought she looked adorable; nobody else really agreed with him. *No accounting for taste.*

Mowiat said she had briefly belonged to one of the lost trappers, but his family hadn't wanted to take her with them when they fled the village. He had bought her back for a few gold. Regrettably, he really didn't have enough food to keep her through another (or continual) winter. It was either sell him to someone that really needed an equine companion, or Ronlin's would have something fresh to butcher at his store. A few more gold got the last of Mowiat's feed, too.

In other words, Nayli was just about perfect for what everyone wanted.

The lovely filly was up to carrying around a couple of saddlebags, which was just the thing he needed. He gave the sweet thing a soft stroke through her hair before digging out a jar full of some utterly vile smelling grayish paste and went to work. The instructions were fairly simple: put the salve on first, then empty the contents of the second pouch onto it.

The reaction was vigorous, to say the least.

As the powder met the paste, his immediate thought was that she could have warned him to stand the bloody pits as far away as he possibly could when the alchemy started to work. The entire mess caught fire in a blazing reaction that burned clear through the melted lock and several of the iron bars below it. He wasn't entirely convinced that it didn't burn through the stone wall the mess had been anchored to (nor did he have the courage to bend down close enough to look after it finished).

Three walking corpses. Can feel them from here... something else is around here, too. Can't tell what but there **is** *something else. Hopefully it's whatever animated them to begin with. Odd though, that they'd get up and walk away from the village right after the soldiers made it back. Odder that they walked* **away** *from everyone, instead of going into the town. That's not... sure, the damned undead want to hide but to run away from the living? The* **mindless** *dead don't usually do that... they mill about, carry on whatever mischief that fits their liking at any given* *moment.*

This is an ill omen if there ever was one.

The marsh outside was indicative of the reason that the mine had been abandoned. The deeper he went into the mine, the worse it looked. Slushy water filled small pits in side rooms and more of it seeped through cracks in the walls and ceilings. Wooden beams showed signs of rot. One hallway had already caved in.

Muck was quickly accumulating on his boots and the lower edges of his chausses. It didn't stink, at least, so it had that much going for it. *Doubt I'll be so lucky when I catch up to the wretches. Zombies. Actual, honest-to-Goddess zombies infesting the area.* A disturbing thought passed through his mind as he rounded a curve and started to descend another level into the mine. *At least... I hope. Can't imagine that the old bint would have been able to fight them off if they were anything worse.*

Most people would go their entire lives never seeing one, or even believe that such things existed in this day and age. To the rest of the world, they were mythical – tales to frighten little children. To the people in his particular profession... they weren't exactly common, but they weren't all-too-rare.

A few things could cause them to pop up. They were known to occur in areas where uncontrolled magic ran rampant – or controlled magic animated them on purpose. Distortions from wild discharges of spells at random allowed for Abyssian influence to seep through the walls between worlds, past the veil and into the mortal realm.

Were that to be the case, then the bodies would simply become corrupt. Defiled. Mindless shambling things with no desire but to wreak havoc wherever they popped up. Easy enough to dispose of, unsettling as it may be.

Or, should the ether become too disrupted, souls that had no peace in death could break through. That presented another issue: intention. A soul desperate enough to return to this plane of existence may not even be the soul that used to inhabit the body in life and merely take the first one that it was offered.

Of course, it could be the original owner come back for reasons that rarely had a happy ending. Either way, it brought a whole new slew of complications. Be it to escape the wrath of the Abyss or a need to seek vengeance, the wrong spirit could transform a corpse into something worse. A lot worse.

Unless they've grown up substantially over the last few days, doubt it's going to be a zenorat... mutant corpses, all the things wrong with death repackaged and disfigured and so much harder to put down. Still have nightmares from the one that Brother Steelhom arranged to have conjured up for us to poke at. Can't tell if the other instructors hated him for that as much as I did, but damned if it isn't close.

Revenants? Maybe? You'd think that Hirshma would have seen them wandering back around a few minutes later when they regenerated. Probably just nothing of note. Some lost spirits around attracted by this unholy winter.

While he mused on what the nature of the dead, details of the mine jumped out at him... when he could see them. Bolintop Mine didn't seem to go too deep, at first. A modicum of passages stayed close to the surface, while a few side-rooms had been carved out of the rock. This feat of engineering had obviously taken a great deal of time to work through. *Someone made a lot of gold working this. This had to have taken decades of effort, at least.*

There were the usual tools of the trade left laying here and there; carts, tables with chunks of iron and coal scattered all around the man-made cave. There was no shortage of picks, shovels, and hammers that had been tossed about haphazardly. Mildewing sacks had been left to rot in puddles. Crates half-filled with various musty tools were stacked haphazardly at irregular intervals through the tunnels.

Strangely enough there were rusty iron pipes partially submerged in the areas where the flooding was the worst. Every now and again he'd catch sight of one with a grate on the top of it. They appeared to travel towards the same hidden destination deeper into the industrial excavation. A few had rusted and broken with chunks of rock serving to crack them open as they fell from increasingly muddy walls.

Torches, on the other hand? Wall sconces, braziers? There were some scattered about at odd intervals but there was no sense in trying to light one and then be stuck carrying it around. If the extermination went bad, there was going to be the need for something more reliable in his hands than just a lit oily rag.

He had to settle for casting a very small, very simple spell. It caused his left hand to emit a faint, soft glow. It was a rule – in order to beat back the dark, you must know how to summon the light. It was such a simple thing. He was at a loss why it wasn't taught to everyone, mundane or not. Magic came from within, and everyone had at least a little bit of it in them.

The downside was that it did help the dark see where he was. Or at least, it made a ripple in the ether. If anything was in here that was strong enough to feel that ripple, it would take away any kind of surprise he might have had. However, it did let him see the things in the darkness, so it was a worthy trade-off.

Easier to handle than carrying around a torch, too.

What caught his eye in the middle of one of those scattered piles of rock were a handful of partially obscured stones that glittered in the light of his magic. It had a silvery sheen with an amber tint and looked unlike anything he'd seen before. It seemed completely out-of-place in a mine that was full of coal and scattered chunks of something that looked like raw tin. *That looks like the same stuff that Eos'eno's clasp was made from. Interesting.*

He debated trying to chip a chunk free while he walked into a sloped shaft that led deeper into the bowels of the mine. The further in he got, the worse the flooding was. Eventually, he was wading through water that was almost over his shins. In the back of his mind, he cursed himself a second time for not asking why the workers had abandoned it before he left.

All of these thoughts hung in his mind as he rounded a corner and ran into a mass of tangled, gnarled roots that had grown through cracks in the roof of the hallway. There didn't seem to be any way through them – at least, not at first. When he turned to look for another way around, his sword brushed against a tattered vine. As he tugged it free, there was a slight rustle that he ignored.

He could not ignore the hand that fell on his shoulder.

Cursing, he whipped around and thrust his glowing fist into the center of the mass that was clogging the tunnel. Mouth agape, a grinning skull tore free and dangled an inch away from his face. Hollowed out eye sockets looked like they were impossibly full of life; the jaw flapped open then broke free from desiccated tendons that couldn't hold it in place any longer.

A spell flared out of his hand reflexively, albeit to no real result. Purple and blue light coursed through the shell and left barely a single ember anywhere on or in the dangling corpse. He snarled as he pulled away from it; and his lurch back was all it took for the rest of the body to hit the ground with a dull thud.

After a few minutes of foul looks and efforts to look back down the passageway he had come from (to make sure nothing new had made an arrival), he was more-or-less convinced that what danger there was had long since passed. The body, as far as he could tell, had not had much such luck. *Mangled would be an understatement*, he quietly mused under his breath.

Thick claw marks had left divots in the bone along the back and base of the skull and over the spine. Something or someone had crushed the ribs, leaving most of them broken or missing. The dead man had been wearing some kind of thick leather armor that hadn't spared it from a gash over the sternum that he could have easily stuck his head through.

That wasn't all, either. There were tattered scraps of desiccated skin still on his bones. Every single one was charred and streaked with broken blisters and worse. *Oh this poor fisker **really** pissed someone off. Clawed, beaten, burned? I wonder how much of it was done when he was alive. I hope it was a he. No lady should have to experience this.*

Well, no man either. Just... He let the thought die in his head as he continued to look over the body. *Who or what brought this thing here? And who would just abandon it? Did they run out of power, was animating it too taxing? Did it simply get stuck and forgotten?*

Whatever magics that had animated it were long gone with barely a tingle of toxic magic or despoiled ether. There was just a little, a very little, flicker of Abyssian aura left behind. It was so faint that Akaran wasn't even sure that his magic was identifying something unholy left in the body or if he was picking up the scent of the zombies that made their way into the mine.

He knelt down next to it and pressed his hand into the shell, sliding it under the broken ribs to see what might have been left behind. Only shredded chunks of rotted muscle remained where his heart should have been. A subsequent check did not give him much hope that any of the other (mostly) missing organs had remained intact for more than a few minutes after (if not before) the man had died.

In the state that it was in, he wasn't even going to try to take a guess when the previous occupant had left its mortal coil. Could have been a year ago. Could have been fifty. However long ago it was, his soul wasn't here anymore. *Nor has it been here for a long time now, I think.*

Looks like he was moved. No, looks like he moved himself. Doesn't look like anyone tried to set anything on fire in this part of the mine... damn. Something used this guy as a meat puppet. For his sake, really hope it wasn't an effort that his own soul made after... I'm guessing pretty damn painful... death.

Who or what that had made the body get up and walk around for a while was as important of a question as who or what killed him. *Not going to find out much more, I don't think.* Trying to find evidence from a ravaged corpse was hard enough under normal circumstances. These were obviously not even remotely 'normal.'

Being forced to walk around after it died – and who knows what other postmortem activities it had been up to? No. Those were never easy on a body under even perfect conditions. A thought that finding anything else out was going to be next to impossible started to grow in the back of his mind – and he did well to ignore it. One more hard look removed the impossibility and replaced it with raw confusion. A mark on the victim's skull gave both a clue *and* a fresh set of questions.

It was a dead giveaway for *where* the body had come from. Or at least, who it had served in life. Someone had etched a pair of circles – one on each side of his temples – with two jagged triangles carved inside. It almost looked like a crude carving of a mountain peak, and maybe when he had been alive, it would have looked majestic. Assuredly it would be unique. Just as assuredly, it identified him and where he came from.

Actually, that wasn't a maybe. It would have. *Before decay took him, that circle would have been filled with pale blue ink, and those mountains would have been ivory white. So why in the world would a Steward of Blizzards be **here**? They're... scholars. Archivists. They never stray too far from the fjords of Namaria, halfway across the Nightmare Sea.*

They don't get involved in Dawnfire's affairs or give a shit about the Queen's people. He'd need to travel by magic or cross the sea and then trek through the Civan Empire... and pretty sure that teleportation is not their area of expertise. Bet a year's worth of pay that the Civans, followers of the Goddess of Flames as they are, wouldn't have given him any kind of assistance if he waltzed down from up north. They'd sooner kill him without feeling even one little bit of remorse.

*Visiting some worthless village in the asscrack of the mainland? Please. They don't even like this **continent**. What in the name of Niasmis would entice one to come here? More importantly, what was he doing? Gah. Well. I suppose this speaks to the kind of magic at play here, as if there was any doubt left at this point. If Eos'eno is really from Tundrala, that would be all the excuse they would want to take a vacation.*

One more mystery added to the plate was just what he needed.

No, it was the exact opposite of that.

With absolutely everything he could possibly hope to ascertain from the corpse at an end, he forced himself to calm down and focus on the next task at hand. Methodically and respectfully, the exorcist gently pulled the remnants out of the vines. Carefully, he laid the body down on the floor.

Sighing, Akaran gave a silent prayer to the Goddess to beg Her to guide his soul to a place of rest, wherever it may be (assuming it wasn't already there). He'd have to come back for it later for disposal; the zombies he was here for could be anywhere. If he wasted any more time, they might even find him first. That probably wouldn't have worked out for the best.

The task done, Akaran cast a different spell. *Tired of this. Job to do – want it done.* The hole behind his eyepatch flashed once, a dull white flash with just a tinge of blue about the edges. The tunnel ahead flickered black and white in his good eye for several heartbeats. Then the world's color returned to normal, albeit with an addition that he and only he would be able to see.

A thin tendril of light danced in the air before slipping through the passages ahead. *Got you. Whatever you dead things are, I bring word from my Goddess.* He hand squeezed the hilt of his sword tightly, a sneer popping onto his lips. *She wants me to give you a hello, send you Her regards, and then tell the lot of you to kiss off and go rot in burning piles of ash.*

Less than ten minutes later, the mine coughed up the answer to the nagging question of why it had been abandoned. Whoever built it had installed a series of pumps in a larger chamber, all connected to a water mill. If he had to guess it would have served to pump out anything that started to flood the mine, and provide water to sluice through parts of the pit. It wasn't abnormal construction by any means. It was just more than he expected to find this far away from what he considered civilization.

Luck, on the other hand, had not decided to grace the miners. The mill had broken; half of the water wheel had shattered. Chunks of wooden debris clogged up a small drainage ditch in the cave, causing water to flow everywhere in the chamber. One of the three pumps that connected to it was nearly buried under a pile of rubble.

A steady stream of water poured down from above, completely soaking all of it. *I bet there were pumps scattered in some of those side halls. They would divert the water into here, where the mill would have helped pump it back out of the mine or into some underground stream.*

All of that would have changed when part of the roof collapsed. A deep, ragged hole had opened up overhead. Why the entire place hadn't ended up completely submersed was beyond him; his only guess was that it had to have found a way to pour into some deeper cave system. Another year or two and he'd be surprised if the whole mine wouldn't be a brand new lake in the Queen's lands.

Size wise, the cave was big enough to comfortably house a noble's overbuilt manor with room for a third floor for extra beds. Snowdrifts had piled up in higher (drier) corners, and icicles dangled precariously from what was left of the roof. Granite walls had long-since frosted over just so Nature could prove Her point: it was fisking cold.

There wasn't much light left in the day, but enough reflected off of the snow to just barely illuminate the inside of it. Mining equipment filled almost a solid third of the chamber. None of it looked usable and all of it looked like someone had destroyed them out of spite.

Not that any of it fisking matters. THEY do.

A trio of shambling corpses were milling about not too far away from where the ruined mill was. They were congregated around a buck that had fallen through the shattered roof. If it hadn't died on impact alone, those three wouldn't have given it much time to get away. He checked his surprise that they might have been able to kill it on their own.

With their focus on the deer, it gave him a chance to size up the competition before committing to the exorcism. They were just zombies. Why should he bother taking a few extra moments to observe them?

One hard look was all it took to size them up and realize that they didn't have enough strength to last long in the imminent fight. He didn't think anything of these particular dead, and why should he? Nothing jumped out at him that they were anything more than just aimless, mindless corpses. A quick charge and it would all be over.

Really, they were just zombies.

However, there *were* rules to be followed. Uncharacteristically, he opted to follow them to the letter. After he took a long and deep breath, he buckled down and started to get to work.

Before he took another step, he did one simple thing. He pulled a small piece of charcoal out of a pouch on his belt and carefully drew a slightly intricate rune at the mouth of the cavern. When he was done, he placed his hand flat against the series of circles and the crosshatch markings in the middle of it. A soft pulse of pale lavender light blinked out from between his fingers and under his palm to infuse the scribbles. Containment was key.

Even when facing the weakest of the weak, containment was *always* key.

He made it about halfway into the cave before they saw him. There wasn't much to them; desiccated skin was tinted light blue and dusty gray from the cold. Their flesh was taught and torn on their bodies. They had been buried with clothes on, although one of the three had somehow managed to tear that last little bit of dignity away. The longer he looked, the more their ruined state cut into his heart.

The smallest of them still had a head of ratty brown hair. She looked young. Someone's daughter, he wagered, taken by death far too soon. And now she was being defiled, cursed, and pulled from her rest. It offended him on so many levels that he completely disregarded the rest of the room (and ignored something he really shouldn't have).

All three had bits of deer stuck to their hands and teeth. The mess was beyond comprehension. It would stick with him for the rest of his life, although he never would figure out why. While the sight was too disgusting to describe, the aura that the three possessed was not. They were weak, they were simple, and they appeared to be mindless. He thought that he could put all them down with a few strikes of his sword and be done with it.

They were just simple zombies.

What was there for someone like him to worry about?

His first two assessments *were* right. He was right about his sword, too. He wasn't right about the mindless. He would regret storming in without using his training to fully get a grasp on what lay ahead. He wouldn't even have to wait long to do hate himself for it.

Because he *wasn't* right about if they were alone.

As the trio of walking corpses stopped what they were doing and started to turn to face him, the deer pushed itself upright and *lunged* at him, charging across the partially flooded chamber like it still had all four legs and a pulse. Entrails hit rubble on the ground with an awful wet thud as it bounced across the ruined mine after him.

All three of the zombies charged right along with it. Desperate haunting moans and wails filled the air as they shambled to him as quick as they could. One of them suffered either bad luck or divine intervention aimed at Akaran's behalf that caused the one of them to get tripped up in the mess and fell forward onto a jagged rock.

That might keep it out of the fight for a few minutes. Maybe.

Oh, shit.

At the last second, he brought his sword up with one hand on the end of the edge of it and the other on the pommel. The beast had just enough momentum going that it couldn't stop even if it wanted to – and it was too stupid to realize what he was about to do. One quick thrust and he caught the deer (*What kind of monster reanimates DEER?!*) right across its broken face.

An already-cracked antler took the brunt of the blade and cleanly sheered off as he sidestepped out of the way. With a sound that was almost animal but somehow not (and entirely perverse), it reared up on one leg to kick at the exorcist to no avail. He started to slip as he moved away, concern for where he was standing getting pushed out of his inexperienced mind.

As it pulled back, Akaran caught his balance and made his own push. With his full weight behind his swing, he slashed clear through its leg mid-kick. It didn't do anything to slow it down – until it tried to land and regain its balance. While its leg slid off of his dry outcropping to land in a splash in the frigid water, the rest of the animal hit the stone floor and completely shattered its neck.

He didn't have time to savor his victory or see what happened with it next. He really should've. He didn't see the first arm that pulled itself out of the deer's mouth. Nor did he see the second, or the third. He didn't see the pale, moldy blue and black speckled skin on whatever it was that was leaving the body. All he saw was the next defiled corpse waiting its turn in line.

The first human corpse shambled closer with one arm extended and gnarled fingers clutching at the air. It made a quiet gargling sound from a hole in its throat as it lunged for him. The exorcist swung his elbow out to batter the creature back. Rotted teeth cracked and fell to the floor while the depressing monstrosity tried to latch on to him.

Behind him, something started mumbling while he grabbed the back of the zombie's head with his left hand and aimed his sword at it with his right. "*So cold too cold always cold never warm never heat snow ice sleet no heat no warm cold in shadows...*"

His sword flashed a cool lavender as he thrust the blade into the ruined mouth of the zombie and out the back of its head. It must have missed what passed for the brain, because the dead thing reached up with its other ruined arm to grab at the weapon. Akaran snarled, and said a single Word. "*EXPEL!*"

The creature shuddered once and went slack. Its eyes flashed blue and acrid smoke erupted from every crack, tear, and hole in its head. A wail started to build up inside its chest as the light faded from its eyes. A heartbeat later and the creature slid off of his sword and landed in a lifeless heap at his feet.

"Two down, two to go," he grunted under his breath. "Pathetic."

If the damned things heard him, they didn't care. The one that tripped over the deer's bowels wasn't able to make it back to its feet yet. Although, that didn't stop it from eagerly crawling through the rancid floodwaters towards the holy man. It gave a valiant effort. A worthless effort, but a valiant one. The dead girl, on the other hand, was under no such impairments.

She was surprisingly agile, and she acted like she wanted to skip as she limped towards him, a sad mimicry of what her body had done when it was still alive. That was far too long ago though, and what was left of her now couldn't quite keep up with what her enfeebled mind wanted. Even if the perverse nature of her very being wasn't enough of a demonstration to show that her innocence was long lost, the chunks of bloody deer still hanging from her gaping mouth did the trick.

That was when he realized he should have paid more attention to what was left of the buck. Half-solid tentacles wrapped around his sword arm and pulled him back. Barbed ethereal feelers went right through his armor and sank into his skin like he wasn't wearing anything at all.

He screamed. He had no choice *but* to scream. He screamed as the touch sent jagged bolts of a mix of white-hot but freezing agony from his wrist to his shoulder and into his chest. *"Cold you're not cold you're warm you have warm you are warm you will be home!"*

He dropped his sword and unleashed a torrent of curses as he turned to face the new challenger. The damned thing was just that – a damned *thing*. A half-solid wraith floated in the air, almost inches from his face. It was covered in tentacles and a mass of grasping arms protruding from the center of a shifting mottled black mass at its core.

There was a central face to it, masked by shadows and grotesquely distorted; an odious mockery of a man. Dark blue eyes stared at him with no iris or eyelid to be seen. Chunks of ice and gray pebbles of some brittle stone infested each tentacle and arm. Melting snow and slush dripped off of it as it attempted to wrap the exorcist up tighter with several more tentacles and arms.

It didn't get the chance.

"LUMINOSO!"

No sooner than the Word left his lips than a brilliant white dome blossomed into being at his feet. It spread over him like a protective shield. The light was a soft whitish pink and blue and it bathed the room in glorious light.

The light drove the spirit back and forced it to let go of its prey. It made a mad dash for the entrance to the room from the mine proper, but the ward at the door stopped it before it could escape. The marks Akaran had carved in the wall flared to life and matched the glow flowing over the priest and his immediate surroundings. The damned soul spun about and apparently realized that the roof was the only way out it had left.

There was no way that the exorcist could have warded it, was there? It would be safe. It would be a quick exit. The wraith launched itself through the air, ignoring the daylight that filtered down through it.

But Akaran wasn't even remotely done. "*LUMINOSO CORSINAR!*"

When the last syllable left his mouth, the light around him faded and coiled into a brilliant ball of pure white mana that rolled off of his fingers as he flung his hand. Translated simply as "light at range," the spell exploded to life on the rocks at the edge of the ruined roof. Agonized by the glow and seemingly too solid to pass through the walls of the mine, the wraith suddenly found itself completely (and utterly) trapped.

Sobbing manically and crying out at a pitch so high it made his ears hurt, the spirit flitted back and forth at the back of the cave. "*Half-breed girl gets home! Daringol gets no home! Daringol can find no home in man with light! Man is warm! No peace while cold, none! Half-breed is one with ice! Half-breed wants to keep Daringol cold forever! Daringol hates the half-breed! Daringol will see it **vanquished**!*" it incessantly wailed.

Akaran didn't care.

Neither did what was animating the little girl. Even stunned and knocked back from the multiple explosions of light, she had almost made it back into range to bite him. In a desperate act (either out hunger or simply a desire for murder) she lunged at him with a wordless cry. That was a mistake. Just because *she* had no words left to scream...

...he wasn't suffering any such penalty. "Goddess of Love, Matron, Mother, Lover, grant me a boon to return these wretches to their place of rest!" he shouted. As he did, his left hand took a glow that matched the one that had been on his now-discarded bade. The agony in his arm melted to a tolerable ache. The wraith shrunk back deeper into the cave. The husk of a girl did not.

Akaran caught her with his hand clamped down over her mouth.

She bit down into his palm, managing to draw blood through his glove. The pain throbbed through his hand but it didn't stop him. With an angry snarl, he used her own momentum to jerk her forward and throw her onto the ground. He dropped down onto her spine with his knees to the sound of a dry crack as brittle bones shattered.

Without any further ado, he shoved raw mana into her with one hand over her mouth and the other one on the back of her head. Flames erupted everywhere he touched. He ignored her desperate attempts to chew his fingers off and her attempts to claw at anything she thought she could reach. Her skull burned away in moments. The rest of her body quickly ignited from the inside out. There wasn't anything left to fight against him in a matter of heartbeats.

He stayed on top of her until the blaze caused her body to crumble under his weight. Embers flared up as his knees painfully hit the scorched ground. The second customer sent barreling back to the Abyss, the exorcist turned his full attention back to the damned soul hovering nearby.

Whatever this "Daringol" thing was, it bounced between the ward and the illumination spell. With no place to go and no other options, it finally gave a desperate rushed towards the priest while he was still kneeling on the ground. Maybe it thought that he could catch the young man unaware. Maybe it thought that he had used all of his power on the second zombie.

Whatever it thought, it thought wrong.

It couldn't help itself. It made one final and desperate plea when it got close to him. *"Daringol needs warm!"*

Akaran whipped about and shoved his hand into the center of the swirling mess. It burned, badly, but it hurt the wraith a whole lot more than that. He clenched his fist as he shouted a different Word at it. *"**DISPERSE!**"*

A flood of warm lavender light spilled into the twisting tentacles. Shards of the spirit broke off and shattered into nothingness. Tentacles vanished as the light made them evaporate. Spectral arms fell apart. The shadows in its core disappeared and revealed a twisted mockery of a human face with sickly white eyes and rough ridges across the forehead, cheekbones, and jaw. Smoke poured out of the holes where its nostrils should have been.

The spell didn't destroy it entirely. But it did come damn close. *"NO! NO LIGHT NO PAIN JUST WARM NEED **WARM!**"*

"WARM?" the exorcist bellowed. *"**I** will send you someplace* *warm!"*

Realizing that it was faced with imminent banishment, Daringol flew back and tried to plead its case. *"No no, no! You've destroyed our homes! We did nothing wrong! Took what they not needed! Sought for you but you are warm so warm! Not perfect homes but homes! Shelter, shelters from the cold, but no shelter now! We are lost with no home! Daringol gets no home! No shelter no warmth no home!"* it cried.

"No, you sure as all in the heavens do *not* get to have a home here!" he spat back at it. Tendrils of steam drifted off of his glowing fist. Little rivulets of energy wormed halfway up and down his forearm. Behind him and off to the side, the final zombie struggled to crawl towards the exorcist and the damned soul.

Torn halfway to shreds, the spirit shrieked in terror. It was doomed, and it knew it. *"No please no Daringol causes no harm! Daringol just wishes warmth! Accursed cold, cold and accursed!"*

"Damned thing! Whatever your part in this blasted freeze was, I am *sure* the Warden is going to take it out of your hide." He smiled as he willed magic down both arms. Akaran started to walk over to it, flexing his hands and cracking his fingers.

*"The freeze? Daringol have no part in storm! Daringol is many, many together! Many for warmth! All we wish no snow no cold just warmth! Half-breed girl makes cold! She makes cold! Daringol will take the cold all the cold the **true** cold! Daringol will make the **true** cold be warm!"*

Only marginally interested in what it had to say, he continued to stalk his prey. The exorcist spit out a mouthful of dirt and bits of ash from first two corpses. "Then I hope the four of you get to warm up together."

"Four? No! More than four! We are more -" it tried to scream.

It didn't have the chance to finish. Divine wrath lanced down Akaran's arms and lunched from his palms. "I said **DISPERSE!**" This time, there wasn't any chance for the wraith to hold itself together. The beams of light simply obliterated the ghost. There was absolutely nothing left as the spell-born brilliance faded from the mine.

Suddenly drained and out of breath, the young priest collected his sword before he leaned back against a stone wall and slid down to the ground. He watched the last zombie continue to crawl over to him. Anger faded slowly as he watched it, a stabbing jolt of pity joining dull throbs of pain that radiated up his arm.

With a small snort, Akaran picked up a rock and flung it at the corpse. It connected solidly against the side of its head. Soundlessly, the zombie quit trying to crawl. However, what it did next was not-quite unexpected by this point. Tentacles and arms pushed out of its mouth and latched onto the ground. Enough of it pulled free for him to see that it was almost exactly the same as the first one.

He might have paid more attention to Daringol's rants than the wraith had thought.

Glaring, the priest was on top of it before it had the opportunity to get loose. Even in pain, he moved faster than it could, and his sword cut through the zombie's skull and right through the squirming mass of tendrils and the upturned face taking form in the middle of it. The blade lit up with blue and white flames as it incinerated boiled away both flesh and spirit. "Don't even try."

There was a short but pained moan from around the edges of his weapon. The tendrils hit the ground and shattered into pieces like they were made of phantom glass, and then they vanished completely. The corpse itself fared no better. Its upper torso was reduced to smoldering embers before the spell ran its course.

Confident that everything dead in the mine actually *was* dead, he gave himself time to catch his breath. As he looked around at the mess he had made through the battle the gravity of the encounter began to weigh down on his shoulders. As the aura around his sword and hand bled away into nothing, he tried to comprehend everything that had just happened.

Absolutely no comforting answers were forthcoming.

Sighing, he pulled a handful of small canvas bags from his belt pouch. The blessed mixtures of herbs, metal shavings, and a couple clods of sanctified soil would do well enough to keep the dead down for good... just to be safe. The bodies would be rendered inhospitable for any wraith to ever touch again and not even the ashes would emit even a hint of toxic aura (and he gave serious thought to digging up the remainder of the corpses at the village to give them the same treatment before he called his trip quits).

A few spells (and prayers) later would keep the mine sanctified for generations to come. He was absolutely sure that nothing dead would be able to break the seals he was laying down for the next few hundred years. By the time he was finished, he was more than confident that the mine would be purified for good.

Akaran was wrong, of course, but he was absolutely sure that it would work.

It really wasn't his best week.

Really though, all of the precautions were just overkill. Then again – this 'simple haunting' was no longer all that simple. Would it hurt to be a bit more cautious? The flames he was about to consign them to wouldn't even leave enough of them behind for anyone to stumble across and wonder who or what had left teeth laying on the ground. Even the special packages of sanctified material he was stuffing into the bodies would go up in smoke.

At least it would make them smell a little better. Maybe. Though there was a great deal of cold misery to be enjoyed as he fished bits and pieces of them out from the watery muck in the cave. By the time he was done the exorcist was just about certain that maybe Daringol had a point. He had a feeling he was about to be willing to do just about anything to warm up himself.

That was easily solved by sticking around and letting the bonfire of bodies dry him out before he continued on his way. One other thing that he took the time to do was recover the body of that Steward of Blizzards he had found earlier. Theologically speaking, setting the body of a worshiper of the Lady of Pure Frost on fire would probably be frowned upon.

Circumstances outweighed protocol in the end. The Steward joined the other remains without any immediate feelings of guilt to be had (a decision Akaran would hear about at length later on). Hopefully nobody would make a big fuss out of it.

Hopefully.

He stayed around long enough to make sure that the bodies were completely reduced to cinders before he left to make his way back to town. Those zombies weren't the first he'd culled. The small one though, that was his first child. It was hard to think of it as anything else. It had a child's body, it had a child's size. He knew it wasn't really one. It had been one once, sure, but it wasn't one now.

Knowing, and *knowing* are always two different things. It didn't make it any easier. All he could do was hope that the thing that had taken possession of it really *hadn't* been the little girl. There were things that could snag souls and force them to do awful things. That was true in life and true in death.

Those wraiths though? They had him worried. They weren't even the first lost souls he'd ever seen (the Temple made sure that there was no shortage of horrors that they introduced exorcists-to-be to). Surely not the first spirit. Yet each of those times, it had always been under a controlled setting. A single lost soul was what he had been expecting to run across. Whatever those things were though...

At the Temple, he'd seen a few. They never looked like that. They never acted like that.

Somehow, he felt that Hirshma had been right – this land may have been pure, once. It wasn't now, and it never would be again. He looked over at a small pool of blood left behind from the deer carcass and sighed. *Yeah, it never will be again.*

The thought left a very sick feeling in his stomach the entire trip back to town.

And of all the things he could have been right about...

VI. FROST'S BITE

The trip back from the cave was even less enjoyable than the trip to it. His white tabard was coated in foul-smelling ash and other unpleasantness. Burning the herbs with the corpses did absolutely nothing to improve the stench from incinerating the bodies (*dammit*). He supposed there was no way he was going to get the odor out of his hair, either. Getting a bath in *this* cold? Oh no. That was *completely* out of the question.

Trying to dry out from the flooded mine was bad enough. Doing it again out here in the wild? Turning into an exorcist-sized-icicle? He wasn't even enamored with the idea of doing it back in Toniki in front of a roaring fireplace. *Then again, if Rmaci helps, then maybe...*

Really, picking between that and reeking of charred corpses suddenly didn't seem all that bad.

Even still. The stench did manage to kill his appetite. Spoiled his mood, too. The longer he thought about it, it probably killed his chances to be warmed up by that barmaid on top of it. Not that the wraith did anything to make him give more than a passing thought to the wench and her steamy ways.

Ghosts were *far* more common than the average peasant (or even nobility) thought. By their very nature, one could pop up anywhere someone died. A soul is a soul, and every man and beast born of this world has one. For that matter, there were quite a few beasts that were thought to have souls that originated in the other planes of existence – divine or otherwise.

There was an oft-disputed theological question as to if trees and plants did; followers of Kora'thi said yes, and everyone else said that

Nature's druids were a crazy bunch of twits. So, there was room to argue it. Don't *even* get started on what the diminutive freaks in the dwarven kingdoms thought about *rocks.*

Usually, the vast majority of souls freed from their physical bodies went off to their next life without any convincing from mere mortals. Typically, it happened within the blink of an eye. If you were *incredibly* in tune with the spirit world, you might even be able to see someone's aura flicker into the ether when someone gave up the ghost.

Sure, every now and again you'd run across someone no longer breathing that preferred to be guided into the afterlife by a kindly priest willing to hold their metaphysical hand on the way out. Or you'd run into one so stubborn about moving on that they would manifest and cause all kinds of trouble, leading to a situation much like this one: an exorcist being summoned to dispose of the spirit before it could cause any more mischief.

So while it was usually just the unhappy dead that would hang around at times...

...it was just a *lot* more unusual for them to be able to crawl back into a body.

Then there was the question of what it was saying, and what it seemed to want. The more he considered it, the nastier the thought turned. That creature, Daringol... there was a lot to the encounter to feel unsettled over.

*It named itself. Names **do** have power. The most base of the damned rank-and-file don't have one or don't remember what it was in life. It was sentient, too. Desperate, focused, able to engage in some kind of conversation. Let's not discount "We are many."*

*We are many? We are many what? **That** is **not** how you define reassuring.*

He doubted it was just simple circumstance that the last zombie seemed to be possessed by the same type of wraith that had been hiding in the deer. That meant that the walking corpses weren't restless because of ill-borne or even wild magic. They were restless because three other wraiths had made them get up and start moving.

Explains how that Steward made it into the cave. I think.

That didn't answer the question as to why they were trying to gorge themselves on the deer that their friend had been trying to take over. It surely looked like they weren't working together, or at least, that they weren't happy with their companion's effort to possess the fresh kill.

He wondered if they were also after 'warmth,' like the freely-floating spirit said it was. The deer's blood wasn't warm, but it wasn't frigid. It was warmer than the rest of the room, at least. Even then, if they did want the warmth of a body, why did the wraiths wait until the last second to free themselves and fight without being encumbered by a rotting sack of meat and bones? The unbound one moved freely on its own. Was it controlling the other three? Or was there a simple reason behind it?

Maybe they must have just really wanted to keep those bodies all to themselves.

Four in total in the mine, and that frigid bitch from last night makes five. Hirshma said she had personally put down five more. So, ten. Plus whatever tore up the garrison soldiers. Those zombies couldn't have done that. There's no way. The army would have walked through them and brushed them off without a second thought.

Unless these wraiths managed to infest something really big with a lot of teeth, they aren't the culprits. They didn't want to give up a child's body or a broken animal. I can't see them giving up a couple of bears for a handful of old carcasses. Or at least, **those** *wraiths. Hard to say how many more are out there. There could* **be** *re-animated bears stalking the mountain for all I know.*

Ugly thought, that.

Well. Even without Ronlin's complaints about the weather, it's pretty obvious that there's something out there with a pretty strong pull to lead them. Or at least, to bring them into this world. The cold is just a symptom of the taint on the land around here. He really didn't like the thought but all signs pointed to it being right. As a symptom though, it was a weird one.

So. The wraiths like the cold as much as I do. That girl from last night is terrified of fire. Two entirely different entities with completely different metaphysical traits. With everything else that it said, I'm willing to bet that there's a power play going on that doesn't particularly care about the local villagers. Or it least, they didn't, before they started eating people.

What changed?

What changed was the wrong question to ask right at the moment. What kind of spirits were they? Figuring that out was much more important. What those spirits did moved them from just being simple apparitions and into an entirely new category. Figuring out their reasons could wait. Figuring out what they were…

Lost souls tended to look like humans (or animals, depending on what they had been in life). Those things? No. Not even close. Maybe in the face – maybe. It didn't change the fact that they were still ghosts (and were disposable using the standard set of rites and spells). Still. That opened up a slew of other complications.

Full-blown wraiths were a lot harder to cope with than some meandering soul that wasn't aware it was dead. Simple spirits could show up and scare people, sometimes make things fall over. *Wraiths* could directly interact with the physical world, and there were few limits to the things they couldn't do. When they interacted they were pretty focused on the how, based off of what had given them power.

Died in a blaze? Your angry spirit could set fires. Drowned? Aside from making a room reek of dead fish, you could expect a waterlogged evening of macabre entertainment. (A few years ago, a trainer that summoned one outside of the Academy barracks as an 'example' was punched out by one of the students just for the smell alone.) Everyone (the trainer included) learned the lesson *real* fast: inherent abilities could be a source of great anguish.

This is a breed of them. What kind, I don't know. I've never heard of damned souls that looked like that. Nothing in the of the Damned and Divine. They didn't look like any of the usual servants of the Fallen, not that I can tell. They didn't smell of rot and weren't interested in fighting for the sake of fighting. They didn't act like they were fueled by hate or made desperate from lust.

Dammit. That alone takes out half of the Lower Pantheon. Could be something new that owes allegiance to one of the Archdukes, if not to one of the Fallen? How bad would my luck have to be to run into something freshly cooked up from the Pit? It can't be that convoluted, can it?

Sometimes spirits would arrive in the Abyss take on characteristics of their newly-found environment. Or sometimes they manifested (somewhat) naturally in the living world, and would be similar in appearance to other lost souls in the area. But they still should look a *little* human. These didn't.

Damn.

Those wraiths just looked like someone had taken as many arms and legs as they could find and shoved them into a void in the air and told each one to try and claw free of it all at the same time. Seeing as absolutely none of that made any kind of sense to his inexperienced mind, that changed the game in a lot of miserable ways. *Miserable isn't even the right word for it. Starting to think that it's a bloody blessing that the village hasn't been wiped off the map already.*

Though I suppose... Eos'eno, whatever she called herself, said she was from Tundrala – the Upper Elemental Plane of Ice. These things are agonized over the cold. Makes you wonder where they're from. Frosel? If I had been condemned to the Lower Plane? If I had pissed off the Goddess of Frost bad enough to be sent into that awful torment? I'd be desperate to find warmth myself.

Safe to say that if there's at least two of them – no, ten – I'm going to find more of them up in the mountain the higher I go. I'm probably going to end up spending the rest of my life prying these vile things out of the rocks up here. I just can feel it in every inch of my body.

Lady above, this is a mess. Wraiths, minds somewhat intact, drawn to corpses to reanimate them. Around ten of them. Unknown breed, unknown patronage, unknown cause of death that would leave them in such an odd state. Or even if they were alive once, and not just patched together down in the Pit.

Then the girl. Whatever she is. Too much of my guesswork depends on her being from where she said she is. If I'm wrong I don't have any idea what I'm dealing with here. Not that I have much of an idea anyways... "Cold" is their only similarity. If those things are Frosel escapees, that's the closest thing that I can think of that would make sense.

A brand new bad thought popped into his head as he rode into the outskirts of the village.

Okay, say she is from Tundrala. How is she here? Did Usaic summon her? Did she cross into our world on her own? Why is she here? Protecting her master's work, she said. Trying to recover her lord? Said she needed help, seemed to think I was it. Is she alone? Are there more of her?

*In the name of all, **why**?*

The Sisters wouldn't have sent me if they thought this was going to be this ugly. I mean I know I'm a tool of the Temple. We all are. Can't see them throwing me away like this, not if they knew. So if they didn't think that this would be this complicated, that meant that the wraiths and their masters were able to hide their auras. Same with Eos.

That, or the Sisters have much more faith in me than I do.

*Wait. For that matter, not only did they hide it well enough to keep it from being felt at a distance by the most powerful seers in **any** kingdom, they did it well enough to hide from me up close. The ether barely rippled, even when I was inside their chamber. It just felt like wild* *magic. Not something focused. They're powerful enough as a group, at least, to block a scrying. Weak enough to banish without drastic measures.*

This gets worse by the minute.

Damn. If those things can possess corpses, makes you wonder what else they can grab. Should be grateful that they were only after dead bodies this time around. Could be worse. They could be animating rocks. **That** *would probably hurt a lot.*

He looked down at his wrist and rubbed it absentmindedly. It still burned from where the pitspawn had touched him. *Or maybe they're not just after dead bodies. The first one did try to push itself into me.* His stomach lurched a little as he considered what would have happened if it had succeeded. If he had tripped coming in, or slid on the wet rocks and hit his head... there wouldn't have been a thing he could have done to stop it.

Akaran had to bring Nayli to a slow stop for a few minutes while he pondered the implications about how close he came to a brush with something that suddenly felt like would have been a lot worse than just death. *It wanted warmth, needed it. That implies the others did too. So why are they here if they're so cold? This isn't a hot spring. Couldn't they just... fly for a few weeks and find a beach somewhere south of the mountains?*

A new thought – just as confusing as the rest – popped in his head. *Really? Ghosts get cold? Even* **if** *they're from Frosel, you'd think that being* **here** *would make life easier on them for that fact alone.*

But, okay. That one hates the cold. I know that the girl reacted poorly to the tavern fire. What am I not seeing? By the Grace of the Goddess, what are these things up to? Is she hunting or... haunting them? Are they hunting her? If I can figure out why they're at war maybe I can figure out what they actually are. But... dammit, no. She wasn't strong enough to cause a long-term change of weather either. At least, I don't think she is.

It keeps coming back to the snow. You can't both be too weak to be felt and strong enough to change the weather at the same time. Storm magic of **any** *kind is notoriously complex. Then to make it last over the long-term? Even simple disruptions require a lot of power. Or if not direct power, indirect effects from something of sizable impact.*

I mean... oh, fisk it all. How DOES a ghost get cold, anyways? It's not like they have skin.

He looked up to the cloudy, cold sky with a sigh. *Goddess? Why*

74

would you send me here? This is more than just I can handle, isn't it? The Sisters had to have looked for danger, that there would be little here to be much of a threat. They are rarely wrong, so what makes this time different? Wait...

Almost back to the village, he brought his horse to a second complete stop before he looked back over his shoulder. Any and all thoughts of merriment vanished on the spot. *Usaic. That wizard is the wildcard. Until I can figure out what he was doing, there's no point in trying to figure out the rest.*

That's when he stumbled on a thought that was right in ways he wouldn't realize for a few more hours. Long, painful hours, but he'd eventually realize how right he was. *Wait. The wraiths are a **symptom** – so's the cold. They're not the **cause**. If Usaic's work is what's causing the weather, then it stands to reason that it would be strong enough to attract the attention of creatures already wandering in the ether. Or his work let them break through the veil.*

*It wouldn't even have to be necromantic in nature. An elementalist with a specialization in planar manipulation would be enough to wake the dead for hundreds of miles if he made something that got out of his hands. Say he breached the walls into Tundrala, then say something happened to him. Or his spell. Containment of magic is key. It is **always** key.*

If he breached the elemental planes and didn't seal the hole wraiths flying about everywhere would make perfect sense. Everything would. Including the fisking weather.

Oh, shit. If his magic is strong enough to screw with the seasons it would be strong enough to mask itself. Fisk, I would've masked it. Putting down heavy-duty spellwork attracts attention from anyone with their eye even half-turned to the next world. Assuming he did, and he blocked it from sight? Nobody could have known if they weren't looking directly at it.

Fisk me. Oh I do not like where this is going. If they're masked – even by accident – there's no telling how many of them there are. One or two at a time is one thing. What if more come? What if they figure out there's a lot more warmth to be had in fresh serfs than in their dead bodies? Or... whatever else could be loose.

*If I'm right, you can start that list with the things that ate the garrison. That means whatever else is out there could be absolutely **anything** at all. Absolutely fisking **wonderful**. I am making way too much sense to be wrong. Until someone can prove to me otherwise, this* *is what I'm basing this haunting off of.*

He couldn't help but entertain another thought. *Now I just need to figure out what changed. Why did they suddenly come to the graveyard? As desperate as that thing seemed to be to find a shell, why did it only recently start looking at the local graveyard? Did I miss something there? I had to have.*

There's no warding to speak of. The ground wasn't consecrated. Some of the graves had been blessed, but just... barely. Old graves, old blessings. Simple magic that fades over the years. If they could take corpses, they could have easily pushed through what was left there. There were more than eight bodies in that field.

So what's taken them so long? Unless there was something old enough there that would keep them from probing too close to Toniki? But what? Blessings fade over time. There wasn't a single person in the village that looked like they wouldn't consider lynching to be the only appropriate way to welcome anyone an affinity towards magic. So is this all just lucky timing on my part?

So much of this is conjecture. Probably wrong about all of it. The Sisters always did hate it when we'd jump to conclusions. Doesn't mean we were wrong. Just means they liked us to have something more solid to go on.

So... where do I go from here?

He forced himself to clear his mind and meditate as he traveled back towards the village. With the bodies disposed of, the next step was to ensure their place of burial would remain undisturbed. Normally, he'd have waited to say a prayer over each grave as the occupants were returned to rest. Normally, there wouldn't be this many bodies left unattended. Normally, you would bring back the ash. What was left behind in the mine was too waterlogged to bag up and drag back to sanctified ground.

Without knowing who should have been where, he'd have to go through each one to reinforce the sanctification ritual he had used earlier in the day. Even if not for the safety of the village, but for the souls that the restless bodies had belonged to. *Nobody likes it when someone moves into their old house*, he mused, *and I can't see that this is much different.*

The graveyard wasn't too far away from the village wall. So, at least it had that much going for it. All he wanted at this point was just to find a fire, clean the dusty and disgusting remnants of long lost villagers off of his armor, and pray for guidance. That was what he wanted. Cold, wet, and miserable had all the hallmarks of a cough starting if he didn't find shelter soon.

What he saw when he got there made his own complaints irrelevant. At first, he thought it was a snowdrift against a gravestone. Just another drift, a mess of this white misery, dotting another grave. It took him a moment to realize what was so very wrong about it, because no, it wasn't a drift.

It was a boy's body. Even when he stood over it, it was hard to really tell much about it. If he had to guess, he figured that he was no older than eleven years, maybe twelve. His neck had been twisted almost completely around, and his back had been broken backward. The neck had been the killing injury; the rest could have been caused by the impact against the grave-marker.

No, that wasn't true. It had been done by hand. A very large, inhuman hand. As he quietly worked to brush away snow and dirt from the child, he took notice of deep claw marks into his side and scalp. They were too big to be done by anything human. He honestly didn't know if that made him feel relieved or worse. The fact that the hands were the size of his own and half as much more was making him lean towards worse.

He worked quietly by torchlight. The smell of oily rags burning beside him helped mask odors he didn't recognize coming from the boy's body. For what he needed to see, the light itself wouldn't have done him any good. Unfortunately, there wasn't anything in the ether that gave off a clue either. Try as hard as he could the best he could feel were little wisps of anger and darkness – and a pungent hint of a toxic, vile aura that he didn't think came from the zombies in the mine.

It wasn't the same poisonous, foul *wrongness* from the wraiths in the mine or the taint that had taken over Lativus's body. If an aura could be aloof, this one was. It was the only word he had for it and it didn't make much more sense either. Less when he realized that this meant that there was yet another player active in the area. *Until I can figure out otherwise... "Aloof" will do for a name.*

A big player. He had no idea how far back that the kid had been thrown from. It could have been five feet away. It could have been twenty. Either way, that made it bigger than the exorcist, and Akaran didn't like that thought.

"I knew the boy, you know. Grew up here. Since a babe."

He had heard her coming so it wasn't a surprise. It wasn't a welcome voice, but it wasn't a surprise. "I'm sorry."

"I know. You didn't do this, you didn't cause this. Don't..."

"Something did. It won't live to see the end of the next moon." He looked up at the sky. "What was his name?"

Hirshma walked closer. "Julianos. His mother passed. Two years back. His father left... some time before then. Just some trader. Last anyone saw, fool went off to the Midlands." Her voice trembled a little bit as she looked down at the body. "Whole town always took care of him. It's what we did. We were a happy people before."

"I am sorry."

"Sorry won't bring him back."

"No, it won't. It won't bring anyone back." Akaran looked up at her with a grave but exhausted glare in his eye. "We can't leave him here."

She gave a weak "Yes," in response, and then added: "I'll let the others know. Set him... set him here peaceful like, please? They'll need to hear from you. Again. You're starting to have a calling to that. They'll want to come take him home."

"Can't."

"Hm?"

Akaran carefully picked the child up and walked towards his horse. "I can't leave him where he is. Whatever took him wasn't the same as the wraiths in the cave. Can't risk it."

"Wraiths? What wraiths?"

"Not important right now. We can't leave the body here." Gently, he set the boy on Nayli's back and covered the child with his cloak.

As he did, Ronlin's sister caught sight of the blood and bandages on his hand and finally noticed all of the blackened gore on his tabard. "What... what did you find out there? What did you do?"

"Your missing dead. We can discuss it later." Hindsight being the mother of all misfortune, he'd realize that he might have made his life a lot easier if he talked about everything then with her in private (which possibly could have won her over to his cause) – instead of springing it on everyone as a whole a few minutes later.

The pair approached the town proper without saying another word to each other. The exorcist felt wracked with guilt; he couldn't quit blaming himself for not finding the source of the disturbance before the child died. Her heart broken, the woman next to him could barely manage to think of what to say.

People went from door to door, waking up other members of the township to give them word of the terrible news. They quickly assembled at the village square, with Julianos's body being taken off of Nayli's back almost immediately. Vestranis took the body out of Akaran's custody with a foul look towards the priest.

The body was somberly delivered to a small shrine dedicated to the Upper Pantheon of Light – a shrine that included idols of the likes of Pristi, Melia, and even Kora'thi. It had three-quarters of a dozen others to join them. Niasmis was not included in that list, of course.

Istalla was, though. He wondered how many people appreciated that. Her bust looked newer and in far better conditions than the others. That was odd; he would have guessed that the Goddess of Ice would not exactly be in high regard around here. *I wonder if that Eos'eno creature... girl... whatever... is somehow responsible for that.*

For a brief moment, it made the exorcist ponder the idea of if he should even attempt to enter for fear of offending his hosts. It was only a brief moment. The work to be done superseded any other concerns. He was going to end up offending them anyways so why did something so small matter?

On the outside, it was a small building, only slightly bigger than the town hall. Shaped like a layered pyramid that went up a little less than two stories tall, the busts of the Gods of Pantheon decorated small pillars on either side of the walkway leading into the temple. It was, by far, the most ornate building in the village.

He had no problems believing that it was also the largest example of ego-stroking to be found in these mountains, with the possible exception of the provincial capital's brothel. (*Gonta, isn't it? Lador?*)

Ornate or not, however, it was in disrepair. Dead vines had wrapped themselves around the pillars and cracks where old mortar had broken free gaped open along the lower parts of the wall. Nobody had been performing any kind of upkeep on anything.

Except for that bust of Istalla.

*Somebody's not even **trying** to be subtle.*

That aside, this felt incredibly odd. The people here seemed to have no love for the Gods but the very presence of the shrine spoke differently and screamed out their hypocrisy. He voiced these concerns to the innkeeper's wife when she stopped to linger next to him. Her reply was as simple as her voice was quiet.

"We've no want for the priests and the charlatans that speak their names. But the Gods? They say every man and woman needs one in their life."

"I was just expecting Melia here... not almost all of the Pantheon," he whispered back.

"The Goddess of Destruction?" She failed to hold back an irritated grunt and spat her name out in utter revulsion. "Just because the Queen worships Her and named Her the 'Benefactress of the Kingdom' doesn't mean we have to do the same."

He accepted her answer for what it was and didn't plan on pressing further. "I see. Thank you." *Fine. Let them tell themselves whatever. It's obvious their derision is only aimed at me and mine. Everyone needs a God in their life. Bullshit. If they did, I might get along with them better. No, just a bunch of sanctimonious pricks that only call for a God when they need something. Well tough shit you hypocrites,* **my** *Goddess sent* **me***, like it or not.*

Then she added the other, more concise answer when she looked at him with a faint smile on her lips. "The Order of Light offered Ronlin's father a pile of gold a mule could barely carry to put this gaudy blight here, dedicated to Gods that don't give a shit about us any more than we do them."

That, sadly, made a lot more sense. With an irritated inward sigh, he retracted his unvoiced condemnations. Most of them, anyways. *Still a bunch of pricks. Greedy pricks now. All I needed to know.*

Only a few people entered the shrine. Rmaci lingered for a moment with him before speaking to the nine or so that had gathered outside the door. He overheard one of them say that they were waiting for someone to give them permission to enter. That was just as well. He really wasn't looking forward to the talk he'd have to have in there.

The fewer to yell at me, the better.

With a wary look, one of them gave him a bleary state through bloodshot eyes. He recognized him from earlier – Moulborke, the fat woodsman and one of several drunks that the town had to offer. "Your Goddess. She ain't liked all that much by the others. Heard rumors, tales about that. Her people abandoned Illiya's armies in Agromah? Set them up to fall way back when?"

Akaran shook his head and sighed. "No. She didn't. We lost as many as everyone else."

"But then why are Hers so hated?"

"The rest of the Pantheon blame Her for something She didn't have a hand in. They blamed Her, condemned Her followers, cast Her to the lowest parts of the Heavenly Mount. Her people, my people... we were shoved into a great deal of suffering. Wasn't until we grounded

80

ourselves in southern Dawnfire did we get a home to call our own again."

"Oh." The look in her eyes made him think she was going to ask for more, but then Rmaci put a hand on his shoulder. The moment he stepped inside he was taken aback by some of the excesses that the Orders of Light filled their shrines with. Even this one, in a town far away from the hubs of the Kingdom, even in one that gave no love to the Gods as a whole? They treated *every* temple as if it was the only one in the world.

Everywhere he looked, tarnished silver and dull gold attempted to glint in the torchlight. It lined every curve and every corner of the shrine, including the tall altar against the far side of the room where every God and Goddess in the Pantheon had been cast in white marble. Each bust had a platform jutting out from the wall, and the platforms were arranged in the same triangular layer as the shrine outside.

If you could ignore the cobwebs, dust, and small plumes of dried mold in the corners, it would *almost* pass as a place of worship. It didn't. Could pass as a hideout for a gang of murderers and thieves, surely. *Oh wait. That seems perfectly fitting for these hypocritical Godlings. I stand corrected.*

He had to force himself to not remark on his missing Goddess. Not only was She not included, the men that built the shrine had purposefully left Her space on it empty. It was supposed to be just below the top of the pyramid, with two other platforms below her visage. Love was once the focus, the catalyst, for the acts by all of the other Gods.

But now?

The other two Gods that had pledged direct allegiance to Her and Her glory that made the world work were present – Kora'thi, the Goddess of Nature and the Majesty of the Elements and Solinal, the God of Peace and the Patron of the Weary. Yet Niasmis Herself? The Lady that both were once said to answer to?

No, She was intentionally left empty.

He had to presume it was to serve as a reminder for any of Her followers that neither She nor Her people were welcome here. It got the point across nicely. A disgusted voice somewhere in the back of his head suggested that he should come back and spit on the blank face of the Origin, the God atop the shrine. It was an ill-advised idea, true, but it *was* a tempting one.

The Origin. The God that all Gods honor as the True Beginning.

*Faceless, formless, and with a name too supposedly holy to be uttered by 'mere' mortals. Sanctimonious prick. Absolutely just one huge sanctimonious cosmic **prick**.*

Inwardly, he let himself grumble as he stepped back into a corner and watched the proceedings. *The one that the other members of the Pantheon claimed They were honoring when They threw the Lady out of Their ranks. He's just nothing more than an egotistic voice in the light that doesn't give a damn about anyone or what people or Gods do in His name. For an all-powerful, all-knowing God, He COULD have stopped His children from turning on His most beautiful daughter.*

Fuming, he turned his attention to everyone gathered in the room. Ronlin and four other men stood by Julianos's corpse. Vestranis looked down at the both with tears in his otherwise dull brown eyes while Yothargi had a laid his scarred hand on the boy's brow. The other two weren't important enough to the town to even mention. They were there because they wanted to be, and had no apparent use to the situation at hand. The elder appeared to be calling for the divine in a quiet prayer.

Akaran's needs were too immediate to wait.

He kept his voice low enough that only the men beside him would hear him. Word would make it around the town fast enough – and right now he needed permission to work more than he needed a village full of morose mundanes civilians crying over the corpse. "Elder. The body needs to be consigned to the flames. Now, not later."

All eyes snapped over to him. It was difficult to say if their ire was because of his interruption or because of his request. Yothargi's ire was probably born from other incidents since the exorcist's arrival and he spoke up first. "Burnt to ash? That isn't our way."

"You've no right to tell us how we bury our own," one of the two nameless fools added.

"Yes, I do," Akaran corrected. "Something unholy claimed his life. He's been defiled. I'd like us to not make it worse than what it is."

The elder protectively placed a hand on Julianos's chest. "And who's fault is that? You were sent to help us. Not to go wander out in the wilds. Now he's dead – how much worse can it be?"

"I went where your sister told me," the exorcist snapped back. "And that doesn't matter. What *does* is that something came here and murdered this boy. *Just* this boy."

Vestranis wiped away his tears with a calloused hand. "Then we count ourselves lucky to still be among the living. That doesn't -"

"Yes, it does. I don't know what did this but it *wasn't* something human. I don't know why and I don't wish to find out tonight. I've already seen things in the dark that don't belong here. Without knowing why the rest of you were spared? Ensuring that the child isn't used for worse is an *absolute* must."

Ronlin shook his head. "Then go back into the dark. This boy is here with us in the light."

If only they knew, he sighed inwardly. "I just banished a spirit that was able to reanimate a body on its own. It didn't have help. It didn't have instructions. It wasn't doing a task. It was trying to survive. It was sentient. You have a *very* serious threat here. A simple burial will not be enough." That worked to shut them up. Their eyes darted between each other before finally returning to his. "Do you really want to risk his soul, too?"

A shade paler than he had been a moment ago, Ronlin began to change his tune. "Evil can't enter a shrine, can it? Spirits of the damned have no hold in a place devoted to the Order."

"I suppose that depends on what's out there," Akaran countered. "And how strong your faith in the Divine is. I gather it isn't much." The men looked back and forth at each other while they each debated the truth of his statement. "His body *must* be purified in flame."

"Can't you do something else? Anything else?" the blacksmith asked. "He was one of us. He deserves a sendoff from all of the village befitting that. We failed him in life. Please do not make us dishonor him in his death."

"There is no dishonor in ensuring he won't rise again."

"Julianos was a son to everyone," Ronlin argued. "At least let everyone see him one last time before he is sent away."

Hirshma stepped into the fray while the exorcist stifled a groan. "I need to tend to the body before it goes anywhere," she snapped with a tired-but-furious stare. "You'll not consign him to any flame nor grave before he is made proper to be returned to the land. It is our way. It is Kora's way."

"Kora's way? I thought you -"

"I don't," she snapped – suddenly a *lot* angrier than she had cause to be. "The land should still be honored."

One of the nameless twits behind her started to say something before Vestranis quieted him with a hand on his shoulder. Akaran was too tired to notice him standing up for him. "I'm not going to say I understand your traditions. I can't say I care. Please understand mine. I cannot let this boy lay here unattended and vulnerable. You wouldn't want to see what would happen if he was defiled and ends up as one of the risen."

"We won't set his body ablaze here and now. We will not let you." Ronlin argued. "We asked for your aid but we did not agree to let you have your way with our dead."

"Yes. You did. I'm not here to plant flowers and sing hymns." Glaring at all of them, he gave up with a sigh. "Fine. Then let me prepare him – and then I'll keep watch over him through the night."

"You'll keep watch over the dead? What about keeping watch over us?"

Akaran shrugged. "The thing that killed the boy didn't bother taking the time to come in and kill anyone else. I don't feel an abyssian aura in the town, so whatever it did it left. For now. That doesn't mean that it won't be back or that the wraiths in the mountains won't try to use the child as a vessel."

"A vessel? What do you mean...?" Yothargi asked as he stared at him, not even remotely comprehending the severity of the situation at hand.

The alchemist stopped the answer before Akaran could give it. "It doesn't matter what he means. *I* will prepare the body, and *we* will have a ceremony for him come morning."

"The only way I am going to allow you to touch his body is if you let me do my work first." Trying to hold back a growl of his own, the priest just about bit Hirshma's head off. "We already had this fight. His body is the newest and the most immediate threat to your safety. If you won't let me do what *needs* to be done, then let me do the only other thing I *can* do."

She wavered for what felt like an age before giving in. "He's right. We *did* ask for his aid. I'll let him give it. We'll send him to ashes tomorrow. You may work your... whatever it is you think you need to do... now."

"To what end? How do we even know he's telling the truth?" Ronlin challenged.

"We *will* let him do it," his sister snapped. All but Rmaci – who was silent through the entire discussion – tried to argue their cases, but Hirshma shut them down each in turn. "I don't want him here any more than the rest of you do but whatever is going on here is more than any one of us can handle. The sooner we let him do his work the sooner we can be rid of him and whatever it is out there tormenting the land."

*Tormenting the land? Not tormenting the people? She **should** be a priestess of Kora'thi.* Wearily, Akaran took a step back. "The Temple is sanctified. It should be safe from outside influences. Or it may not be. I'm here by your request – and by request of the army – *and* by the authority of the Queen. If you want to argue that with *them*, go ahead, but we're not going to argue it with *me* any longer."

Defeated, Ronlin had to consent. "Then do what you need – but that body will *not* be burned until *after* the village has a chance to wish him a safe passage into the next world.*"*

"Fine." He swept his eye over every single one of them. "I need quiet to do this. If you can't, be outside. Be home. Be something. But be *not here*," he ordered.

They really didn't like his tone. For their credit though, they finally took him seriously and stopped their bickering. He imagined the only reason they didn't argue longer was due to the alchemist – but his edict didn't fail to include her.

One after another, they all stormed out (albeit somewhat quietly, out of reverence for the boy, even if not for the Gods), until only Hirshma remained behind. "Just because I know you have a duty of your own does not mean I have to enjoy watching you do it."

"Lady, there are no shortage of things in this world that those in my Order are called upon to do that people would not enjoy watching." He kept her gaze with one of his own, though his eyelid was drooping and his shoulders were sagging. "I don't expect this to be any different."

Hirshma's glare continued throughout. "He's already been murdered and mutilated. Now you plan on defiling him too? You've no shame, do you?"

There was probably no chance of a victory against her. Instead, Akaran reached under his coat and pulled out the last of the herbal concoctions he had prepared for the 'simple haunting' he had been sent to dispatch. *Goddess only knows if I can find what I need to resupply.* As he held it in his hand, he placed the other on the boy's chest. "Blessed be this child, blessed be his path. Blessed be his journey into the next life, blessed may it be and blessed will it be his last," he prayed, his eye closed and his voice barely above a whisper.

"Praying to your Goddess ain't done a shit-lot of good so far. What makes you think it will now?"

He ignored her. "Blessed be, Lady of Love, blessed be Your guidance, and blessed be Your light. Sanctify this body, sanctify his heart. Let none touch it, let none defile it, let none use it for the dark."

As he finished, he carefully opened Julianos's mouth and placed the pouch into it.

The alchemist growled as he pushed it inside and didn't bother holding back her curses as he carefully shut his mouth. "Not enough that he's dead, now you have to...? What? Cram him full of garbage? Charlatan playing as a 'holy warrior.' Do you really think that -"

That's when she saw the light from his fingers, and words failed her.

Akaran lifted his head up and affixed her with a stare that would have stopped a rampaging boar in its tracks. He didn't say anything. He didn't need to. A glow began to emanate from the body. As a pale blue light ebbed out of Julianos's mouth and out of the scratches covering his skin, the exorcist just looked at her with undisguised annoyance.

She eventually found the courage to speak, although it was little more than a whisper. "You're... not a fraud, are you?"

"I'm tired," he snapped, "and I don't have time for this. Do as you need for the boy. There's more going on here than any of us know, and I've got more to take care of before I can sleep."

"You do? What?"

He stepped away from the altar and brushed against her as he stormed out. "You wouldn't care even if I told you, so don't bother asking," he spat. "We've no more business to discuss."

Hirshma said something to him. It wasn't entirely polite but it was far more muted than her outbursts had been before. He just didn't care about it at all. The night wasn't getting any warmer and there was a lot more work to do.

What he didn't know, and what she didn't know, was that the death had just set into motion a series of progressively fouler events and even worse decisions. What they also didn't know was that outside the shrine, in a small fountain that had long ago iced over, water bubbled and trickled down the sides of its bowl. While not inherently unusual...

...the fact that it bubbled with every word of the blessing he said was.

Lost in thought outside the shrine, he didn't see the alchemist walk out of the temple after she had finished her preparations. Up until that point, his mare had been his only companion (and he liked it that way). So far, she had heard every profane opinion he had on the snow, the village, the people, the wraiths, and even the wizard that had dropped him in the mud at the start of this particular quest.

The poor mare showed far more patience than he had, and had

resisted smacking him with her tail just to get him to shut up. "I don't suppose *you* have any ideas, do you Nayli? How long do you suppose it'll be before they start getting more adventurous?"

His horse just snorted back at him. It was the equine version of 'damned if I know.'

"Not helpful."

She answered with another derisive snort.

"Well of course not," Hirshma snipped. "It's a horse. Did you get hit on your head out there or does your Goddess teach you to love all manners of beasts?"

"She teaches the value of manners. I think that's lesson you'd be wise to learn. Please, no bickering. Usaic – I have questions, I need answers, and I need them now." Akaran paused for a moment, and looked at her with his head half-tilted to the side. "And a few about what you did to those zombies."

The alchemist crossed her arms over her chest. Gray hair couldn't hide the ill-amused brown eyes that glared at him. "Oh of course you do. Well. I've got a warm fire at home waiting for me, so don't expect me to waste a lot of time out here."

He almost dared to hope that there really was a chance she'd act somewhat human. "Then I don't suppose we could talk in front of it, maybe? I'm not sure I can feel my fingers."

There was absolutely no hesitation in her reply. "No."

"Blessed be, why not? Do you hate everyone, or do you just hate **me**?" It was almost enough to make him cry in frustration... if he didn't think that the tears would freeze his eye shut, anyways.

"For all I know you're as bad as the creatures you hunt. Who knows what kind of mischief you Love followers do behind closed doors. Trust a follower of the Great Harlot? Pft. You could be thinking of doing untold depravity to my flesh."

Even his horse gave her a slack-jawed look. "Hirshma. I promise you. I have no intention of doing anything depraved to you on you or with you. Or near you. Ever."

"Oh, and why not? Afraid of a real woman? You only go for whorish tavern wenches already beholden to someone?"

Blessed. Be. "Please. I just want to get out of the cold. If you're not going to help with that, please at least just answer my questions?"

She shook her head and huffed. "Absolutely not."

"*WHY?*" It almost came out like a scream.

"The sun went down hours ago. It's the middle of the night. Only reason I came out was to make sure none of my kinsfolk hadn't come around to kick your one-eyed ass halfway down the mountain."

"With my mood? You've no idea how badly I wish one would try."

"Harrumph. Well. Maybe I have questions for you. You truly took care of our lost souls? Or was that just something you said?"

"Yes. Those weren't simple animates. The ones you culled – how did you destroy them?"

"Your life is a strange one if you can call abominations like that 'simple.' And no, I ain't telling you what I did with them. They're back at peace. Didn't give too much trouble. Did what had to be done. Nothing more, nothing less." She pursed her lips a little and looked him over. "You know you smell funny, right?"

Akaran shrugged his shoulders and stretched his neck, unleashing enough curses muttered under his breath to almost melt all the snow in a mile radius around the valley. "You're not going to willingly help in any way right now, are you?"

With a shrug, Hirshma told him what he already knew. "No. Too late. Too cold."

"Too bad. I *need* to know something."

"Oh, please. What kind of question could you *possibly* have that would be so important to make me stand out here yammering about it on the dead of night?"

When he caught her eye, there was something burning in it that all but compelled her to back off a bit. Paying no heed to her refusals, he asked anyways. "When you put them down, did anything come out of them?"

"Put them down? Come out of them? What kind of monster do you think I am to tear open our fallen and start ripping out their innards?"

"Don't ask that question." He gave her a short, curt huff of annoyance. "Listen to me, and answer true. Did anything try to crawl out of their bodies when you put them back to rest? I don't know any other way to say it. Maybe fly out? Seep out? Did some creature pop out and go bouncing across the mountain ecstatically or did a shadow spring forth and mope around like you just took sweetrolls from them after you caved in their faces with your ever-so-charming personality?"

She was completely puzzled, and it showed. "Well, no. They do that?"

"*These* do. When you culled them, what did you do? Crush their heads? Cut their heads off? Set them on fire? Fired a cannon at them? Fired them *out* of a cannon? *What did you do?*"

"Culled them? I... well, I..."

No. No. No. Oh, Goddess. No. "You didn't destroy them, did you. You've been lying to me ever since you sent me away. You've been lying to me since you took your first breath."

"I... well. I put some of them to rest. I'm just an old lady. What do you think I did?"

Oh you have GOT to be... "I think you lied. I think that they're still wandering around out there. I think you just wanted to see if I could deal with three you trapped before you'd tell me where the others went." It was all he could do to keep from storming over and shaking the old bint until her head came off. She knew it, too.

The alchemist looked away and gave him an answer more honest than anything else she had said so far. "Four of them were making their way towards Usaic's cabin. We wanted to catch them before they got far. I had one of my students with me. One of them came after us, went right for her. She panicked."

"She dead?"

"What? No, oh, no." The crone looked up at him, almost apologetic. "She had an old mining pick. Her father gave it to her. She swung it and hit the thing right in the chest. It crumbled. Eyes flashed a few times. Made a dreadful smell. That was it."

That made it his turn to blink a few times. "In the chest? And it didn't get back up? Did it do anything else at all?"

"No, no it didn't. Stayed down. We... there was a howl. It was long, loud. Awful. The other three... our people. They turned from us and went off after it. We ran, made it halfway back here before we caught sight of a trail leading to the mine."

This part, he didn't doubt. "I saw that one. That one, you destroyed."

"Yeah, boy, we did. She did. She caught it in the side of its head. Didn't move again. Covered it in burn-dust. Lit it up and let the dust take care of the rest."

"Not very well," he sighed, looking forlorn while his anger growled in the back of his mind. "I stepped in parts of it." In what he could *only* hope was a display of sympathy for his plight, she cringed and took a step back. Suddenly feeling so tired he felt the air itself would crush him, Akaran let out a long breath. "Those three zombies. They went after the howling?" She answered with a wordless nod. "Did you see what made it?"

"No, no we didn't. We've heard that howl before. Same one that kept taking our people. We got back on our horses and we ran as fast as we could. Didn't ever look back. Not in any rush to end up like those garrison boys. You want to find out what made that noise? Be my guest. Take a sword. Take a friend. Pits, take a *regiment* with you. Just want to see them gone before anyone..."

While Hirshma let her thought trail off, the young man just shook his head. "Do you have any idea how close you came to getting killed? Or worse?"

There was a flicker of a smile on her lips as she answered. "Not close enough to be unable to answer your questions out here in the cold. But boy, that's the last of them. Ain't gonna say another word, not about the restless, not about Usaic. Not tonight."

"I want that pick she had," he stated, with a tone that left nothing negotiable.

Hirshma shrugged. "Then take it from her if you can. She's being all kinds of protective of it."

"I bet she is," he sighed. "Thank you, for this much, at least. Wish you would have bothered to mention all of this a few hours ago."

"Didn't know if I could trust you with it. Still don't."

"I'm sure you didn't. Get over it. I'm here to save as many lives as possible and you people aren't making it any easier. Before you give me another rude answer, let me tell you one more thing."

She scoffed and continued to glare at him. "Typical boy. Always wanting more after getting just a little. Nothing new there. Fine, ask away."

Akaran gave a snort as he looked around. "Don't lie to me again."

"Excuse me?"

"It's simple. Don't lie to me again. When I ask a question, it isn't to waste my breath or flaunt my rank or because I'm too lazy to go find out myself. I don't like these things any more than you do. Abominations, the lot of them, and there isn't a one that I won't be glad to send back to the next world."

The alchemist tried to interject in the middle of his tirade. "Now wait just a -"

He didn't give her the chance to continue. "When you lie to me, I can't be prepared. If I'm not ready, the rest of your people aren't going to be protected. Then I'm going to die, and they're probably going to die, you might well die if there's any justice in this world, and there won't be any time to try to figure out why I failed, or who's to blame. Just who gets buried first – if there's enough of us to bury. Or if we're not wandering about as mindless shells under someone elses's control. You've already lost one more innocent that you didn't have to. Do you *really* want to lose another?"

In her defense, she took the scathing rebuke with only a mild grunt of displeasure. Truthfully, he was sure it was just a matter of time before he had to repeat the point. "You're right boy, I shouldn't've. You really put down those three on your own?"

"And a fourth one, an uninvited guest."

"Another corpse? Wasn't any from here, couldn't have been..."

He shook his head. "No. It wasn't another villager. Four different wraiths. Three in the corpses, one that was... it was, leave it at that, you don't want to know and I don't want to think about what it felt like."

She blinked. "Wraiths? Oh please, say it ain't our people..."

"I don't know. I don't know. *That's* why I'm asking questions."

"Well then what do you know?"

"Why I don't get paid enough for this?" the exorcist grunted.

The alchemist gave him a bemused glower. "Oh, you get paid? I knew there wasn't much of a difference between you and the Hunters."

"No, we don't get paid. That's why I don't get paid enough. Now. I can't waste any more time on banter. Tomorrow, you will tell me about Usaic, you will tell me everything you do know, and so help me, if you're lying, I will see you and your brother and everyone else that's living here pulled before a tribunal when this is over."

"A tribunal? We're not part of the army!"

"Indirectly. You're in the way of someone that outranks about two-thirds of the Queen's biggest and brawniest. Do you really want to see if I'm as full of shit as you think I am? I *have* to get back to work, so if you're *refusing* to be helpful, piss off."

Stunned, Hirshma looked at him like he'd grown a second head. "Work? You're really daft, aren't you? First you're too cold to stay outside, and now you're gonna do what instead? Walk around here freezin' your Temple-ly bits off?"

He allowed himself a moment to stretch and look at the various homes around the center of the village. Before she could waste his time with another taunting word, he brought both of his fists together with the knuckles pointed at the ground. A hushed roar echoed around him as a light blue glow raced from fingertip to elbow. It wasn't warm and it didn't sizzle. It didn't even make a snowflake melt.

"I'm going to do what your people asked me to do."

Even though she was utterly unimpressed by seeing his hands glow again, she started to cave just a little. "Boy, it's so late. Fine. If you want a warm fire, I'll let you in. Just this once."

That was almost the last straw. "Lady. Go back inside, and enjoy your fire. I've survived almost the entire day out in this. I'll sleep when I'm done. Things around here are going to get a lot worse before they get better."

"What does that mean?"

Akaran clenched his teeth and answered her with a question. "What does it sound like? Whatever out there isn't what I was expecting and I don't know what to do about it yet and as plain as day, there's no way this won't get nastier before I'm done. Pretty certain that once more of these things realize I'm here, they won't like me none too much either."

At that, he knelt down to the ground and placed his fists on the dirt. The air shimmered over them as the soil started to warm up slightly. As she stewed, he would have sworn he heard a woman mutter from the inn behind him that they'd have plenty of good company. A glance up towards the window was too late to see any more than a figure step away and curtains close in her wake.

"So you expect me to believe that you went out and put a couple of restless souls back to sleep and now you've come to find some threat so grave that you have to put all other things aside and slap the dirt around a bit like you're trying to impress anyone dumb enough to look out and see what kind of racket you're causing?"

"Yes."

"So, what? You think that whatever ate the soldiers is going to be coming for us next? Ain't nothing got even close to the town, 'cept for the graveyard. Everything else only happened if people went north. Anyone that went east or south came back just fine."

"Yes. If they don't come sooner, they'll come later. But mark my words, they *will* come."

Mulling it over for a few long minutes, she spoke up. "You are well and truly serious, aren't you?"

He gave a shrug with his answer. "Yes."

The alchemist looked at him like she was finally seeing the boy as someone that might actually, Heaven forbid, know what he was doing. "You know if you stay out here you're going to get sick, and then what help will you be?"

"If these wards work, it won't matter if I'm sick." He pressed down even harder and a circle of light rolled over the ground in a wave. "Protecting the village is the only priority now. Whatever *I* need can

92

wait until later." Akaran looked up and gave her a dirty look. "Of course, some of what I could really use right now are the rest of my questions *answered*, but I already know your stance. So, if you don't mind, I have things to do."

Chastised utterly and completely, Hirshma, for once, shut up and watched him work. Not long after, she left to go back home. Focused in thought and silent prayer, he didn't even notice it when she came creeping back a half-candlemark later. She set a small package down next to him and then retreated back to her cabin.

When he looked in it, he had to smile, even if just a little. The still-warm chunk of roasted something-or-other and broth-dipped bread within didn't last long enough to even begin to cool down. The wine she served with it didn't stick around either. Warmed and grateful for small favors, he went back to work without any other interruptions.

Even better, that roast wasn't venison.

And as he worked in the center of the village, on his hands and knees, brushing away snow and ice and mud from the town square, he felt something else. He kept his sword close by and made an effort to use his magic to sense if there was anything unholy nearby. Every time he tried, he couldn't detect a single soul out of place. That didn't change the fact that he swore someone else was watching him, and it was probably an ill tiding of horrible things to come.

He wasn't wrong; off in the dark, a pair of crystal blue eyes watched his every move.

Those eyes weren't an ill-tiding – but he was right.

Horror was soon to come.

Sleep brought no comfort. Nor did the light of the morning.

He didn't really care by the time the night finished if anyone in the village gave a damn that he spent another hour attempting to divine any sign of *anything* near the village that could have ruined the lives of so many people. He didn't care if any of them gave a shit as to the mess he made in the town square as he put down the largest ward he could think of. Then he put down two more – one at the graveyard and one inside the tavern.

It may have been a little self-serving, and he may have waited until everyone else went to bed, but he put one inside it anyways. There was already one in his room but a little extra never hurt anyone. He had a feeling he'd have to remind himself that when the innkeeper found where he had carved it in, but really, was anyone going to look under his counter anyways? The cobwebs implied that nobody did.

He really didn't even care by the time that dawn rolled about, he had only slept for a scant three hours – and all three in a pew furthest from a fire. Someone had come in and taken the time to drape a blanket over him as he rested, at least. Adorned with shades of soft blues that he couldn't name even if he wanted, there was a gorgeous silver and gold mountain embroidered on the center of it... exactly like the etching he found on the Steward's skull.

So there's at least one follower of Istalla around here. And that Eos'eno creature said she's from Tundrala. So she's got an ally in these walls. That's just wonderful. I wonder who. And why. It couldn't be that bitch of an alchemist, and that, he imagined, was the only guess he could take. *But... whatever was left in the graveyard **isn't** from one of the Upper Planes, so for now, I'm not going to pry.*

For now.

Some nameless young boy shook him awake as the rest of the village began to assemble outside of the shrine. It was all he could do to make it to his feet and out the door before mourners could make it inside. To say that he felt out of place in the proceedings was an understatement, and he was more than happy to wait for everything to finish.

Who would want him inside anyways?

The lovely woman that had so far been his only real friend in the village was the last one to approach the entrance to the shrine. While everyone else wore woolen cloaks that were matted gray with fur along the trim, she somehow appeared to stand the test of the chill with a robe that had far more colors than the rest of the village put together.

True, it wasn't *much* brighter, but the fact that there were a few reds and a shade of gray that was a bit brighter than the misery-incarnate that everyone else wore with pride... well, it made a difference. Even if but for a heartbeat, it made a difference.

So did her hand on his shoulder. "They'll be waiting for me in there before we start."

Confused, he didn't know what to say. "I won't keep you then, m'lady." It was the only thing that popped in his mind and the last thing that could possibly have made sense.

Taking pity on him, she squeezed his arm. "You... you have a job that is both horrible and hateful. People will never welcome you into their homes with open arms for who you are and they'll never wish to see you around their dead for what you do."

That remark didn't help him figure out what she was after, either. "I know. It's why I'm here and not inside there."

"No, you're out here because you fear for what they will think of you. I'm not a fool, Akaran, and I'm not so set in my ways that I think you should be kept at arm's length. Only a few wanted a priest to come here and I know that *nobody* wanted an exorcist."

"Then why did you send word for one? If you didn't want me and you don't think you need me, why did you call for me and mine?"

"The soldier begged for one. A priest, I mean. And..." She bent forward and placed her lips on his forehead. "...and because despite how they act, we're not all so stupid to think that all in this world can be fixed by men who mine stone, women who dig for plants, and elders who preach that we don't need others to preach to us."

He tried to study her face but in his youth and inexperience, he couldn't make sense of what it was he saw in it. Instead, he looked at the shrine and the inscription over it. Try as he might, he just couldn't read what it said, though he remembered by heart what it was supposed to be. "*In Light, hope is offered to all those welcome here.*"

Rmaci gave him the kindest of smiles as he read it out loud, though he missed a flicker of something along the corners of her mouth as he did. "I never knew if that should be believed."

"The Pantheon doesn't seem to believe it about my Order, no."

"They say that Gods made us in their image. If we are imperfect, then aren't they as well?" She didn't let him answer her before giving his hand a soft squeeze. "Please, come inside. Whatever grievance the other Gods have with you, it isn't ours. Will you? Please?"

It didn't even take five minutes before he hated himself for falling prey to her charms.

His heartache was leagues away from the sadness that the villagers expressed. Ronlin stepped up to the altar and laid his hands on a blanket that had been draped over the poor child's corpse. "We... we have all suffered in this cold, this unceasing winter. We have lost the lives we once had; trappers with so few animals to hunt, blacksmiths with no ore from our mine. Our mulemen have had no way to feed new foals and neither my sister nor her charges have had herbs and flowers and leaves or the smallest of creatures to gather to practice the honored trade of alchemy.

"We have lost our wives, our sisters, our mothers – all to sickness brought by this misery. We have lost our brothers and fathers and husbands and those men who had none to carry their names on; those? Those we have lost to creatures in the woods, creatures in the dark.

"Our way of life has been stolen from us. We know not if it will ever return or if we will always be in this morass until Istalla Herself decides to take the last of us from here to pull us away from Her freezing punishment. I do not know what it is we are being made to atone for, but we must atone for it."

He thinks Istalla is punishing them? Atone for what? Does he think they slighted her somehow? That's a strange take on this mess from a town that doesn't profess to care much of or for the Gods. It's almost understandable... almost.

Wonder if he gave me the blanket... nah. I doubt that.

Ronlin continued on, utterly oblivious to the wheels turning in Akaran's head. "We do not ask for much; we ask only for what is due. We had a hard life, a hardy life. A life where we lost people, true. But it was still a life, and one we fought for, and one we fight to keep.

"It's a life that a babe has now lost. A life that will never be lived. Never to know the trials of herding goats in the mountains or building a barn with the brief summer sun beating down on us. Never to know the trials of trading with the Free City States to the east or the Midland Wastes to the North. Never to serve in the army of Dawnfire and never to explore the world and return to his home with tales and stories of greatness.

"This one is not one taken by the beasts or the sick. Not taken by any of the old ways to spill blood. A new way, another way, a way that is no more natural than this endless winter. We could've left. Many did. Many thought it best. If we had, this babe would not be on this altar. If we had, who knows the lives that would still be with us.

"But we have kept fighting. We have kept trudging through our trials. Our fathers lived here. Our fathers' fathers lived here. We tamed this land long ago. It was given to us by the Queen who came before the last three Queens. It is our birthright and our home. We will keep it.

"We fought and battled within our own to ask for help. It came. It came too late for Julianos. It's here. Our hope is here our help is here. That man, the priest in the back. Look to him and look to what he must do, what we must do."

Everyone turned and did just that. The world chose just that moment to suddenly shrink around him, one lone man with what felt like a thousand eyes upon him at once. *Oh no. Oh please, oh no. Don't ask me to...*

"He does not have an easy task. He has already saved a soldier; and where he has been, what he has done leading to this dark night? You had blood on your hands when you delivered our child to our arms. That blood was not all from our child, was it, boy?"

Akaran shook his head. Not speaking seemed like the best option.

A voice spoke up before Ronlin could continue. "His or not, enough belongs Julianos!" Another, then another, added to it. Half-murmured epithets were aimed at him while some townsfolk made their catcalls much louder. "He said he's here to protect us. Leaves for a day. Back and one of us is dead and gone."

The exorcist looked at the crowd and tried to figure out where each one was coming from. "There's more than one defiled soul out there. I don't know how many but I do know that there are now a few less."

"A few less?" a random voice from a random person shouted out. "One less of us!"

He heard Mowiat unleash a snarling curse from a few pews ahead of him. He made a mental note not to secure his horse back at that particular stable anymore. Then one of the two trappers (*Talaoc, maybe? Isn't that what I heard someone call him?*) made an accusation that nobody else had. "How do we know he even did anything? He could be no more a priest than I'm a king!"

That earned a few more agreements from the villagers, some muttered, some shouted. It continued on as Ronlin looked at the priest with a defeated look in his eyes. Without saying anything else to the mob, Akaran moved away from his corner and approached the altar. He made sure that his steps were measured and that each one he took made his sword jingle against his leggings. Moments away from making a very bad decision, he gave up giving a damn about what they thought.

As more people shouted their disgust and anger at him, the priest quit hiding his real feelings on the matter. "He didn't have to die," Akaran finally interrupted. Whatever patience he had started with had been reduced to tatters. He spoke firmly but quietly, and only a few people heard him at first. "*HE DIDN'T HAVE TO DIE.*"

The outburst was so forceful that it shut everyone up at once, except for one person up front that made some whispered remark about "How dare he speak like that to us!"

"Don't ask me what I fisking *dare* to *do*," he hissed, air barely making it from between clenched teeth, "or so help me, I'll make sure *you* find out *first*. I haven't exercised my authority yet. Do not mistake 'haven't' for 'won't.'"

The threat worked. Chatter and accusations stopped without any more objections. The village elder touched his wrist to try to reign him back in before he said something that assuredly wouldn't go over well. It was too late for that and it didn't do any good.

Akaran pushed him off and planted his hands on the altar and gave each of the villagers a deathly glare. "This boy did *not* need to die. And maybe, just maybe, instead of blaming me, you people can come to terms with your own failings first. You understand that magic exists. You understand that spells can go bad or do the unexpected. *And you didn't do anything about it!*"

"Didn't do anything about it? We agreed to call for help from the Orders of Light! We got you instead!"

"Oh? And when? When you started calling it an 'endless winter'? Was it then? Did you call for anyone with an inkling of magic anywhere from inside or outside of the Kingdom? Did you? No? What about when you started losing people to the cold. How about then? Or when the wizard started asking questions about 'fire in ice' and then a forest in the valley sprung ablaze for no apparent reason? Or that the local 'simple wizard' *maybe* put it out? That didn't make you think there was more to him than he had admitted to?"

Ronlin tried to stop him with an urgent word, but he couldn't. Akaran just wouldn't let him.

"*No. You. Didn't.* You didn't send a message to the Granalchi Academy, did you? There's no shortage of their colleges along the Ameressa border. All you would have had to say was 'there's a wizard missing and winter hasn't stopped.' You'd have had one of their mage-hunters here before your messenger even got back!" His fingers gripped the altar tight enough to make the wood creak. "AND I can see plainly enough that you didn't turn to the Gods until the army told you to!"

The innkeeper stood up and issued a challenge. "And how do you think you know that? How do you know that we weren't praying every day, day in, day out, for some kind of interference?"

"Yothargi's right!" Talaoc blared. He was short, dark haired, and not much younger than the elder and his sister. "I prayed! My wife prayed too! She prayed every day 'till she got sick from the cold!"

"I'm sorry for your loss. I am. She shouldn't have died either. But do you want to know how I know that you didn't trust the Gods?"

"The Gods haven't done us any favors, not for a one of us! Not for a long, long time!" the stable-boy angrily shouted.

That was when the exorcist pointed at the busts behind him and then at the corners of the shrine. "You don't wonder *why?* Maybe it's because if you gave a half-solid *shit* about the Pantheon, this place wouldn't look like nobody's been in it for a decade," he snarled. "You people are so stuck in your prejudiced fears... your distrust of the very people that could have *stopped this* before a simple chilly *inconvenience* became a *nightmare!* Now the bodies have piled up. Well guess what, you idiots? Now you're paying th-"

Hirshma got up and marched down the aisle, her hands shaking in rage. "How *dare* you think you can lecture *us* at Julianos's funeral!" she shouted at the absolute top of her lungs. "What gives you the *right* to take that tone to us?"

Akaran pulled his necklace out from under his leathers and dangled his in the air. "This does. By the order of the Queen of Dawnfire, this insignia gives me the right to do any damn thing I want to do."

She wasn't impressed. "The Queen can go fisk herself and you can too. You've done nothing but insult and demean us since you got here and enough is enough!"

"WHAT I'VE DONE?" The alchemist was right in his face, Julianos's body resting in state between them. "If *you* had called for help earlier, he might still be alive. His death is on *you*. It is *not* on me."

It had taken Ronlin this long to find the courage to push them both back. "Stop it! Stop it both of you!"

Simmering with naked fury, Akaran let him shove him away from the altar. Hirshma did the same and backed off for a moment. "All you've done is make accusations and get beaten up by a little girl," his sister spat at him.

In the torchlight of the shrine, shadows bounced on one-eyed exorcist's face. "Really? Then what about the bodies you lost? Let's lay out some of your secrets. Eight of them were up and walking, wasn't it?"

A few people whipped their heads from him to her at the accusation. Rmaci could be heard making a remark that went along the lines of "Even more secrets? How fun."

"*That's enough!*" the village elder finally shouted. Both of them shut up while he looked over the head of his portly sister and at the crowd behind her. "There is darkness in this world and darkness in this village and darkness in the woods and -"

Someone stood up and shouted at Ronlin and the exorcist. "In the woods? Then send him into them! Let this bloody fool go blame the trees for all we care, but either he leaves or..."

"If he doesn't leave right now, I'll kill him myself," Peoran promised, standing up with a few of the other villagers. A disconcertingly large number of murmured agreements resonated within the infrequently-cared-for shrine.

Ronlin turned back to the young priest and mouthed to him that maybe leaving right now wouldn't be a bad idea. As a few more people made a call for his hanging, Akaran had to reluctantly agree. Keeping his mouth shut about it? That was impossibly difficult.

"Then I will," he whispered, lowering his head with his hands still shaking. "You want me gone, I'm gone. I'm done." He looked at the poor child on the altar and had to stop himself from reaching out to him and touching his cheek.

He didn't say anything else even as catcalls from the audience continued. Someone tried to take a swing at him as he made his way out. He ducked it, just barely, and all but ran to get out of the shrine as more people called for his skull on a silver platter. Vestranis stood between him and the door and moved just enough to the side to let the exorcist escape.

The blacksmith didn't let him get out that easily though. He grabbed Akaran's right arm and squeezed it tightly enough to stop him from leaving. He kept his voice to a conspiratorial whisper – although he could have shouted, and nobody would have heard him over the din. Expecting (and suddenly feeling like he actually deserved) the worst, the exorcist didn't even try to pull away.

"What you said last night. The boy. Something worse could take him?"

"Yes."

"But he's dead."

"If that was a deterrent, people like you wouldn't need people like me."

Vestranis's scarred-up hand clenched a little tighter on Akaran's sleeve. "Flames the only way?"

The exorcist gave a slow answer. "No, but the other ways... you wouldn't like them."

His captor chewed on the thought for a few heartbeats. "Don't like you. Don't like your Goddess. Don't like any of the Gods too much. But I don't doubt you."

"Not a fan of most of them either."

Someone came up behind them as Ronlin desperately tried to get order restored. Vestranis shouted and waved his other hand at the approaching crowd, threatening them with the same beating they wanted him to give to the exorcist. "You promise to stop whatever's been killing us off?"

Slowly, Akaran lifted his gaze up to the man with the almond eyes and answered slowly, succinctly, and with every word filled with conviction. "Or die trying."

That was enough for the blacksmith. "I don't let someone else tell me how to forge a sword. I won't tell you how to hunt monsters. You send those things off to the pit and I'll get the boy sent to ash."

Filled with more than a little feeling of gratitude, Akaran thanked him quietly but at length. "Even if they don't want it, my sword is theirs. Convince them not to kill me so *if* I get back here in one piece, I can sleep on something that looks like a bed, next to a fire... and not in one, if they have their way about it."

"I'll do what I can."

"Thank you."

The blacksmith didn't have anything else to add, so he let the neophyte pass without another word. He didn't realize that not everyone was angry with him – or that a few agreed with him on every point. Rmaci squeezed her husband's hand as the two of them chewed on what he said (albeit more for Yothargi's benefit more than her own).

His temper had made him no shortage of enemies.

Apparently though, it made him a few friends. Only thing was... not all of them were inside. In fact, not only was she not inside, she shouldn't have been able to be outside where she was. But she was there, in the middle of sanctified ground, hidden behind a pillar. She watched, and she waited. She skittered in the shadows between the scattered buildings like so much snow drifting through the air as she followed him.

When he stopped at the edge of a simple wooden wall that protected the village from the wolves and the bears and the foxes that ran rampant in the forest beyond, she watched him there, too. She watched and was watched by yet another party – and the exorcist was far too focused on his task to notice any of it. He didn't even bother to glance around to see if anyone would care as he pulled out a knife and went to work carving one more rune at the bottom of the wooden gateway.

Etching the symbol only took a moment. Imbuing it with magic a heartbeat or two more. It was strong enough to serve to ward something slightly unpleasant away or to warn him if truly foul creature passed by. It wasn't much more than that and it didn't have much range. It should have been enough to send a signal that a girl with shards of ice on her breath knelt beside it after he left.

It really should have done something... anything... at all.

VII. HAILSTORM

The villagers had taken to calling it Garrison's Folly. It was an apt, if not understated, name (and one they had decided on it surprisingly quickly). After looking at it, he felt something bleaker would have been far more suitable.

The directions that Ronlin had given him earlier in the week to where the Dawnfire patrol had been decimated were spot-on. While the village itself was in the middle of a glade (possibly man-made), the rest of the region was not. The trees were tall with few low-hanging limbs to dodge, but they were also thin, and he thought he could easily wrap his arms around half of them. They were also fairly hardy to boot, with most of them still sprouting the occasional leaf even in the chronic cold. In fact, he couldn't even say that the ones that had died weren't from causes more natural than abnormal in nature.

The rest of the plantlife in the area hadn't taken the onset of near-constant winter so well. Bushes and shrubs had been stripped bare and slaughtered like someone had decided to commit an act of green genocide. The grass was all but gone, though there were some particularly aggressive weeds with drab flowers on their ends that had taken control where the more cheerful colors had vanished.

There was also snow, as a matter of course.

Snowfall was getting significantly heavier the further to the north he traveled. *Closer to Usaic's home. Coincidence? Blessed be, oh holy Matron, how could these people have been this stupid? Once I figure out what's waiting for me up there...*

His approach was not a comfortable one. Honestly, he was surprised that the patrol had even attempted to venture out in this direction. They were either very brave or very stupid, or maybe simply they felt it necessary to show that they were willing to risk life and limb in the mountains to protect the daughters of Toniki. He didn't exactly hold the army in the highest esteem, and it showed.

Aside from the snow being horrid, the mountain didn't waste time in growing steeper. The land was strewn with rocks and uneven terrain that would have been a pain to navigate at the best of times. This... was not the best of times. Nothing proved that more than when he approached a sluggish stream and made it halfway across a short wooden bridge built long ago in much warmer weather. He could smell it before he could see it; there was only so much ice could do to mask the odor of a mauled corpse.

There was even less the chill could do when the thing was disemboweled... yet it was still making a valiant effort to crawl out of the stream. The discovery jarred him from his internal commentary and forced him to carefully examine the monster. It had been torn apart, with large chunks simply missing from its torso and what was left of its singular leg.

It wore the red and gold colors of the Queen's Army stained across chainmail armor that had once been swaddled by hardened leather. *Well. What's left of the armor*, he muttered to himself. The state of it gave the exorcist a wonderfully warm feeling that anything *he* bothered to put on wouldn't matter worth a damn when it came time for a fight. (He was right, too.)

The wretched thing either didn't notice nor care that the exorcist was there. All it wanted to do was to crawl out of the frigid waters it had gotten stuck and half-submerged in. It made a soft sigh as he placed a hand on the back of its helmeted head and used a Word to put it to rest.

What was worrisome was that the zombie was so steeped in an abyssian aura that the entire thing burned away into a pile of flickering ash that floated downstream with just a single, simple spell. There wasn't enough left behind to bury even if he had wanted to, not counting a few pieces of bloody armor left behind in its passing.

That was an even harder fate than what had happened to the ones in the mine. It came with an ugly implication that the corruption in a corpse would grow worse with time instead of dissipating into the ether on its own. *Abyssian magic doesn't like to go anywhere once it gains a foothold. Still, it doesn't normally grow stronger on its own. Another abnormality. Quaint.*

Even though nothing tried to crawl free, it did at least feel like the other zombies. So... at least I'm still working with just three breeds of monstrosities from the pit. It's a small blessing... but I'm gonna take it anyways. Well. Rest quietly, soldier. Your battles are done.

Any unease Akaran had about the land took an immediate back seat to the rest. He *had* kept his ears open for the howling that supposedly preceded the worst of the attacks. He *hadn't* been using magical tricks to make sure that there weren't any other lesser undead this way through, since none had ever been spotted. It wasn't a mistake he was going to make twice.

When he reached what was obviously the Folly, it didn't take him more than a minute of looking around at the evidence from the massacre to make him wish that lesser undead were all he had to deal with. Almost a week and a half worth of light snow had managed to cover up most of what had gone down. It didn't hide all of it.

It couldn't.

Blood had completely drenched the tree trunks from the neck down (and in some places, a few heads higher up). Dried or not, you couldn't miss them on the lighter bits of bark all around. You couldn't miss some of the bits of people left behind in the desiccated fauna.

Even though Ronlin had said that the medic had come up here after he arrived in town, he was either too rushed or too cowardly to stick around to try to bury the bodies. It didn't even look like he had done anything with them at all. *How fun.*

Maybe he had been expecting woodland creatures to come clear away the small bits of Dawnfire's finest. Or maybe he thought that they were all fated to walk the mountains in death no matter what he could do. Or maybe he simply had a fear of the dead (though that would be an odd position for a medic to take, the longer he thought about it). Whatever his reason, it left a mess behind.

Still, there was at least one reason he could think to be been grateful for the cold – if it hadn't been so frozen, he could only take a miserable guess as to how *foul* the area would have reeked. The sight alone was enough to churn the hardiest of stomachs. His wasn't any more immune to the odor of viscera than anyone else would've been.

Maybe in time he'd learn to tolerate it.

This was not that time.

Whatever had torn the soldiers apart appeared to be long gone. A steady walk around the edges of the worst of the battlefield didn't let him see too far into the woods. Feeling over-exposed, he caved and began to focus entirely on magic to be assured that he would be left alone enough to fully take command of the slaughter.

There wasn't enough left behind for anything short of a pure-bred Daemon to be able to resurrect and play with. The wraiths and wild magic that crackled through the shadows did not have even a tenth of that power. *Not that I'd be surprised to find one skulking about. Why not? I've seen just about everything else unexpected so far. I suppose next it'll be resurrected squirrels nipping at the back of my neck?*

While he walked around and through the battlefield, more than a few things caught his wandering eye. There were tracks left behind, deep ones that would have cut into the land even if they had been walking across a slab of solid iron. For once, he was able to start making identifications. While most of the prints left behind were ruined from either snowfall and some brief melts, there were a few on the outskirts of the battle that he could clearly identify as inhuman... and not even bipedal.

The ground had been torn up by something with large paws and larger nails. There were two sets of them, leading in from somewhere deeper in the woods and to the northwest. From the spacing, they were moving so fast that the patrol couldn't have run away even if they had wanted to. *Handful of soldiers dead and the trees look like they suffered the wraith of a thousand drunk beavers. Pleasant.*

These are too widely spaced for just one thing... it has to be a pair. From the size of the mess they left behind, they have to be more beast than man, and the tracks say these are really beasts, not spirits. These are the monsters Tornias claimed to have seen.

Four legs, forked claws, and a howl you can hear down the mountain. And who can forget the poison they left behind in Lativus? I swear, if it wasn't so miserably wet out here, I'd think that they're abyssian hounds.

*Oh no. Oh **no**.* He loathed himself the second the thought hit him. *These **are** pit hounds. And I have two of them to deal with. Goddess above, this just keeps getting worse. A **lot** worse. The wards I put down last night... those might work. **Might**. They should be enough to give out a warning if I'm close enough to... I don't know. Die horribly, probably.*

Abyssian hounds were another one of those topics covered at the Temple by people that had seen too much and remembered all of it. As the hierarchy of demons went, the hounds were on the lower end of the spectrum – but that didn't mean that they weren't kept around as pets by a legion of nasty things. Outside of that, conjuring one wasn't too terribly difficult; meaning that they were one of the favorite guardians used by practitioners of twisted spells across all of history.

Usaic, Usaic, Usaic. Reasons to have a chat with you keep piling up, don't they?

Progressively darker and darker thoughts cascaded through his mind one after the other. Killing *one* hound wasn't a fun endeavor even with help. Killing **two** by himself? *Even if I put down a rune of warning, they're still going to get me killed. I'm... dammit. Well. The people were right: they DO need someone better.*

No. I can't do this. I just **can't** *do this on my own. Not if I'm supposed to hunt these down and protect the village at the same time. The best I can do on my own is to get everyone out of here as fast as possible and send a call to the Temple to get a pair of paladins deployed before this gets completely out of control. There is* **far** *too much going on here for just* **me**.

No, it's already out of control. I'm insane to think otherwise. But... dammit.

I don't dare leave them out here in the wild. I **have** *to find them. If I can take them one at a time I might be able to contain them. If they're going to kill me then hopefully I can bog them down out here and buy the villagers a little more time for the army to hurry up and get here. Can't do that if I go running back to Toniki.*

Shit.

Miserable from the idea, at least there was one thing he could do right now. *I am NOT leaving myself open for any more surprises.* Glumly, Akaran knelt in the middle of the slaughter's leftovers. With both hands on the ground, a simple Word aimed at detecting magic in general slipped past his lips and into the soggy dirt. He should have used it earlier. Overconfidence was quickly becoming his downfall.

What it found was surprising for three different reasons.

There was more than just corruption here from the hounds here. Though there was plenty of that, there were traces of three other actors as well. The first (and the easiest) to detect was only easy because of its familiarity.

Jagged shards of ice and pieces of thicker-than-normal hail had faint echoes of the magic that the girl in the blizzard had used on him two days prior. Everywhere he found her ice, there was black blood congealed near or on it.

Touching the chilled piles of ashen gray and black gore that had been left behind gave him a flicker of dread in his heart – and that was simply from touching it. *The hounds. She got into a fight with the hounds.*

*You thought I was your 'help' and out here you've attacked the dogs. Were you trying to save the soldiers? Or just hunting these demons yourself? Who are you? What **are** you?*

Unsure what to make of that discovery, he focused on the second scent of magic that was sending out ripples into the ether. This was different than anything else. There was no taste of the undead, no taste of the defiled, and no taste of the energy that Eos had been using.

Well, now, this doesn't make any sense either. The magic was there, faint, but there – like the person who had cast it was barely more than mundane. It wasn't strong enough to be a ward or some kind of rune. It wasn't anything that had a purpose that he could discern.

What he was able to realize was that it was something good, something holy, and something pure. He searched through the area for the cause of it and quickly discovered the source of it. There wasn't much to it. *Pure* was right. Pure, as in Pristi; pure, as in the Goddess of Purity.

Someone had written a prayer to the souls of the departed on a broken branch at the furthest edge of the massacre. Except it wasn't just a prayer. Somehow, it was a spell. The log itself didn't look like it had been on the ground too terribly long.

There was snow under it although not over it. The base of it still had a little bit of yet-frozen sap just inside the end. Chunks of dirt and several large rocks were around it in divots, as if someone had been throwing stones to try to destroy it.

Confused, he spent a few minutes looking around for the tree it had come from. That was when he found it, and the tracks that were near it. It was freshly fallen because the tree it belonged to had been recently mangled (and by that, he meant 'nearly reduced to splinters'). Something had come along and gone after the tree, just the tree, well after the dogs had left.

Nearby tracks confirmed it. The aura left behind on that particular tree did too; it was the feeling of dull malice that had permeated the graveyard around Julianos's body. The same thing that had murdered the boy had attempted to destroy the spell. The dogs had come here after the soldiers, then someone had come along to put them to rest and laid the enchantment down.

The last remnants of magic in the ether is from here, right here. Hello, Aloof, you asshole. The other demon had come to bring an end to that. He was willing to bet that it had gone after the village immediately after. The prints for the hounds and the demon both went off in different directions and vanished into the deeper snowfall.

So. Aloof is probably acting in concert with the hounds, but wasn't here when they attacked. So either they both are serving the same master and were carrying out different tasks, or they're both just drawn to the area for different reasons. So where was it when the hounds found the soldiers? Why did it come to Toniki a week later?

Doesn't explain why it stopped with the boy. The hounds would have killed everyone they ran across, unless someone had a tight chain on them. So why the boy at all? Was Aloof interrupted, or... what? It's trying to get rid of a spell that would be innately opposed to its nature, then when it gets to the village, it stops at murdering a child.

You'd think it would go after the shrine, if that was the case. It isn't confident enough it can destroy it? Did Julianos find something in the graveyard... and was just there because of bad timing? I don't understand any of this.

It was going to be difficult to say exactly where any of them went next or how long they had been gone. The only thing that left him completely convinced that they didn't arrive at the same time were the different directions that they had approached and left the battle from. *Beautiful. I can track the hounds from here, or Aloof. Not both. Aloof could have hit the village last night and been back here this morning. Or here first, then Toniki. No way to know.*

Inwardly, he gave a deep sigh. *I don't know what Aloof can do, other than throw small children and apparently destroy small trees. Only thing I can blame him for so far is just Julianos. The dogs have a much higher kill total... damn be all. They're first. They'll have to be first. If I can get lucky enough to banish them both somehow... I might even get an understanding about their friend.*

Abyssian hounds weren't known for being thoughtful predators. They were more along the lines of a "maul you if they see you," type, not the "lead a siege" variety. If they went for the soldiers either they were attracted to them or they were just handy playthings. Considering that the village had lost a few people that had gone north into the mountains prior to that... it was likely that the soldiers were handy and the dogs were hungry. *I almost appreciate the simplicity of their motives.*

That, or the soldiers were getting too close to something that the dogs trying to protect.

They do make excellent guard... well. Dogs.

Usaic's cabin. They said it was a ways north of the village, and this is a ways north of it. What was it they had said? That anyone that got near the cabin felt like they were enveloped in a feeling of dread? That wouldn't be a trick unknown to the Abyss, or a symptom of magic that comes from it.

These things don't like anyone getting close to the cabin – and I guess they really don't like magic being used near it. Magic attracts magic. Are these things hunting mages? Did they catch Usaic? He stopped and looked down at the branch in his hand as he remembered something. *Magic attracts magic. You know...*

He sat back on his laurels for several moments before cocking his head off to the side. *If the locals are as disinterested in the Order of Light as they seem... I know that medic said he followed Pristi. He said he doesn't have any skill with magic, but maybe he doesn't know...*

The dogs caught these sad pukes first, and wiped them out. Then Tornias came, moved the bodies, unwittingly cast a spell of purification somehow and kept the words etched on a local log. Like... a prayer, asking for aid from his Goddess.

*This caught the attention of the wraiths, who followed him back. The wraiths didn't take **these** bodies... because there wasn't enough left of them to let the bulk of them walk after the fact. Then Aloof came here, and tried to destroy that enchantment before going to the village a few days later.*

So while I hunted the corpses, the demon came about to... find something someone either put in the graveyard, or had left there. Julianos was there as... a fluke. An absolutely abhorrent feeling sank into his stomach as he realized that everything he had done to this point was making everything worse.

*Magic attracts magic and that is **all** I have done since I got here. The village... Julianos... did that child die because I tried to sanctify the graveyard? Is Aloof out there, scouring the mine while I freeze my sack to my thigh here in the woods?*

Goddess, what have I done?

*He could be there now, killing everyone. Or the dogs. Or all three of them. No. **No**. If they were there I'd feel my words screaming. Or shattering. I didn't put a ward down on the first trip. Sanctified the ground to keep more dead from rising. But no wards. I can still feel that my spell is intact so these three demons are still out here.*

Somewhere.

Wracked with a sudden onslaught of guilt, he couldn't rush back yet even if he wanted to. He felt like he had been wrong about everything else so far, so what was the point in trusting his instincts that nothing would be able to rouse a party from what was left of the soldiers? In truth, he should've trusted them. The time he spent pulling the larger parts of used-to-be people towards the center of the Folly before covering them with logs and limbs would have been better spent elsewhere.

Instincts be damned, he worked the task as quickly as he could. By the time he finished and left, he was confident that the spells he left behind would be enough to deter anything from getting too close to the remains until more could be done with them. That much, thankfully, he was right about.

Sanctifying them would have to be enough for the time being. Setting them aflame? While the heat would be enjoyable it would also be a horrible idea to start the fire then up and leave. *I can almost hear the General screaming at me for burning the mountain down.*

Actually... it's not that bad of an idea. Torch it all and go home? Would the Sisters approve?

He was also right that the hounds were protecting the area from interlopers – and right that magic did attract magic. It was a trick he hoped would buy him time to get to the cabin and confront the source. It did, and it would, but it was also close enough to Usaic's home that it caught the attention of more than just the hounds.

It was just another item on a long list of regrets he'd entertain after all of this was over.

While he tried to clean the pile of corpses up, the villagers were trying to decide if his should be added to the stack. Elders and innocents throughout the village conferred; some happy, some not. At a house not far from the shrine, Romazalin and Mariah-Anne talked over a cauldron of stew. It was *not* one of the happier conversations.

"Ain't nothing good gonna come from this. He went and spit on everything we've done here, lived here for, loved here for," the farmer bitched. "And he thinks he can just walk in and start accusing us of what? Gettin' a boy murdered, getting folks killed?"

Mariah shook her head. "Maybe accusing us of not being afraid when we should be? Of not seeking aid? Of not taking this threat seriously? We *all* should have left, *ages* ago. You know what he is, don't you?"

"He's an ignorant, self-absorbed, whining child. That stunt at

Julianos's funeral was all I could take." Off in the corner, two dirty-blonde brats squabbled over some misshapen wooden toy. One of them turned around to watch the women argue, a finger idly picking at his runny nose.

The younger girl didn't accept her response. "That stunt was a passionate man hitting the edge of his patience. Patience, that may I add, you and nearly everyone else has been very reluctant to show towards him."

"Why should we? Boy walks in like he owns the place, does some magical mystical stuff with his hands and suddenly that Lativus fellow is supposedly 'cured.' But he isn't healed. He's not up not walking around. Doubt he did anything."

Mariah set the ladle down and looked Romazalin in her cloudy-blue eyes. "But he's not mumbling insanity in his sleep anymore. He's not thrashing about. He's recovering."

"Getting better? He ain't even awake yet. You aren't a healer, you ain't a templar or whatever they call themselves at the capital."

"A cleric? No. I am not. This is true. But Hirshma is a good teacher... and she's taught me how to treat the sick. But you don't need to know anything about any of that to tell when someone isn't in a pitched battle against something worse than a fever."

Stepping away from the pot, Romazalin wrapped her arms around her youngest child's shoulders. "Well. If he ever gets up and starts walking and talking again? Maybe then I'll believe it." Thinking about it for a second, she stopped and corrected herself. "No. No, I won't. He walks and talks again, all credit goes to your miss."

"You didn't see the things I saw. I watched him through the barn window. I saw what he did, saw the mist that lifted from the soldier. I was out in the woods with my miss when we found the dead, too."

"The dead? There's always dead about in the woods. The world is full of the dead. All you saw were animals. Just animals. Or trees, plants. Things always look odd in the dark. That's all it was. You know better."

Hirshma's student stopped stirring and crossed her arms. "*Bodies don't get up and walk around*. It's not *natural*."

Squeezing her son tight, the farmer with ratty hair started to lose her temper with the alchemist's apprentice. "What does a girl your age know about natural? For all you know you and your miss fixed up a bad potion. How do you know that it wasn't in your head?"

"In my head? It wasn't -"

"Even my boys don't like him. You know them. They've never been wrong about a stranger that comes up here. Isn't that right?"

The youngest of her brood clutched at the hem of her dirty dress and nodded while Maria tried to continue to argue her point. "We haven't had enough strangers coming up here for your boys to know much of anything about much of anyone."

Oblivious to the point Mariah was trying to make, the ugly little boy went back to exploring his nostrils, sniffling into his mother's dress. Visually, it was not appealing. "Well. We will after this winter fades. All it is. Just a bad winter."

"What about everyone that's gone... well... missing? Even a bad winter doesn't claim this many!"

Showing a surprising level of willful ignorance, Romazalin dismissed her with a wave of her hand. "There's bad things that live in the peaks. Everyone knows that. When it warms up they'll go back where they should be. As long as we're safe and stay in our walls, no harm will come to us. No more harm. It won't. If any of that nasty whatever it is out there sticks around after, the army will take care of it."

"So you admit! There *is* something!"

"At worst, trolls. Never been never will be anything worse than trolls."

"But Julianos... that could have been any one of us. You. Me. Your boys."

Hugging her dirty child all the tighter, the farmer was refusing to let her opinion be changed. "Girl, you don't know the stories about his Order. Where they go, bad things follow. Always. Julianos is dead because we let him into our homes. If we had turned him away, the boy would be alive. We'd be at a lot less risk. Where his people go, suffering follows. Chaos follows. It ALWAYS follows."

Reaching for her friend's hand, Mariah tried to calm the older woman down. "Rom... you don't know the things that we... I... saw out there. You don't know what it looks like to see people walking around, already dead?"

"Nor do you! Quit telling stories like that. You *know* that Milin don't sleep right from nightmares as is. Going to add to his worries and that means I won't be sleeping either."

"Momma's right," her son added in a nasal whine. "No sleep, can't sleep. Keep seein' things when I close my eyes. That man, he's scary. See him somewhere bad! A tower in th' water! I see 'im in it!"

"See that? Nightmares. Ever since. Tower in water? Makes no sense. He won't listen. You won't listen none either."

"But... Hirshma saw it too... it wasn't just me..."

Shutting her down, Romazalin affixed the younger girl with a nasty snarl on her lips. "She's old. Give her credit where it's due, but that woman is old, and if *she* told *you* to tell people that she saw dead bodies up an' walking around out there, then you're a right fool for repeating it."

"She didn't tell me to do anything of the sort!"

Livid, the farmer stormed over and threw the cabin door wide open. "You know, think you better leave."

Shocked, Mariah stood there with her mouth wide open. "Leave? What? Why?"

"Oh please. Of course you'd want to slide up on him. Young man, professes to be something better than most. I was a young girl too. You wanna suckle on the boy, you go right ahead, but quit making up tales just so we'll think better of him."

Unable to hide an indignant response any longer, Mariah-Anne lost it with a shout. "SUCKLE? Are you *mad*, woman? He's a... I wouldn't dare ever...! Thank you but no thank you! I only speak for him because -"

"- because that's what young girls do. You charm boys with your legs spread and then tell everyone you see that the young cock is so wonderful and that he can't do no harm. You think I don't know better? How do you think these bastards came to be?"

Her son looked up at her and blinked. "I'm a bastard?"

Ignoring him, Romazalin grabbed Mariah by her arm and forcibly shoved her out of her home. "Go! Out! When you get tired of being let down by fools and their foolish ways, you can come back here! Until then... **get out!**"

Fuming and frustrated, the alchemist's apprentice did just that. Storming off to Hirshma's house, she didn't really care that a handful of Toniki's backwards citizenry overheard her answer. "Inbreeding. That's how I think they came to be."

Finding the cabin wasn't an easy task. Even if the woods had their vibrant, summer colors, it would have been far too easy to get lost. In this muck? The only reason that he even found it at all was because he had picked up on the hounds' trail. The directions from the village were worthless when half of the landmarks were covered in white slush.

His tracking spell hadn't been worth all that much back in town, but this far from comforting fires and equally-comforting innkeeper's wives, it was another story. It didn't hurt that now he knew more about what he was hunting for. It would hurt when he found them, but it didn't hurt when it came to tracking them down.

Still, an encounter with the demonic puppies wasn't high on his list of things he was looking forward to. Worst case scenario was that they already knew he was coming and were circling him while he explored. *No, that's the second worst. The real worst is that they know I'm coming and they're waiting for Aloof to join them.*

Best case scenario was that they weren't even there.

That – oddly enough – ended up being the case. Yet somehow, he wondered if that was such a good thing. *Wherever they are, I doubt I am going to be happy about it.*

The cabin, on the other hand, was a welcome sight for cold bones. It stood on top of a small hill with a much denser line of trees flanking it on all sides. There was a simple stone well at the base of it and the remnants of a small, untended garden nearby. *Or what used to be one,* he glumly observed. There were a handful of rusted tools – a shovel here, an axe there – laying about on the ground, and a snow-covered pile of firewood next to the door.

One thing was for certain: there was more here than just a foul aura. The entire area put off a feeling of impending doom that rocked him to his heart the moment he caught sight of it. It was quickly joined by a rolling wave of nausea that brought an immediate rush of bile into his throat. If he hadn't been expecting it, it would have sent him running in abject terror.

Expecting or not, that wasn't to say it was a good feeling by *any* means. Akaran quickly brought his hand to his eyepatch and focused on the area, half his mind still reeling. It only took a moment of focusing on the ethereal to see the cause of his suffering.

It stuck out to him like a sore thumb – a trio of old, decaying, children's skulls covered by snow and encased in that sickly ice Aloof had flung everywhere at the Folly. *Oh **damn**. That thing knows **magic**.* Rocked with the effects of the demon's trap, he got close enough to kick the snow off of the totem. The sight of it was utterly repulsive to the point that the feeling of dread was replaced by a feeling of deep personal *offense*.

With a snarl colder than the omnipresent snow, the priest picked up a thick branch laying nearby and shattered the skulls with extreme prejudice. Shards of ice and bone flew about him with each clubbing blow. *I can match you skill for skill, asshole. Just wait until we meet...*

Enchantment destroyed, the hut awaited his attention.

He gave the cabin a quick circle around before giving up on any hope to find any exterior clues about what lay inside. There was no sign of the hounds anywhere he could see although the area was steeped in enough of their essence that he could almost retch. It reeked of sulfur the closer he got to the dense woods behind it. He spied a small path cut through the dense brush leading farther up the mountain, although to where, he couldn't tell.

An urge to go down the path to find them before they could do any more damage briefly bounced around inside his head. Frozen fingertips that had long started to go numb from the cold, on the other hand, convinced him to hang back and seek temporary shelter. A look through one of two windows gave him cautious hope that finding warmth inside might just be possible.

From what he could see from outside, there was a fireplace against the back wall and a wooden door opposite it. A pair of bookcases and an unassuming wooden table decorated one corner; a dining table set with clay dishes stood not too far from the bed.

Nothing about it looked out of place or in any way special. It could have belonged to thousands of people throughout the Kingdom. For as important as the place seemed to be, he felt let down by it. *He's an 'elementalist of great power,' huh? I don't even smell so much as a hex here. Maybe there's something worth finding on the inside.*

Regretfully, the door was locked. Worse, he had never mastered the art of picking locks back at the Temple. While he had been forced to admit that sometimes evil resides behind a locked door, he had countered that if evil was attempting hide behind a simple iron bolt, then the lock was worth breaking. It was a sentiment embraced by many in his class.

It also earned him a stint emptying chamberpots after half of the class had stood up for him.

He still liked his way better – buckets of shit or not. When a kick to the latch didn't solve the problem, another log from the pile of firewood did. Alas, the door didn't shut quite as snugly as it had after he got inside. It was a situation easily remedied by putting the lone chair in the cottage up against it.

A few minutes later, a warm fire roared to life in the cabin. That didn't mean he allowed himself the time to enjoy it properly though. While a cursory search turned up little, a more intent one discovered a latch half-hidden behind the bed that opened a passageway to a lower level. At first, it filled him with hope when he heard the sound of a lock

116

unhitching, and then greater hope when he found a door in the floor covered by a rug. *Mages and merchants. Always hiding things.*

Those hopes were dashed aside almost immediately when all he found was just a basement made of the same cobblestone walls as the upper floor, and decorated almost entirely the same. There were a few wine casks stacked against a wall, and a few wardrobes opposite that. The first thing that struck him as odd was a lack of furs, rugs, blankets – anything that would protect a hovel like this from the cold on the inside. *Surely whoever owned this would need more than just a fireplace?*

For that matter, it was the *lack* of things that was catching his attention. Yes, the wardrobes were there, yes, there were a couple of crates and casks. There were dried out vegetables hanging from the rafters. Those looked absolutely awful – shriveled and twisted with dust coating them. If it wasn't so cold, they'd have turned to moldy mush.

It was easy to tell that *nobody* had lived here for a long time.

So why the spell outside? Why are the dogs attacking anything that gets near?

There weren't any weapons, not even a walking stick. There were only a few sparse pieces of clothing stored in the dressers. There was one bookcase that was full of tomes although not a one of them was written in any language he could decipher. Three others were empty shy the occasional scroll, or in one case, a small journal filled with recipes.

If he hadn't found one small, simple thing, he would have given up all hope that this was even the right house. It could have been coincidental, true, though possible. At least the fire had started to make the cottage warm up enough he could take off his cloak, gloves, and boots. While they dried out next to the roaring fire, he caught sight of something glinting under the edge of a pillow on the bed.

When he uncovered it, he realized it was a small bracelet made of alternating cloudy crystal beads and jade pebbles. It was roughly hewn yet pretty; not gaudy, but striking in complex simplicity. In a home so sparsely filled to say that it was a strange find was an understatement. When he picked it up, he smiled to himself at the feeling of serenity and peace that flowed into his fingertips.

This is magework... magework that doesn't want to eat me. I could get used to that.

It felt cool to the touch – but a different kind of cold than the straw underneath it. It wasn't enough of a chill to hurt but it was there. In fact, it felt comfortable against the skin. It was a truly odd feeling though not one that was entirely unwelcome. There was no trace of any kind of hostile or malicious aura to it (a fact he wasn't at all unhappy with).

Those crystals. Wherever they're from, they're soaked in elemental magic. This, the hidden cellar, and the stench of those damned hounds so close by? This has to be his home. A question popped into his mind before the first thought was even finished. *He took everything else of importance with him when he left. Why leave this here? All these tricks to hide a single piece of jewelry? I doubt it.*

*And where did the fisker **go**?*

While he held it up to the fire, he noticed something else. The closer he moved it to the flames, the chill in it began to fade. What replaced it was a soft feeling that made him immediately think of a blooming garden. It was as if he had dipped his fingers into freshly-tilled soil.

In fact, he swore he could even smell the very land itself. He even tried to test it a few different times – away from the fire, it felt comfortably cool and refreshing. Closer to it, it felt like he was digging his fingers into the dirt.

*Dual-imbuement. Someone's overcompensating. Magework, assuredly. But not... there's more. That odd smell of soil... that's **not** cyro-kinesis. That means he didn't do it by himself. So who did? Nature magic and ice magic. Weird.*

*Usually druids tend to avoid the colder parts of the world. It's not their 'thing.' Yes, ice **is** part of natural magic and the Goddess of Ice was given birth by Kora'thi Herself, but people find that it's hard to make fisking flowers and roses and medalia-fruit grow in the bloody permafrost...*

The answer was not forthcoming even as he sat there and stared at it.

*So where, for the sake of all, is this bastard at, if not **here**? Why are the dogs still so focused on guarding it? Why is the freeze so much more pronounced here than it is in the village, if this isn't where he's hiding?*

Those questions – and the lack of reasonable explanations – did little to settle him while he picked at a small bag of rations he had brought with him. *More fisking questions. Can I please just find something big and banish it already?*

At least there were the hounds to look forward to. Even if they weren't here, they had to be near. He could sense them still, and they would not get to hide for long. They also weren't the only things that had taken it upon themselves to stay near the cabin. The good news was that the dogs were kind enough to leave him alone through his lunch.

The other guardian was not.

Howling broke his reverie. All thoughts about what flavors of magic were safe to mix together and dozens of unanswerable questions were tossed out the second that he heard the first one. A second one encouraged him to step outside, as ready for a fight with the hounds as he could be. He got a fight, too.

Just not the one he expected. Apparently Aloof and the puppies left the house protected with a creature that would have pounded your average mundane soldier into squishy bits. While it was true that Akaran was none of those things, he really didn't like the look of the threat.

He couldn't even call it much of a guardian. While he felt it coming in time to put his clothes back on, it arrived before he could exit his commandeered shelter. It stood at just above his own height and was covered head to toe in white fur. In spite of the hole in its throat or the gaping pit where its left lung should have been, it roared a challenge at him.

All Akaran did was stand there and stare at it in disbelief. *You. Have. Got. To. Be. **Kidding**. Me.* It had curved black teeth that started on the outside of its mouth and pointed inward filled a gaping maw just below its beady black eyes. Thick mottled black and brown claws adorned its hands and its feet. Three of them had snapped off of its right hand but the rest looked to be in perfect condition.

Nope. Nope. Not... nope.

The beast gave another howl while it attempted to intimidate the holy man. Sadly for it, the exorcist wasn't even so much as flinching. *A mountain troll. These things killed, then animated, a mountain troll. I can't tell if they're that bored or that cocky or if they just simply don't give a damn. So. Wonderful. If this thing was drawing breath, I'd happily go hide in the cellar for the rest of the week.*

*Bloody fisking absolutely **wonderful**.*

*What's next? Are these blasted things going to find a way to posses my fisking **dinner**?*

When it roared at him a third time, he finally gave up trying to discern rhyme or reason from the seemingly random encounter. In a fight that was sure to prove the existence of a Goddess that both loved him and watched out for him, the troll-come-zombie had not been returned to life with the combat acumen and ferocity that its kind are known for. *Thankfully...*

True, most of that acumen was built around basic decisions like 'see something, eat it,' and 'slice it with claws,' or even just 'keep hurting until it moves no more.' Mountain trolls also had speed and attitude. And grace. They weren't the lumbering beasts that many an unlucky traveler gave them credit for.

(Lowland trolls, as should be noted, were a much more evolved beast. They were known to integrate into certain societies. The world was an odd place. Even for those in his line of work.)

This one just had the urge to try to hit things with its front paws. It could barely manage to stand upright, making its attacks both laughable and more than a little ineffective. Akaran didn't let the fight last long though – which wasn't too different from how it would have been if the beast was still alive.

That was the other thing. A living troll would have won.

What he didn't do was use magic against it. Not directly, at least. The zombies in the cave had realized that his sword was imbued with a heavy-duty enchantment that the Temple had provided him on his way out. The living would shrug it off as a mild shock to the skin.

The defiled? They had a slightly different reaction. The blade left steaming gashes everywhere it touched the lumbering monster and his shield was enough protection against the beast to keep it from even getting a *chance* to scratch him.

The battle ended when he got behind it and pulled the edge of his sword up across its throat. With a hand on the hilt and the other against the end of the weapon, he gave a hard pull towards his chest that was met with a satisfying wet a crunch as he cleaved the troll's head from its shoulders. Like the other creatures that he had disposed of with head trauma, tendrils appeared and then evaporated as he executed its host.

At least they're consistent. I'd hate to – "**FISK, OW**!"

His cry spooked the thing away that had landed on his neck from one of the trees above. It landed on the ground a few feet off to his side and sat there, chittering away in anger while it glared daggers at him. The sight of it was nearly as bad as what he felt when he had seen the troll.

No, he briefly mused, *this is... worse. Somehow, this is so much worse.*

This time he used magic. The undead squirrel (*A SQUIRREL! They actually reanimated a SQUIRREL!*) that had tried to take a bite out of the back of his neck boiled away on impact. It didn't leave so much as a whisker behind, let alone tendrils. *Well. If I had any lingering doubt left about this cabin belonging to Usaic, I don't anymore. Too many of those wraiths around here. Of course, if these blasted things are attracted to magic, I imagine...*

Shit. He looked at the smoldering ash pile and the slightly rotten troll remnants and sighed. *Think before acting, you idiot.*

The idea was equal parts welcome and not so much. The more wraiths that decided that here and now was an ideal place bask in holy magic or to fit into the warm body that was using it? That was a good way to start actively reducing their numbers. *I wonder how many of them are out here. I should probably try to figure that out soon.*

The downside was that the more of them that hunted him down, the greater the odds that the hounds wouldn't be alone when they realized that someone was busy making a mess out of their territory. *I want them alone. One at a time. No wraiths, no Aloof, just the dogs, one after the other.*

The squad from the garrison didn't last this long out here. Since they're not hunting me down right now, I think it's safe to say that either they're waiting or they're busy with someone else. I can't think of any other reason they would hold back, if my spells at the village aren't being disturbed. Whoever else they're after, I will say a prayer for.

Yeah. Said it before, I will say it again. (He would. Repeatedly, and with great gusto.) *Shit.*

He made his way back into the cabin once he was satisfied that the rodent was gone for good and the troll was really done for. A few minutes later, and he had all of his gear (plus the bracelet) gathered together. The decision not to put down any wards or runes was a difficult one to make, even though his reasoning was sound. *When the time comes, I'll burn this place down myself. Not ready to risk Aloof or its minions doing the job before I'm ready. Leaving a second toxic mess behind. I really hope I don't live to regret this.*

There wasn't any point in dragging it out any longer. Without another word or thought, he worked his way into the denser woods behind the cottage and resumed his hunt. The woods made travel difficult but not impossible; the snow made it worse. He could feel little spirits in the wild watching him, and could sense little ebbs and flows of magic in the air. With the sun already going down, there was no good that would come from any of this.

It was fortunate that he didn't have to take long to find the next place of interest.

It was also fortunate that the villagers weren't done talking about him, too.

If you wanted to call it that.

In its heyday, the Rutting Goat was the bustling hub of the village. There wasn't a night that went by that someone wasn't dancing on a table, or someone was getting into a drunken brawl. Every evening had rancorous laughter and men slinging ale down their gullets while women of dubious morality were more than happy to help alleviate them of any loose coin that may fall down their trousers.

Or just their trousers.

Anymore, such thoughts were buried deep within the recesses and hallways of depressed minds and subdued whispers. The drinking hadn't stopped but the ale was watered down to a bare froth. Even the roasts over the central spit – roasts once well-renowned by anyone and everyone in the region – barely had a touch of warmth and none of the old taste.

Yothargi rested his elbows on his counter and sighed, head hung low in his only good hand. "I just don't know what to think of him."

A few stools away, drinking a mug of that watered-down swill, the blacksmith wasn't much help. "Your wife does."

"Yeah but his wife thinks of everyone that way," Talaoc tossed in, sitting next to him and grinning through desperation-laced drunkenness. "No offense." It was the first thing he's said since arguing with Akaran at the shrine. Everyone would have been happier if the drunk had just stayed silent.

Yothargi slapped his right hand down on the counter and growled a warning at him. "Watch your tongue, or I'll throw it to those dogs soldier-boy over there swears he saw."

Tornias looked over at the grumbling villagers from the corner of the tavern. He'd been cowering back there since last night, and the circles under his eyes made it apparent that he hadn't been getting any sleep. "Those dogs ARE real. I swear upon the lives of my mother and my mother's mother that -"

"Those dogs ain't here, so quit actin' like a baby. You know what? They ain't here, and you are. Things didn't get this bad until you hauled your worthless ass back from that patrol," Vestranis spat.

Off to the side, an otherwise inconsequential young woman looked up from the smoldering fire and disputed that. "Now that's not right. People left because of the cold, sure. But what about Kena, Kyoi, or Malabe? They went missing when the howling started..."

She was ignored, of course, by closed-minded men that thought they knew everything.

The innkeeper piled it on. "Yeah. For all we know this could be all the worse because of you."

It wasn't an accusation that the cowardly medic took kindly. "Now, now wait. You called for *us* to come aid you! We came! *We* were attacked! I didn't make anything worse! We didn't! I am a medical attendant in the army of the Queen herself, assigned to -"

Smirking, Talaoc was only happy to join his companions in telling the soldier exactly what they thought of him. "You're assigned to wander about the border and pray nobody up in the midlands decides they're bored fightin' each other up in the mountains. That's all you are."

"I serve the Queen with honor, dignity, respect," Tornias countered. He was attempting to sound brave, but the way his voice cracked while he fidgeted with the pendant around his neck made him sound like anything else.

Vestranis couldn't help but bark out a laugh. "Cowardice and stubbornness, too. Least he clings to his tale."

Indignant, the medic continued to protest. "My faults are no greater than yours. Less, in a multitude of ways."

Yothargi drew himself up to his full (even if short) height and joined the blacksmith with another bark of laughter. "You just like to try and impress everyone, don't you, soldier-boy. A time will come when someone's gonna make you eat those words. Hope I'm there for it."

The laughter from the thinner, badly scarred innkeeper helped give Vestranis a nastier edge to his growl of warning towards the would-be-hero in the corner. "And your shit ain't the issue at hand, either. So shut up and let us talk."

That did it, and for a few minutes, Tornias did just that.

Vestranis looked at Talaoc and Yothargi in turn, dull brown eyes glinting in the torchlight. "That priest."

"Which one?" the trapper grunted (with an ale-powered belch for effect). "The psychotic one, right? Not the coward? Not our supposed elder or his sister?"

"Just rumors that those two ever served the Gods though, ain't it?" Yothargi asked.

The blacksmith clarified his statement with a shrug of his shoulders. "Yeah, just rumors. Never saw either of 'em worshiping anything but their own egos. So, yeah. The psychotic one. At least he's honest about who he serves."

"What's to say? That prick's crazy. Rantin' and ravin' about all manners of darkness out there. I still say that a long winter is just a bad winter. It'll pass."

"You only think he's a lunatic because your wife took a shine to him the minute he walked in," the heavy-set woodsman giggled.

Vestranis tried to ignore him while the owner of the fine establishment made a foul gesture in the trapper's general direction. "Then explain the attack on the garrison. Explain the people we lost in the forest. Explain why we haven't seen that wizard the last few years. Explain any of it."

Half to himself, Tornias answered the question in a nearly-hushed whisper. "Dogs. I swear, huge, huge dogs, faster than anything..."

Glowering at everyone, Yothargi dismissed him. "Big wild dogs on a mountain. That ain't nothing we've never seen before, even if the winter is hangin' on lots longer than we should. I bet that those poor pups were hungry as all else. No offense, soldier-boy."

Tornias did his best to argue his case, and was simply ignored.

"Big dogs don't wake the dead."

"You really believe that?" Yothargi asked, suddenly feeling unsure in the face of the bulky blacksmith's conviction.

"I do. Checked the graves. Some were disturbed. Some were sunk down, like the ground got emptied. Something ain't right. More than dogs. More than a bad winter. Shouldn't be pissed at him until we know there's reason we should be."

Talaoc tried to shrug it off. "Oh he did it himself. Priests. Do anything they can to convince you they know what's what and what's real. Ain't nothing but bullshit."

"Maybe." Vestranis pushed his mug towards the lanky, gimped innkeeper. "You think he'll make it back?"

"Hope not," his friend muttered.

The trapper grinned up at him. "You only say that because your woman wants to bend him over a cask."

Vestranis had to laugh. "Sure he'd go willingly. She might even let him return the favor."

Fuming, Yothargi swiped the blacksmith's mug and didn't fill it back up. "Speak a word about my saint of a wife again like that and I'll do more than feed those hungry hounds your tongues. We clear?"

"Yeah. We're clear. But... I wonder."

"No need to wonder! She's pegged more holes than –!" Talaoc didn't get anything more out before Yothargi lunged over and slammed a wooden mug right into his mouth.

Over the sound of the fight, Tornias found his voice again. "Your worries are misplaced. The army will be here in nothing more than three days time. When they arrive, I will be sure to tell all of them to know how brave and heroic the townspeople have been. Nobody will dare say a word about you. It'll all fall upon Akaran's shoulders."

Amused by all of it, the barmaid spoke up with a pipe full of every opiate that the village had to offer packed between her lips. "Oh you will, huh? I suppose you don't want us to tell them how you jump at every shadow?"

Tornias glared back at her. "Say what you must. It is hard to say what Commander Xandros will do to or with everyone when he arrives based upon what he may or may not hear. He may decide that you are too independent to be governed by yourselves any longer. The Queen would do well to have this territory under tighter control. Or he may not. Depends on what it is he hears."

If the threat phased Vestranis any, the blacksmith didn't show it. "I've heard some travelers mention that name. Man is something of a 'kill 'em all, who cares if anyone sorts the corpses,' type, isn't he?"

Tornias smiled smugly. "Oh yes. He and his wife will come here and scrub this shit from the mountain. You just wait..."

Elsewhere, Akaran was going to have to wait for his quarry as well. But not for long.

The overwhelming stench of sulfur was the first giveaway that he was about to stumble into their lair. It was quickly followed by the unmistakable order of raw shit and putrescent viscera. His sword had almost magically appeared in his hand before he got close enough to smell it. Much the pity, he didn't need it.

Their lair was in a small cave less than a twenty-minute walk away (even in the snow). If he had even been an inch taller, he wouldn't have been able to fit inside it. Nor was it all that deep; he had seen dungeon cells that had more room to move about. A quick Word to illuminate the cave showed him everything he needed to see, except for the dogs themselves.

In their stead he found a pool of tar and shredded remains of people that he guessed were the brave souls sent to talk to Usaic a couple of months ago. They weren't moving about or in any other way obviously possessed, which was one less thing to worry about. He had to assume that the dogs had torn them apart so badly that there wasn't enough left behind for any of the wraiths to try to infect.

That was *all* he could assume about the remains, too. It did track with what he had seen at the Folly, at least. *So they need somewhat intact shells to make them move around. Nice to have a little confirmation about it.*

It was also the hottest place he'd been since arriving on this blasted mountain. The hounds evidently liked things to be warm. Or maybe they had found a way to bring a bit of their home here with them. Either way, it was so oppressively hot that he wished he had left his cloak outside.

While he hadn't really expected different, finding their lair took away any doubts as to the nature of his quarry. Without them there though, it did little good. On the other hand, without them there, he thought up a way that would assuredly ruin their day when they made it back. There wouldn't be a need to hunt them down after this – they'd come looking for him.

He knelt down with his knees resting on the edge of the sulfur-and-tar muck and recited the same prayer he had used to sanctify the graveyard. This time, he also added a few extra Words to aid the blessing in removing the unholy mess from the face of the world.

The effects took hold right away. The tar started to turn ashen and gray and the chewed up bits of people scattered around the back of the small cave began to fall in on themselves. Little bit by little bit, their nest dissolved. A few minutes later, and a fresh rune carved into the dirt ensured that not only would their home be destroyed, they'd burn if they attempted to move back in.

Fisking hounds have chased people out of their homes and ensured that many more would never see them again. This may be petty, but dammit, fisk 'em. Turnabout is fair play, he mused. Even the sludge on his knees sloughed off and disintegrated into nothing. *Even Pristi's angels wouldn't be able to clean this up any better. Besides...*

...if I do end up killing them, I'd have to come back to do this later anyways.

With at least one (albeit currently unimportant and possibly petulant) job done (one that would be akin to going to your neighbor's cottage and pissing on their bed) he exited quickly and resumed his job. The *important* job. The dogs left one thing behind worth noting though: fresh tracks.

Really fresh tracks. They had rushed out of their lair so fast that the ground was gouged up and wet sludge (***Please** just be mud, **please** don't* *be more shit...*) was scattered along the trail. They went deeper into the woods and away from the direction of the town, which was a massive saving grace.

The only path they apparently followed was what they had managed to carve out of the forest itself. Tree after tree and frozen bush after frozen bush had been torn asunder. He could only think that they were chasing something that they couldn't quite catch.

It was another thought that didn't sit well in his frost-addled brain. Abyssian hounds are notoriously fast. There was *nobody* human that could outrun them for more than a minute or two. If you could manage to do even a little more than that? That meant what you had was a head start.

A more pronounced feeling of dread started to fill him as he realized that not only were the hounds after something, someone was fighting back. Shards of ice as sharp as broken glass decorated tree-stumps everywhere he looked. Small puddles of steaming black blood had splashed every few feet through the woods.

Whatever happened here was in the last hour... no... whatever happened is happening right now.

The further along the trail he went the more frequent the puddles became. So did the shards of ice. If there was any kind of saving grace to calm his borderline-terrified nerves, it was who the shards of ice belonged to. They weren't black; they were almost clear. They didn't have Aloof's aura; they had something softer.

Eos'eno. That answers that. They don't like each other. Either she found them or they found her. Don't know what she is but at least she doesn't make my skin burn to touch her spellwork. Whatever was going on looked like it had turned into a running battle through the woodlands.

Try as the dogs might've, they didn't make traversing the forest any easier for him. That didn't stop him from doing his best and charging right along after them like a desperate child running after his parents. The hem of his cloak and tabard were ripped to shreds even before he got halfway to them – and when he stumbled across them, he didn't like what he heard.

He really didn't like what he couldn't see.

Dense fog covered the area. He could smell fresh water and heard waves lap against a rocky shoreline. Not that he could see it, but he could hear it. He could also hear shouting. Very, very, *angry* inhuman shouting. And since pit hounds weren't known to speak... "Why... why must you hide from me?!"

Aloof! The eager grin that blossomed over his lips came unbidden but it was entirely heartfelt. *Time to bring you to justice you son of a...!* He started to shout a challenge at the damned thing, but before he could even utter a single word, someone shut his mouth.

Literally. She shut his mouth. Painfully, too.

A pale hand smacked his jaw and slid over his lips to muffle him. The coolness in her touch overwhelmed his outrage and the whispered voice in his ear stopped his thoughts in their tracks. "*No, no speak! Listen!*" Before he could move or push away, the girl took hold of him by the back of his neck and quickly dragged him deeper into the fog.

She hadn't changed much – just her clothes. Her ratty cloak had been replaced with a silvery gown that hung loosely on her shoulders with pale blue ribbons streaming out of her hair and off of her long sleeves. Apparel aside, there was one thing for certain: the poor thing wasn't happy to see him.

Eos'eno, whatever she was, was terrified.

When he tried to talk, he realized that her touch had actually sealed his mouth shut. She hadn't just closed it; the supernatural woman had frozen his lips together. In a panic, he tried to struggle away from her grip and shove her hands away with his own before she slammed him into some kind of rocky cleft. Eos squeezed the side of his neck and another jolt of something cold stabbed through his spine and down his shoulders.

"*Hide here. They won't sense you wearing this they won't! Please, please you must you have to you must hide! I can only protect for so long, you are not the help that protects, you need **my** protect, not me **yours**! Makolichi will kill **all**, kill **you** kill **them** kill **ALL** if he finds **you** here!*"

Off in the distance, the other voice (*Makolichi? At least it's a name...*) droned on.

"*You make me send... master's dogs for you... now you are here... speak, say to me... why, why must you do this? Why must you make... make me, make us hunt you? Why must... must you stay involved? We are... not unalike!*"

"*I am hiding you, hiding **all** you. You must not speak must not say. Please no harm I mean none please listen run or listen but do **not** act!*" she continued to whisper, pleading and begging him. The sheer terror in her soft face brought any objections he may have had to a heel.

With a dim nod, Akaran agreed to stay quiet – reluctantly, and not for long – but he agreed.

There were heavy footfalls and the sound of something large being thrown into the lake. Ice broke and water splashed upon impact, close enough that he could almost feel the waves hit him. He still couldn't *see* the damn lake but at least he could feel it now. "You know that his work is... so pure, so strong. We could be so much more. We will be... so much more..."

Eos'eno flipped away from his sight and shouted back at Aloof. "Master's work is *his!* Not ours, *his!*"

"His work is ours... he made it, ours, for us..."

"His work is his! He is not gone, he is ours!"

She must have struck a nerve. "His work! He brought **us** forth! Did what he must **WITH OUR AID!** He has crossed the veil! Left us! Now home in... our home...! He has left us behind... to take our... **our birthright!**"

Usaic's dead? Damn. Well. Whatever his work is I don't really feel inclined to let either of them have it, Akaran groused. Bucking her instructions, he smashed his fist against his lips and painfully broke her muzzle apart. Spitting a small touch of blood aside, he still kept quiet – though it was getting harder by the heartbeat, with Aloof's heavy footfalls getting closer.

Eos continued to challenge the demon while the exorcist readied his shield and sword, a few prayers filling his head for assistance he was sure he was going to need. "Our birthright? Ours is to the mountain, the ice, the people! The ones that make the beauty of the frost so much more!"

"Beauty to be buried in eternal snow? No! Warped! Master made you *warped!* There is no beauty here! There is only death! There is only the endless death... and the endless cold!"

Can't argue the sentiment... the exorcist mused, wrapping his hand tight around the hilt of his sword and gripping the inner edge of his shield. *Though I can promise the endless death is gonna come real soon... Goddess, protect me, may Your Love guide my sword...*

"If all you see is the death then you are warped, not I! Look about! Look at the shine of the light, look at the softness of the snow! Look at the crystals that glitter in each flake! See it? Look at it all, and do not condemn! Water from snow brings life to the mountains! It is the cool comfort that brings life to the world!"

"Beauty? That is **POWER! POWER** brings **POWER!** It does not bring life! Where power is men will come! They will come, as they always do!

They seek to make beauty theirs? They seek to make the **POWER** theirs!"

"No!" she screamed. "They mean no harm! The mortals, the living! They are of this world, we are of ours! Master's work is a gift to them! That is what it is, a gift! To *them!* To those that need it to those that must have it!"

A roaring shout met her cry. "**We are no gift to be given!** Our world is no slave to theirs! No slave to any of them... They seek to bring their magic about it. They touch the cold... and they **die**. They stain the ice... they turn the snow red! **ALL THEY ARE! JUST STAINS** in the **SNOW!** They... they are all like... the wretched bleeding **thing** you hide here!"

A bleeding thing? That was when he looked down at the blood he spit out, and saw that it had crystallized in the snow. *Ohhhh... oh I wonder, did... hope he didn't smell that. Some demons do and...*

...and as a rule, dogs do.

Shit.

Akaran could hear the panic in Eos'eno's voice. "A thing? I hide no thing! I keep the work locked away! Not hidden, locked! For when master awakens!"

Aloof/Makolichi *screamed* a reply. If they didn't hear it in Toniki, he'd be surprised. "**LOCKED FROM ME, LOCKED FROM THE GROWING SOUL! Locked from the... thing... you hide here. Locked from...! YOU AID THEM! YOU LIE! THEY DIE!**"

Growing soul? What in the pits is that? That wraith... thing? The fog and the thick snowfall all around had gotten worse to the point that he could barely see his hand in front of his face, let alone either of the bickering creatures. Goddess only knew what they were, but he was **done** listening to the one that had that raspy, painful voice.

Akaran stepped away from the relative safety of the cleft and faced the direction where the argument emanated. Barely visible – but emanating enough raw hate to boil the air – two dark and hunched over shapes started to pace in the distance, distressingly too far to do anything about but *way* too close to ignore.

*The hounds! How did I not sense them?! Alo... Makolichi and the hounds, both? No matter. Time to end this. I am **done**.* He lifted his shield and started to slowly advance on one of them with a quiet thought running in his head. ***Are Eos and Mako the hounds? Can they shift forms like some kind of werewolf? Only one way to find out.***

His shout alone could have blown the cottony fog apart. His Word did it instead. "**LUMINOSO!**"

The answer was an immediate and unforgettable *no*.

There wasn't time to do anything else but grip his shield a little tighter and bring it up to cover half of his face. Bearing more than a minor resemblance to a craggy mountain peak, a massive lumbering form charged through the fog at him. *Oh he's a BIG bitch, isn't he! Shit!*

His body was encased in seaweed-green ice that allowed impending victims to see an entombed mangled skeletal frame completely suspended under his frozen shell. A mottled fleshy skull shouted out horrific sounds at him, sickly green eyes illuminating the ice encasing it. A pair of squid-like tentacles floated in the brine, grafted onto its carob-brown skull by whatever malevolent being that had given birth to the demon.

It only had one arm, but one arm was enough. His massive right hand caught Akaran's shield and *twisted*, wrenching his arm and turning his body to the side. Bones fractured as wood shattered and the metal frame around it buckled. With a forceful jerk and *crunch*, the giant shattered the escutcheon and sent the debris flying.

He heard the scream that cut through the fog for long heartbeats as he stumbled after the splinters. Akaran only had a moment to realize the noise came from his own mouth before Makolichi grabbed him by his cloak and pulled him back the opposite way. That grinning maniacal skull screeched at him, its un-tethered jaw flapping in the brine under the ice, eyes burning with a piss-yellow glow.

Pain blossoming out of his left hand, he did the unthinkable with it – and *punched* the demon right in the jagged crystal it called a face. He felt his wrist snap the rest of the way when chainmail met shell and stunned the beast for just a moment. A moment was all he wanted. *"EXPULSE!"*

Makolichi didn't take the impact well. Briefly offended that someone would *dare* punch him, the spell cracked ice and snapped its head back. Divine magic tore into the cracks and ripped them open. Its constant screaming took a new, anguish-laden tone as it coursed through the ice and sent shards of ice spitting out of it head to toe.

That was not even close to enough to put the demon down. The exorcist caught his bearings and dove forward with his sword in hand and attempted to stab it right in its thigh. Mako twisted and shoved Akaran back, the blade doing little more than nicking his frozen armor. The impact felt like he had hit something harder than steel. The shock knocked the blade from his grip and sent it sliding away into the snow.

Off to the side and out of the corner of his eye, he saw the pair of dogs rush towards him, molten globs of fiery spittle shining in their horrific maws through the rapidly returning fog. He tried to bring his hands together with a new spell on his lips to bear on the new threat, but just as suddenly, he saw Eos'eno speed through the snow. Just as she touched the two hounds, all three of them vanished in a cloud of snow to mark their passing.

There wasn't time to think about what she had done or why. Countering Akaran's ill-advised attack, Makolichi grabbed the priest by his midriff and *screamed* at him so loud that it all-but deafened him. The touch did something else too, something that nearly ended the fight then and there.

His aura had been toxic before. Actually being held by him? Feeling it direct that awful, burning, freezing evil right into his gut? Akaran's world shrunk to a singular point of pain that tore right through him, worse than any other pain he had ever felt in his life. It was by the grace of the Goddess Herself that it didn't make him black out.

Makolichi kept a tight grip on his stomach even while the exorcist desperately tried to break free. Sensing his desperation, the demon threw him several yards away and face first onto the ice. It broke and scratched at his skin while he took a deep breath on instinct, and ended up inhaling a mouthful of fresh water. Coughing and choking, he swallowed mouthfuls of it before he could push away from the frigid pool.

Crystal-clear water coursed down his face as he pushed his battered helmet away. The demon picked him up again, but this time, something felt different. More pain stabbed through in his left arm as the demon lifted him back into the air and screamed raw hatred right to his face. Pain or not, when he started to channel Her power for an urgent act of Holy violence...

...he felt *good*.

For whatever reason it was – and he'd wonder about it a lot over the next couple of days to come – he managed to clutch Makolichi's side with his sword-hand to give one last desperate response to the assault kind. Only it wasn't just a response, it was a *response*. Energy he didn't know he possessed coursed down his arm and right above the mountainous demon's left hip. Ice didn't just crack this time.

Ice shattered.

Somehow supercharged, the spell caused something white hot to detonate out of his palm. Before either of them could comprehend what had happened, it shot through the other side of the monstrosity that had him in such agonizing pain. Chunks of frozen armor shattered and exploded out of Makolichi's back with a gush of rancid salty water that burned through the snow all around them. Bone shards followed and the demon was blown back and sent down to its knees.

Both of them screamed in wordless pain. The eruption of conflicting magic launched the combatants away from each other. When Akaran landed, his head cracked against a smoothed over rock that sent the world into a hazy fog that eclipsed his vision. All he could remember next was that Makolichi jumped over and landed just above him a minute later, virulent slush streaming out of the cracks along its body.

"DOGS! FEED YOU TO THE DOGS!"

...then Eos'eno was there, her hands on Aloof's frozen shell. Gleaming silver light blossomed around her, and then both of them were gone in a blizzard's worth of snowflakes. Akaran tried to shout at them, tried to say something. All he got out was "I'M HERE TO HEL... lp... yo... u..."

That was when the blistering pain in his chest and throbbing agony in his head caught up to him, and that was the last thing he had to say for a little bit. Not long, but, long enough for his body to catch a (miserable) respite.

Although, it was a good thing that he had some allies making their way north.

Eventually.

Hours prior, a trio of people had congregated next to the smoldering ash where Julianos had been cremated. Hirshma had doused his young body with a diluted mix of the dust that Akaran had used to melt the door to Bolintop Mine the day before, which made a grisly task an hour instead of most of a day. Most of the village had gone back to their homes or their jobs; these three just weren't ready to go – miserable chill be damned.

Moulborke felt crushed by the child's passing, and blamed himself for much of it (even though he was far from at fault). "He shouldn't have died. The priest is right. He shouldn't have."

"Yeah. If he had stayed in whatever plush temple he preaches from, then someone smarter would've gotten here and done the job of *protecting* us," Mowiat groused. A cold drizzle of sleet had started a quarter-candlemark back, leaving his course auburn hair looking like a depressed hedgehog.

"No. He was right. We've brought much of this on ourselves," the woodsman argued with a defeated sigh.

Mowiat stared at him, disbelief in his eye. "Are... are you mad?"

"Maybe. I've seen stuff out there. Stuff you haven't. Stuff that nobody else has."

Wresting her eyes away from the pyre, Rmaci finally spoke up. "What kind of 'stuff' did you see?"

"Even before things got bad? Woods weren't right. Onset of winter wasn't right. Animals weren't right. Things were running away long before it got so cold. Talaoc won't admit it. Peoran probably won't. Go ask Walthershin. Go ask Hirshma, or her apprentice. Well. Walthershin, at least. Maybe the apprentice. Not Hirshma."

Mowiat had to agree (even if he really didn't want to) "Hirshma won't admit to anything that goes on outside these walls. She acts like she's got some kind of right of ownership to anything in the woods and beyond."

Nodding her head slightly, the woman with jet-black hair voiced her own opinion. "Always with secrets, that one. Always with secrets."

"She swore we'd be safe if we stayed in the walls. None of us have ever died in the village. Only when we leave do we go missing... or... worse."

"She was wrong on that," Mowiat sighed. "So very wrong."

"Maybe Julianos did something wrong? What if he was being punished by the Gods?"

Rmaci looked at Moulborke, surprised at his thought. "Punished? What sort of sin could a boy his age have done to warrant such punishment? Battered, beaten? Thrown on top of a grave? Even the Queen's inquisitors are not so cruel."

"We don't even know what did it," he said, shoulders slumped forward in abject defeat. "Maybe he went into the woods? Could have left the village and died out there. She could have drug him back here to be found, just to scare us into staying put."

"Or maybe it is as simple as that old witch is wrong. Simply, as it is, we now know she cannot protect us. It was all bluster. Nothing more. Nothing less," she snipped, the tone in her voice laden with venomous disdain for the alchemist.

Mowiat kept looking back and forth between the two of them, trying to decide if he believed either of them. "You think she's been lying to us all along."

"*Always* with secrets, that one. *Always*," she said, making careful sure that her companions paid close attention to her emphasis. "The boy did not deserve this. Neither did our other fallen. This is no punishment for the Gods. You know as well as I do that they simply don't care."

Nodding, the woodsman continued his earlier testimony. "I mean this in my heart," Moulborke sighed, water dripping off of his muddy hairline. "Things out there were foul long before. Thought it was just something moving in. Spoke to Amilia, spoke to Jodian about it, before they vanished. Talaoc's brother, too. They *all* knew it was getting... *wrong* out there. We should've called for help from the Orders of Light a year ago. More."

"The capital wouldn't have believed us even if we had said anything," the stable-master replied with a sad sigh.

Moulborke had a different opinion. "The garrison did."

"Those thugs just wished an excuse to play soldier. Had nothing to do with us, just their own egos."

Looking back at the pyre, the woodsman shook his head again. "We had proof before then."

Nobody spoke up for a few long minutes after, until Rmaci broke the uncomfortable silence. "Whatever that exorcist is doing... if we're to trust him... he needs to be watched."

Disgusted at the slight reverence that she gave his title, Mowiat's response was curt and pointed. "Someone should have been watching him the moment he stepped into town."

"Someone was," she said, her voice barely above a whisper.

Moulborke had to fight an annoyed smirk. "Of course you were. Do you think anyone thought you wouldn't be?"

Refusing to raise her voice even a little, Rmaci simply looked at him. "I have my reasons."

"Yeah. I bet. His name is Yothargi. I'd be watching someone else too."

Mowiat spoke up in her defense. "Watch yourself Moul. She's a lady."

Giving the auburn-haired horseman a dirty look out of the corner of his eye, Moulborke piled it on. "A lady with a husband with a burned-off dick."

The scorn that filled her voice could have cut through solid steel. "The Civans have a saying: *'Passion needs no touch to make a woman burn with joy.'* Neither of you need to be concerned with what I do or whom I do it with or *how*."

"The whole town knows what you do and who you do it with," the pudgy, hunched over pig of a man snipped back. "First you drool over some boy from the Great Harlot, now you quote those ash-sucking Imperials? Maybe we're wrong and your husband got tired of *you.*"

Stepping between them, Mowiat grabbed the woodsman by his arm and squeezed painfully hard. "The only reason I'm not laying you out on your ass for speaking to her that way is because we're *all* torn up over Julianos's death. I know he was like a son to you but *mind your mouth,* or I will do it for you," he promised, wiping the sleet off of his face and away from his eye.

Taking a deep breath, the woodsman almost dared the boy to say that again — but settled on apologizing instead. "He's right. My... I was out of turn, Rmaci."

Mowiat didn't give Yothargi's wife a chance to accept the apology or not. "*Either way,* what we need to do *isn't* to concern ourselves with who is doing what or where. Only one thing left for us *to* worry about, I suppose."

Rmaci looked to her current champion and raised an eyebrow. "Oh?"

He answered with the only logical conclusion he could think to reach. "Where we go to from here. I'm not sticking around for that... those... things... to come back for the rest of us. You know they will. They will."

"Stable-boy has a point," Moulborke said with a sigh of frustration. "Think all we need to do now is pack our bags and drag our asses south. There's no home here for us anymore."

Unimpressed, Rmaci didn't share the same opinion. "Do you think that running will solve anything? Do you think there's a point to that? We leave and then what? The Queen sends the might of her army? She throws away the history of this town? I may've not lived here for long but I do not believe that any of you wish to see all you have accomplished here become fodder for her war machine."

"She is the *Queen.* It *is* fodder for her, anything she wishes."

"It doesn't have to be. Not like this," she answered, her eyes dark and arms crossed.

Mowiat couldn't quite wrap his head around what she meant, and tried to drag her to reason. "We stay and what then? Not having to listen to people argue if I should be buried or burned is a good enough point for me..."

"The state of our souls is a greater concern," she snapped. "We threw that priest out. A *priest.*"

The woodsman turned to face her and lifted his hands up in the air. "His *job* was to go out. Not stand around and preach to us!"

"*We* know this land. *He* doesn't. We sent him with no guide and no care. Rough landmarks and vague directions. This mountain can be treacherous in the best of times, and we are *not* in the best of times," she argued, frustration at their simple-mindedness finally bringing an edge to her own voice.

Mowiat looked at her and blinked in surprise. "Rmaci... don't tell me you find yourself *concerned* about him. Not *you*, of all people? Didn't you -"

"For him, for us, is there a difference at this point?"

"Of course there is. If he doesn't come back that means we leave even faster," the older woodsman contested. "No sense in waiting for the next disaster. He wants to go play a hero, let him go play one. As for me...? Mowiat, do we even have any horses left that can pull a cart?"

"He left the one I sold him when he stormed out. We can use her."

Rmaci's head whipped around to focus on him, alarm in her voice. "He did? Why?"

"He didn't exactly feel the need to tell me."

"That's one way to be assured he won't come back," the woodsman grunted, almost happy at the news. "Whatever's out there won't just let him walk back safely after the sun sets. Things out there... they get mean after dark."

Frustration bleeding away into actual anger, the innkeeper's wife let her interest in the priest guide her resolve. "Yes. It is. Well. That settles all of that – Moulborke, if you wish to run away, then by all means. Mowiat..."

Swallowing, he refused to meet her gaze. "Don't look at me that way. Whatever it is you're thinking, I want no part of it."

All she did was smile sweetly at him. "You don't? What about our *agreement?*"

"We don't have one," he protested.

Moulborke's laugh was as cold as the icy rain that fell on their shoulders. "Oh, now, I remember this. She always did say she was going to find a way to use that night against you."

Desperate for some kind of footing, Mowiat tried to tuck his auburn hair back into his cloak. "She swore she wouldn't. YOU swore she wouldn't!"

Rmaci followed suit and pulled her cloak tighter around her body as the sleet started to pelt down even harder. "Desperate times. Will you help or do I need to use the lips that the Gods blessed me with?"

Smirking, the woodsman threw more of his ample weight behind her. "Wasn't your lips that got him in trouble."

"Suppose that's really only something he and I know. And his sister. Can't forget his sister. What was it she..."

"She does *not*...!"

The woodsman slapped Mowiat on his shoulder. "You know as well as I do she already did."

"Then it's settled," Rmaci chirped with a happy smile that belittled the nature of their situation. "Go find his horse and saddle her. We need to find him before the other things do."

Stunned, it was all Mowiat could do to find his voice. "Excuse me, what?"

In the space of a heartbeat, her voice went from delighted to deadly. "When one of their own goes *missing*, his Order will send down the strength of an army, an *angry* army, to this village. It won't be more of those man-children from the garrison. It'll be the Knights of the Dawn. It will be a Maiden. It will be a Paladin-Commander. You *do* understand the difference, do you not?"

"They won't send anyone of the sort up here," Moulborke growled.

"Are you so sure? Are you so willing to risk your homes on that? We won't have a village when this is done with, and I have no plans on leaving my home up to the good graces of the Queen and her so-called *Holy General*."

"But... he'll make it back. Assholes like him always live."

"You didn't seem to think so a few minutes ago, did you?" Moulborke countered.

It didn't matter to Rmaci what he thought. "I know that if he doesn't, someone worse will come a calling, and then we'll all have our necks on the headsman's block."

Mouth open in shock, Mowiat stared at her. "Maybe yours! I've never done a thing out of place!"

"Do you think it will matter?"

Swallowing nervously, he looked at the woodsman, trying desperately to find any ally. "We haven't done anything wrong... we didn't call for aid but that doesn't mean we were complicit in anything..."

She gave him the sweetest of smiles. "If you believe that, then you have nothing to fear."

"You really think they would? For things we had no control over?"

"We threw out one of their own. We didn't call for help when we knew there was something of ill-magic out there. Of *course* I expect them to blame us! No matter how they make it sound, the Order has no shortage of authority in the kingdom. If such a lowly boy feels the need to threaten us, his superiors – people with *actual* power – will not stop at *threats.*"

Moulborke couldn't hide his disgust at that. "That sounds wonderful. You two – go do that. Now as far as I am concerned, I have no part in this. Whatever you two do, be safe with it. I'll see if Ronlin has a goat that can still shamble down to Gonta that he'd sell me. Not that I have much to leave here with anymore."

"Only dead ones," Mowiat spitefully snapped. "I don't think you'll get any of them to get up and walk around to drag your fat ass away."

Done with dealing with the two men, Rmaci put her foot down both literally and figuratively. "We've talked enough. We need to take action, or we will regret it. I promise. We *will* regret it."

She was right – they would regret it.

Oh, would they ever regret it.

VIII. RIME'S AWAKENING

Say what you will about the cold, but after a while, it'll either kill you or make you ache so bad you wake up. The latter was – thankfully – the option his body took. The aches didn't need much help to hurt and what he did for the next five minutes was nothing more than to just lay in the snow, and listen to his heartbeat pound in his ears in time with the tinkling of ice breaking along the shore.

A quiet assessment of his wounds did not help improve anything. Blood from his scalp had frozen against his cheek, and his left wrist felt all-but useless (and *Goddess* did it hurt). His lower gut absolutely throbbed all the way through and he did not even *want* to think of how badly he was torn up down there. The other after-effects from the jolt of Abyssian corruption were bad enough on their own, and that was the most he was willing to deal with right this very moment.

Fisk me, I just want to vomit. **Please** *Goddess,* **please** *just let me vomit.*

The blizzard, and the fog, had mostly vanished along the water's edge. If he'd been dropped by Aloof (*No, Makolichi,* he silently corrected himself) half a yard more to the right, he'd have fallen victim to the waves and drowned. It looked like a surprisingly large body of water – though as thick as the fog was that still hung over the center of it, there was no way he could see the other side.

At least it tastes fresh... tastes... surprisingly good, actually, for water. Cold. Sweet. But good.

All the magic he had left in him went to two different tasks after he pushed himself to his knees. The fight with Makolichi drained almost

140

absolutely everything in his personal stores. Until he had a long chance to pray and sleep, there wasn't a lot more he could do, even for himself.

A small spell though? A pained, begging prayer left his lips – and was, blessedly, answered. A soothing pale glow lifted up from the ground and bathed him in the softest of lights. It wouldn't repair anything, but it would abate the pain for a few hours.

The Temple was long-winded on the subject, but it was one of the most important things that they had been taught. One of the earliest lessons, too. It wasn't perfect (by any means) and good bloody luck if you expected it to last longer than a hopefully short hobble back towards friendly territory.

Brother Steelhom had started the lecture with an Arch-Templar standing by waiting to demonstrate. The lesson even converted two exorcists-to-be to join the ranks of the healers in their vaunted ivory tower as they hung onto the Templar's every word. Akaran, on the other hand? All he could think of was wonder about hanging off of a young blonde girl that had been in attendance.

"How can we expect you to fight, if we know that the things you battle only exist through magic of the dead? How can we expect you to survive if you do not know the magic of life? You, your lot, you will not be healers. You will not be Templars – you have opted for a different path.

"But as a mundane soldier would know how to bandage an ally, as they would know the most base of poultices to use, or would know to cauterize a shorn limb – you will be taught how to dull the pain of the Abyss, how to ease the ache in your bones, how to stand up once you are knocked down.

"There are no old exorcists. You have heard this saying. You know it to be true.

*"Though we've no wish for you to die **too** young."*

The rest of his fading strength went to making sure that he was alone again. Hastily cast spells gave no sign of anything dead or damned left in the area, which was just one more thing he couldn't tell if he liked or not.

Not exactly a lot to be happy about. Damn them all. There wasn't any time to give the area the attention he felt certain it deserved. If he didn't get somewhere warm, and soon, Makolichi's efforts to put him down wouldn't have been in vain.

There was time enough to do two things before he left – both of which he would thank himself for later. His water-skin was still intact (a small blessing), and filling it up at the lake did not take more than a few moments. *All of these things having a quaint little chat by the water's edge? Maybe there's a reason for that. Maybe not. Either way... I am ruling out **nothing**.*

Besides, it tastes good. Tingles a little in your throat.

Almost at his wits' end, he also took a moment to collect one of the shards of ice free from a random log that he had seen on his way here. It didn't melt at his touch nor did it send the same kind of searing pain into his hands that the shards from Makolichi had. He pocketed it on the hope that it would last long enough to study it – or at least pray over it for guidance.

One of Eos'eno's. I don't even think it's ice. It's almost... pure crystal.

Defeated, depressed, and drained from the fight and the cold, he turned and slunk back towards Usaic's cabin. Whatever else would come of it, there weren't any more answers to be found here right now. If that woman (**Whatever** she is, he groused) hadn't killed the hounds when she spirited them away, he was sure that they would be back. When they did, they wouldn't be happy.

Neither will Aloo... Makolichi. That thing was intimidating to think about before I met it... what in the pits IS that demon? Whatever I thought about it before... that thing... until I can figure out what it is... I'm not going to be able to...

He attempted to flex his wrist and his shout of pain split through the quiet air. *DAMMIT. Not that I can do anything about it **now** anyways. DAMMIT.* Cursing – lots, and lots, of cursing - filled his thoughts as he started to work his way back to the cabin (and its fireplace).

Feeling hopelessly out of his league, the priest reconsidered his approach to the battle. All he could imagine accomplishing at this point was just trying to save as many people as he could before the demons decided that a village full of witnesses (*What had Makolichi called them? Red stains in the snow?*) would not aid their cause.

At least there were things he could do back at Toniki that might make a difference.

Might. At some point. When he got back.

That was going to take a smidgen longer than expected.

He saw the figure moving through the cabin as he approached. The glass was so frosted over and fogged so he couldn't tell who it was. Fresh smoke billowed out of the smokestack though, so he guessed that the occupant was human.

Akaran really, really, hoped it was human. A living human would be a plus, too.

For a change he was spot on – not only was it human, it was a friendly one. That didn't stop her from greeting him with a long dagger aimed at his throat when he opened the cottage door. She looked better than he did, but not by much. Her hair was a fright and her clothes were just short of ruined.

While she wasn't the first person to threaten violence since he got there, she *was* the first to lower her weapon immediately when she saw him. She also expressed shock over the bloody scrape on his temple and the bruising along his eyepatch.

The sheer abundance of ice and snow was the only thing that had helped keep the injuries from swelling more than they should. It hadn't done anything for the burning pain that radiated up his arm or the black ache that throbbed in his chest. But, at least it helped keep the swelling down.

Rmaci was also the first person to hug him. It was a kindness that wouldn't soon be forgotten – even if it should have been. "By the love of the Divine, are you okay? You smell of blood... and is that piss?"

Oh Goddess, of course she'd smell that. Dammit you fisking... The exorcist had to stop himself from giving a reply that would have been heartfelt, albeit sarcastic. Instead, he answered with a simple, "I'll live." It was true even if it didn't speak to the rest of his mood. "What are you doing here?"

She looked scared, almost terrified. There was blood on her woolen shirt and her unimpressive gray fur cloak had been tossed into a corner. A cursory look didn't show any obvious wounds on her skin or tears in her clothes, which he took as a good sign. It was a flicker of hope that vanished no sooner than it appeared.

"I... we... we left the village not long after you did. It wasn't right what they did to you, wasn't right what they said. You aren't responsible for... you didn't..."

"We?"

A flicker of pain danced across her face. "Mowiat came with... he was with me..."

Akaran's stomach started to knot up. "Where is he now?" He didn't want to ask.

"We... we had your horse. I got away while it... Mowiat... I saw it, one of those... things... drag him..."

He closed his eye and tried to keep from crying out of a feeling of utter hopelessness. *Dammit...*

Swallowing nervously, the innkeeper's wife looked outside the cabin window and refused to look him dead on. "We... we were attacked. A wolf, some... some kind of dog. It didn't look... it wasn't natural. We heard the howling before we saw..."

Dammit. "How did you get away?" *I knew it, I knew it, they were hunting someone else.*

"I... I don't know. It launched itself at him and... I ran, I had to run, I had to. I... didn't, I didn't see what happened after."

"Just as well," he sighed. "DAMMIT! You knew that there was something out there. *Why* did you two come after me?" As he spoke, he slowly started to unwrap his cloak and then gingerly removed his left glove. The look of the mottling, swelling skin under it did nothing for his mood. *Oh Goddess. Ohhhh, Goddess.*

Rmaci continued to stare out the window as she wrung her pale hands in the fading light of day. "We hoped we could find you, catch up with you. We followed your tracks and made it to Tinarik's Creek when we were... we saw the burnt armor on the bank and figured you were the one that..."

The spell that kept the pain at tolerable thresholds wasn't going to last forever. There was also no chance that he was going to leave the cabin until he warmed up. *As... Goddess. As long as I'm careful, maybe she doesn't have to know how bad...? I don't want her to think that I can't defend... I can't, but I don't want her to* **think** *it...*

Before she could see it, he pushed his hand back into his glove and just barely kept a blasphemous oath from escaping his lips from the wonderful feelings that were sent shooting through his arm. Her skin was cold where he touched her shoulder with his other hand, and her sleek black hair smelled sweetly of fresh juniper berries and pine cones. "I'm grateful for your efforts and sorry for your loss. But you had to know..."

"We did. I swear, we knew the risk but we couldn't let you venture alone. Not after what happened at the shrine. If you're here then the Sisters had to have sent you. Yes? They wouldn't send a boy if he wasn't up to the task. If they can have faith in you, why can't we?"

"The vote of confidence is appreciated but let's be honest – it's not like many people give a damn what the Sisters say or do or who they support." He'd be lying if he said he wasn't surprised that she evoked the name of the high priestesses from back home.

"I know. I know," she quietly sighed, almost matching his tired tone.

"But I am not most people. The followers of Love are scattered far and wide; you know this."

Carefully, he guided her away from the window and back to the fireplace. Any other time and the circumstances would have been romantic. Right now? It felt ominous and reeked of terror-to-be. The flames cast a pale yellow light against her skin and glittered in her pale brown eyes. "You're one of Hers?"

"I am. Yothargi is not but I have been one for as long as I can remember. My mother's mother constantly told the tales of the Hardening and how we can never freely admit what we are and who we seek the favor of. I couldn't say it at the village not with so many eyes and ears. Goddess knows what would have happened."

There wasn't any reason to disagree. While more than two centuries had passed since the Goddess had fallen out of favor with the Divine, there was no shortage of ire directed at every single one of Her followers. It was part of Her punishment from those sanctimonious pricks, and one that had cost the lives of thousands of Her people.

The ensuing years were ripe with condemnation and persecution. Followers of Niasmis were forced out of their homes while Her shrines and temples were burned. The entirety of the Civan Empire turned against their former allies so violently that they murdered any of Her people that they could catch in the alleys and practiced public executions in the streets.

They called it the Hardening of Hearts. Those that could escape the wrath of the Pantheon (and Illiyans, specifically) fled to Dawnfire from all around the world. It was a safe harbor that was far from ideal but there was protection to be had there for a price. A steep price at the time – but it was better than extermination.

Even now, there were parts of the world that were so inhospitable to Her followers that they simply couldn't go without fear of being imprisoned, beaten, tortured, or outright murdered. In the midst of it all, the Goddess was able to forge a special niche that made Her invaluable at times – under the right conditions. If *She* was going to be cast out and tormented, why not pay it forward and deliver retribution to the Fallen that *actually* deserved it?

Well then.

The old saying is right: Love *is* a bitch.

"If you are... then why did you ask me about Her at the boy's wake?"

"To be sure you were who you said you were."

He couldn't fault her logic. He couldn't do much else, either. There was only so much the benumbing spell could do for so long. Rmaci wasn't making it easier, either. Akaran looked around and tried to look at anything but her. She had an aura that made it painfully tempting to just touch her. That's all. Just... touch.

This was neither the time nor the place and a little voice in the back of his head told him that if he started, he wouldn't be able to stop. *She could make me feel so much better. She could*, he sighed. It was stupid and he *knew* it was stupid, but there it was.

The innkeeper's wife appeared to have no interest in *letting* him keep his hands to himself, either. As the fire warmed her skin she scooted closer and closer until her head nestled itself against his shoulder. Reflexively, he nestled her close and held her against his armor even as that little voice continued to blare a klaxon all through his mind.

If she cared about the rough feel of leather and chainmail against the woolen tunic she wore, she didn't show it. "Exorcist... are we safe?"

"Safe? Here? No. The moment we're warm, we're leaving."

She made a soft little sound of worry and pressed her lips against his arm. "You came this far and survived. You've stopped them, haven't you? Killed all beasts roaming the woods?"

In his defense, he tried to push her away. He *did* try. "Couple of things. Small things. Not the dogs. Not the demon controlling them."

"What dogs? What demon?" Her soft kisses stopped immediately (to both his relief and chagrin).

It only took him a few minutes to explain what he found and what he blamed for the ills that had befallen the village. He even went on to really open up about the zombies that had pulled themselves out of Toniki's graveyard, and his irritation with how Hirshma had wanted him to stay quiet about it.

The gentle concern in her voice changed first to slight agitation and then outright frustration. Her hands quit wandering over his chest too – instead, she gripped at his leg like a woman possessed with far more scorn than seduction. "The alchemist is keeping more secrets, is she? I have no stomach for that woman."

"She isn't the easiest to like, won't argue you there. With how she treats me I can't be surprised with how she must treat you."

"Treat me? Why do... Oh, yes. You mean because of Niasmis?"

"Of course. What did you think I meant?"

"No matter, none at all. Of course, the Hardening. Please, I beg of you to listen. Don't trust that woman. She holds her secrets tight to her chest and has shown no qualms in twisting truths to suit her own needs. If half of the township knew what I know... and..."

"And?"

She swallowed softly and tucked herself in closer to him. "And you should know that I lobbied Ronlin to call for aid from the Temple. I didn't expect to get so lucky to get one of ours, but... he and his sister, that bitch... they didn't want anyone to come. You should know that."

"Thank you..." Akaran cleared his throat and felt the hairs on his neck start to stiffen as he wondered what things the alchemist had been hiding from him. "Secrets have been getting people killed. What is it she's hiding?"

"What isn't she?" she quipped, then tucked herself in tighter to his side like she was clutching at him for dear life. "I bet she told you she barely remembered the route here, didn't she?"

"Or words to that effect. I had to ask her brother..."

"Oh of course, she would. If she ever did tell you herself, she'd find a way to absolve herself if you never found it or got lost and never made it back. If that hag could figure out a way to send the hounds after you, there's no doubt she'd have done that too."

Slightly taken aback by the vitriol in her voice, he had to give careful thought to what he said next. "You being here does imply that more people know how to make the trip. Is it safe to say that everyone does?"

"Most do. Not everyone has a need to come this far but there are several that have trekked out here in the past. Not as many now as there were but so many of us have already left the village... none of us have ever had much want or love of the man. He was a hermit. We've been satisfied with that."

He realized he was absentmindedly brushing his fingers through her hair as she talked. When he stopped, Rmaci took his hand back in hers and returned it to the back of her neck. "An odd secret to keep. I wonder why..."

She smiled to herself even as her tone continued to simmer with anger. "The hag used to love the man; used to be his and he hers. Her father disapproved and disavowed it. Hated the magic that Usaic cloaked himself in. Banished the wizard after the relationship became public knowledge."

Akaran's brow furrowed. "Not everyone is a fan of magecraft, I suppose. There are those that believe that only the Gods should have the right to wield it."

"Not every father is thrilled when their daughter is deflowered by a vagabond, skills in magic be damned."

The truth of the remark made him painfully groan. "No. They aren't."

"Even after Usaic was banished she continued to sneak from town to see him time and time again. The relationship between her father and the mage thawed over time until her lies were discovered anew."

Far too familiar with the cost of flawed judgment in his own personal life, there wasn't much room for him to disagree there either. "Hard to imagine she could go missing for as long as it takes to get here without him noticing she was gone."

With a sarcastic little chuckle, the innkeeper's wife (he had to remind himself of her attachment so frequently that the word was losing what importance his body felt constrained by) clarified her meaning. "Alchemists take time to gather their ingredients. Trips of a day or more were not uncommon. It was when he discovered that the Gods saw fit to grant the blessing of new life in his unwed daughter that he realized what a deceitful bitch she had been."

"Ah. Shit."

"Indeed. I don't know if they continued to see each other even after he threatened the mage with his life or not, but I do know that tragedy struck her twice in quick succession a few scant years down the line."

Focused on her story more than anything else her wandering hands were doing, he felt his back go rigid. "What kind of tragedy?"

"The kind that one would not wish on anyone's heart. Soon after the baby's eleventh year, the Gods saw fit to end her life. They say she always had an affinity for animals; no matter where she went the peaceful creatures of the woods always flocked to her. One day, a wolf did – and it carried with it a rotting disease on frothing lips. Her passing was slow and agonizing and tore Hirshma's poor heart to ribbons."

"Goddess," he whispered. "No mother should see that happen to her child."

"That wasn't it all. Days later her father fell off of the bridge leading to Anthor's Pass. His body wasn't found until it washed ashore not too far from Gonta, in the lowlands."

He could almost feel the sense of loss that the alchemist had to have felt. "Gonta is... days away from here, isn't it? How did anyone know who he was?"

"Yes, it's nearly half a week away by foot. He still wore the village emblem about his neck."

"That's... pure luck that it survived, especially if the rest of him didn't hold up as well."

She had to agree. "It is. Yet it gave Hirshma some closure; as much as a broken body can. Her grief was compounded when they weren't able to even recover all of his remains, so badly had it been dashed against the rocks. The state of his corpse drove the woman into a catatonic state that she didn't resurface from for months after."

"Blessed be... that is..."

With a resigned sigh, Rmaci slipped her hand against his thigh and stroked it slowly. His breath caught in the back of his throat while the rest of him responded the way young men are known to do. "She has lied to anyone that has ever asked her for more, be they travelers or be they her neighbors. Even when the mage started to make regular yearly visits to the village – well after her father's demise – she refused to speak to him or of him. He often asked for her but the answer was always a reception that was colder than the void and harder than stone."

"The poor woman."

"Not too poor. You shouldn't trust her. You just shouldn't. Who knows what she discovered or learned? She wasn't in the village when he went missing. The others remember her saying that she had left for this cabin, but how do anyone know that? What if she had been the one to throw her father off?"

Akaran chewed on the thought while she started to lightly tug and chew on the edge of his tabard. It was almost impossible to concentrate on the story at hand. "You mean as a way to get back to him for keeping her away from her mate? Why wouldn't she speak to him after, if that was the case?"

"What if they had done it together?"

"And no proof to prove it either way."

She sighed into his armor and started to push him onto his back. All thoughts of the nightmares outside the cabin were dashed away at the insistence of her hands on his chest. "None... but we've spoken enough of such awfulness. It will be dark soon. Whatever monsters out there will surely be worse if they find us after the sun falls."

It took all (absolutely all) of his willpower to push her back. "Light or dark, it won't matter," he sighed in exhausted frustration. "We need to be back in the village, behind the wards. Goddess knows what Eos'eno – whatever she is – is doing with those monsters. I don't think she can kill them. Or even if she really wants to. So... either now or later, they'll be here. I'm sure of it"

"They could be dead at her hands for all you know. A magical being of ice attacking creatures of shadow and even more ice? Fighting each other, battling, locked in mortal combat? If what you've said is true, she can always fly above them and slay them from afar."

"But she hasn't yet. I don't think she can. Ice against ice? She's got power in her, but..."

"You worry about the wrong things. Even if somehow the dogs come here, we are protected, yes? I've heard tales of what your people do. You've cast spells to protect us here, yes? You'll protect us both. It's your nature, it's what you do."

"I want to, but..." Akaran shook his head and tried to stand up. "It is, but that's if they come *here*. I still don't know why that big fisker went to Toniki and killed Julianos. If it knows where the town is I imagine the hounds do too."

She cast her eyes to him and looked at him – then realized how much worse the injuries had to be where she couldn't see them. "You've hurt yourself too bad to fight." That was when she paid attention to how he was favoring his left arm; his weak little almost-apologetic smile did nothing to brace him against the withering stare that came from rapidly darkening eyes.

"I... can't. Not now. No."

Insistently, she tugged at his armor until he lifted his arms up for her to pull it up over his stomach. Hissing to herself, she made him help her take it off the rest of the way. He winced as she ran her fingertips over the dark bruises along his ribs and his stomach. When she pulled his sleeve up and his glove slightly down those insistent tugs turned painfully rough.

For the first time since he'd met her the touch didn't feel enticing or welcoming. He could just *sense* simmering fury (although at what, he didn't know) radiating out of her fingertips. "Dammit. I can't use you like this."

"Use me?" As she guided him back down to the fire (and wincing again while he did it), he slowly shook his head. "Rmaci, wait. It'll heal. I don't have the strength to call on enough of Her to do more than to keep walking, but..."

"If all you can do is walk, you cannot fight. If you cannot fight, you cannot live. You're no good to me dead." She stood up and started to rummage through the dresser by the bed, then gave up and settled for taking her knife to the musty bedsheets – makeshift bandages that would simply have to do. She came back over to him and carefully started to wrap his left wrist and hand still.

"Tell that to Ronlin and his sister." He rested his right hand on the center of his stomach, right where Aloof's toxic aura poured into him. "I've had worse."

Rmaci looked at him and didn't even bother to hide the skeptical nature in her stare. "You're an untested neophyte. You have said this many a time, and I am not so foolish to think that you've been downplaying your experience."

Slightly taken aback, he looked her in the eyes and shrugged. "I entered the Temple when I was... twelve years, maybe thirteen. When I was fifteen, I took a limited apprenticeship to a local blacksmith. We were all encouraged to learn from tradesmen, either to broaden our skills or determine if we should truly be on a warrior's path."

"I'd not have pegged you for a metalworker."

He had to clear his throat slightly while the absolute dregs of his personal well of magic gave up the energy to make a dull glow of white began to throb under his palm. "Let's just say there's a reason I do *this* and not hammer out blades. At any rate, one day not long after he took me on, I was tasked to melt down some broken swords, armor. Junk.

"Down the hill and solid jog away from the smithy, we had a practice pit... they would bring in Adepts from the Granalchi Academy to summon certain *things*. They did it in a controlled environment, so that we can practice and grow stronger."

That particular revelation about his training set her aback and made her pause her own efforts to try to wrap up his hand. "They... spawn... demons? At the Temple of *Love?* Your... instructors? They did this? This is condoned? With the knowledge and permission of the Queen?"

"Better to learn to encounter evil where it can be controlled as to not be surprised by them outside of the Grand Temple's halls. Not knowing what we'll be called upon to face is terror enough. Seeing things can be... unsettling enough in safety. But in the wild? Thank you, but no. Things in the wild... you see me, here, now. Inexperience... with what we do, it... gets people killed. There are no old exorcists, they say."

Repulsed, she continued to stare at him, mouth agape. "True demons? They actually brought forth *true* demons? There's evil in this world true, but surely not enough to warrant such... such... excess?"

Akaran snorted in derision. "My hand would beg to differ."

"Well..." Otherwise rebuked, she continued her efforts to help patch him up.

"But. One day, there was an accident. Well, not an accident. They said that the summoner had developed a grudge against the Brother that was teaching the lesson... no idea what it was all about. Infidelity. Money. Someone's horse shit in a garden somewhere. And... anyways. He was supposed to just bring forth a small little imp for us to study."

Rmaci watched him continue to pulse light against his stomach and squeezed his leg encouragingly. "Wasn't an imp?"

"Wasn't an imp. Asshole summoned a *chinikari* – as pure of a demon as demons get. About seven feet tall, they walk on two legs like you and me, but they're bloody giant lizards. Scales and all, elongated jaw... It ripped the binding stones apart like they were made of parchment and then went after the students. When it finished with *them* it went on a rampage through the courtyard."

"Oh no. Goddesses above, that sounds awful..."

"It was." He looked off into the distance, like he was looking at something that just wasn't there. When he continued, his hand clenched up and his voice changed pitch. She had the faintest flicker of a smile when she saw the light under his fingers take on a deeper, darker intensity. "The smithy was the third stop on its tour."

She went back to work on wrapping his wrist and arm, shaking her head. "You poor thing, you must have been absolutely terrified."

"Should've. More angry than anything else. The smith panicked and ran off. I didn't... and it liked what it saw when it got there. Could see the absolute delight that thing had in its blazing yellow eyes. It hurt. It hurt a lot."

"How bad did it..."

"Bad. Spent the rest of that summer hobbled. Got stuck helping the maids clean bedding for months before they'd let me pick up a sword again. Was glad when they did." It was a half-truth – he *was* glad they let him pick up a sword, but just touching one made him remember what it felt like when the *chinikari* held him down and slowly impaled his arm with two of them, one above his elbow and one below it.

It wasn't a fond memory.

"Is that when you lost your eye?" It came out in a blurt, and she looked almost shocked that she even said it.

Blinking, he relaxed a little. "No... no, but they said it nearly killed me. I don't remember all of what it did. I remember claws, remember scales. Other than that... just what they told me. A few other fragments. It took an Arch Templar a week to get me to wake back up."

"You must have been truly blessed then, to survive. I hope they were able to catch it before it hurt anyone else? Were they?"

"Ah... no."

Her green eyes shot open. "*What?* They let it get *loose?*"

"Oh... no. I mean that by the time that the Brothers were able to reach it, there wasn't a need. It was dead."

"Well that's a relief, I suppose." Her eyes never left his face, and they didn't quit shining. Rmaci even looked like she was gaining some kind of victory hearing him relate the tale. "Good to know that the Order puts proper safeguards on their summoned monstrosities. I take it someone ended its miserable life from afar?"

Akaran cleared his throat and relaxed his grip on his bruises and gimped wrist. They weren't going to get any better than the throbbing they were at now, but... at least he was mostly convinced there weren't any internal wounds that would kill him in the immediate future. With a cough that hurt *a lot* more than he was going to admit before the buxom tavern wench, he clarified what he meant. "It didn't make it past me."

One more time, she went completely still. "You... a boy. You just said that it nearly killed you. You said it did kill several others. You expect me to believe that *you* ended it?"

"Yes. It hurt me. I hurt it back." That was the *other* thing he remembered but didn't feel like it was worth sharing: the scream the *chinikari* made after he flung a small crucible of molten copper at its head. Most of the rest was a blur of blood and scales. Most.

He still remembered how desperately it screeched when he paid it back for his arm. He also remembered how much he enjoyed hearing that cry of anguish, even if he never admitted it to anyone. *And never will*, he quietly reminded himself. *Not... exactly priestly.*

"After that, the blacksmith never let me back as his apprentice. Said my talents were far better elsewhere. The whole thing ruined his workshop. Ended up burning it down, something about bits of lizard embedded in the walls. Don't know what to think of it. Didn't see the end result."

"Your people are mad."

He scoffed a little bit and gave her an overconfident smirk that he really didn't believe. "I thought you said you had heard tales about the Order? I mean, you're a follower, and... we don't keep secrets from our people."

"I have... just... not about your... about the training... I've never been to the grand temple."

"The things the Sisters put us through in training?"

"That, yes." With a tired sigh, Rmaci rolled back onto her heels and looked at the bandages on his arm and the handful she had wrapped around his ribs. "That's not going to do much good. I hope Mowiat dying was worth this."

Frowning, he started to push himself up off the floor. "He didn't have to come out. You didn't."

"You didn't take your horse and you came back here looking half dead. By your own admission, you can't fight." She stood up and helped him get to his feet, an unabashedly agitated look on her face. "I doubt you'd make it all the way back from here on your own."

Akaran grabbed his cloak and pulled it up over his shoulders, bristling. "I didn't ask you to come rescue me."

Rmaci put her hand on her cheek and sighed. "Then none of us got what we wanted. If you're ready, we'll go. The sun is already going down. It's sure to set before we get back in the village walls."

"Fine," the exorcist replied, sagging a little. "Just... let's go. Get the horse ready to leave."

He watched her look out the window and poke her head outside before she stepped back out into the cold. *Goddess above. I do not know what to think of that woman.* While he extinguished the smoldering fire, he had to agree with her opinion. *Nobody got what we wanted.*

Dammit.

154

IX. WARM WELCOME

The horse was a blessing in disguise. She spent the entire trip back moving carefully between every chunk of frozen rock and divot in the landscape like she knew how bad he had been hurt. There wasn't a stumble or bump to be found as they slowly worked their way back to the village. Akaran could not stress how much he appreciated that mare to anyone that would listen.

Not that anyone *would* listen.

Nothing new there.

Only a few people were happy to see him back at Toniki – although after they saw the shape he was in, even the hardest of hearts melted a little. Hirshma wasn't the first person to welcome him back but she was the loudest and most insistent about getting him under her care. "Don't know what you did but I can tell you damn well fisked it up." Then she looked over at his companion, and her next remark was far more terse: "Or fisked someone."

It didn't even warrant a response. Romazalin had one of her own when Rmaci quietly apologized for losing the stable-boy along the expedition after the priest. "He was a good man, risked his life..."

The farmer's wailing and crying cut the exorcist to his core while he limped along behind the healer. As Hirshma guided her newest charge to her hut, she spoke in a quiet voice. "Mowiat had been courting her... it's why she hadn't taken her kids and left..."

"What do you think she'll do now?"

The alchemist scoffed at him. "Leave. Kill herself. Drink. Does it matter? Nothing else for us to do."

Akaran just shook his head (and immediately regretted moving it).

They spent more than an hour in quasi-silence as she worked on him. When she was done, his left arm was in a tighter sling than Rmaci had fixed up and his scalp had ten stitches that were not at all pleasant to have sewn in. When she saw the bruising along his gut, she offered a few choice words about him and the cow she presumed was his mother. A few thick bandages were wrapped around his ribs and upper abs no matter how much he told her that it wasn't necessary.

All of his complaints earned him a severe rebuke that he had to agree with. "Fine. You say you can heal some of this. Then heal it." He tried – but there wasn't enough left in him to even give a flicker of relief. "Then you'll take the bandages and shut up about it. We've buried enough. Bad enough you brought back word of another we'll have to mourn. *And* then hope that we don't have to put him back in the ground later, apparently. *If* we're ever lucky enough to find the body to start with."

To his credit, he shut up about her care – but he did tell her about the rest of what he found out. He did not, however, tell her about any of the less-than-flattering things that Rmaci had said about her, or the story she had spun about Hirshma's family. *Never anger the physician. Not when you still need their care*, that wonderful voice in the back of his head quietly suggested.

He also skipped over the bracelet *and* the water. If the raven-haired beauty was right and the alchemist couldn't be trusted... the less she had to know about his investigation the better. Then again, it didn't seem right to leave her in the dark about the rest of it. Specifically?

Telling her about Makolichi.

"The thing that killed Julianos. It did this to you?"

"It did."

She looked at him, staring into his eye, and kept her voice steady the entire time. "Vestranis said you promised to kill it."

"I did."

"But you didn't."

Akaran ran his fingers over the stitches on his head and sighed in exhausted frustration. "But I will. One way or another, I'll see it dead. Either by my hand, or by one of the Brothers of the Order. Probably going to have to be helped by someone bigger than me but I *will* see it dead."

"So you aren't able to protect us?"

He struggled to answer and hated himself for it. "I can delay him. Them. But I don't think I can kill all of them on my own. One or two at a time. Not all at once, if they come like that."

Hirshma slowly put her tools down and almost bored a hole through his face with her unflinching and almost unblinking stare. "You... need to tell Ronlin. I assume you'll be giving him the same doom and gloom and begging him to tell everyone to leave their homes?"

"That depends."

"On?"

The exorcist stood up and wrapped his cloak around his upper body as tight as he could with one hand. "Do you want to die peacefully somewhere warm or die screaming while freezing here?"

She made him leave without replying.

Ronlin was in the back of what was left of the town's slaughterhouse when Akaran caught back up with him. There were enough hooks dangling from the ceiling to string up twenty pieces of large game. Now? All that was left were a pair of skinny foxes and a half-carved goat.

"I know it seems like a place this far out of the way could never be prosperous. It was. The large stables, the blacksmith's hut. The barns. All of it. Not a day went by that we weren't doing well out here. We were, before all this. We really were."

"No sin in being successful," Akaran answered with a soft smile. "No fault in wishing to live on the border, either. You've no idea how lucky you are to be away from the bullshit that drenches the capital."

The elder had to stifle a laugh, a chore that seemed odd to have to do with his hands buried in the front half of the goat that was dangling behind him. "There's enough issues here with keeping the peace between one another. Thank you, but I will defer to statesmen, lords, ladies, and those in dresses and robes to deal with matters that impact thousands. Or matters that they think do."

"Just as well. I've no love for them either. I've always had an issue with authority – or at least, that's what my instructors say. If I disagree, I'm lying. If I don't, then I'm agreeing with their authority. It's confusing."

With a small smile of his own, Ronlin kept his eyes focused on his work. "Young men always are. But. I suspect you've other things on your mind than the egos of our beloved rulers?"

Akaran cleared his throat and looked around the room to make sure that nobody was hiding in a corner somewhere. Confident that everyone was out of earshot, he took a deep breath and laid out his case for an evacuation. He didn't spare anything; the animated dead he had to dispose of, the wraiths in the cave and what made them so odd. He told the elder about the tracks at the graveyard and how they were different from the ones in the woods.

When he talked about what he discovered at Garrison's Folly, the elder had to stop his work and listen intently. He took the news of what Akaran thought had happened to Julianos well enough. The elder even interrupted him long enough to admit equal blame of his own. "Boy, if we had called for aid earlier, many more of us would still be alive. I admit that. But now you think that your own magic made these things come closer?"

"I am sorry... so sorry for that. I had no idea, no way to know."

Ronlin's tone didn't lead Akaran to think he believed his sincere apology. "I know your duty, heard tales about how your people have failed before. Just be mindful to remember his face the rest of your life. He may be the first you get killed, but if you live through this, you gotta know that boy won't be your last."

The admonition sank Akaran's heart further in his chest and did absolutely nothing to help clear his mind for the argument that he was about to lay forward next. Before he reached the end of his explanation and started his plea, he did stop and ask Toniki's leader if he had been the one to place the enchantment in the woods.

Ronlin looked taken aback by the question. "Me? Magic? I thought men like you could sense the presence of such skills."

"We can. It's harder if there's only a little of it in a person. Sometimes it doesn't take magic to ask for the aids of the Gods. A pious soul can request help too. Once in a while, it's granted."

Continuing his job unabated, the elder dismissed the thought completely. "I've spent a long life in the mountains. Pious? Never. Too many winters with too much wine. Too many fights with rough men and too many nights with rougher women. There's no hope for a God to answer any request I'd make." He gave the carcass a hard squeeze, almost like he was angry at it. "Far more likely I'll end up as one of those damned souls your people claim to be tasked to banish."

"There's always hope, and there's always a chance to turn around. Even in death, the damned are granted peace if they seek absolution." The words of encouragement did nothing to address the more urgent matter at hand. "That sermon though – when you gave respect to Julianos. That wasn't one of a man that gives no thought to the Heavens."

"Oh there's thought given. Just not by me. The village looks up to me to make the hard decisions and to guide them. When someone passes, people need guidance of the spirit, not the guidance of an old drunk with an aging cleaver. It's a pity you decided to lecture us instead of guiding us. You're a priest. You could have done so much better."

"I'm an exorcist. What I do better would have done no good in that room." Pained, he sighed. "I'm not here to make converts or offer salvation. I'm here to condemn the damned. Playing up the righteousness of heaven is not my task, and now isn't the time even if it was."

"No, time for such talks later. If there is a later for any of us. I can hear the uncertainty in your voice, young man. You need to learn to hide your anxiety if you're going to convince anyone to follow along behind you."

"Right now I don't want anyone to follow me. I want them to run away from me."

"The duty you've taken on would demand them to at least listen wouldn't it? Frightened men don't always make the most convincing."

"Maybe. Or maybe you seeing that I'm scared should be enough to convince you to get everyone else to listen. Please, tell me honestly. The blessing? Did you place it, did you ask any of the Gods or Goddesses for aid?"

Ronlin didn't have to think about it. "No, sir exorcist, I didn't."

"Please tell me that there's someone else here that would. Tornias swears he doesn't have any in him. That shrine your people have looks to have been used a little bit, even if not much. It wouldn't take a lot of effort for the right person."

Again, the elder didn't have a useful answer. "The last family that I knew that had any devotion to one of the Pantheon left three months back. They weren't followers of Pristi. For some reason, they cast their lot in with Matron of the Kingdom. Melian followers, I'll never..."

It was Akaran's turn to try to stifle a laugh. "Nor I."

"Well, if the soldier says he isn't involved, is there a chance that someone else in town would be worshiping Her in secret? That's what your people do with yours, isn't it?"

"Nobody would have a reason for worshiping the Goddess of Purity in secret."

"Then you have your answer."

Then he looked down at his feet and sighed. "Damn. It has to be Tornias then. Lying little shit."

"Your language is far too colorful for a priest of your stature."

"I'm not a priest that has any stature." Frustrated he strummed his fingers against the hilt of his sword. "Can't think of a reason why any of Pristi's followers wouldn't admit to their involvement though. Bunch of stuck-up holier-than-thou twats. They'd brag about taking a shit if they thought it would honor their Goddess."

There was absolutely no way that Ronlin could stop from laughing at that. That laugh turned to a dim look of unhappiness a few moments later. "Say I believe you, son. You truly do think we need to leave, all of us."

"Yes."

He looked up at the exorcist and stared into his eye. For a moment, it felt like he was trying to look directly into his heart. "I know you heard me say that this was our home and that we have not yet abandoned it and couldn't even if we wished."

"I did."

"You still want us to throw all of that aside?"

"I do."

Ronlin kept his voice steady, although there was a hint of anger behind it. "You know I won't tell them to go. You know they won't go if you tell them too, either."

"If I thought they would – I'd be out there, not in here with you," he answered slowly. "They're not safe here. They won't be safe. I don't know how much time you have left before..." He let it trail off to empty silence.

"Before things attack that you can't even name."

That made Akaran's skin prickle a little, and it showed. "Wraiths, hounds, and animated corpses. Plus the thing that killed the boy and damn near put me in the ground. This isn't a case where a pack of rabid boars are menacing your doorstep." He cleared his throat a little to add some weight to it. "Dawnfire already lost men to trying to exterminate the vermin hounding your people. The Queen will be very upset if she loses a township because of petty stubbornness."

"She'll lose one if we leave, too."

"There's leaving, then there's *leaving*. One of which has a way you can get back from."

Ronlin gave up trying to bore into the one-eyed man's heart through his eye and turned his attention back to the bloody harvest on his table. "From what you've said? We can return from both." Akaran tried for a retort, but the elder shut it down before it could even begin.

"No. I will not tell our people to leave just because you feel that you're too weak to fight for us. Maybe Rmaci was right and we shouldn't have bothered."

"Rmaci? She said she... whatever, it doesn't matter." It took all of his willpower not to unleash a torrent of blistering curses at the stubborn fool. "I can't make you go. I simply make no promises that you'll leave if I do. You saw what happened to the soldiers. They were many. I'm just one."

"If the threat had been bandits and the patrol had been wiped out by them then I would be worried. The threat is something supernatural. If it chews you up and spits you out like unripened berries – again – then I'll consider an exit. Until then? No. I trust you will serve your Kingdom and your Goddess and *us* until the threat is gone... or you are."

Akaran couldn't help the bile that welled in his throat. His response to that wasn't helpful to his cause. "Well. Seems you and your sister both have something in common."

"Oh we do?"

His anger barely contained, the exorcist gave his answer as he turned his back and left the butcher's shop. "You both seem like you'd be happier if I was dead."

Whatever Ronlin's reply was, he didn't catch it.

He was barely three yards away from the butcher before a young girl with a melodic voice stopped him. "If you're looking for the healer, he's off in the tavern. My miss made him go eat and take a bath on pain of death if he didn't go."

Lost in dark thoughts and startled, Akaran almost jumped out of his skin when she interrupted his internal fury. She was bundled up pretty tight even though today was a bit warmer than the last few had been. "If I'm right, she should have killed him then and saved me the trouble."

"If you're right, he won't have long to regret not doing it."

"I don't want to be right."

The girl just looked at him and shrugged. "Then don't be. Just start asking the right questions."

A closer look at her made him realize that there wasn't much to her that would set her aside from anyone else in the village. She looked like she was roughly his age and height, though as bundled up as she was, he wasn't convinced of anything. Even though she was keeping her head covered by a heavy wool cap that accentuated the long gray woolen coat she wore, there were little tufts of pale blonde hair that stuck out from under it.

Akaran gave her a frown that he swore until the day he died that made her giggle at him. *The Sisters didn't send me out here to test me. It's a punishment. Has to be.* "Lady..."

"A lady? I know you're not enough of a gentleman to think that highly of me already."

"Listen, lady... girl... whatever..."

"Oh, I like 'whatevers.' Those can be fun."

That was the last of that he was willing to swallow, and he said as much. "Okay. I give up. Can we skip the riddles and the veiled hints and the half-truths and the scorn that everyone has been dangling in front of me so they can make me seem the fool? I am so tired of it."

Nodding, she just smiled at him. Her blonde hair covered half of her face, and her little smile was a thing of slight beauty. "I said where he was. But you're not going to go see him right now. My miss sent me to find you."

"Who is... oh." The name left a sour taste in his mouth before he even said it. "Hirshma?"

"Yes."

Shutting his throbbing eye, Akaran couldn't even begin to think he'd enjoy any of this. "And what does she want this time?"

"You," she answered. "In bed, specifically."

That wasn't quite what he was expecting. "I ah... no offense, but..."

She snickered at him and pressed her back against the butcher's shack. "She wants you in bed. *Your* bed. To sleep."

"As much as I appreciate the suggestion, I -"

"You *are* going to go to bed. She ordered it, so you have to do it. That's the way it works."

Akaran stared at her dumbfounded. "She's not my miss, so no, it isn't."

She pushed away and walked right up to him, placing a hand on his sling. When he winced, she started to whisper at him. "You don't have many friends here. But the ones you do have want you to stop these things. You can't do that if you're barely able to stand on your feet. Some of us have lost loved ones. Friends. Family."

"From what I've heard, most of you have."

She shook her head and squeezed his arm for a second, making him bite his lip and wince again. "Some of us have lost friends *defending* you. We will watch over you if you promise to watch over us. You can't do that when you're half-dead."

"I'm perfectly..." Looking into her shining eyes, he stopped. There was something faintly almost magical to them – shades of ivy around a pale blue center. No, not magical. Just... pretty. *She's right, but... Makolichi...*

"You're perfectly beaten. Whatever your training is, it won't help you much right now. Not while you're walking around looking like a heard of swine just ran roughshod over you."

Trying to avoid admitting that she was right, he took a different approach. "Those things are coming, they'll be here soon. You gotta know that."

"If they come now, we'll be dead or we won't be. If you keep pressing yourself, you'll be dead either way. Then what? If you're dead, then we're all dead. So, you need to get some rest so *you* won't be dead so *we* won't be dead."

She's right. Really, really right. Dammit. Giving up, he felt his shoulders sag.

Hirshma's apprentice picked up on his defeat right away. She squeezed the bandages holding his arm and gave him another little smile. "Don't get any ideas, but I'm taking you to your room. Hirshma will have my head if I don't."

"She can have it. In the meantime, Tornias and I have business. I need to know what he did."

"You two don't have business until you start asking the right questions. You don't even know that you're asking the wrong ones."

"I gathered that. I'll figure them out. Inside. I promise, inside, and not out here. But I'm not going to bed so if you don't mind would you please step out of the way so I can -" While he tried to brush past her, she reached up and put a mitten-covered hand on his chest.

This time there was no question at all about what she did: she actually *did* giggle at him – though it was just a nervous tick (not that he realized it; he thought she was mocking him). It preceded the most useful bit of information he was about to be given so far on this miserable excursion. "Wait. I'm going to regret telling you this but... you know that three soldiers came back from the excursion. Yes?"

His frown shifted to a look of slight interest as his eyebrow slowly arched up. "Yes..."

"The one that died. He couldn't talk much. Wasn't left much of him that could talk. All he did was just clutch at a silvery crest and thanked it again and again for saving him." There was a short pause and another little giggle (a sound that didn't help soothe Akaran's nerves any).

"Guess it didn't work. Miss barely managed to pry it from his fingers. We ended up hanging it on his grave-marker.

There was a brief heartbeat's worth of internal argument before he asked her if she noticed anything remarkable about it. *Not all of us go gently. Poor soul could've gone mad from pain, or...*

"I think I recognized the face on it. Belongs to that Goddess that overlooks the Temple. Pristi. It's one of Her idols. Man just absolutely had no wish to let go of it. Not that I can say as I blame him."

You could almost hear the pieces fall into place in his mind at the sudden revelation. "Please tell me you know which grave is his."

"Didn't see it. Just know that he didn't get a proper burial. They covered him with stones instead of trying to dig through the mush. Remember Vestranis saying that the garrison would send more men up here and they'd take care of their dead, so no sense in doing something that they'd undo a few days later."

"It's a given they'd send more soldiers, true. I got sent first so they'd be able to be safe."

"Oh yes. Brave soldier boys. That medic was very clear on it. Surprised they aren't here yet. He seemed to think they'd be here... um... only a couple of days from now, really. Didn't really like the ones that came the first time. Kept looking at me like I was a walking piece of meat with lips."

She had absolutely *no* idea how right she was (and never would, thankfully). "That would make sense. I wonder why the delay."

"Don't know, sir priest... no, not sir. You don't like that, do you? Don't want to give you any more grief, you've been given enough from us."

Three days later and I've finally found the second person who's willing to be nice to me. "No, but... not important right now."

"Oh, no, not even close. I'm Mariah-Anne, by the way. Never met someone from the southern side of the Kingdom. Glad I have."

Akaran looked over at the entrance to the Rutting Goat. It was so close, yet so far away. In the torchlight, Mariah's quirky little smile looked so innocent, so welcoming. He was also struck by the thought that the witty girl could clearly see through any bullshit anyone put in front of her. His own included.

The buzz his spellwork had coated him with long gone, and there was only so much that Hirshma's foul-tasting medicine could do to help numb his body the from the beating at Makolichi's hands. Every inch of him, every bone, every piece of skin, everything and everywhere, wanted him – was screaming at him – to go to sleep.

Ideally somewhere far away from here. Preferably on a beach. Maybe with this girl. *Wishful thinking.*

In that moment, he could see that she knew it too. That didn't stop her from blurting out something else. "Do you *promise* you're going to bed after you search the graveyard?"

"Yeah. My word. I promise."

She giggled again and started to walk with him in the dark. "Good... because I imagine that in short order you're going to want to hunt Tornias down and beat the idiocy out of him. I might watch. He was the last person to see Julianos alive, you know."

Akaran's eye twitched. "He was?"

"He was. I yelled at him myself. Won't say why he asked him to go there, but... he did. The last one to see him and nobody here gives a damn. They think that he just went off exploring on his own like he does now and again."

"Tornias sent him to the graveyard."

"He did."

It clicked. "After the amulet."

"Think so."

"Did you go after it?"

Mariah looked at him like he'd just grown a second head. "Just because I'm stuck in this ruined town, do you think that I'm eager to get myself killed?"

"Makolichi went there after that soldier's amulet, and the boy was there, and... it was timing. A fluke. The kid wasn't prey. He was in the way."

She quietly agreed with him and waved her torch in the dark. "You already think that Tornias worked some magic out in the wild that attracted the thing that killed Julianos – even after swearing he had none. Then he got my friend killed."

Pain now a distant thought in his mind, Akaran trudged forward, growing anger giving him a stronger bounce in his step. "You can watch when I punch him."

"Thank you. Oh... and exorcist?"

"Yes?"

"I overheard a couple of the mourners. When they put my friend to rest... they said that something had thrown rocks up on some of the graves and... that they came from Destin's area. Think they had to go cover him back up."

"Destin is Tornias's companion?"

"Yeah."

They were almost to the entrance to the graveyard when he stopped and looked at her. "Why are you helping me? Rmaci did... now you. But... nobody else. So, why?"

She answered him without missing a beat. "You're admitting you're scared, but you're doing your job anyways. That medic tried to impress me with stories of his time with the army. All he made me realize was that he was a fearful little fool, just that he won't admit it."

"I think I've figured that much out."

"Yeappers. Men who *admit* that they are scared are men that will not tolerate other men who *lie* about their bravery. Am I right?"

Even on the best of days, he didn't have the least bit of strength to argue that. "You know if your people don't start running away, now, more of them are going to die, right? You included. You shouldn't stick around. You people need to pack your shit and leave."

"*If* I left now, it would piss my mistress off to no end, and I've seen how badly *you* do. I do think she likes you, even if she won't admit it." The remark left him stunned, and the bigger grin she flashed after it scrambled his thoughts a little bit more.

"She likes me? Rmaci said she..."

Mariah faced him and then leaned in close to his ear. If anyone saw them, they would have thought she was giving him a kiss. "And if you believe anything that woman says, you're an idiot. Don't."

"But she -"

"- is full of more shit than a barn full of stomach-sick pigs. *Don't* trust her." She backed away and faced the grate to the graveyard. "I'm not going in there. I'll wait out here, but I'm not going in there. Whatever you need to do, do it fast. It ain't getting any warmer."

Akaran stopped and took a deep breath, fingering the hilt of his broken sword. "Yeah. Fast."

She smiled and opened the gate for him, then stepped back well away from it. One last nervous giggle on her lips, she looked into it. "I'm holding you to your word. You're going to bed after you do this."

"Bed. Right." It was the last thing on his mind.

Thoughts of beaches and girls with star-flecked eyes be damned.

X. LOST IN THE FROST

Standing in the graveyard felt like the first time that the world decided to greet Akaran's ears with peace and quiet since he had gotten there. No horse, no animals, no villagers, no intrusions. The only thing that made a noise was the sound of his boots softly crunching in the snow and the sound of his sword gently bouncing off of his hip.

For all of those reasons, there was a sense of unease that persisted. It wasn't that there was something innately wrong. It was that there was something that was missing. A glance across the graves didn't show any fresh evidence that they had been disturbed again. The area had been half-trampled down from the shoes of the well-wishers that had come to mourn the child, but that said nothing more than to reinforce that the boy had been well-loved in the town.

Vestranis had been true to his word. At the far end of the graveyard, in a corner, wood still smoldered under the raised iron platform. There was still some ash residue in the oblong basin that they had placed his body in, along with a plethora of footprints all around the crematory. *At least the boy is at peace now.*

Oddly though, he couldn't tell where or what they had done with the ashes after the fact. None of the existing graves had been bothered at all and there was no sign that he had been buried elsewhere within the graveyard. *Probably interred in the shrine for the time being. With these people, who bloody well knows.*

He stood as close to dead center of the burial plots as he could and looked around. The efforts of the last two days were taking their toll on him, and the cold wasn't helping. Still, he kept his breath steady, he kept his shoulders tight, even though all he wanted to do was take a few minutes to relax. He had sanctified it just last night, so this was a safe place, wasn't it? He could take some time, look around, and enjoy the quiet. The graveyard had been sanctified to ward off evil, so it should have been safe.

No sooner than the thought enter his mind than he realized the source of his unease. The heartbeat after that, his eye snapped open wide and his sword was in his hand (and the torch that Mariah had given him dropped to the ground). He spun around, looking, hunting, searching for a reason. Any reason.

Any reason at all to explain why the ward he had cast had lost all of its strength while he was gone.

Nothing presented itself right away, nor did anything challenge him. He really, truly, deeply, wished something had (he was also grateful that the torch hadn't gone out right after it hit the snow). With a weary, wary eye, he walked to his ward and brushed away the snow he had covered it with. It was intact, but several of the runes that surrounded it had been... burned away. The ground where they had been had been blackened but the snow that had covered them hadn't melted.

Nobody attempted to destroy it. Something taxed it until it could take no more. Why didn't I feel it fail? I wasn't that far. That... masking spell? Did it mute everything? What in Niasmis's holy name is going on?

There was a warning that the instructors at the Academy had beaten into the heads of every prospective exorcist, priest, cleric, or anyone else that wished how to call upon the Goddess to protect a place from the machinations of the Abyss. Their wards were simply Words written in the tongue of the Divine, carved onto a surface and infused with power from of the Goddess. Simple was a misnomer compared to everything else...

"Wards are many things," Brother Steelhom had said, *"and you will learn each of them. They exist to warn you of the damned as much as they do to drive them back. They may be used to protect, or they may be used to condemn. They may be used to contain – or they may be used to draw forth the things that live in the dark.*

"They have their limits. They will fade, over time, as no magic is eternal. The strength they have is the strength you have; you are still the conduit for what power the Goddess sees fit to grant you. They are imperfect; as we are imperfect, the things we do, the magic we use, are all imperfect."

Akaran kept sweeping his gaze over the defiled graveyard as he remembered the look on Steelhom's stoic face when the man spoke the next part of the lesson. *"There are things that will drain them. The longer they are exposed to corruption, the more energy they will use up. Over time, the magic that imbues them will be siphoned off into the ether. When that happens, will feel it fade, for it is an extension of you.*

*"**Do not** rely solely upon them. Should you do so, you will have made a fatal error. Should you die from blindly expecting them to be all of what we do, you die a fool's death, because now you know better. Always check them, always look for them. Always expect that they may be overpowered or drained or disenchanted by something stronger than you when you return to them. **Do not** take their power for granted."*

"I am **not** in the mood to deal with something bigger than me right now!" Akaran half-shouted. "Dammit **all!**" *Then again, maybe I am. Fine, just fine. Whatever drained the ward had better not be lurking about if it knows what's good for it. Don't care if I do hurt like fisking rabid thundering rampaging cock-sucking swine...*

His search began immediately. The crematorium was fine, as was the gate itself leading into the hallowed ground. He checked each grave, each marking, each wall. Even when he found the grave he had been looking for, he didn't sense anything. Not at first.

That changed when he found the other thing he had been looking for.

The chunk of wood that served as the grave marker read "Destin," with no indication if it was his first name or his last name. He supposed it didn't really matter. What did matter was that the apprentice alchemist was right about how he had been buried; they had dumped him as far from the other graves as they could. His place of (temporary) rest was slightly below the rest of the cemetery, down a minor slope that kept it out of sight (and effectively kept it hidden from him his first trip).

She was spot on that the villagers had done little more than give him a shallow grave covered by stones. Honestly, it looked less like they had covered him with care and more like they just threw rocks at him without giving much of a damn if they actually stacked up on the body or not. He was grateful that they had, at least, bound his remains in a thick swath of canvas (which was a discovery made when he started a particularly unpleasant task).

At least he's not up and moving around. I'll take that as a victory. If Tornias wanted the crest back, I wonder if he had the courage to come get it himself after his errand-boy was murdered. If it's still here, I swear to the Goddess I am going to shatter his jaw.

Disgust at the medic hastily overpowered his disgust for what he had to do next. That crest had to be here, and that left only one way to find it. *I might damn well break them anyways.*

Resigned to the job, he grit his teeth and set to work. After planting his torch on the ground next to him, he cautiously started to uncover the grave. Stone by stone, he stripped the grave down from the head down towards the feet. Nothing turned up until he started digging towards Destin's midsection. What he found he didn't like.

His search came to an immediate halt when his hand brushed over something that sent a wave of nausea rolling through his body and a jolt of searing pain right behind it. He unleashed epithet after epithet as he recoiled and threw himself back on the rocks that littered the area. His arm gave a silent curse of its own when he slammed his wrist against a large chunk of stone, though the pain went half-noticed in the face of the discovery.

Hello, Makolichi.

Please Goddess, give me the strength...

A short, desperate prayer later, and She did. The next word out of his mouth was literally just that. It was one that set his hand ablaze with a brilliant lavender glow that illuminated everything around him under the night sky.

Carefully, he resumed his task – removing every rock, branch, clod of dirt, and bits of scavenged brush that was near where he felt the burn. However, the source of the supernatural toxin didn't plan on waiting that long to expose itself. A silvery chunk of metal slid out from under the stones and clattered onto the rock beside the exorcist.

Another piece fell right after – and he barely managed to move his hands away before the final piece joined them. The shattered pieces of Pristi's crest did not slip free alone. The last piece had been speared with a chunk of what appeared to be shining onyx. It wasn't.

Showing an excessive desire for safety, Akaran didn't touch it again. He bent down and looked at it – and gave a soft whistle as he realized what it was. *I really do not like you, you son of a demonic bitch.*

The chunk of rock was the same stuff that Makolichi had thrown at the enchantment in the woods. It steamed as the light from his spell illuminated it and the smell from that was acrid and disgusting. It had melded perfectly with the remnants of the crest and little black vein-like crystals had spread halfway over it.

Makes sense. He doesn't like holy symbols in his hunting grounds. Odd that it stopped here and didn't go for the temple. If it hates the holy enough to tear down a tree and lay siege to a graveyard, why not tear apart the shrine? I don't know what he is – but the villagers wouldn't be able to stop it. With or without the hounds at his side. What's been chasing him off before now?

Eos'eno.

Assorted other obscenities and a handful of borderline blasphemous grumbles followed one after the other. All of them were directed at the garrison's medic. *He would have probably died instead of Julianos, if he had come himself.*

*Why didn't he? That's easy. He was afraid of whatever butchered his troop. He thought it might lurk out here... so he sent a little kid to go get this. Then he didn't want to speak up and take the blame for his death... that son of a **bitch**.*

Didn't want anyone to think that he knew more than he was letting on. Or was afraid that whatever was out there would see him take it. There was little tolerance for cowardice to be found in Akaran's mind (a truth that Tornias was soon to learn) and this was just... too much.

If he hadn't been so obsessed with running through every curse and condemnation he knew, he might have made out what the soft voice just past the graveyard wall that made a mournful cry of "Oh, my kin, oh no, you did, you did..."

The sound interrupted him for a moment. He couldn't quite tell what it was – but he wasn't the only one there. Rmaci had also arrived on the outskirts of the cemetery a handful of minutes after he found Destin's grave. She didn't know what to make of the whisper or see who said it, but the sadness it conveyed touched her heart and gave her plenty of pause.

Any doubts *she* might have had about the skill Akaran possessed were swept away in the next instant. She hadn't seen his hands take on a glow from where she had been standing, but after she crept around him and kept to the woods, she was clearly able to see what he did next. Honestly, she had wondered if he was all he claimed to be, just like everyone else had.

It wasn't easy to decide what to do about the remnants of Makolichi's destructive rage. It was telling that it had lasted for as long as it did and was still this potent. The shards at the Folly only had a flicker of some taint left to them compared to this shard... then again, this was several days more recent.

He came to the slow conclusion that the shard was somehow feeding off of whatever energy was left in the crest and that it might have even been growing on it. Despite a particularly strong desire to rush it back to town and shove it down Tornias's throat, what it would do if it got in proximity to the stronger wards he had put down in the center of town? It could have been fine, or it could be disastrous.

Who knew?

He didn't – and he wasn't going to take that risk.

Pain flooded up his arm to his shoulder when he grabbed the concentration of black magic with his good hand. Even with holy light enveloping his fingers, it still burned to the touch. Hissing through his teeth, he wasted no time in issuing an edict against it. Even if it had been feeding off of the crest, it couldn't feed on his spell. It was too much, too fast, powered with unrestrained and exhausted anger.

He made the rocky ice choke on it.

When it fractured, shattered, and melted away into the glow that covered his gloves, he set it down and touched the other two parts of the crest in turn. Enough residue from the demon's magic covered them that they also steamed up under his touch as the corruption boiled away to nothing. *He's not going to like this.*

Good.

Finished with the crest, he took the time to send a pulse of the magic through Destin's body as well. When an all-too-familiar tentacle sprouted up out of his chest just before it dissolved, not only was he not surprised, he even expected it. *They're drawn to magic. Black or white, it doesn't matter, though I'd bet that black is much easier for them to stomach. Less likely to hurt... but the hurt isn't enough to dissuade them, if the holy is kept in small doses.*

Even shattered, the crest kept the wraith contained. They're weak, at least. Not going to complain about that. They're going hand in hand with Mako and his puppies though, so... safe to say that they'll be around next fight... but I can work with weak. Wonder why they weren't at the lake.

*No, no reason to wonder. Eos'eno chased them off. **That** makes sense – if she's fighting them, they're going to run from her. She's got a lot more power than the wraiths, and even more than the hounds. Good. I think.*

All those thoughts firmly in his mind, he took a little time to cover the fallen soldier up and then offered a prayer to bless his passageway through the next life. Hopefully it hadn't been interrupted, but that was all he could do. Just hope.

Both Rmaci and Eos'eno saw him do it, although neither of them were privy to the next two thoughts that popped into his head. One of them was a good idea, and the other not so much. He'd regret both to a degree – one significantly more than the other.

Enough's enough. I'm done playing defense with these things. I think it's time that I made myself more attractive to them. ***After*** *I deal with that sad little shit of a medic.*

A dark cloud hung over his head as he stormed out of the graveyard, thick in disgust and rolling in self-loathing for not figuring all of this out well before now. Mariah took one look at him and shied away with a quiet little prayer of her own that none of his attitude was going to be aimed at her. It didn't stop her from calling out to him though, as much as she wished she didn't have to.

"Hey. You promised."

It didn't stop him. "Things change."

"And you gave your word."

"I did. Things changed."

Frowning, Hirshma's apprentice scurried after him. "If you run off that fast, I'm not going to get to watch you hit him. You are still going to hit him, right?"

"If you want to help with that, find me a heavy rock."

Grabbing his arm, she stopped him in his tracks. He started to shove her off before she grabbed his hand in her own. "I don't think you're able to pick up a rock right now."

Whipping his head around to snarl at her, he jerked himself free of her grip. "I re-buried that soldier. I cleared out the mess that Makolichi left behind. The one that Tornias is responsible for. I'm *fine.*"

"No, you're too pissed off to know what you're doing. What? You think you're the only person upset over Julianos? What about Mowiat? What about *everyone else I know* that died to these... things?! You don't see me throwing a fit over it? Do you?"

Seething, he pulled his coat tighter, absolutely freezing in the night air. "You don't understand. It's not your *job* to deal with this kind of shit. It's *mine.* The kid's death is on my head. Mowiat's is on my head. Anyone else that dies right now is on *my* head because I didn't do *my* job to keep them alive! It's my fault!"

"We were dying before you got here. You've been blaming us for these deaths since you showed up, now suddenly...? What now? You missed something and suddenly you're at fault for everything that happened? You're bloody lucky to be alive, that's what you are."

"Dammit, no. Those things are still out there. I didn't catch them, I didn't kill them, I didn't stop them. What do you think is going to happen when they make their way down here? They're going to want to sit around a campfire and sing bawdy drinking songs?"

"I think that if you don't take the time to take care of yourself the first thing they're going to do is make you watch. If you're going to be this pissed about it, maybe that's what you deserve. Maybe it's what *we* deserve."

Softening a little at her confession, his tirade died on his lips. "What? Of course it isn't."

Her voice cracked as she spoke, and she stepped back as she finished. "You said it. Again and again. We're guilty."

"Maybe but... you don't deserve to..."

"What we deserve isn't up to you. You don't get to decide that. Probably just as well; you'd have half of us hanging from the rafters if it was. Or strung out in the woods."

Akaran grit his teeth and tried to force his temper back in check before he tore the girl's head off. "I wouldn't do that. Even if I could."

Tears had started to well up in the corner of her eyes, and there was no mistaking her sniffle. "Really? Because that's what everyone thinks that's what you'd do. Some of us think that you're just waiting for the army to arrive to have us all thrown into a dungeon because we didn't call for aid from your vaunted Order to start with. You've not been the most calming of voices."

"I wouldn't..."

"Not to me. Not to Rmaci, though I am sure she'd deserve it. Or Vestranis. Or to Yothargi, though the Gods know he'd string you up by your cock if he was given so much as a slight chance. Can you tell me you wouldn't do the same to my miss? To Ronlin? What about to Tornias?"

She was far more right than he wanted to admit. "Tornias should have told me everything about that attack from the start. He didn't. The boy is dead because of that. And even if not tell *me*, he could have gone after... Destin? His amulet, that amulet. He could have gone for it himself."

Clenching and un-clenching her hands as she spoke, Mariah looked him dead in the eye. "Like some piece of jewelry is all that important."

A little half smile curled at the corner of his mouth as he pulled the shards of it out of his sling and dropped them, one by one, into her hands. "An amulet of Pristi, a ward against the Abyss. There's not much that sulks in the shadows that could be around someone carrying it... or at the very least, not that wouldn't be in a world of pain from touching it."

She looked at it, not entirely comprehending what he meant (and she didn't entirely believe him). "I don't believe you." She also didn't believe in tact. He liked that about her, to be honest.

"Believe or not believe. This is why Makolichi went to the graveyard. This is why he came here. He destroyed it, which doesn't bode well for anyone else. So. Yeah. Tornias. I could have had this out of town, or even put it on myself, and..."

"It would work for you? I seem to recall everyone saying for all and ever that your Goddess and the rest don't exactly get along..."

He had to admit that she had a point. "Pristi hates the damned more than she hates Niasmis. Enemy of my... intolerable relative. I guess. It doesn't hurt me to touch it so I'm guessing..."

"Well. Quit guessing. Honor your word, go to the inn, go to bed. Don't go looking for him tonight. Surprised you're up and walking around. What in the world did miss give you for pain?"

"It doesn't hurt that bad..."

His lie earned him a sharp rebuke and a mitten on his sling. "Bullshit, I saw your arm. What did she give you?"

Her tone caught him off guard and made him think. "Um... belistand wort and larochi tea?"

Mariah didn't even try to hide her surprise – she just answered with a slow and soft whistle as she slipped a hand under her coat. "You know that's what she gives pregnant women as they give birth, yes?"

"No...? I pity your expectant mothers-to-be then. I feel fine."

That lie went ignored. "Well. I can't stop you from going and beating the shit out of him, can I? Even though you look like a stiff breeze would knock you on your ass?"

"A breeze won't, he won't, and no, you can't."

"Fine. At least will you drink this? Just... it's some wine to help keep you warm. You look like you're about to turn into a human icicle."

Sighing in marginal defeat, he took her offered flask and made a show of taking a long draw off of it. The taste of it, however, was almost enough to do to him what she thought a gust of air could. "*Blessed be!* Is this *wine* or is it *mule piss?!*"

"We have some very talented mules, haven't you heard? Now drink the rest. It won't do much for your mood but it's not going to hurt you any. I give my word." She crossed her arms and glared at him. "My word is more dependable than yours is, too."

"You really are Hirshma's apprentice, aren't you?"

The blonde-haired girl didn't dignify that with a response. "She is a wise woman who does not deserve your scorn. I'd appreciate it if you would stop."

He gave her a dirty look as he took another swig of the so-called 'wine' and tried to choke it down. *It could be worse, could be worse...* "I don't appreciate her shoveling bullshit down my throat and putting her foot up my ass."

"She's an old woman on the edge of the frontier. She puts her foot up everyone's ass. Should have seen the things she made me do when I got here."

Akaran tried not to laugh around the swill, but he did start walking back towards the Rutting Goat. "Why are you here, anyways?"

"Don't know if I should tell you."

"Unless you're hiding a secret alliance with one of the Fallen, you've got nothing to fear from me." He stopped, looked at the flask, looked at her, then back at the flask. "You aren't, are you?"

"Just with my miss."

For a change, he showed enough wisdom not to say the first thing that popped into his mind. *Same thing, isn't it?* "Then you're safe."

"Well..." Shaking her head, she kept off in the direction of the inn while he started to lag behind. "I wasn't supposed to be here. Not for this long. My family wanted a better life. We left the Province of Kralos... started a trek up through here. Father wanted us to move to Ameressa."

"That's a long trip. Months, isn't it?" *This stuff tastes like how I imagined week-old horse shit in a jungle would, but... does make a man warm.*

"We joined a caravan. But... then father took ill halfway. When he didn't make it... my mother didn't want to keep going. So, she stayed... trading post, near Treifragur."

Sipping more and more from the flask as they walked, the warm feeling was quickly and happily buzzing all through his body. *I want more of this.* "Why didn't you stay behind with her?"

"My brother did. He and I... we've never seen eye to eye. Father wanted me in Ameressa, so Ameressa I will go."

"But this isn't Ameressa."

She looked around the village courtyard and looked at the piles of slush and snow. "I got stranded here when the snow started to fall. I stayed with the caravan. They were nice enough, all told. They kept going even after. Hope they made it. I do."

"So... why didn't you?"

Mariah shrugged. "Had a feeling. Wasn't a good one. Thought if I stayed one winter through, the next caravan along these parts would head deeper into the mountains, and I'd be back on the path in the spring."

He stood beside the door to the inn and tiredly leaned against the wall, the entirety of the day catching up to him in a hurry. "So you stayed."

"So I stayed. Thought it'd just be one winter... needed a place to call home, did odd jobs and services at first... worked off my rent... then... guess it got obvious things weren't gonna change. Told my miss about it one day, my father's plans, his hopes. Then what happened? She took me in. Cared for me ever since, better than my mother."

"I... yeah. I guess so. Reasonable." Stifling a yawn, he looked down at the flask in his hand... and realized it had slipped out of his fingers without him noticing it. "Hey... wait..."

Hirshma's apprentice let out a relieved sigh. "Finally."

Blinking slowly, he tried to stand up a little straighter. For the life of him, he just couldn't. "What did... why do I..."

She slipped over next to him and lifted his right arm over her neck to keep him from falling down. "Because we both figured you'd try to do something this foolish. So, we're helping you keep your word."

"Y... you... drugged me..."

Clearing her throat, she leaned in as close to his ear as she could get. "I didn't wait out here in the cold just because I like you. My miss or not, she's gonna owe me for making me freeze my tits off."

A few mumbled words that were entirely unfit for repetition slipped out of his mouth, although for his credit, he did take the time to compliment her on how nice he was sure her frozen tits were. "Dammit I... they could come back at any time... why would you...? Wai... you like me?"

"I told you. You're no good to us dead. *Miss* will continue to protect us on her own until *you're* able to help her." Whatever his response was, it was lost in her shout as she tugged the Goat's door open. "Hey! The idiot finally wore himself out! Can someone give me a hand getting him back to his room?"

He missed hearing the answer she got.

He *also* missed the venomous exchange between Mariah and Rmaci while Vestranis dumped his unconscious ass onto his bed with absolutely no care for his overall well-being. Or dignity. As both women smiled faintly at the sight, the innkeeper's wife spoke down to the younger girl in quiet, hushed tones.

"Wore him out did you? Aren't you the lucky one?"

"You're only upset that he fell asleep with me, and not under you."

"He's young enough still. Not the kind to need much rest between time spent with a woman that knows what she's doing and a mewling child like you."

Mariah smiled and worked her hair out from under her coat. "I'd say he's all yours, but I'm sure you've got your hands full with... how many cocks is it now? You're down one, since Ronlin took that last goat, I know."

"Oh yes, poor little baby alchemist. Having to satisfy your urges with my scraps?"

"You can't call someone your scraps if you never wanted them to start with."

Rmaci let her gaze flip over to towards her challenger and smiled again. "Claiming to speak for me? Isn't that adorable."

"If only more people would speak for you, I wouldn't have to hear your voice so often."

"There are ways to ensure you don't. I can help you with some of them. There's plenty out in the woods that needs to be done these days. Maybe you and I can venture out there some time soon. Think you could help me feed the dogs?"

Smiling wide at the tavern wench, Mariah gave her an answer befitting a woman three times her age. "Oh let's! I'm sure the hounds would welcome the sight of a bitch in heat. They just don't know what they missed. Heartburn, likely, but even still. They wouldn't be the first beastly tail you've tucked between your legs, would they?"

"Maybe we can stick the both of you out there," Vestranis growled as he slid the door shut in their faces. "Let the boy sleep, fisking idiot looks like he went through a war. Not that either of you two cackling harpies would have noticed."

Scolded – but far from done – the blonde took Rmaci's hands in hers and squeezed. "Whatever your designs on him are, don't. Whatever you want from him, don't. You didn't want anyone from the Orders of Light here, you didn't want Ronlin to let him stay when he got here, and now you're trying to slip his cock down your throat and your tongue up his ass. He's a self-righteous jerk, and it's a miracle he didn't get killed fighting for us. At least *he* is trying to do something *helpful*."

All Rmaci did was just smile sweetly to her. "He fought, he lost. There's nothing he has left that I could possibly be interested in. You can play with him all you like, little baby alchemist. You won't have any competition from me."

Keeping a smile nailed to her own face, Mariah dropped her hands and started to walk off. "You aren't any kind of competition to start with."

XI. GLACIER'S PEAK

Morning came with a thunderous bang.

Or at least, that's what it felt like in his head.

It was just about all he could do to crawl down the tavern stairs and keep his head up at the same time. Vestranis hadn't disrobed him before putting him into bed and he felt no reason to strip down now. His left arm felt like he'd never want to use it again, his ribs felt like someone dropped a tree on them, and his head, well...

Who keeps firing a cannon in my skull?

Yothargi wasn't to be seen, but Moulborke was. "Boy. You hurt as bad as you look?"

"Goddess above, I hope not. Water?"

With a little smirk, the woodsman pointed to a cask behind the counter. "Ale. Has water in it."

Akaran ran his tongue over his cracked and dry lips and debated the wisdom in adding to what already felt like a hangover. *Desperate times call for desperate measures.* He poured out enough for one cup, then quickly chugged it down. While the older and far-drunker man laughed at him, he downed half of a second flagon's worth.

"More water than ale."

"Well it sure as all ain't the thick piss they call booze down towards the capital."

Rubbing his temple, the exorcist looked down into his flagon and sighed. "Thick piss... we used to call it slightly-damp shit." Then, sighing, he looked over at the somewhat jolly fat man. "You're not dead."

"You wishing I was? Odd thing for a priest to hope."

"I'm not dead, you're not dead, the ale smells rancid. So nothing changed last night? The dogs, the demon, the wraiths, that... snow-tittied ice queen? They didn't show up?"

Moulborke gave a small nod and turned his attention back to his own drink. "Snow-tittied ice queen? You did have a rough night, didn't you? HAH! Nothing new. Wind still is cold as my wife's mother's ass, ice is still as prevalent as lice on whores. Last creature that came a callin' and walked into these walls was you."

"Small blessing." Grumbling under his breath he gave the room a long glance and set his flask down on the counter. Pushing away, he looked over at the woodsman and gave him a (painful) nod. "Thanks to Yothargi when he comes around next. To you, too."

"To me? I ain't done a damned thing." After a short pause, the woodsman sized up his injuries and tilted his head a little to the side. "Leaving already? No impassioned speeches? No accusations? Not even an argument?"

If his head would quit throbbing so hard, Akaran might have given a damn. It didn't, so he didn't. "Would it do any good?"

The woodsman shrugged in response.

"Then I won't waste your time, or mine."

"Fair enough, boy. But... boy?"

Looking back over, Akaran raised an eyebrow just slightly. "If you're going to chew my ass out as well, could we not? I'm done with it."

Sighing against the lip of his cup, the woodsman shrunk a little bit into his seat. "Suppose you've got a right to feel that way. But be honest with me. You come back, lookin' like you'd gotten stepped on by a God. You really of the mind that these things can kill all of us? This shit ain't some kind of act to try to convince all of us how much safer we'd be if the Queen had her enforcers down here ruling all over us?"

"I look like I've been in a war, and out of all of you? I'm the only one that knows how to kill them."

"So did you kill them?"

Cringing slightly, the priest had to admit his failure. "Not yet."

"Then you sure you know how to put 'em down?"

Akaran reached for the door and opted to brave the cold instead of going with a conversation that would be as drawn out as it would depressing. "No. I know who does though."

"More bravado?"

"Nope. Going to have a talk about it now."

Giving his own nod, Moulborke belched out a response and then took another swig of the watered-down horse piss that doubled as liquid courage. "Don't like you, boy, but can't fault your heart. If you think we're to blame for all this, then don't get killed for us. Sure we all got sins to answer for. Or... just don't get dead, in general. Don't dislike you that much. Alright?"

"Yeah. I'll try that."

The wind outside had calmed down, and if anything, it was the warmest day he'd felt since he walked into this accursed town. Even the sun was shining, and there wasn't a snowflake to be seen. *Small bloody miracles. I'll take whatever ones I can get.*

He wasn't lying to the gruff critic at the inn – he was going to go talk to someone that he knew would know how to deal with this out-of-control calamity. *Still cannot believe that they thought this was a simple haunting. Big enough to eat a few soldiers but not big enough to cause the rest of this. Blessed be unto all if I make it back the Sisters and I are gonna have a talk.*

Not that I'd expect them to **listen**...

They wouldn't.

A simple question to a random child told him where to find where it was he was looking for. When he got there, he had to admit that it wasn't all that bad. The northernmost tip of the town overlooked a cliff – probably thirty, forty feet down, ending in a half-frozen river that tricked down from Goddess-only-knows-where up in the mountains.

Unsurprisingly, the locals didn't care enough for the Gods to hold ceremonies of any kind (except, apparently, funerals) at the shrine. Instead, they carried them out here, where a ruined stone archway-formerly-gazebo had been built long ago. Like the rest of the town, it had seen better days, with chunks of it laying about what was once a pristine clearing flanked by trees and encircled with rusted iron braziers.

The archway sat on a smooth stone platform, and overlooked the drop-off. Creeping up to it and looking out into the valley beyond, he couldn't deny the view. The old adage of 'you can't see the forest for the trees' was openly on display. *Well, if I was going to get married, this... doesn't look to be that bad of a spot.*

Not only could he see over this valley, he could see the dip and crest of the next two. Above all of it, the frosted peaks of the Equalin Mountains looked down over everything below – with vaunted, snow covered majesty. *I really am on the frontier of the Kingdom. The Midland Wastes are up there somewhere. The Free Cities of Ameressa on the eastern edge of that mess. The Civan Empire to the north of all of*

it, past the Midlands, on the other side of the mountains.
Yet it feels like I'm looking at the edge of the world.
Why did I have to get stuck with assholes on this side of it?

He really hadn't lied to Moulborke; there *was* someone up here that could help him out. What he didn't say was that it wasn't any of the locals, or that it was anyone that was likely to make an actual physical appearance. In fact, if anyone saw what he was about to do, they might throw him off the cliff on general principle. Ultimately, it didn't matter what they thought.

The villagers probably wouldn't be happy about him dragging one of those braziers across the clearing or lighting it close to the stonework that someone had once taken great pains to carve out of the rock. They'd get over it. He had no intention of freezing to death out here, and this *was* Temple business.

He set the small statuette on the edge of the platform and sat down next to it. He'd given a passing thought to asking Rmaci where she worshiped, but her tone on the way back to town hadn't endeared her to him any. Plus, if someone had overheard him ask, it might do her more harm than good.

There was a pretty simple rule that was written out in the first chapter of the Tenants of Love: even if the Goddess was shunned, She would be wherever Love was the strongest. You could find Her in a midwife's hut, or comforting a camp of refugees, or even a small cove where a man or woman would discretely meet. Or...

...you could also find Her where a pair of lovers would give their vows under the gaze of all the Gods in the sky. *Even if the bulk of them are just glorified pricks on a celestial scale.* Really, you could find Her anywhere – the nature of Her being and all of that metaphysical spiritual stuff that was hard to comprehend on the best of days – although places like this one made reaching up and out to Her realm a little easier. Again, he was sure that someone much brighter, wiser, older, and attuned to the minutiae nature of such things knew all of the myriad reasons why.

They didn't tell him what all of those reasons were and the few times someone had tried, it gave him a headache. Seeing as his head didn't need any help to hurt today, skipping the *why* was better than trying to puzzle through it. *A velvet glove or a hardened fist; know which I want you to be,* he mused, reciting the centuries-old mantra drilled into his skull.

Once he had the statue settled and the fire in the brazer going, the only thing left to do was close his eyes and pray. "Goddess of Love, Goddess of Passion, Goddess of Warmth; Lady of Lovers, Queen of the Star-crossed, Matron of Mothers; Home-tender, Caregiver, and Comforter of the Lost. I beseech You to listen, and I beg of Your aid. I come before You as one of Yours, as one who needs Your touch, Your guidance, and Your counsel. I am far from Your reach – but I am where Your will sent me.

"And my Lady – I need answers, and I need Your help. Please."

Elsewhere, answers were already starting to come to pass.

Not that anyone was going to *tell* him about them anytime soon. When they did? He wouldn't like them.

The alchemist's hut was filled to the brim with crates, canisters, sacks, and assorted compounds that had reactions with each other so interesting that they should probably be kept in different provinces – and *definitely not* in the same building. Here they were though, even if they were almost universally depleted. There was enough work for the two of them to keep busy, and today's focus was solely on preparing enough poultices to supply an army.

Or at least, that's what it felt like to Mariah.

She wasn't that far off. "He looked like someone threw him down the mountainside," she whined.

Looking up from a well-worn mortar and pestle, Hirshma didn't seem interested. "From what we were told, Mowiat likely was."

"If you had been out with him, either of them, he'd still be safe."

"Or I'd have suffered their own fate. If not worse. I'm not a young woman anymore."

Frowning, Mariah worked her hands through a sack of dried out panacain-weed and refused to meet the glare on her mentor's face. "You say that, but you also say that you can protect us if we stay in the walls."

"They were outside them," the elder answered as she pointed at jar behind her apprentice's head. "The sirnah powder, please."

"Outside them? The village walls touch the graveyard walls, and it's walled up itself. There's no difference there." It was all that Mariah could do to keep from throwing it at her. "Julianos wasn't. You told me – again, and again – that we'd be safe here, and that we'd be able to take care of the people until this cold reversed itself, that the natural order would be restored."

"And it will. I fail to see how what I am doing now somehow

impedes upon that promise, or even fails to live up to it. Perhaps you could tell me what, or how, you feel that I have let us down?"

"I can't believe you'd ask that. He was like a little brother to me!"

Looking down at her desk, the alchemist shook her head sadly. "Julianos was no fault of mine. The graveyard is past our walls, and he had no reason to be out there. He didn't listen."

"No fault of yours? If he had listened? But he was still out there, he's still gone. And why are you treating that exorcist so poorly? Why are you complaining so bitterly about him? He's no threat to you, no threat to the village."

"He's a threat to himself and I am tired of burying people. I've seen his type. I know them. Reckless. Cocky. Playing with powers, playing with *things* they don't understand. Don't you understand what people like him are capable of? The type of devastation that follows in their tracks?"

The girl flicked her hair out of her face and continued to dig through three different a musty sacks on the floor. "I'm seeing the kind of devastation that's going on *without* the help of people like him. He was dead on his feet last night with that... that... *woman* hanging all over him when he got back. And even then he still kept going!"

The emphasis drew a slight laugh. "Feeling jealous, are we?"

"Jealous? Why does everyone think I'm jealous? I've simply no wish to hear about how his cock ends up covered with festering boils from bedding that whore."

"So you do admit you think of his cock, do you?" Hirshma laughed – with absolutely no attempt to hide it.

"I think about a great many things," Mariah muttered. "Wouldn't want to hear a bull groaning after bedding her either."

Shifting in her seat, the alchemist was forced to agree with the sentiment (even if just barely). "Your objections give away your feelings. You forget; I was once like you. Young, naive, full of spit and spunk. Dreaming of a strapping young man to come whisk me away from my tired lot in life."

Wrapping her fingers around her prize at the bottom of one of the bags, she went for the elephant in the room. "You mean as you did. With Usaic."

"What I did with *that* man is not to be repeated. Not today, not tomorrow, and *not* by you."

"But it's what you *did* do, isn't it? He's why you're so against having a priest in our midst. He can do real magic. You know it, and that's what bothers you about him. I've seen you flinch every time someone even *suggests* it. He reminds you of Mayabille's father."

Hirshma leaned forward and looked at the mess of herbs and dust on her plate like it was the most important thing in the world. "What bothers me about him is that he's not the kind to give up. How much Iarochi did we dose him with yesterday before he finally slowed down?"

Sighing, Mariah sat back and looked at her miss. "Enough to have knocked out Moulborke and Vestranis both."

"At the same time."

"At the same time," she agreed. "But doesn't that mean that he's the man for the task at hand? If he won't quit fighting until someone drops a slab of granite on his chest, doesn't that mean he's the one that can stop those... whatever those things are out there?"

If the pile of stuff on her counter gave any indication that it was concerned with how intently the alchemist was staring at it, it didn't show. Then again, dust wasn't usually the thoughtful-feeling type. "Those things are an affront to nature. Nature will not tolerate them any longer than it takes for the cycle to run its course. They should be left alone until that time. Nature will deal with them when it is in nature's time to do so."

Her apprentice thought about it – and then shot it down. "What's going on isn't natural. You've taught me enough about the world the last three years to know that. The *world* taught me enough to know that this is wrong. Demons don't come about because nature is working right, they come about because nature has gone *wrong*."

"The world was here before demons, before angels, before magic. Maybe before the Gods. I don't know. The world will be here after all of them – after all of *us* – are dead and gone. Who are we to question it?"

"*We* are. You taught *that* to me too. *We* are here to question. *We* are here to understand."

"To question and understand. We are not here to change."

Standing up, Mariah ran her hands through her hair again. "Men make the world in their own image. What we do is to aid men, and aid them so that men like *him* aren't needed except in the direst of circumstances. Miss, I hate to argue with you, but these *are* the direst of circumstances! So why don't we do more to make him welcome? That's all I ask. He's not the villain."

"He isn't the villain, but he is dangerous. I have protected everyone in Toniki just fine before he came, and I will after. Those that leave the township do so at their own peril. I have protected us for years, and I will protect us for years yet to come."

The girl walked over and put her hands on Hirshma's desk. "But miss, you *haven't*. The cold is still out there. It's in here. It's not just the demons that are killing people and making us miserable. It's all of it, and you cannot protect all of us against the entire world."

"I can protect us against everything out there that would seek to do us harm! Now sit back down and get back to work before I task you with shoveling the shit out of the stables. We're short of black powder, and that -"

"*What shit?* There's no horses left! No cattle, no sheep. Ronlin cut the throat of his last goat this morning! *There's nothing left!*"

Stunned by her absolutely uncharacteristic outburst, Hirshma quietly set down her tools and watched her apprentice seethe in righteous anger. "I knew... a man. Once. Yes, Usaic. He had magic, he had power. He said he was one with nature. I believed him. I believed *in* him. But he didn't. He didn't have a mandate from nature, he didn't have the power he thought he had."

"You were young. We're all young, we're all allowed to make mistakes. As long as nobody dies -"

"Somebody *did*. A mistake? No. It wasn't a mistake. That wasn't the case. He was reckless and dangerous. He looked at the things I believed and the things I could do and all he did was use them to his own ends. Don't you wonder why there's none of us left that openly worship the Gods? We were lead astray by him. I was. My brother was. Our father, may the Gods bless his soul. We all were."

"Akaran isn't him though, miss! He's... he's *good*. Cocky, dangerous, deadly. I can see that. Everyone can see that. He doesn't hide it. There's something in him... I have no doubt that he'd slit the throat of anyone that stood between him and the people he protects without a moment's hesitation. Part of me... part of me thinks he'd enjoy it, too. The Gods only know if he's going to kill us all or not and the scary part is that he's on the side of the Divine."

Hirshma folded her hands over each other and cocked her head slightly off to the side. "If he kills us all with his recklessness, what makes you think that him killing us out of an effort to be *good* is any different than if he did it out of malevolence? He's a zealot in the making, if he lives long enough."

"Because someone that was doing it out of malevolence would just sit back and watch us die off one at a time and play on our fears and make us scared and miserable and hungry and tired and paranoid.

Exactly like those *things* out there are doing now."

"Those things won't be there forever. You're too young to see how the world works. The Queen's men will be here within another day. Two, at most. They will deal with what is out there, if it can be dealt with. I am certain I can keep our township together for another day or two until they purge the mountainside."

Maria was far less than impressed by the argument. "Say they do. Purge with what though? Mere violence? Simple swords, simple arrows? The army is full of Melia and Makaral followers. Don't you think they'll bring far more strife than a man of Love?"

"They will purge. It's what the army is made to do. We will provide shelter, medicine, comforts. Me included. You included. The less time they spend here the best, the less magic they use the best. For everyone."

"Or they'll purge with magic. Worse than the kind of magic that that man has in him. Is that any more natural than what he can do himself? Is waiting on one group of spell-slingers to arrive more *natural* than letting the one that's already here deal with it?"

The alchemist shook her head. "He is not one of the people. The army is made of the people, made of people like us. Not... like the type that he aligns himself to."

"*His* type?" That did it; that gave it away, as far as her apprentice was concerned. With her thoughts racing at a league a minute, she continued on. "Say that more of them don't get killed. What life is there for us after that? Will the traders return? Will the animals? Will our people?"

"Villages come and go. I will stay here until my last breath. You aren't going to be judged harshly if you take my lessons and run. I'd no sooner blame those that already ran than I would blame those that opted to stay. But you will stay until it is safe outside, past the walls."

"But that's the thing! I don't want the village to go anywhere. I don't want our people to give up on Toniki! So why have you given that priest such an awful time of it? You say it's because of people like him. ONLY people like him. HIS people. I don't understand – you're like a mother to me and I don't understand! Is it solely because of whom he prays to? Do you loathe him because of where he casts his heart?"

Setting aside her finished poultice, Hirshma leaned over and took her apprentice's hands in her own. "When I was a girl, your age, I knew magic. I had it."

The admonition caught her completely off guard, and she didn't know how to comprehend it. "Miss? You, a mage? You've never spoken anything kind about magecraft since I met you, and longer than that, or that's what our people said..."

Hirshma shook her head. "I gave it up when it all turned against me. Magic, the Gods, all of it. The world will correct itself. It does not need our aid to exist. It doesn't, so what cause do I have to use it anymore?"

Confused, Mariah slipped them out of Hirshma's hands and put them on her hips. "What does that have to do with Akaran?"

"Everything, of course. The undead have no desire to come here and risk fighting a Warden of Kora, current or past. They know that I am here, but they do not come in our walls. Denying the power doesn't mean that I don't feel it still. They must as well. It's why they haven't come into our homes before now, and why they won't still."

"Wait... miss? You place your confidence that... these things won't attack because of something you said you *used* to be? Something you're no longer? You told all of us that you could keep us safe, and now it's an untested... **maybe**? And you turn away Akaran...? Someone that *can?*"

The alchemist answered simply. "Those demons do not care to tangle with me. With him? He nearly died fighting three, and now he expects to win? As bloodied as he is? They'll come for him. He should not be here when they do. He puts us at risk."

"The same risk you say isn't here for anyone *within* the walls? He's in them now! You were against him from the day it was discussed! Give the boy aid and he will be gone soon enough! You'll have nothing to worry about after, and less once the creatures are destroyed! You want me to provide 'comforts' to the mages in the army yet you argue about supporting a priest just because you hate his Goddess!"

"Mariah... my motives..." Hirshma sighed and stood up, picking her words carefully as she thought about the best way to explain. "There's more things that are stirring than a few lost souls and a pair of rabid hounds. Me, you, my brother, Toniki... it will all come down on our heads if he is given cause to look for things he has no business searching for."

"Miss – no. Just... no. I will not condemn him for being here simply because he has magic or because he may discover things you and your brother may want to keep quiet. Too many secrets. Secrets will be the death of all of us!"

"My brother is a fool. They aren't his secrets. He's too dense to keep one. I don't let them be known because it *will* ruin us all." she replied, a slight sneer replacing the gloomy frown on her lips. "Do you know that he once fought with the Queen's Army?"

Slightly surprised by the admission, the blonde apprentice couldn't find the right words to say. "He fought? Which war? Which battle?"

"One that is long done. One that ruined his back and neck. He shouldn't have gone and he did. What he saw when he served is enough for him to know that the army is more than capable of disposing of what is here. Nature has not yet, the army will."

"Akaran is *part* of that army. His Order has *sway* over it! The army is known to answer to the Temple of Love before they answer to anyone else! Their leader – the Holy General? You know as well as I do where she casts her soul!"

Hirshma's anger started to boil. "The Queen heads that army. She may have a cause for those violent thugs in his Order but we do not have a cause to have them *here*. The soldiers in the army, soldiers like the man that Ronlin used to be, they are enough. That... those freaks... his freaks... their influence will not touch our homes!"

"The only way that their influence won't touch us is if he's dead or... if he can't fight." Blinking, she started to chew on the thought, and prayed she was wrong. "As if... if he's too hurt to fight, or... too drugged." Realization hit her hard, and she pulled as far away from her mentor as she possibly could, aghast. "You knew that. That's why..."

"That's why I what? Choose your words carefully Mariah, you are on the edge of my patience."

"There was enough belistand in the tea you made him last night to put a grown man to sleep for days. You *want* him to be comatose until the army gets here. You weren't trying to help him, you were trying to *poison* him!"

"And what of it? He gets to live, and we aren't bothered by him. Then we aid the army. It's that simple. You and I, however, are no more. Do what he says and leave, girl, because you've no longer a home *here*."

With her back against the wall of Hirshma's hut, the girl wanted to say something more – a lot more – but she couldn't. It wasn't because she was afraid that Hirshma would yell at her or hurt her or whatever else.

It was because someone else spoke up first.

Or more aptly said, it shouted.

"BLEEEET!!!"

...if you could call that a shout.

For most people, prayer wasn't a complex thing. You kneel down, you open up your heart and confess your sins to the God of your choice, you beg for forgiveness and/or guidance, then you go about your merry way. If you were insanely lucky, They never ever talked back (most of the world was that lucky, a fact most did not complain about). For a priest, it should be even easier than that. They tend to speak for their Benefactors, so speaking *to* isn't usually difficult.

That wasn't the case for everyone.

There were at least twenty other things that Akaran wanted to do this morning. Most of those options involved being indoors, away from the breeze, away from wet ground, and near something other than a small torch to keep his fingers warm. He wasn't asked if he wanted to do this or not – but he had to.

No, it was the monotony of it. Sit down, clear your mind, focus on Her voice, focus on Her words, let Her speak to you, let Her find a way to guide you. That's how it had been done for centuries. It was a tradition that he didn't feel up to. The sheer boredom of all of it was just...

Let me just find a way to hurry this up, he sighed.

Prayer was for far more than just questions (or idolization or general worship). The entire idea was to make yourself in tune with the Goddess for one reason or another. In the process, it started to help him recharge. The longer he spent with his head bowed, the better he felt – reaching for Her home let priests of any stripe in the Order refill their stores of personal magic. Their power would slowly recover themselves over time *without* praying, but...

Prayer helped speed up the process. True, it was going to take a *lot* of prayer to restore his completely tapped-out reserves. It was still leagues faster than just waiting for his body to do it on his own. How he managed to keep pumping spells out last night was a testament to his devotion/willpower/attitude problem.

After a certain point it quit being a specific prayer and started to drift into uncertain meditation. Meditation helped him steer away from the obvious questions - "What am I facing?" the most popular one, with a few rounds of "Where should I look for them?" and a not-entirely unpopular question of "What will stop them?" That wasn't to say that he didn't ask those questions. He did.

His other questions were slightly more roundabout. "Who hides the worst secret?" "Who is my strongest ally here?" "Who is my weakest?" "What do I need to break this curse?"

When he finally let go enough to feel Her comforting aura in the altar all around him, the meditative prayer did what it was designed to: it started to guide him. His eye closed as his vision started to be obscured by a misty fog. At that moment, you could have fired a cannon at his head and he wouldn't have noticed it.

The Goddess didn't speak to him personally.

At least, not directly.

The moment the world vanished from his eye, he saw a new one. Parts of one. Instances, events that were carved out of the gray fog in his mind. The first scene was so real, he was convinced he was there.

He stood in front of a tower, a massive lumbering behemoth of an edifice that poured snow from the ramparts as it pushed itself up through the ground. *No, not out of the ground. Out of the water. No, ice.* The size of the building would have put the Queen's palace to shame, although it bore no markings and no sign that it belonged to the crown. Then he saw the thing that had claimed it as its own: a familiar mass of tentacles and shadows that started to extrude themselves through varied windows that adorned the stone.

Except this one wasn't a tiny and borderline inconsequential spirit. It was a **huge** one that was able to wrap its limbs completely around the tower – a feat that wouldn't have been possible for even sixty men strung arm to arm. It was still the same mass of shadows and deformed faces; the same conglomeration of arms squirming and grasping in the darkness.

As he watched, a figure emerged from the base of the tower and he recognized her right away – Eos'eno. Her clothes had been ripped apart and her body was covered in blisters and claw marks from head to toe. She looked up at him, dim eyes suddenly flaring to life in shock as she realized he was there, even though he wasn't.

The vision shifted as she started to call out for him. What he saw next was Tornias, hunched over and furiously scribbling runic symbols on the edge of his companion's sickbed. *He does know magic, he does know spellwork. He could have stepped up, but he hid...* That image faded as quickly as it came.

He wished the last one lasted less time than that.

He saw himself scrambling on the ground, unarmed, not even wearing a shirt. There was a fresh gash across his chest and blood covered everything. His vision-self stumbled as he reached for a pickaxe on the ground where someone held it tightly. In the vision, he saw the arm first. The pick came into focus immediately after. *No... that's... not a person... that's...*

Shit, that's just an arm. Who's? What is this? What am I seeing? When?

Then he heard himself shout out a challenge and he knew exactly what he screamed at without hearing a name or seeing a thing. "**COME ON, YOU SON OF A BITCH! COME TO JUDGMENT!**"

It all vanished into a gray mist – nothing left to see, no more messages, no more warnings. It was completely quiet as he opened his eyes and recovered his senses. While his mind reeled and tried to comprehend what had just happened, he heard someone.

A whisper on the wind.

You *always* pay attention to a whisper on the wind.

"{*Ask when you are first lost – not when it is nearly too late to change paths.*}"

The voice came from nowhere but everywhere at once. With the reproachful rebuke rattling around in his addled mind, fate wasn't interested in giving him any time to recover his senses. As the sound in the back of his head faded to nothing, an unpleasant and unwelcome feeling blossomed in the palm on his left hand.

The bandages covered the rune tattooed on his palm – but he didn't have to see it to know that it had just turned a furious shade of crimson. *The wards! They're here!*

"PLEASE! PRIEST EXORCIST COME QUICK PLEASE!"

"What... what's going on...?"

He saw him then – Tornias. The medic was absolutely terrified, blood on his face and down the front of his coat. "AKARAN PLEASE – IT'S HERE, IT'S HERE!"

Shoving himself to his feet, the priest gave one last desperate attempt to recover his senses. He didn't have a sword, didn't have a weapon. He gave a desperate grab for a burning stick out of the brazier (and tried to hope for the best with it). "What is here? TELL ME!"

"GOAT!"

He stopped in his tracks and looked at the coward with his mouth agape. "A... goat? Do I look like a herdsman?"

The answer was apparently a resounding 'yes.'

The town square was a disaster. The villagers were falling suit in short order as the Abyss announced its very existence in front of them. The Gods were about to have a whole bunch of new converts today – people gained 'faith' real fast when evidence of pitborn malevolence was shoved right in their faces.

Right now, it was being shoved in their faces and down their throats.

Ronlin was on his back down the street, almost a third of the way towards the shrine. He had his apron on, slick and covered in congealed blood. He was shouting at the top of his lungs and desperately trying to scramble away from the *thing* that was accosting him.

The exorcist held his burning torch and *really* wished he had his sword. Or anyone's sword. Or an axe. Maybe even a crossbow, if his left arm didn't hurt so damn bad.

"It lives it lives how does it live?!"

Rushing from the shrine, he heard Rmaci call out to them both. "How does *what* live?" she shouted, just a few octaves short of the top of her lungs.

"*BLEET! BLEEEEEET!*"

He stopped, again, just... simply stopped. Not even his hair moved. "Bleet?"

There was lots of bleating. Too much bleating. Every single time it reached their ears it made Akaran's stomach churn as he listened to the elder spit out clods of mud and madness. "The thing, the monster! It's there, in my shop! In there!"

An answer popped in his head well before he wanted to know it. "Oh. Oh, Goddess. They... animals. They *really* like animals."

The innkeeper's wife looked at the one-eyed priest as his face started to darken. This was it. Every inch of his body told him that he was about to experience the last indignity he was going to be able to tolerate. While he stared at it, a deep-seated anger *issue* he had took hold. It wasn't a good look for him and it did little to encourage her to help.

"What are you talking about?" she demanded from the elder, her mood turning just as dark (and just as quickly).

Another pained 'bleet' blasted out between Ronlin's shouts. "Demon! A demon! The only excuse, a demon!"

Without a word of his own, Akaran dropped his torch and scooped a rock up in his right hand as he cleared to within five yards from the door to the shop. A spell wasn't needed this time. The missile crashed through a window overlooking a fenced-off stall, shattering the thin glass with ease. As soon as it did, part of a goat's head and a horn poked through the hole and *bleeted* in an odd mix of fright, pain, and inhuman confusion.

"THAT THING THAT THING! IT MOVES!" Ronlin shouted as he made it to his feet, scrambling backwards until he was almost hiding behind the raven-haired woman. "IT MOVES AND IT SHOULDN'T!"

"Rmaci! Shut him up before he drives me to damned distraction," the exorcist snapped, a cool blue glow enveloping his fist.

She didn't pay attention to him. The rest of the goat's head popped out through the broken window, animal sounds sounding hollow and forced. Its mouth was wide open and didn't move as it made each awful sound; its tongue hung loose and flopped in the air as it struggled. It wasn't doing much more than trying (and failing) to force its way out through the shattered window.

It didn't even seem to care that a jagged piece of the window frame was digging into where its left eye was. It just kept bleating, and scrambling, and pushing against the wood like it thought that it should be able to pass through it.

That thing is... disgusting. Just... disgusting.

That thought came to a quick end when it was able to drive a single hoof through the window-frame and break free just as he could get to it. The exorcist grabbed for a horn to try and hold it still. The dead thing had more strength in it than he expected though, and while the glow on his hand caused its head to sizzle where he touched it, it didn't quite work as planned. Instead of letting him catch the goat, it gave the beast leverage to pull itself through the wall and broke free of his grip.

Akaran muttered a few curses of his own while the sad creature flopped on the ground. It was in much the same shape as it had been when the village elder had insulted him a yesterday, except now, the damned thing was doing everything it could to run away (or hop away, more appropriately). There wasn't anything left to the back half of it aside from a few bits of lung and bowel. Ronlin had skinned it from the neck down, leaving a head covered in bloodstained and matted fur.

Still, it worked on doing the absolute best it could to climb over the stall's fence. "Goddess, blessed be, these things *really* like to lean towards animals, don't they..." he continued to half-growl under his breath.

Rmaci grabbed Ronlin by his smock and shook him, shouting into his face. "You doubted him, you did! You doubted that there really was anything that a priest could deal with. I heard it, your sister heard it, we all heard it and *you* put doubt in the minds of every man woman and child here and now *you* can see that the boy ain't so full of shit and what are *you* doing? Hiding behind me, crying in my coattails?"

"But you said...!"

"Look at him now! Does it matter what I said? Do you see it you old fool?! This is on *you!*" If he wasn't so busy, the exorcist would have appreciated her rant. As it was...

Akaran grabbed at the should-be-dead goat by its horn and managed to reign it in for a moment. A spell started on his lips while he tried to keep his grip. Distressingly, he didn't say it fast enough. With one irritated and painful "**BLEET!**" it jerked its head away hard enough to make the exorcist stumble.

That was when it took the initiative and started to hobble away. It trampled Akaran and sent him sprawling onto the ground. He only had a moment to turn his head before its gaping chest covered his upper torso and smeared gore all over his face. He attempted to get a grip on it but his efforts were failures. The curses he was uttering, however, should have been enough to set the air aflame and turn the village into a barren desert.

It was a small miracle that they weren't actually spells. Everyone should've been thankful for that.

"It can't be real that can't be real those things don't exist they never have they don't they can't..." Ronlin cried, rocking back and forth on his knees behind Rmaci. For what it was worth, she took the situation in stride and shouted at other villagers that were starting to get a little too close to the fight (if you could call it that).

Far more lively than it should have been (given the circumstances), the goat kept bouncing away as quickly as it could. Akaran sprinted right after it, soaked in its juices, cursing every step of the way. As it ran, it drew spectators from everywhere. One poor family stepped outside just in time for the youngest of their two children to nearly get blindsided by the foul creature.

It would have been funny, if the child hadn't nearly died of fright on the spot.

Vile and spraying bloody froth everywhere it went, the goat bore down on the shrine – where an entirely different scene was unfolding. A body spun haphazardly in the air over the fountain. It was (had been) human, but was mutating into something else moment by moment. Long black tendrils whipped out from his mouth and out of his hands while it lashed at the two people in front of it.

Mariah had been knocked onto the ground, with Hirshma over her, hands up in to try to ward off the flying body stalking the pair. Akaran watched as brambles sprouted out of thin air around her head and a wall of vines exploded from the ground. The body lunged into the plantlife and was immediately turned away as a rain of thorns shot out of the wall at it, lacerating frostbitten skin halfway to the bone.

SHE'S A MAGE?! THAT LYING BITCH!

The goat didn't notice, or it didn't care. It rushed headlong at the fountain and then jumped into it as fast as it possibly could go. Whatever its *intentions* were was an utter mystery. What it *succeeded* in doing was to crash into the stone – and then both the sculpture *and* the goat shattered on impact. Its entire body crumbled into a mess of broken bones and shredded muscle. The frozen pool at its feet cracked and a small geyser of water spurted out of the wreckage, showering everything and everyone in a ten-foot radius.

Everything the water touched reacted to it. Immediately, and violently.

The flying body overhead dropped to the ground and affixed Akaran with a hate-filled stare as a small forest of black hands ripped out of the skin on its back. He had enough time to realize that the corpse had once been the stable-master, and that was all the time he had to spare.

More massive tendrils sprayed out of the broken goat as its body sucked up a steady spray of water from the ruined fountain. Bleets were replaced with unholy roars as the beast transformed before his eye.

"DARINGOL SEES ALL SOULS, FEELS ALL SOULS, WILL BE ALL SOULS!"

When the mix of bloody froth and icy water splashed onto the vines, dull brown strands swelled up and turned a vibrant green. Flowers blossomed at the edges, and it was seconds later that the vines completely obscured the alchemist and her apprentice. The goat made an attempt to battered its way into the foliage after Hirshma – but Mowiat turned and saw someone in the crowd. With a twisted echoing cry, the stable-master launched itself after the innkeeper's wife.

It was a horrific mistake on the part of both of the monsters, because everything that the spraying fountain touched ended up supercharged. It made the vines erupt in lush green leaves. It made the wraiths grow into real monsters. It enhanced the magic in *everything* it touched.

Including Akaran.

Nobody else in the Order could use the same spell he did. Well, that's not entirely true – they could, just not the *way* he could. For most, it was just a pale tendril of light that could serve to briefly entrap a demon at a distance. Its range was short and its ability was limited.

That is, for everyone else but him.

His instructors couldn't figure it out, so it was written off as one of those things that the Goddess had planned for him. He was *gently discouraged* from using it (although that wouldn't ever stop him). It sure as all was not what the wretched zombie expected to happen (if it had any idea that anything could happen to it).

"*BONDS!*"

While it was true that light did a wonderful job of chasing off the dark and the damned, sometimes you didn't really want them to run away. Ethereal silver chains spun into existence from his left elbow and to his palm, and he lashed them out at the damned soul. The chains snapped around its midsection as Rmaci produced a blade hidden in her dress. Screaming in rage, the dead man clawed at the air in a desperate attempt to reach her that came up just a hair too short.

"*LUMINOSO – EXPULSE!*"

His spellwork made Mowiat's upper body explode in a single flash of light. His legs continued moving for a few staggering kicks before they burned away in a cloud of black ash with the rest of him. The ruined goat turned away from Hirshma and attempted to rush the exorcist, which didn't do much good either.

It twisted and lunged; Akaran grabbed it by its throat and screamed a Word at it. "**EXPEL!**" For the most part, it had the desired effect. Most of the ruined body caught fire and the wraith started to rip itself free of the disintegrating shell. That wasn't enough of a punishment.

Not even remotely enough of one.

He shoved his battered arm (bandages and all) into the center of the mass of tentacles and limbs that twisted inches from his face. Divine light poured through every crack and hole, banishing shadows and smoke with its very touch. Try as it might, the wraith couldn't pull itself away from the grip he had on its former host or from the grip it had in its core.

He bent down and placed his lips just next to the goat's ear as the struggling slowed down and more arms appeared from inside of its midsection. "I am *done* playing with you little *shits*. If you do not give up your true name to me before the full might of my Goddess *right now* I will *burn* you with flames so hot that will make you long for all the wonderful *comforts* of the Abyss!"

"*Daringol seeks warmth that is all Daringol seeks just warmth just warmth!*"

"I said *your* true name. *Yours*. I want *your* name and my patience **isn't** limitless!" he continued to whisper, quiet enough that nobody else could have heard him. "That name belonged to the one in the cave."

A face appeared, and it looked like an almost perfect match to the wraith in the mine. *"Daringol is one of many and many of one I am Daringol we are Daringol, Daringol needs warm, Daringol needs safe..."*

"So I've heard," came the muttered reply. "Let me help with that." The eyes of the wraith shot open as the exorcist thrust his hands deeper into the goat, just below its neck. *"**PURGE!**"*

There wasn't any time for the wraith to spirit itself away. The soft glow that had been pouring into the goat turned into a nearly-blinding flash of light that poured out of every cut and tear the corpse had. In front of half of the village, even the horns dissolved into nothingness as the purifying magic ripped the creature asunder.

Bloodied, hurting, and thoroughly repulsed, Akaran stood there as oily smoke rolled over his feet. Nonchalantly, he reached into the vines and wrapped his hand around one of the brambles – not even wincing at the barbs digging into his skin – and whispered a Word. The glow returned to his fingers but the vines didn't register anything at first. When *"Expulse,"* didn't work, the second Word did.

"Disenchant."

The vines quickly started to wither away and fell apart while more and more people started to congregate around the edge of the temple path and small courtyard. The look on Hirshma's face was one of dismayed surprise and guilt as she took the brunt of the cold fury burning in Akaran's eye. Under his glare, she slowly knelt down and cradled Mariah's head in her hands. "Exorcist... please, she's hurt..."

He joined her on the ground, and carefully cupped Mariah's cheek in his hand. She was out cold, with a trickling gash dripping off of her temple. His fingers danced across the wound, and he gave a relieved sigh when he realized there wasn't a sign of any of the wraith's corruption in her aura. "You're lucky she isn't dead."

"I... I know. I'm sorry. I'm so so sorry."

The apology fell on deaf ears. "You'll be caring for her."

Nodding slowly, she continued to hug the girl against her lap. "I will, you don't need to ask..."

Cutting her off, he snapped his glare right back to her eyes. "I wasn't asking." She started to respond, but Akaran just didn't care anymore. As he stood up, he looked around the throng of terrified and horrified villagers. "Is anyone else hurt? Did those things touch anyone at all?"

Nobody was and nobody had been. And absolutely nobody took their eyes off of him as he stepped into the bubbling trickle of water that gurgled out of the ground around the shattered fountain. A small rush of energy drifted through his boot and up his leg with a strangely pleasant chill that banished the frigid ache in his bones. As he enjoyed the sensation, he covered his broken wrist with his right hand and encouraged a small spell into the bones.

His fingers twitched involuntarily and the pain in it died off after a few moments of concentration. *This is some kind of wellspring... a magical fount. Same water as at the lake. This isn't... abyssian. Sure as all it isn't a natural phenomenon. It's... from somewhere aligned with the Mount of Heaven. I think I just discovered why so many things are playing here. It's from Tundrala. Has to be.*

Oh. Goddess.

*Someone tapped into the Upper Elemental Plane of Ice and **left the damn door open**?! How fisking... **stupid**?! No wonder this area is steeped in wild magic! **It's literally being steeped in wild magic like the whole damn mountain is a giant teabag dropped into a lake!***

He came to a hard internal pause and blinked. *The lake. It's diluted. But it's in the lake. This isn't diluted, so it's got a direct line, or... the concentration is different because it's... smaller stream, something.*

*Well. That explains **that** part of the vision. I don't think I like where the rest of this is going. Usaic's magic is in that tower, under that lake, and... that's where I'm going to find the source of all of this. Damn him, and damn these idiots. SOMEBODY had to know!*

When someone had the courage to speak up, it snapped his attention back to the immediate problem at hand. "Exorcist... what... what were those things? Are they gone for good? Is that the last of them?"

"Ronlin. Don't talk right now. You're last on my list."

The elder choked back a nervous lump in his throat and backed up into the throng of villagers behind him. They always seemed to come crawling out of the woodwork at the worst times instead of running away like anyone sane should.

Then Hirshma found her spine again, spoke up, and *immediately* wished she hadn't. "Well. If you're done standing around there and looking the fool, give me a hand carrying this poor girl back to my hut and -"

And then he did what Mariah-Anne said she was afraid he'd do.

He cut her off before she could get anything else out. "**Hirshma**. By order of an agent of the Temple of Love and under the dully granted authority of the Queen of Dawnfire, you are remanded into custody to be bound to the nearest Provincial Justiciar under accusation of obstruction of an inquisition *and* intentionally refusing to disclose your ability to use, *and* active use of magica."

"WHAT?!"

"Your disregard of the Queen's law in that regard has resulted in the death of *at least* one innocent child *and* it served to cover the nature of the deaths of at least six soldiers attached to the local garrison and *Goddess* only knows how many other dead or wounded your *bullshit* has been responsible for!"

"Remanded unto...?! You're *arresting* me?! Who do you think is going to stand around and let you lock me up?"

"Anyone that doesn't wish to answer to the Justiciar with you. If any of these *wonderful* people wants to see if they can stop me from handing you over, they are welcome to try. *One* try is all they're going to get, but they are welcome to try."

It was bravado that *nobody* thought was false. Nobody stepped forward. Nobody wanted to risk it. Hirshma's face turned crestfallen as they abandoned her, one by one, to her fate. "After all of the things I've done, sacrificed..."

"The *only* reason I'm not taking your head from your neck right now is that there's not a single hint of darkness in your spellwork. Do not take that as an argument for your innocence. You're as guilty as these damn wraiths – and *they* are at least honest about what it is that they want. I need you alive to treat the injured. You and I are having a *talk* tonight and so help me, DO NOT test me any further! *Do you understand me* or do I need to try you here and now on the spot because *I'm* allowed to do that too!"

"All I did was -"

"Lie. You have lied with every single breath you've taken and I am *done* putting up with it," he seethed, every word slipping out of his lips with a hiss that would have done a cobra proud. "I don't have anyone that I can spare to put a guard on you but I promise you that if you try to run the beasts in the woods will be the very least of the things you have to worry about – *am I understood*?"

Defeated (and forced to admit it), all she could do was just give a single meek nod.

More than one person behind him grumbled at his edict – but most just stood there in stunned silence. Against any and all *possible* rationality, it was Tornias that objected the loudest. "How dare you! She was here, she protected these people!"

You could almost feel the world groan as Akaran slowly turned from the alchemist-come-druid and looked at the medic. "And **you**. Oh, **you**."

Everyone that stood near the soldier moved away from him like he had just been outed as having the plague. In that moment, in that instant, there wasn't a single person there that was anything other than utterly terrified of the priest and everything he embodied within the kingdom. "Nobody has had any reason to trust you! You come here you swing your sigil you act like you know everything and you think there isn't a single soul here that would... not think that... you should be told... anything?"

His voice cracked as Akaran just stood there and smiled. "You don't understand how big of a shit-mess you are in, do you."

It was another non-question.

That didn't stop Tornias from answering. "I am a Lieutenant in the Queen's Army. My word carries much more weight than yours ever will!"

"I am an Exorcist under the direct command of the *Holy General*, you fisking **moron!**" he roared at the absolute top of his lungs as he stormed over to him and *punched* the medic in the jaw. The blow knocked Tornias to the ground and flat on his ass while everyone just watched.

Somewhere to the side, Yothargi started to complain about the rough treatment. "You can't -!" he shouted, just before Romazalin grabbed him by his arm and shut him up before his mouth made the situation even worse.

"By order of the Temple of Love and under the granted authority of the Queen of Dawnfire and under the *express permission* of the bloody Holy General *herself*, you are remanded into custody to be bound to a *tribunal* under the hand of the Provincial Maiden for insubordination, dereliction of duty, wanton disregard of the safety of your countrymen, actions resulting in the death of a child, actions resulting in a rising threat of an enemy of the state *and* an enemy of the Divine and *Goddess* help me if I can talk them into it I will find a way to have you tried for sedition, aiding a demonic influence and outright **stupidity** unbefitting an Officer of the Crown!"

The fact that he got all of it out in a single breath was worth admiration, if nothing else. He wasn't even done. "**NOT** to mention failing to inform **me**, and by extension, the *damn army itself* of your **own** magical affinity!"

Mouth agape and eyes wide in shock, Tornias tried (tried) to object and beg off Akaran's fury.

It did *not* work.

"Unlike why I am keeping *her* around, the **only** reason I am not having you hung from the rafters right now is because I have heard horror stories about Maiden Piata that would make the Prince of Fear shit His bed and piss His boots. I cannot think of anyone in this entire Kingdom, no, on this *planet*, that I would not want to cross more than her and the very *idea* of putting your cowardly ass in her hands absolutely fills me with so much *delight* that I could just about keep myself warm and happy in bed just *thinking* about it for the next year even here in this frozen mudbog!"

"Piata?! The Madwoman? You can't possibly be -!"

Seething, absolutely seething and covered in gore, Akaran raked his glare over the assembled throng of the people under the Queen's protection before Romazalin squeaked a question from the back of the mob. "What... what were those things? That... that was my Mowiat..."

Glancing at her and trying to temper his voice, he gave her the only answer he could. "That was something that took over his corpse. It calls itself Daringol. Does that mean anything to anyone?"

Unsurprisingly, nobody was able to connect the name to anyone that they knew, or anything they had ever heard of. Vestranis said as much and Hirshma agreed while Yothargi walked forward and helped her pick Mariah-Anne off of the ground. "Never heard that name. Never seen that thing."

"That's the... sixth? seventh? ...that I've condemned since I got here. *Someone* has to know what they are. Where they're from. Why they're here. Does *anyone* know *anything* at all? I will spare you from a trial, I will spare you from a lecture, I'll even have you paid – but *please, please tell me* what they are."

Akaran was right – somebody knew.

But the brown-haired woman with the crystal-blue eyes hiding off behind the shrine didn't exactly feel comfortable speaking up right just then. So she did the next best thing, and channeled just enough energy that he felt it at the side of his neck. The little mark she had placed right under his hairline pulsed on his skin, a cool and comforting touch that made his eye twitch.

So. She does, and she's here. And she didn't want to interfere. Fine. Now what? Do I have to drop dead before I can get her to sit down and talk to me? He sighed in frustration and kept looking around the crowd. Tornias hadn't tried to get up yet for fear of immediate reprisal, but the village elder was nice enough to pull his head out of his ass and make himself the next target of the exorcist's ire.

"Don't do this to Hirshma, please. I know I cannot speak for my sister. I can only say that I know she never had any ill-will towards any of us. She's always been here, always been willing to help, and our family has paid a great cost, greater than you would know, to protect the people that live within our walls."

"Live in them, die outside of them. Yeah. I got the picture. *You* aren't immune to my *irritation* either." Going a shade or two pale, the elder nervous swallowed and took a couple of steps back. "Vestranis!"

The blacksmith stepped forward and crossed his arms. If he was unhappy with the proceedings, he didn't show it – if anything, he looked grimly pleased. "Exorcist?"

Akaran pointed his finger at him but didn't let his eyes off of Ronlin. "You said if I killed the things that killed your friends, you'd help me here, didn't you?"

"More or less."

"I've been killing them."

"I saw. You gonna kill more of them?"

"I'm gonna kill all of them."

Vestranis gave him a pencil-thin smile. "Then what do you need?"

"Effective immediately you are to take charge of this damn village. No. It's not a village anymore. As far as I'm concerned, it's an outpost. Effective right this moment, marshal law is in effect and you should consider yourself drafted to the Grand Army of the Dawn."

That was an unexpected edict but to his credit, he took it in stride. "I am?"

"You are. I want to know how much longer Toniki can sustain itself with the food reserves you have left and if there are any beasts of burden that could handle an evacuation. I want... I don't know. I need a wall, I need a guard, I need something or someone to watch over this fountain and this shrine. Nobody's to touch the water nobody's to enter the shrine and nobody's to get near any of it."

Hirshma paused as she and Yothargi made their way through the throng and looked back at him. "The... fountain? Whatever for...?"

Looking down at the spreading pool behind him, the exorcist just barely hid his own trepidation over it. "Because that 'elementalist of great power' didn't just tap into something extra-planar, he installed a gateway to the here-after right in the middle of your town. Do you have any idea what that means?"

Hirshma did. "Oh... no. Oh *no*." Nobody else had a clue, but she surely did. All she could get out was a strangled whisper. "Usaic... Usaic you bastard... you..."

"Ronlin. I'm still not done with you."

Much like they had done with Tornias, the people of the tired village took a few steps away from their former leader and let him take the bulk of what wrath Akaran had left in him. "Your butchery – burn it. Burn it down, burn everything in it."

"WHAT? That's... that's my home, my trade, my -!"

"That *was* your home. You're evicted. Set it aflame, burn it down, leave nothing but ash. If you don't I will and I might well make you stand in it while I do."

Mouth agape and eyes wide, he couldn't grasp the reasoning behind it. Any of it. "WHY? Do you hate me so? Hate my family?"

"Yes. I do. But that's not why. These things. They like dead bodies. They like animals. Do I need to spell it out further? Do you get my point yet? That slaughterhouse is one of the best things they're gonna see. I can *only* pray you've been burning the remnants of your work and not just dumping it into a ditch somewhere."

He didn't follow the logic. Moulborke did. "Elder... if more of those things come, they'll go to you first. We just saw them, all of them. You have to do what he says. You have to. That boy just made a believer out of me and if he says it has to go, it has to go."

"Finally. Someone else that's going to be helpful. Now I need to know one more thing."

Vestranis walked over and grabbed Tornias by his shoulder and pulled him up to his feet. "I never liked this idiot. If he knows something, I'll help you find out what."

That made him smile. A lot. Ear to ear. "I've got questions for him later. Right now – where is Rmaci?"

Almost out of earshot, Yothargi stopped in his tracks. "You. Keep. Your. Hands. Off. Of. My. Wife."

"She said Mowiat had been mauled to death by the dogs. Did his body look mauled to you?"

Hirshma had stopped with the innkeeper and slowly shook her head. "No... no he didn't. He looked..."

"He looked like someone had slit his throat and put a knife in his chest. Now, *where is she?*"

That was another question that nobody had an answer to.

Dammit.

XII. BLIZZARD OF TRUTHS

Everything was a mess. Policing the bodies took more time than he wanted to invest, but making sure the remnants of the two corpses were dumped as far away from the fountain as they quickly could be felt like an immediate necessity. Dealing with the fountain itself was another story entirely – while there were some methods to deal with wild magic, a discovery like *this* simply wasn't covered in the rule-book.

It wasn't helping that there was a thick cloud of black smoke and the stench of smoldering charnel throughout the village. Ronlin did set his shop aflame (with Vestranis right behind him, enforcing Akaran's edict), but now, well. Now there was just a particular smell that was filling the village, much to the chagrin of literally everyone left in Toniki. It only added to the misery the poor folk were suffering through and he just *knew* he'd never hear the end of it.

Nor would he for what he was about to do next. Rule-book *be damned. Rules are made to be broken anyways, aren't they?* he sighed to himself, right before he broke a big one.

*"Never tap into magic you do not know; never play with that which you do not understand. We – exorcists, priests, paladins, and templars – we **exist** because of the folly of men and their drive to experiment with the dangerous and the unknown. If it were not for man, demons would hold far less sway in this world."*

There weren't many people left around to watch, but a couple of well-meaning children (and Romazalin) had stuck around to see if they could help. "Well. If it keeps us in business, who am I to bloody well argue?"

Thankfully, the ground was soaking up most of the water, keeping it from flooding everywhere. It was turning the path to the shrine into a muddy bog – but one problem at a time. *At least I won't have to clean it up. The Sisters won't be that mad when they find out what I've been up to, will they?*

The farmer started to ask what he meant, but opted to keep her council to herself. It wouldn't have done much even if she hadn't. Akaran quietly shooed everyone away from the slowly-growing puddle and pulled a small idol of Niasmis from one of the bags he had brought with him to this loathsome town.

She – and her kids – scooted even further away when they heard the short muttered prayer that followed. "Goddess above, if this does damage to Your image, please forgive me. If it doesn't, please let this stupid idea work. Your servant is tired of getting his ass kicked."

Stepping into the middle of the ruined fountain, he felt that surge of magic start to flow up into his bones through the soles of his feet all over again. His body started to pleasantly tingle and his breath turned to steam. Gently (oh so very gently) he set Her bust down into the center of the ruins and made sure Her beautiful form was in direct contact with the water. Akaran closed his eye and carefully willed the magic that was infusing his essence to focus into his palms.

Saying *"Purify,"* was all it took.

It did. She did. She didn't even make him wait.

A ripple of pure lavender spread through over the stone and coursed over the water like a flame across oil. Everything it touched was awash in the glow, even as it poured up and over his skin. He gave a short cry as Her aura filled him and met his broken arm – and promptly fixed it.

Painfully. He hadn't been the most respectful to Her since he got here... and Love *is* a bitch.

Then She fixed a problem he didn't know he had.

The bones knit themselves together at once and *pushed* a black mass out of his arm and into the air. His shout was joined by a screech of pain from the toxic fog just before it withered away to nothing. As he fell backwards, more of the light coursed over him and sent his head reeling from the violent reaction to the spell.

When his vision cleared up, he felt hands on his shoulders dragging him out of the midst of his poorly-thought-out decision. The pain in his head was gone and his arm felt better, though the rest of it left him feeling like someone had punched him in the crotch. "What was all that? What did you *do?*" Romazalin cried, all but shouting in his ear.

Pulling himself up to his knees, he looked at the glowing remnants of the fountain. The wreckage was still there, and the water was still quietly bubbling out of it. The idol was still there too, though it wasn't just the crafted piece of bronze it had started out as. The metal had taken on a silver and blue sheen that was matched by a glowing fog that rolled out around it.

"Fixed my arm," he muttered, then smiled as he felt the charge in the air around them. "And... don't let those wraiths touch you. Ever. Ow. Just... ow. How in the world did it survive in me? Insidious, siphoning, magic-hungry little shits..."

Someone out there was surely going to be furiously pissed at him for breaking the rule (and *oh* was he going to make them even angrier soon) for it – but in the short term? "Nothing Abyssian is going to be able to come near that. The idol and the magic are going to keep purifying it until someone shuts off the flow, breaks the idol, or breaks the spell."

"That... that sounds... dangerous?"

Shaking his head he managed to get himself back to his feet with a very smug feeling overtaking him. "Can't believe I did it, actually. Not dangerous for you and me, but *damn* is that going to burn anything pit-born. Bet it'll feel like shoving your hand into a vat of molten steel." *Wonder if I can give Makolichi a bath in it.*

Nervously trying to show that she understood what he was saying (she didn't), the farmer huddled her kids up to her coat. "Now... now what do you do? I'm not so stupid that to think that the threat is abated? If that water healed you, will it help the other injured? Mariah and the soldier? Lativus?"

The thought hadn't hit him yet, so he had to give her a little more credit than he thought she might be due. "That's a bad idea but... it's the best one I've heard yet. We're not going to be able to get everyone out of here if that soldier is unconscious, or if Hirshma can't rouse Mariah..."

"But... but would it help? You need all the help you can get, don't you?"

"You're not wrong," he agreed. A slowly-forming sick feeling took hold in his gut as he looked at the idol and shrugged. *Forget hanging Tornias. They're gonna hang **me** if I let her do this.* "Alright. Go fill a few bottles of it and... who was taking care of Lativus, anyways? That fisking medic or the alchemist?"

Romazalin shook her head. "Neither. Mariah had been tending to him. Hirshma tossed Tornias out of the barn after she heard him praying a little too loudly. Said he was inviting trouble. Mowiat had been, but... guess it's just... me now."

"Probably was. Fine. Take it to him, give it to him yourself. Pour it on his wounds directly. If something unpleasant arises, scream."

"Scream? That's your best advice, scream? Is it safe or is it not?"

"It's not. I'd really appreciate it if you did it anyways. Might make a difference."

"Why can't you? What are you going to do that's so important?"

Stretching and working the stiffness out of his arm, he looked around for a minute as he wondered that same exact thing. "Need to speak with those two idiots."

"Hirshma and Tornias?"

"Those would be the two. Ronlin, as well. I'm done being lied to."

Nodding slowly, the farmer decided to offer up a few truths of her own – though she kept her worried eyes locked on his. "You won't get much from Ronlin. He styles himself a font of wisdom for all of us and some great leader but the honest truth is that he only has the title because he was born into it. Not much different than the nobility in the Capitol he despises."

"I gathered that. I've met his type," Akaran remarked with a grunt. "You'd think that people would be more willing to talk when their lives were being threatened."

"You would, but that means they either have a great deal of faith in you -"

"I doubt it."

"- or they don't think their issues matter to the problem at hand."

"That's more like it."

Romazalin grabbed his hand again and held on tight. "Exorcist... Akaran? If you find Rmaci? Steer clear of her. Kill her, if she did as you think she did – avenge Mowiat's death, punish her for what she's done to my heart – but do not believe a word she utters."

"So far she's been about the only person that hasn't wanted to stab me in the throat. Though... guess that doesn't matter much now, does it? She's more the stab you in the chest/silt the throat type, it looks. Mariah said the same, so... go on."

Her voice had a grim growl to it that made him ignore her soiled grip.

"I don't know what her game is. She isn't well-liked around here, and if she's made you her next pet project? I can promise that you won't like the outcome. She was the most vocal of anyone here to *not* call for a priest – *any* priest – and now suddenly she's got her mouth on your ear? Can't imagine the sweet nothings she's been filling your head with."

Confused by the accusation, he chewed on her words for a minute before answering. "That's... more or less the exact opposite of what she's been telling me. She said Ronlin was opposed, most of the rest of you people were too, and she was only one of a couple of people that tried to make a case for me."

"Oh, she tried to make a case alright. Mainly, to have an arrow put in the face of any 'outsider' that would try to 'convert us all by a blade or by a lie.' She has been *lying* to you and us all. Ronlin only had minor concerns. Hirshma and Rmaci? Nearly had fits."

"She's been lying? Who hasn't? Why should I believe you? Why should I think you're not lying to me too?"

Bereft of any proof, all that the farmer could do was beg him to listen. "You don't know me, you don't have any reason to trust me. I understand. Ask Vestranis. Ask Peoran. Ask Hirshma. Ask *anyone*."

"The smith doesn't really like me, does he? Peoran all but called for my head. Hirshma has hated me since I stepped foot in here. Strange you'd mention her, *she's* the one that Rmaci said I shouldn't listen to."

"Of *course* she did," the farmer growled. "Though, really... guess she's not wrong. That woman *does* have more skeletons buried in her closet than we've got in the graveyard."

Akaran took that with a grunt. "The best lies always have a glimmer of truth with them."

"Oh you poor boy, there's more than a glimmer. Follow your heart though, please, not your cock. *Listen to it.* Remember what you were taught: *Love* always finds a way. *Don't trust her*, whatever else you do, *don't trust her*. Please."

"Why are you so opposed to her? And why the sudden interest in who or what I talk to around here?" Then, blinking, he sized her up anew. "And how does a farmer out in the middle of the mountains in a village that is full of people that say they all despise the Gods know what I was taught?"

"Because Ronlin is lying to you too. He said he's no holy man, said he follows no God. He's lying to your face, and you deserve to know the truth. *All* of it. You are so right that you can't do your job if everyone around here is filling your head with bullshit."

While he tried to hide the anger in his heart, his mind unleashed a torrent into the back of his head. *Yay! More riddles! Do the people in this fisking village not know how to get to a bloody point?! Oh he's lying, oh she's lying! Oh for fisking sake all if I don't get this shit done with SOON I'm going to lose my damn mind!*

"Fine. He's lying too. What? He some closet follower of Illiya? Afraid that I'm going to turn him in to what's left of the local garrison?"

Nonplussed, Romazalin shook her head. "Kora'thi. Him, his sister, their father. Every. Single. One. Of. Them. *Wardens of Kora'thi.*"

He couldn't have felt like he'd been slapped any harder if he had tried. "Druids. The vines... explains them but... *druids?*"

"Druids!"

"Those two *hate* the Gods... did you not notice that?" *Well. Now I have a crazy person trying to woo me over. Wonderful. What next? Someone going to tell me that the animals are all filled with angst because these people really are the mule-fisking idiots I think they are?*

Oh. Wait. Animals.

*The wraiths **really** like animals. Hirshma is a closeted nature-worshiper, this woman says that Ronlin used to be, and their father was as well. What are the odds that this Daringol creature is here because of something that their family did? Wraiths that dive into animal husks at every opportunity? Oh that **can't** be a coincidence!*

***FISK** these idiots!*

Frustrated at his unwillingness to believe her, an edge started to creep into her voice. "They've got their reasons. Her daughter got killed by a wolf. Their father got blown off of a bridge by a freak storm. Their mother... don't even ask. Blight and rot took her and it did not take her peacefully. You'd be pissed at the Gods too if the one you worshiped suddenly decided to turn Her very nature against everyone in your family."

That wasn't unreasonable, he had to admit. "If they had come clean at the start... if they had..."

"I blame them, I blame them all now. If anyone ever says you shouldn't send them to the gallows, they're the ones wrong, and you should have them all hung. I am so so sorry that I did not trust you myself, we are all fools, and we cannot ever make this up to you. Please... please avenge my Mowiat. Please bring them all to judgment."

"'Bring them to judgment?' That's twice you've said something that makes me think of home. I don't think it's an accident."

She hung her head and teared up, grief and guilt overcoming her. "My grandmother. She followed your Lady. She suffered during the

Hardening. She spoke of the Temple. My father hated your Goddess for what she went through. I... hated Her too. And... you with Her."

"And now?"

"...and now I just want you to kill them all."

Her honesty was refreshing. "I... That's a tempting thought, really. Go on. Take care of Lativus. Don't let anyone else drink that water unless you hear it from me first. Have one of your sons make another bottle ready when I make it to Hirshma's hut. Tornias and I need to have a talk first."

"Talk with your fist again. He deserves it."

"Gladly."

Years down the line there would be one nagging problem that stuck with Akaran that he never quite outgrew. He grew smarter (somewhat), and he grew stronger (a lot stronger). He would rise in rank (eventually), and he would be admired by a close few (even if he was detested by a score many more than that). He'd be broken (badly broken in the far future; moderately maimed in the near) and he'd be rebuilt as a better man (debatable).

Some people would come to him for advice and training (and they'd ignore half of it). Others would come to him because they knew that he would do everything in his ability to defend what he felt was right (even if he was wrong). Others because someone needed something to die (horribly). Quite a few would want him dead (no shortage of people there), though in his line of work, that was to be expected (even if he had *far* more ill-wishers than ever previously thought possible).

Yet, all of that being true, one thing nobody would *ever* accuse him of was having *tact*.

They had detained the medic in the basement of the inn. It was relatively safe, and kept him from meddling in anything else. Some random local with a name he hadn't bothered to learn stood by the door and was only all too happy to go away when the exorcist shooed him off (but he came back with others a few minutes later, because misery loves company and anger loves an audience). Yothargi joined him, though as troubled as he was about the accusations leveled against his wife, he kept silent through the bulk of the interrogation.

The innkeeper was nice enough to make sure that the medic had been securely tied to a chair, though. It was a nice touch. It made this easier. Plus, it gave him a little bit of satisfaction to see the cowardly little bastard humbled.

The conversation started off gently enough. Yes, Tornias admitted that he had gone to the battlefield, "To see if he could determine what had caused so many to lose their lives so grotesquely," he claimed. He also admitted that he had spoken to the boy the night he died. "The child had wanted to know more about the army," he lied.

He denied (lied) that he was the person to even have tried to call for Pristi's favor at the Folly. He also denied (lied some more) about having anything to do with Julianos going to the graveyard. He adamantly refused to allow Akaran to touch him to feel his aura. It was an attempt to gauge if he had enough of an affinity to cause such an enchantment take hold even accidentally.

Tornias also reacted *exceedingly* poorly when the exorcist had put his hand on his shoulder anyways. Words were said (although not the more forceful *Words* the priest was fond of using... there was a difference between a lack of tact and a lack of all decorum). Those words earned the soldier another slap across the face – then when he looked like he was happy to try and force his way out of his ropes, the innkeeper picked up a leg of a broken barstool and made it silently clear who he had cast his allegiance to.

Before the shouting match degenerated further, Akaran pulled out the remnants the shattered crest. "Do you know what this is?"

Even though he blanched at the sight of it, the medic continued to lie through his teeth. "I have no idea, you buffoon."

That caused a look of pure disgust to pop up while he cracked his knuckles and rubbed his hands together. "Alright Tornias, then it's time for us to have a bit of a discussion on the types of magic." Akaran glanced at Yothargi and shrugged. "If you want to call anyone else to come listen, go ahead. You might learn something." *You twits might even realize that I honestly know what I'm doing.*

Mostly.

"Magic? The only one slinging spells about is *you* and that reckless alchemist. What makes you think I give a damn about any of it? I'm no mage."

When the exorcist touched Destin's broken amulet and made the aura around it glow with a whisper, the medic closed his mouth and looked like he had just swallowed a rat. "This does."

"What's that?" the bartender asked.

"This is why we're going to have a lesson. I'll keep this simple so you can understand. There are four basic kinds of magic: Divine, Abyssian, Elemental, and Preternatural. Note that I said *basic*. Each type has a few different branches, and a few even merge together.

"Elemental magic is what's causing the bulk of the chaos around here. You can break it down any way you want but it adheres to the four base elements – and it can align itself with the light, the dark, or it can just simply *be* with no care to which world it exists in. If that sounds complicated, it really isn't. Just can be difficult to control.

"Those pompous know-it-alls at the Granalchi Academy focus on that type of spellwork. Fire, Water, Air, and World make up their skill-sets. Right now, we're dealing with something that's focused on ice. You probably figured that out. I just haven't figured out *what* yet. I'll admit that much. I've got a lot of good ideas now and when I get done *you're* going to help me narrow it down if you want to live to see your next birthday with all of your fingers and toes still attached - to the right spots, at that.

"Some elementalists draw not just on the base power of the element, but also on the specific planar region. Those are the really powerful mages. It's like drinking a jug of mead – sure, you can get drunk, eventually, but the really good stuff has to be sipped out from under the froth on top and the really bad has to come straight from the gunk left in the cask.

"Each element is represented by a Divine or a Fallen deity. An elementalist that draws power from Tundrala siphons their freezing power under the blessing of Istalla. Usually, it's beneficial. So they say. Damned if I know how ice can be beneficial. Apparently some people think it can be. Me? Be happy if I never saw another icicle in what's left of what feels like the very short life I have left.

"Or, if anyone that draws from Frosel, they do so with the permission of Her Fallen counterpart, Zell, the Brineblood. Anyone that can do that generally isn't what most people would consider a 'nice person.' Granted, most mage-types aren't. So, that is what it is."

He stopped a minute and looked down at his still slightly-sore wrist and remembered the smell that Makolichi had given off. *The Brineblood. That was looking at me this whole time, wasn't it? I like you less by the moment.*

When Yothargi noticed the distant look in his eye and tried to get his attention, Akaran shook off his quasi-revelation and continued on. "Of course, because different schools of elemental magic can call upon competing Gods or just use the element as they find it in the mortal world, well... it can result in a schism between mages that use one or another, of course, and it confuses many people as to if they are truly using elemental magic or that of the divine.

"For all I know, there's a second mage out there somewhere that's in the middle of a fight with that Usaic bastard. Nothing else makes much sense, so why not? Anyways.

"I really hope you're not confused yet – the rest of this is pretty easy. I just want to be sure that you understand why dealing with all of this has been such a pain in my damn ass to figure out. Every time I've stepped outside of the village walls, I've regretted it. Part of that regret has been having to come back to deal with people like you."

Tornias answered with a snarl. "Then leave. The rest of the garrison will be here in two days. Maybe less."

"Good. Then I'll leave now and come back in three days to help them bury everyone. Never liked to dig graves but you know, if everyone else listens to me I *could* just leave you nailed down in the town square for the wraiths and the hounds to chew on. Does that work for you or would you like me to stick around instead?"

The medic answered with a glare. Yothargi and his barmaid voiced their approval for the idea. Giving credit where credit is due, they kept their remarks to a low murmur. *Good, they're listening. Would hate to think I'm wasting my time on just this twit.*

"Holy magic comes fully from one of the Divine. There's no question as to the power of it and how it interacts with the other types. The various Gods and Goddesses of the Pantheon each have Their own rites and abilities and Their own requirements that They expect from Their followers before They grant it. The Granalchi bend magic by force of will; the devout channel magic by the blessing of Divinity.

"Abyssian magic is a little more complicated. You see, not only are the Fallen able to grant Their followers vast power – and They have Their own demands that They extract from a supplicant – the Abyss itself is a source of limitless energy. Provided, of course, you're willing to pay the price."

Akaran's focused his smirk right on Tornias bewildered face. "Believe me, there's a very *big* price to pay for asking for aid from the very pit itself. I don't think I need to tell you that Abyssian magic and Holy magic don't get along. That's what makes elemental magic such a pain in the ass... you can't always tell where the lines begin and end.

"Oh, and if you *didn't* notice, something from the Abyss has a very large hand in this mess, too. Where do you think those hounds came from? Or that *thing* that killed the boy? Or those wraiths that are dogging my every step? They weren't just pissed out of the clouds right beside this accursed snowfall."

Off to the side, the bar-waif cleared her throat. "You said there was a fourth kind? I never figured there'd be more to magic than light and dark and just... magic?"

"There are some creatures that defy the Laws of Normality. For whatever reason the Gods saw fit to give them abilities unlike other creatures. G'odorn sharks dissolve wood by touching it, you can't set goblins on fire no matter what you do to them, and zolibi can turn themselves invisible."

Frowning, the waif questioned him a little more. "Doesn't that just... make them demonic?"

"No, some things are close to it though, like... charf rats."

"A charf rat? What's that?"

A look of raw revulsion washed over his face. "Don't ever ask. *Ever.*"

The medic finally stood up and gave him a foul look. "What does any of that have to do with *me?*"

"Oh, I'm getting to you, asshole." Akaran put his hand back on the amulet. "Magic manifests in different ways. Most of it simply just can't last forever. Whatever elementalists do is... fisk me if I know. They make their chosen elements... do stuff. I just know that sometimes we're lucky if everything around them doesn't get destroyed when they do it. I'm not a fan, if you can't tell.

"As for Divine or Fallen magic? You have to continually ask permission from the deity of your choice time and time again to use their spells; permission they don't always grant. Or you might be able to power a ward or a blessing for a few weeks or months. Maybe even years, if you know just the right way to do it. Then there's the joy of dedicating a temple to them, or sanctifying a grave. Or paying a cost – a sacrifice or a labor, or a favor or whatever.

"They give those temples or shrines or works *special* interest and tend to *appreciate* the effort it takes to do it. Makes the area a safe haven, of a sort, and other than giving people like you and me a place to sleep, the innate power they generate can be put to use.

"That amulet is special - and I think you know it. Sometimes, people are able to imbue an item with special properties. Sometimes, those properties last for a very long time. Or, sometimes those properties are enhanced by the magical strength of the person holding it. Or, they can be put to use only by followers of a specific Godling."

Tornias was barely able to keep his own anger in check. "So what of it? You still haven't gotten to your damn *point!*"

He rubbed his temple and sighed. "I'm about to, now shut up and listen. *That* is an Amulet of Cleansing. It had to have been hand-crafted by an Arch-Priestess of Purity, then imbued with the essence of Pristi Herself. They're pretty damn rare and I have absolutely no idea how your fallen comrade got his hands on one. If it wasn't broken, I'd take it for myself.

"As it *is*, it's getting turned over to Brother Steelhom when this is over. He was the most rigorous of our instructors and I can't think of anyone else that would enjoy handling it more. *I* surely don't want to have to deal with turning it over to one of those stuffy Pristi prats."

"So whoever gave Destin the amulet is to blame too?" Yothargi interrupted.

"However he got it doesn't matter. The fact that he *had* it sure as all *does*. He wouldn't let go of it, right? He kept saying that it was the only thing that saved his life, *right?*" Akaran pushed, getting closer and closer his face.

By this point the medic had taken on a deeper shade of red on the furious flush on his cheeks. "It didn't work half as much as you think it did!"

Akaran shook his head at the sheer idiocy of that statement. "Oh, I think it worked just perfectly. It kept the hounds from eating all three of you at once. It bought you enough time to make the hike back to town before their other injuries took them down. Still not sure how Destin got so hurt, but I'll figure it out at some point.

"What *matters* is that *you* figured it out. *You* figured out that the amulet was what kept you alive, and *you* figured out that it was probably the only thing that was going to keep *your* cowardly ass *safe* until the reinforcements from the garrison could get here."

"If it kept us alive long enough to get back here it would keep us alive *in* here! Someone from the army has to be able to tell the others what happened!"

That was a reasonable excuse – if the medic hadn't tried to hide it to start with. "Are you familiar with the phrase 'a sin of omission,' or are you just that damn *dense?*"

"You're talking gibberish!"

"No, you *idiot*, I'm telling you that if you had *told me* about the damn thing, it *might* have helped me figure out this mess before just now! At the very fisking *least*, I could have saved that boy from getting *killed!* Goddess only knows who else, too!" He slapped his hand against the wall hard enough to jar a half-empty cask of mead. While Yothargi scurried over to try to keep it from falling to the floor, Akaran kept at it. "And now what? I sanctified the graveyard, sure. That didn't stop that demon from getting into it.

"I also put wards down in the village. That doesn't tell me if these damn things were attracted to them – which believe me when I say I would *really* like to know if they are or not. I put some down where your friends got killed. Absolutely no idea *what* if *anything* that will do to be any good, either.

"Now that it's been established that I know a *lot* more than you do, let's talk about why you hid your affinity for magic away. Someone with your innate ability should be off... let me think. Right, the Queen is dealing with those upstart rebels in the Missian League, off to the west... on the other side of the Kingdom from here. Isn't that right?"

Furious and glowering, the torrent from the exorcist had finally started to make him crack. In a rare moment of open honesty, he snapped out his reasons. "Because of the rebels. This station, this area – quiet. It's quiet here. The worse that plagues these people is the occasional band of bandits. I serve my time in the army, I collect my pay, and return home."

Slightly taken aback, Akaran couldn't believe it. "You... you have a gift to heal? You can channel even a little magic from Pristi... you can truly use the power of your Goddess? And you do... nothing? You refuse to reveal yourself to keep from being put where your strength can be used for the greatest good? Do you *know* what's going on over there? *I* should be over there!"

"I've no wish to die. Those people in the League... you've heard the stories."

"Yeah. Cultists of the Rot-Bringer. Neph'kor followers. Not nice people. That's why they call them 'upstart rebels.' That's why they need people *like you* and *me* over *there* and not wasting away our talents where nobody over *here* would put them to good use! If you'd been honest to everyone to start with, more people would still be alive *here* and... FISK! Just... *damn!*"

Tornias turned his head and looked away, almost like he was feeling guilty. "I agreed to help the people. The League is not made up of our people. They should clean up their own mess."

"You mean you don't want to risk being in a fight. So you hid over here, and the first time you run across something evil, you lie about it to try to keep your head on your shoulders."

"I didn't just do it for me! I had no idea what that amulet was! I just knew that Destin carried it! After he died I had to have it back, but after what you said I -"

Akaran just looked at him, mouth agape. "After what I said you were afraid that there was more to the story. That's what happened. You didn't want to risk going out and rooting around in his grave after it. So you sent the boy. Then he got killed. I... I can't believe it, I mean I thought maybe, but surely not..."

"I had no idea that would happen!"

"But you EXPECTED it! You thought that there might be something out there looking for it! You sacrificed that boy to try and protect your own hide!"

Shouting right back at him, the medic tried to justify it. "I couldn't risk it! If something ill were to befall me, what would happen to Lativus? He's lost one husband, I didn't dare risk him losing us both!"

Time seemed to stop at the outburst. Not a soul in the room moved. Or breathed. "You couldn't what?" Yothargi asked, breaking the stunned silence.

That took the wind out of him, and Tornias finally cracked with a strangled sob. "He's my husband! Destin, too! He was. They are. I loved them so, we loved each other so. I will not risk Lativus losing us both! Not to those things! I make no apologies and don't expect someone like you to understand!"

Akaran couldn't... he just couldn't wrap his head around the utter foolishness the soldier apparently possessed. "*Blessed be.* Did you really just ask a priest of Love if he understood the desire to protect your husband? I don't care who you rejoice in matrimony with. I *care* that you *lied* again and again! I care that you got a child killed out of your own cowardice! Is it that so hard to understand?"

"Lativus and I aren't alive because of you! We're alive because of that girl!"

"That girl? Which girl?"

Going pale, the truth *finally* started to slip out. "I... no, I can't, she made me swear not to say."

"Oh we are so past the point where I care about who you promised what. Eos'eno. That's who. You met that woman before she showed up here in town. You didn't think that was important to mention? Maybe just a little?"

"She... yes. Yes, that woman intervened. The dogs were only chased away from Destin. They caught Lativus. I watched them rip his arm from his elbow. I couldn't... there wasn't anything I could do. Nothing,

nothing at all, not a movement not a move not a thing, and I watched them start to rip him to shreds. So much blood everywhere just -"

The exorcist waved off the details. "Yes, I saw the end result. What did she do?"

"She appeared in the snow, and threw the dog away from him. She caught the second one and vanished in front of me. Did the same to the other one a moment later. Just... simply vanished in a cloud of... fog."

Akaran bit his lip and muttered a quiet complaint under his breath. "I come here to exorcise a spirit and I end up playing games with a dog-catcher. Quaint. Don't suppose she did anything else, did she?"

"No... I mean... yes... dammit, yes, she did."

"No or yes? Pick one. Stick with it."

Affixing his tormentor with a hateful stare, Tornias shouted his response back at him. "YES, she did! She weaved ice over Lativus's arm. Stalled the bleeding. Swore there was nothing she could do for Destin, though I didn't know what she meant at the time. Then she said '*Work what magic you have or they rise again – DO NOT work a spell outside the walls!*'"

"Do not work outside the...? Oh you have..." The medic should have been grateful that Akaran didn't have his sword on his hip. His fist talked well enough, and knocked Tornias (chair and all) onto the dirty floor.

"Exorcist! No!" Yothargi shouted, grabbing Akaran's fist before he could punch Tornias's teeth in.

"She gave you a warning, she saved your husband, she made the dogs vanish and you knew all of this and *didn't tell me?!* What is *wrong* with you fisking people in this awful town! How is it you are **ALL** so fisking **STUPID**?!"

Cowering, it was all the worthless little shit could do to cry his response. "I tell you and then what? I don't know you! You could have decided that he was toxic, a threat, killed him outright! There are horror stories about people like you! You're just a novice! You don't know what you're doing!"

"You're right. I am. I may not know what I'm doing. But."

"But what?"

"...but *I* know more than *you*."

Tornias tried to break free of his bonds on the floor and pushed himself away from the towering, furious figure in front of him. "I am a ranking officer of the Queen's Army! My word with Commander Xandros carries mountains more weight than your influence! That's all you have! Influence!"

The barmaid shook her head and quietly made a point the medic hadn't quite come to terms with just yet. "Ain't just his. We all know it now too. You ain't gonna silence everyone."

Akaran shook his arm away from the innkeeper and took a few steps back, breathing hard and desperately trying to catch his breath. "You are about to discover why. You are, and I mean this in every bit of seriousness, a dead man walking. *Everything* you've admitted to right now carries a death sentence – and several of those things, a slow one. I'm gonna pray that wherever I end up stationed after this is far enough away that I won't hear your screams."

Yothargi hadn't understood most of the discussion but even he figured out what Tornias's sins of omission had cost everyone. "You need to start running then. Leave him for us. Julianos was one of ours, and if he got him killed..."

"Piata will do things to him that are going to be past the worst that any of us are going to be able to imagine. I'm done here. He tries to run, break his shin. No. Break his knee. Your pick of which one. No, wait. Break both his knees AND his shins. I'm pissed, so be inventive."

Terrified and in disbelief, Tornias looked up at him with his swollen jaw marring some of his words. "Are you truly serious? I've sacrificed everything to keep Vestranis alive and safe and now *you* pass a death sentence to me? There's no justice there! I didn't mean anyone harm! It's not my fault!"

The innkeeper had an entirely different opinion. "You sent that boy on a path to get killed! You might have gotten more of us killed by not telling that priest what you knew! You did those things! Exorcist, I cannot stand the sight of you but I will *beg* you to leave this coward to *us*. We've existed without the Queen's punishers for decades. We don't need one now."

Tempting as the thought was... "You'll wait. If I let you have him, I defy my own duty. I know you seek vengeance but I know that the army will wish to make an example of him. It will do far more good to let them have him. You don't want his death on your soul." With a long, intensely serious stare, Akaran gave him one simply warning. "I don't want to have to deal with any more pit-bound ghosts this trip out. So... don't. Just don't."

Yothargi's barmaid found her voice again. "Will he suffer?"

"I won't suffer anything! I acted to protect my husband and the interests of the Queen!"

"Oh, just shut up," the exorcist sighed. "Or go ahead. Keep talking –

they may ignore me. They may take care of you before you get to Piata. Pits if I know. They're not your friends right now. As far as the Maiden? Yes, they don't call her the 'Madwoman' because of her *kind* and *forgiving* nature."

Tornias tried (tried) to push himself back up off of the floor. "You wouldn't. You're trying to scare me into making me do something. I don't know what, but that's all you're trying to do. Whatever it is, I'll do it. Don't have to threaten me further, don't have to use these simple folk to try to scare me. What is it that you want from me?"

Dumbfounded, Akaran just looked down at him. "You really are an idiot, aren't you?"

The exorcist didn't say anything else as he brushed past Yothargi and went off to go find his next victim, hanging his head in disbelief. The innkeeper, on the other hand, wasn't done. "He said I could break your leg if you tried to run."

"I am not running from you. I can't. Now help me up, I'm a soldier and I deserve far better than to be treated like this. The Maiden will absolve me. She won't take the word of someone like him. For that matter, he'll be back and he'll want me able to fight. I am a good soldier. This town needs soldiers like me to protect you. Now help me up already; don't just stand there looking at me."

Shaking his head, the innkeeper looked at the chunk of wood in his hands and then looked back at the medic. "He's running away."

"You're gonna have to stop him," the wench agreed.

Tornias laid back there, eyes growing wider and wider. "Running?! I'm on the floor!"

The barmaid shook her head as she left the basement, none-too-eager to watch. "Akaran's right. You really are an idiot."

Not long after, Yothargi quietly slipped into a house on the outskirts of the village. The owner had moved on a year ago – and after the proclamation from the exorcist, most people were busy tending to their own belongings in preparation for an evacuation. The innkeeper, on the other hand, had a different task to do.

"Wife? I had Peoran take Akaran's gear to the temple. Made sure that Ipteria knows, too. Stupid girl will stay at that bar 'till the world ends. He goes back to the inn, she'll tell him."

Looking up from a pile of her clothes and a few sundries, his wife feigned surprise. "She's not getting ready to leave?"

"Nope. Stupid wench thinks that when I leave, she'll own the inn all herself. Dumb girl. Can't run an inn if there's nobody to visit it, can you?"

"No... no, you can't. That's what I wanted to speak to you about."

"The inn? What does it matter? We're leaving."

"Yes, I know," she sighed with a roll of her eyes. "Did you find Ronlin? Is he on his way?"

Nodding, he looked back over his shoulder. "Yeah. Right behind me. What do you want from him? You know he's going to go run off and tell that fisking boy that you're here. We're risking you getting caught. For what?"

As she walked over to him, she ducked her hands into the folds of her dress and tried very hard not to berate him. "Because he owes me."

Furrowing his brow, her husband stood there like the simple-minded fool she always thought him to be. "Owes you what? Every man in this fisking village walks around you like you're some kind of whore, you know that, don't you? Sick of it. That's gonna change when we get north of the border. Only eyes anyone is going to have for you are mine. Ain't nobody gonna doubt that."

"Ah, about that..."

Their conversation was abruptly ended when Ronlin finally opened the door. He didn't see her at first, and the soot-covered old man looked completely exhausted. "Yothargi, what is it? What's so important you had to drag me out of -"

"Elder," Rmaci quickly interrupted, "he didn't. I did. Shut the door."

"You! You killed Mowiat! Why should I shut –!"

Yothargi shoved him aside and did it for him, quickly blocking it with his back. "My wife says you owe her. Pay up so we can leave."

Stunned, Hirshma's brother looked back and forth between them with his mouth open. "OWE her? I've never owed this... this... murderous harlot *anything* in my life!"

"You didn't before, but you do now. Oh do you ever owe me now," she seethed, giving him a raw and hateful look. "Do you... do you have *any* idea what you did?"

"Nothing! Yothargi get out of my way; I have nothing to discuss with your bitch. Let me leave now and I won't tell the exorcist you've known where she's been hiding!" The exclamation was met with a poor attempt to push the innkeeper away that didn't work in the slightest.

Grabbing the older man by his shoulders, her scarred husband was quick to turn him around to face his wife. "She says you owe her. Pay up."

"Pay? Pay with *what?* That bastard had my home burned to cinders! I have *nothing!* He took the village from me, he took my home from me, and he's set my sister for trial!"

He hadn't looked back towards the murderess, which was a truly moronic decision. She made him pay for it. With a single swing, Rmaci knocked the elder to the ground with an iron candlestick. Blood splashed as the old man went down with a strangled cry and a horrific gash across his left eye and temple.

"Not just *me* you owe, you utter idiot. Do you have *any* idea how much of this is at your feet? I'd take it out of your sister's hide too, but that bastard beat me to it. *Your* family let that fisking wizard set up shop outside of town. *You* kept letting him come back here. *You* never made him go away, *you* had the chance, but no, *you* thought you'd show your sister some kindness and let him stay around. *You* could have forced the army to remove him from the area. *You* could have stopped *all of this* and I'd have never been sent here to start with! I've wasted *years* in this sad little shit town!"

"Sent here? What are you on about?" her husband tried to interject.

She didn't answer. "*All of this* is on *you.* I don't give a *shit* about that little boy, I don't give a *shit* about this awful frozen rock you call a village, and I don't give a *shit* about your 'I don't want the Queen' whining attitude. Then to make it worse, when you *finally* realized it was a disaster *you* begged your sad little army to send their soldiers and *then* you begged your sad little Queen to send one of her enforcers. Well guess what? He's not here in this room, he's not going to protect you and *you* owe the Empress a debt you are *never* going to be able to repay in what's left of your short, miserable, painful life!"

"Empress?!" Yothargi finally shouted. While Ronlin whimpered on the floor, the realization hit him harder than the second blow that Rmaci gave the village elder across the back of his neck. "You're... you're a Civan?"

Looking up at him with a trickle of Ronlin's blood across her lips, his wife brushed strands of hair out of her face. "Yes, I'm a Civan. The Empress sent me to watch over the affront to Flame being built in these mountains. And everyone in this pathetic little border town has managed to make *everything* worse here day after day after day."

"That... that's why you said you wanted to go north? You're not afraid of being arrested for Mowiat, you're..."

"I want to go home," she snapped, hammering the elder across his upper shoulders with her makeshift club while her husband stood by and did absolutely nothing to stop her. "Home. Home where it's warm. Home where I can pay tribute to the Empress day in and day out. Home where I can be free to speak about Illiya without fear of being spit on."

Crying with broken sobs, Ronlin was able to choke out a plea for mercy. "Please don't... don't do this... didn't do anything wrong, didn't hurt anybody..."

Her next strike broke his jaw. Whatever else he tried to say only came out as unintelligible muffled screams. "Being sent here to watch him and you and the fools you call family took three years from my life. *Three years*. Now there are demons involved, and I will *promise you* that this is something the Queen's little bitch Maidens won't ignore. You think it's bad now with that pussy-hungry child running about out there? Oh my dear, dear husband, you haven't seen a *damn* thing yet."

Content that she had hurt the elder as much as she could with what time she had left, Rmaci walked back to her backpack and pulled her dagger out of it. As she ran her palm down the flat of the blade small orange glyphs lit up along it.

"Wife... I... I don't care. Wherever you go, I will go. I promised we'd run together, and I'll protect you. I... I love you, I'll do as you wish, as you want, whatever you want..."

"As I want? Whatever I want?"

Slowly backing away from Ronlin, he refused to meet her eyes. "I love you. I don't care. I love you, I'll go wherever. I won't ever leave you."

"You won't? You'll do whatever?"

"Whatever you want."

She quickly closed the space between them and flipped her weapon, offering him the hilt. "Then kill him. For that matter, do it in the name of the Goddess of Fire, and in the name of the Empress."

"What?!"

Smiling, Rmaci just shrugged. "You just promised me you'd do anything. So do it. If you want me to trust you, your hands have to be as dirty as mine. Do this, and we will leave, and never look back."

Her husband looked at the elder, and her, and the blade, back and forth, for what felt like an eternity to him. With a resigned, ashamed look, he took the weapon and meekly consented. "For... for the Empress, in the name of Illiya... I'll do it."

Unconscious, Ronlin never saw the sword as it slipped through his ribs, never felt the tip cut his heart into pieces, never smelled the scent of his flesh smoldering from the enchanted blade, and never once heard the sound of Yothargi's broken sobs.

To his absolute lack of surprise, there wasn't anyone stationed outside of Hirshma's hut. She barely even gave him a notice when he stepped inside – instead, she kept her head down as she dug through a barrel on the far side of the room. "You came earlier than I thought. Are you here to take my head like you threatened?"

"No. How is Mariah doing?"

"Better. I gave her some larochi, so she may sleep. That damn... monster... hit her hard. She won't be running about anywhere for a few days without her ears ringing."

Holding up his flask of the fountain's water, he gestured at her with it. "Give her this, too. It'll help."

Hirshma looked at it then at him, eyes slightly narrowed. "What is it?"

"One of your secrets. What exactly happened?"

"She was brave. She stepped between that abomination and sacrificed herself to save one of Romazalin's boys. He was just running around the fountain like he always does when that... when Mowiat's corpse... I couldn't get my brambles up in time to stop it from hitting her... but I... I could use the wind to keep it from getting closer... you saw it when I... when I called for the land to grow the vines..."

Akaran was too tired to feign surprise. "If you expect a reward for that, you're sorely mistaken. You're a druid, aren't you? An actual practitioner of Kora, one of Her priestesses? Tree-worshiping grass-eating warden-of-the-land types?"

"I have never eaten grass."

"Smoked then. Noted. Now that we've established that, don't lie to me again, and we'll work the rest out later. Think I said that at least once or twice already, though."

Sighing, she reluctantly started to open up to him. "You must think me a horrific woman."

"I do. Doesn't matter. Who or what is Makolichi, who or what is Eos'eno, where did the dogs come from and what, exactly, is that Daringol thing?"

"I don't know."

Giving up, he turned away and started to walk out the door. "Then we're done. Good luck with the justic- "

Standing up a little, she tried to stop him with her voice in a half-hushed whisper. "I know what Usaic was doing."

That worked. "You do? Should I believe you?"

Swallowing, she sat back down and looked at the pile of herbs on her desk. "You have to understand him. He wasn't a... bad man. Not by any means. He is brilliant, or... he was. He always loved the cold, the ice. Everything. Hates fire. Hates all things flame. We'd use to... no, it doesn't matter what we used to..."

Akaran faced her and worked his way to a nearby stool to sit. "Even good men can do stupid things. Good women, too. What was he doing?"

"He lost his family, his wife, his brother... to raiders from Civa, back in the last Imperium War... they burned down his home. Illiyan followers... you know the type."

"Worshipers of the Goddess of Flame. Yes. I know of their work. They don't often leave survivors."

"Destroyed everything he had, everything he knew. He watched then burn alive when he was a boy. To hear him say it, he was able to save himself by making a shell of ice about him. The Granalchis took him away after, when they heard his story. They placed him in their Academy."

"Tragic. What was he doing?"

"Have you no pity? I just said..."

"I said it was tragic. I don't have time for more than that."

With another sigh, the elder didn't look back up in his direction. "Please, listen. He was so obsessed with finding a way to stop fire from ever being, but they refused to listen. Said that there was a need for flame in this world – he didn't agree. He didn't care. They threw him out, warned him to never push as hard as he was trying. Never again. *Ever* again."

"He pushed anyways."

Hirshma nodded silently. "He did. I should have seen his madness creeping but I never did. My father knew better, and I never believed him."

Akaran felt a pang of sympathy, albeit not much of one. "I've heard you two were together. You had a daughter by him?"

That name caused a mountain of pain to flicker across her face. "Yes. We named her Mayabille, after his mother. We loved her, she was the light of our lives, even after father expelled him from the village. He vanished for a pair of years after before he resurface. I don't know where he went when he was gone but he came back different, changed.

Older. A lot older than he was."

Grunting, the exorcist just shook his head. "Fisk. Well, you're not telling me much I didn't guess at. Let me cut to the chase: he wanted to make something so cold it could extinguish fire just by waving it in the general direction of a spark, and got obsessed with the idea of it. Probably angry at the world as a whole. That leads a man to do stupid things. Sound right?"

"Al... almost. After our daughter, after she... he threw himself into it. He had to, said it was all he had to live for. I couldn't bear to look at him, I couldn't, just couldn't."

"Grief. Comes from Love. It's a bitch."

Hirshma couldn't deny the honesty of it. "He grew mad at the world, but not just the world, the beasts that roam in it. Usaic couldn't bring himself to look upon... anything wild... after what happened to our girl. You see we had raised them, two of them, found them as cubs... one day one got sick and... it escaped before I could bring Kora's light to it to cure it and..."

"Pits. Please don't say what I think you're about to say."

"It bit... Maya and she... How could the Goddess do that? How could She let that happen? We would have saved our pup, we would have! It couldn't it shouldn't... I never looked to Her again after, never looked to the Gods, never looked, I did all I could, I was a faithful servant, I made things grow! Do you understand that? I was one with Her nature, WITH nature!"

"It happened because part of nature *is* disease and decay. That is the natural order. Nature has two sides – if *I* know this, you should too. There is good and evil in all things, it exists as a balance. *Your* nature is to help things grow but life doesn't *end* with the death of a thing... life continues on *through* it. It's the animals we eat, and the things they eat. It's..."

"Don't you *dare* lecture me on what growth and nature is and isn't! You don't think I know that? You don't think that I understand? I was taught to help provide aid to things sick and rotting, to keep sickness from spreading. *And I couldn't save my own daughter!* Kora forsake me, abandoned me... abandoned *her*."

Akaran couldn't hide his disappointment. "That's between you and Her. Right now you're between me and whatever those things are out there. Did Usaic tell you anything more about his work? Did he give you an idea what he was doing, anything?"

"The last he and I spoke of it, he said that he was attempting to find allies, two people that could help him. Wait, no, he never said people, just... allies."

He thought about it for a minute and played with the end of his goatee. "I have a bad feeling I know where you're going with this. What did he say? Quote him as exactly as you possibly can. It's important."

Thinking back to the look of complete joy and excitement her lover had that day, she recited his exuberant cry. "I think... Yeah. 'I've found the key to the coldstone! An ally of the purest of ice and one of the coldest of caverns!' That's what he said. He was so happy. I didn't risk asking him more."

Coldstone. Going to need to know that name for later. Noted. "Coldest of caverns? Oh, no. No no. He didn't say caverns, did he? He said c*anyons*."

Hirshma gave a quick nod. "Yes. Yes, that's right. Why, what difference does it make? A cavern, a canyon..."

Akaran's head made a little 'thunk' sound on the wall behind him. "Not a 'canyon,' a *Canyon* – an Abyssal Canyon. Eos'eno said she's from Tundrala... the *upper* elemental plane of Ice. Makolichi. *That* damn thing is enjoying a vacation from Frosel. He's not just some low-rank demon that crawled out from under a rock somewhere in our world. He's pitspawn from the *lower* plane. I was right. Zell, the Brineblood. Makolichi is one of His minions. Or... one of His creations."

Some of that condescending tone crept back into her voice. "I suppose you're going to tell me that means something?"

He looked down at his arm and grunted quietly. *I can already feel my bones breaking again next time I see him.* "It means that I shouldn't be surprised I couldn't put it down yesterday, and that it all but absolutely means it has some kind of long-term plan. Can I stress how *fisking useful* this would have been to know about when I first got here?"

"Well *you're* the exorcist, aren't *you* supposed to figure it out?"

"I'm an exorcist, not a psychic. I don't just suddenly know things by getting up in the morning and putting my clothes on. Why do you think they call us inquisitors? It's not because we already know the answers. *Goddess*, this is a mess."

"You... you really mean all this, don't you? Are you really so scared of it now that you know what it is?"

He couldn't believe she even asked that question. "*Yes* I mean all of this! Blessed be unto *all*, you people are *dense*."

Hirshma scoffed back at him. "No need to be insulting."

Akaran bit back the first few words he thought and gave her a foul look instead. "Yes. There is. Lots of reasons. You keep giving me new ones. Okay, so – Usaic was working on something that required the combined power of beings pulled directly out of both sides of the elemental planes, and he... he'd have to know about the mana font. That's coming out of the lake. Which you *also* knew about, didn't you? He's probably the person that made it."

"I... I knew that the lake changed a few years ago. About the time he spoke of his allies. I know that he said he had to hide his tower at the same time and that I wouldn't see him again until all was done. And I haven't."

"Oh now there's no way that could be a coincidence. And what tower?"

"The one he erected on the lake."

"Do we mean the same lake? The one near his cabin? I saw that lake. There wasn't a tower on the shores."

She shook her head and looked up the stairs behind her, quietly hoping they weren't waking her patient. "Not on the shores, on the *lake*... it hovered above it. Filled me with awe every time I approached. He could hide it, he said, away from prying eyes. Didn't want to give away his secrets to anyone he didn't like. Swore me to never speak of it."

"He... he hid a tower on the lake's shore."

"*Over* the lake," she stressed.

"Okay I was there, there wasn't... there wasn't a tower in on or over the lake. I would have seen that even if hidden... didn't feel any magic strong enough to..."

*No, I saw it. That was in the vision the Goddess sent me. Looks like I know where I'm headed. How did it... the masking aura. It **has** to be a **lot** stronger than I thought. Oh, **dammit**. It's powered **by** the lake. The door he opened is right there.*

Hirshma looked at him like she couldn't believe *he* was that dense. "I said he hid it, didn't I?"

His muttered swearing didn't stop as he started to add a few things up to explain away another question. *Oh, I wonder...* "I'm going to ask you a question I won't like the answer to. You had two wolves, right? Pets? Killed them both, fit of rage, all that?"

"Yes...?"

"What did you two do with the bodies?"

"He let me bury them."

"If you say 'by the lake' I'm going to punch something and my hand still hurts from hitting Tornias. Worth it, but it's hurting."

"You hit him? Good." Then, blinking, she looked at him as her mouth started to drop open. "No, you don't think that...? No, they wouldn't. No, they were loving beasts until the end."

Akaran hit his head on the wall again and tried to avoid looking her in the eye. "Two loving wolves – *dogs* – that you two summarily murdered for something one of them had no fault with and the other was too sick to know better. Goddess above, you bloody idiots. Alright. Last question."

"What?"

"Why did you lie to everyone? Not just me, but... everyone? You knew all of this and nobody else had a clue. Trying to save face? Save your own hide? Find validation that you could save them without the aid of your ex-matron? What was *your* motive behind not telling me all of this? *Any* of this?"

"I..."

Standing up as pure annoyance took over, the exorcist kept having to tell himself that hitting *her* was a bad idea. "'I' is not an answer. 'I' is you trying to justify it to yourself and make yourself feel better from the cursing we both know I'm going to do when you answer. So go ahead, get it over with. *Answer me.*"

"You are a nasty, impetuous man."

She wasn't wrong. "A nasty impetuous man who has had his arm broken his ribs cracked and his head rung by something that's leagues worse than what I think I'm able to put down on my own and that's just *one* of them. So. Why? Why did a druid that abandoned her Goddess think she had the ability to better defend the town against *an actual demon and his minions* more than someone that has *spent his entire life* preparing to banish the damned?"

Hirshma tried to keep the sound of her voice wavering from being too obvious. "Because this is my home. Because I know these people and I know these wilds. We like being away from the Kingdom, out here, nobody bothers us. Nobody demands a tithe, nobody sends armored thugs to collect taxes more than once a couple of years. When we quit being able to supply ore to the army, they even quit sending surveyors. The Kingdom has no use for us and we've no use for it."

"And? And what does that have to do with asking for help when you knew you needed it? *You've* known for years how bad this is. *You,* personally! Well before anyone else!"

231

"What do you think happens next? You know our secrets, you know the things we hide, you know about the work that Usaic started. Now you've identified what? Some kind of water that enhances magic? You're a good little soldier boy under the Queen's thumb. You are duty-and-honor-bound to report this to your superiors the moment that you feel it is safe to do so. If the army had come up alone and solved this then they'd never know what he hid; they'd kill the monsters and go back to their wines and whores."

She still wasn't wrong. "I'm a 'good little soldier boy' because I know the kind of things that wild magic attracts. I know what kind of monsters it's *already* attracted and as *bad* as Makolichi and those dogs are *I will promise you* that there are things *a lot worse* that will descend upon this mountain the *second* that they catch a whiff of what's going on here. You think two grumpy puppies are bad? Alchemist, there are things that crawl under this world that will make their fangs in your throat feel like a gentle summer breeze lightly stroking your neck!"

"Not if I could chase them off! Not if the totems stayed intact! Now you know, now the army will know, and now the Queen will move her people here and take everything we've had and ruin our homes!"

Akaran couldn't believe it. "Your homes are *already* ruined, you daft woman. And *what* totems? The only thing anywhere near here that's had an inkling of Kora'thi's magic in it was some bracelet I found in his cabin."

That was beyond unexpected and the sight of it in his hand floored her harder than his fist could've. "He… he kept it? He… he said he lost it…?"

He handed it to her and shook his head. "No, it was on the bed, hidden under a pillow. It was yours, wasn't it?"

"Yes it… we… when I found out I was pregnant with Maya… we… we made it together…"

The emotion in her voice didn't touch him enough to note, so he just shrugged at her. "Whatever fate befell you two, he didn't throw it away."

That was the last she could take. Suddenly exhausted and broken, she caved with tears springing out of the corners of her eyes. "I… I didn't… didn't know…"

"Pity you didn't come to terms with all of this earlier. Yes. You're going to lose your homes. You did the second that Usaic set up shop. Homes can be rebuilt, lives *can't*. Would have thought you had figured that out by now. So. What totems, again, exactly? Where?"

"They were placed all about the town proper. Enough to chase off idle spirits and ward away larger threats."

Frowning anew, he shook his head. "No. There's nothing. I don't know what you did, but there's nothing out there. When was the last time you checked them?"

Confused, she blinked a few times and looked up at him. "When the soldiers came back mauled and ruined. They were fine. I do not know how these things got within the walls, the wards were built into them by my grandfather, then father, then my brother and I. We've renewed them time and time again."

Akaran groaned. "You abandoned your Goddess and you're surprised your magic barely works any longer? You do understand that it is a gift from the Gods, and when it isn't a gift, it's earned through knowledge or tapped into by deep personal will? Why do you think they call it the Granalchi *Academy* – and the rest of us get called a priest in one form or another? How long have you been stuck out here away from civilized society?"

"You call it civilized, I call it -"

"Don't care. Damn it and damn *you*." Fuming, he again fought back that urge to start swinging. "I'm going to make you a deal, and it's a one-time only offer. Accept it, and I don't hand you over to the Justiciar. You and Tornias may well share the same cart to the gallows after you both enjoy a stint at Piata's manor, otherwise."

Hirshma couldn't believe she was hearing him right. "You'd really see me dead? You'd hand me over, just like that?"

"As easily as you sent me into battle without telling me everything going about? That's as close to sending me to my death as I hope anyone ever does. So. Fair is fair. Your choice. Take the deal, or eventually hang with Tornias."

Well-rebuked, she swallowed back the end of her indignation and admitted defeat. "Make your offer."

"When the army arrives, no matter what happens to me, you will explain to them everything – and I do mean *everything* – that has gone on here. *Every. Thing.* You will provide them with any map, any record, and every known threat from the smallest of bug to the riskiest of trails from here to the border."

"You mean make their occupation easier."

"Not that you'll be here to care. Yes."

"Pardon?"

Akaran tried to force his shoulders down to ease the tension in the back of his neck. "This isn't your home anymore. You've all but admitted that. You know it and I know it. When they establish their camp you will help that girl make her way from here to Ameressa, where she wanted to be before she got stuck in this snowy bog of your damn making. "

"Exactly how am I going to be able to take her that far safely...?"

"You'll be provided a stipend. I'll see to it. Won't say it'll be an easy walk but you'll be granted one, and then clear passage north."

Utterly and completely lost, she just looked at him. "I'll be... what? How do you intend to honor that? You've admitted more than once you don't expect to live through this. I could just be as easily promising to walk on water for all the good it'd do you or anyone else. Why do I doubt that you trust me to...?"

"You won't have to wait for me, and you're going to be bound by oath," he sighed, pulling his sigil out of his cloak. "You've seen the things out there. Do you want to risk living them with eternity if you break it?"

She scoffed a little at the thought. "Faith? In the afterlife? If you're willing to see me hung, then I imagine you expect I'll be one of those rotted things out there before long."

"I expect that you won't want to be. Cheer up. You don't have to take it on faith that the heavens exist or worry if your magic comes from another source. You've seen what lurks on the other side. If you want to avoid that fate, I suggest you start making amends."

With a defeated sigh, she lowered her head in submission. "Fine. I'll take your oath. What... what will I have to say?"

"Say? Nothing. You'll be wearing it. It'll get you passage, some supplies, and the stipend. The Crown will reimburse you for the cost of your land as well, I'm sure. Be careful showing it once you make it past the border, but, you'll have it."

"You're giving me this? That makes even less sense. Nobody will believe I am what you are."

"You won't be carrying it, you'll be wearing it. If I don't press charges against you after all this, you will owe me a favor. Not just a favor, but a *debt*. You have a *great deal* to atone for. This is your chance. I can't imagine that the provincial governor will care one whit about your reasons. Really, I shouldn't either but I would like to sleep tonight without fearing you'll sneak into my room to put a knife in my neck."

"If I won't be wearing it, then how will I...?"

Finally, he allowed himself a bit of a smile as he looked over at the fireplace behind her and reached for the prongs. When she followed his gaze, Hirshma turned the same shade of white Tornias had. "You've lost your mind."

He hadn't.

That wasn't to say he wasn't going to enjoy this.

He was almost back to the inn when Moulborke stopped him. "If you're looking for your stuff, Yothargi had it thrown out. Had it taken off to the temple. Guess he doesn't want you anywhere near his wife anymore. Can't imagine why. Everyone else has been."

The only things the priest had to say about that were not repeatable (and certainly not printable).

"Oh, and, boy. Some kid ran into the shrine a bit after that, carrying something wrapped up in a blanket. Expecting a delivery?"

There were a few other words to go with that.

After he sulked back into the shrine, the package in question couldn't be missed. The delivery boy had set the parcel on top of the altar (where someone else had carelessly dumped the rest of his stuff on the floor). It looked to be the length of a shortsword, which made sense for all the wrong reasons. That is to say, it was dripping blood.

It also came with a note.

"*Exorcist:*

"*I wish we had met under different circumstances. I think you and me could have done a lot together. Now is not that time, sadly, and I imagine we won't be able to enjoy each other's company in the future.*

"*I'm sorry for having to lie to you. I admire your dedication even though I hold your Goddess in contempt. This sad world needs people like you, more's the pity. This mess is no longer something that can be contained by the hopes and faiths of these sad idiots and it's grown into something that cannot be ignored either by your Queen or my Empress.*

"*The Civan Empire has known about Usaic and his work for years. My job was to either help him fail or kill him and take the coldstone when he perfected it. At the time, the Empire decided that your Queen having the ability to mitigate the Fires of Illiya would be unacceptable. I still believe that.*

"*However, having a demon of growing strength wandering free will ultimately be a significantly greater threat. It might roam south, or it might roam north. The distance between our nations is vast, this is true; and yes, it would likely do much more damage to your people than mine. Although as history has shown, demons are not weapons – it is simply best to end that thing now instead of risking it grow in strength later.*

"If you haven't already figured it out, I'm certain that whatever magic that Usaic tapped into has managed to spread through the woods and I cannot imagine that it would take it long to spread deeper to the south. To Gonta, most likely, when they finish with Toniki; were I a betting woman. Wild magic attracts vile things. Who's to say these things haven't begun to arrive already? Not I.

"I am also convinced that the wraiths you've been fighting are not part of the elementalist's work. There was a rumor of some kind of shadowy spirit that haunted the region between the midlands and the borders of the Ameressa city-states to the north-east. I don't know anything more about it but call it a hunch that it never left after Usaic caught its attention.

"The Queen discovering this disaster was just a matter of time. Please forgive me for trying to talk Ronlin out of sending you – the sooner she realized what was on her northern border, the greater the potential damage to the Empire. A priest would discover it; a soldier wouldn't. Yet they called for you anyways.

"Please forgive me for Mowiat. I had intended to kill you once you disposed of that interloping spirit – that is all I truly believed it to be at the time, I am not lying to you – and the fool insisted on coming along. Couldn't risk him getting in my way once I found you. It wasn't personal. Taking your life would have been much easier if it was just the two of us. I nearly did, you know. Mowiat was a victim of circumstance. Nothing more, nothing less.

"Ronlin was, though. No matter the need for you, he did set your arrival into motion. I suppose it would be inevitable for one of your kind to be here, true. Still. A price must be paid. Never liked the judgmental fool anyways.

"I am glad I didn't decide to kill you. I ask that you share the same kindness, if our paths ever cross again. Please keep the sword and use it with fond memories of me. At the very least, use it to kill that damned demon that has become such an inconvenience for the Empire. It's the closest I'm going to be able to get to punishing it for interfering in the Empress's wishes.

"I bear you no ill wishes or grim tidings. You and I are alike: we have jobs to do, morbid as they may be. The world rests on the shoulders of people exactly like us – those who do thankless bloody tasks in the shadows for the betterment of our peoples. Be safe in your travels and cast these wretches into the Flame for me, please.

"Glory be to the Empress, curses to your Goddess, and good luck to

you.

"Sincerely, Rmaci."

For everyone in Toniki, the world was a completely different place between when the sun rose and it set behind the cold cloudy skies. There wasn't anyone left that suffered under any misconceptions as to how grave the threat was. There wasn't anyone else that doubted that if anyone could help them, it was Akaran – and all of them regretted not listening earlier.

None more-so than Hirshma. Any semblance of the headstrong and overconfident woman that had been an obstacle in his path since day one was long gone. She didn't say a word to the exorcist when he went to prepare Ronlin's body for cremation, nor did she look him in the eye when he helped carry the elder to the pyre.

The rest of the day, everyone set themselves to either mourning or to tasks he had assigned (or tasks that some of them had come up with to help take their minds off of the mourning). Vestranis pushed everyone to finish preparing what they would need to take with them when the army arrived within the next day or two, while Romazalin and Hirshma simply struggled to go on. The farmer's children were scattered all about the village – set to work by the smith to carry messages from one person to another and back again.

Rmaci's 'gift' ended up being just that – it wasn't a trap of some kind, it was an honest-to-Goddess gift. The blade was sharper than anything Vestranis's hand could craft (much to the blacksmith's chagrin) and there *was* magic attached to it. If it would *work* for him was a good question.

Honestly, it probably wouldn't. The Goddess of Flame did have a special kind of animosity towards the followers of Love. For all he knew, it'd make him burst into flames the first time he swung it. On the other hand, if Makolichi really was from Frosel and the dogs were contaminated by much the same energy, then it might be worth trying to use it.

But at least it was sharp.

For the most part, everyone left him alone. They didn't bother him when he set up a small ring of torches around the shattered well, and they completely ignored him when he prayed for a solid hour to the statuette in the middle of it.

Mariah limped out of bed with a throbbing headache behind her right eye that almost perfectly matched the one that Akaran was currently enjoying. The half-cocky attitude she had been indulging in was a distant memory. While she approached the priest half-subdued, there was an edge of doubt around her.

Their conversation was short, and easily summed up as a "Thank you for protecting us," and an "I will bring you grandpa's pick before you leave in the morning." It was the last 'thank you' he got from anyone – and nobody from the ranks of the village that hadn't tried to talk to him before didn't find the courage to approach him now.

The bar wench that had so far gone out of her way to hide her name from him was the last person to speak to him before he went to find sleep. Ipteria didn't bother to explain herself to answer why she was there, and she wasn't quick to give her name to him even then. "What happens next?"

It was a question born out of curiosity, and not an easy one to answer.

"I stay here until the village can be evacuated. When it is, I leave for Teboria Lake."

"And what then?"

"I try to slow them down."

While everyone else made their beds and many a soul sought to re-align their hearts with the Gods, two others were trying to put the story behind them. The fugitive pair were barely a twenty minutes run outside of the south gate when Rmaci came to a sudden stop. Her husband hadn't stopped complaining since she told him that they'd be leaving as the sun set – something about "It's not safe to be out after dark! The demons will find us!"

"The demons do or the exorcist does," she had snapped back. "We might outrun the demons. We won't outrun the noose. I'm far more scared of him than I am of them."

"He's just a boy!"

"A boy that wants to find those demons and won't think twice about what to do if he finds us. It'll be safe when we get into the lowlands, and once we get off the mountainside, it won't be too hard to stay ahead of riders bearing word of our misdeeds if we head to Anthor's Pass on the way out of this damnable Kingdom. The Empress would love to know about the current troop levels and battlements on this side of the Pass, as an added bonus for which I will be rewarded handsomely for. Even if the rest of this blasted mission has been a complete disaster."

"If we make it to Gonta, what then? You know word will spread..."

Sighing in frustration, she looked at him and leaned against a tree. "Yothargi! We've discussed this already. Once I get to Gonta, I'll be a day ahead – if not more – than anyone tracking me. Nobody will look twice if I scream 'the demons are coming, I must get away!'"

"Tracking *us*, wife. I swore to you I'd never leave your side."

Rolling her eyes, the raven-haired spy slipped right up against him and put her left hand on his chest, just above his heart. "Yes. Of course. You know that I love you. You know all of the things that I did for you before the fire hurt you so, and all the things I did after."

Smiling softly, the innkeeper covered her hand with his and leaned down to kiss her on her forehead. "The wonderful things you've always done and always will."

"Oh yes, the wonderful things. I'll never forget them, I promise... and I've one more to do for you, before we go any farther." His smile faded from joy to shock and pain as she met his kiss with one of her own – and slid a concealed knife into his chest with her other hand. She was so quick and the kill was so sudden that the only thing he could do was to fall backwards when she shoved him to the ground, the blade still firmly lodged just below his heart.

Bloody froth erupted from his lips as words tried to form somewhere in his throat. Try as he might, none of them could make it out. He managed to pull the bejeweled dagger out of his ribs like the fool she thought he was, but that was it. A ruby fountain gushed out as a reward for his efforts.

"All those *wonderful* things. All of those wonderful, disgusting, vile things you had me do to that burnt up stub of a cock when you couldn't get it up. I hate you. I've hated you for years. The only thing that brings me joy about *any* of this nightmare is that the Abyss will take you and I'll never see your charred hide ever again."

Rmaci's admission shocked him enough to talk through the pain and the black fog creeping around his vision. "Hate... hate me? What... why?"

"You turned traitor to your Queen and murdered a man in cold blood. You're aiding a murderess to escape the law. If you thought the burns that ravaged your flesh were bad, wait until you enjoy the ones that are waiting for you down below." Smiling, she picked her weapon up and stepped onto his chest, holding him down as the last of his consciousness faded away. "Illiya will forgive me for acting in defense of Her people. You turned your back on yours."

When he didn't answer, she judged his cheek with the toe of her boot a few times, just to be certain that there would be no more responses coming. "Besides," she went on, "It will be much easier for a widow to find refuge than it will be for a wife and her gimp."

Two hours later, nobody had thought to look outside the village to find the fugitives. Surely they wouldn't be so stupid as to run away after dark, would they? And even if they did, there was no promise that the demons wouldn't find them first. Even Akaran had to settle for that (as much as he detested it).

Rmaci was long gone. She left Yothargi where he lay, and he hadn't moved since she knifed him.

And then he did.

A pale shimmer of gray light took shape a few feet from his corpse. It was burnt, scarred, and looked more and more like her husband by the heartbeat. The wild magic in the area had kept his essence from reconstituting as quick as scholars who knew of such things would consider 'normal,' a fact which did his confusion no favors.

His consciousness hadn't come to terms with what had happened. It wasn't even close to there. Quickly-growing burning pain under his skin that was creeping into his bones wasn't helping, either. A series of painful black cracks started to split open across his ethereal body – an omen of the exciting world full of new delights awaiting him in the next life.

The former innkeeper couldn't comprehend *that* either. Really, all he could think of was what he had lost; not his life, but his wife. She had meant the world to him, she was all he had ever wanted. Now it was gone, and all he could wonder was if he would ever see her again.

There would be plenty of time to think on that, too. He would have all the time in time to dwell on his life, his death, his wife, and every other thing he had ever done or ever wished for. None of it would ever bring him joy.

There was so much that the Abyss could not wait to help him feel. Joy was not one of those things, but it did want to show him so many others. Oh, it wanted to show him a brave new world so very, *very* badly.

While he stared at his body, a creature unlike anything he had ever seen manifested across from him. It was a mammoth, hulking figure, twice his size, dripping with oily black shadows and cloaked in a cloud of icy fog. Tentacles the size of tree limbs lazily flipped through the air and soundlessly cracked in the silent void on the edge of the mortal world. Clawing hands and mutilated faces raked through the center of the mass, too many to count, too many to see.

His scream of terror was as soundless as it was desperate. Running did no good. A smaller blob of tentacles and shadows pulled itself free from the writhing mass and flung itself into Yothargi's corpse while he watched. The larger, hulking beast raced after his spirit and engulfed him thrashing and screaming, twisting and clawing to try and get free.

In a matter of moments, his soul was drowned into an ever-growing sea of freezing darkness, twisting strands of acidic tentacles, and clutching fingers. The last thought that he could make was a simple plea that he repeated again and again. Similar voices shouted similar things all about and around him, all begging for help all begging to get free all begging to find warmth. *Rmaci!! PLEASE!!*

This was not the fate that the Abyss had in mind for him.

Somewhere far below in a void beyond comprehension, something as vast as eternity shrugged.

Damnation could wait – Daringol would suffice for now.

XIII. AVALANCHE OF THE DEAD

The oft-stated rule that "There are no old exorcists, just young corpses," was one that nobody in training enjoyed hearing the first time (or the second, or third, or fourth). None of them wanted to admit that there would come a day when they would likely end up dead (or worse) because of a creature of (probably un-) imaginable horror. Still, about half of them felt that they were destined to prove themselves the exception to the rule.

That helped the instructors separate the stupid from the realists.

He still wasn't sure which he was.

A fresh mangled scream woke him up, coupled with the feeling that half the wards he had put down were all surging to life at once. *The wraiths? Dammit! Couldn't wait until noon?!* He was halfway through the door out of the shrine when he saw that Daringol was the least of his worries.

Chausses and boots, that was it. The only reason he even had those on was because he fell asleep by the fire before he could take them off. He hadn't been at rest long enough to recharge from a long day of steady spellcasting, either. He was half-drained, he was hurt, and he could barely think. And worse?

He was about to get educated on where his personal limits with magic lay. It wasn't going to be one of those 'fun' lessons, either. Because once he got outside? He suddenly quit wondering if he was going to be one of those young corpses when he saw what awaited him.

It appeared to be all-but a given.

When he barreled out the door, there was a very real moment

where he gave serious thought to walking right back inside. He would have, too, if it hadn't seen him. He wasn't a coward. He just wasn't stupid. Just... there might have been something inside that could have helped. A bigger sword, maybe. A shield. Enough wine to deaden the pain he was certainly about to feel.

It was maybe twenty yards away, down the curved path from the shrine towards the village. There wasn't any fog between them this time. No blizzards. No walls, no rocks, no crazy woman from Tundrala. They locked eyes for a minute as they sized each other up.

All of the false bravado he had been trying to show most of the township died in the back of his throat. Hopefully that was all that was going to die, although the mangled corpse laying in a bloody heap behind the dog ruled out that wish on the spot. The dismembered leg it held between its horrible jaws only enforced that feeling of dread.

However it managed to get nestled in the wards deep enough to be stuck between them was anyone's guess. Still, that was the only saving grace. As long as those wards stayed up, as long as Akaran could keep his attention focused on them, that thing was going nowhere fast. On the other hand, that meant he couldn't either. It was a terrible paradox and not one he liked to be in the middle of.

Left hand out, palm forward, he started to recite every binding spell he could think of. It actually worked for a couple of minutes, for good and ill both. Two more people showed up, rushing from behind abandoned houses to go to the one place they thought would be safest (and the worst they could have run to) – the shrine. Then he saw Hirshma join them and watched her eyes go wide at the sight of the beast.

A wise woman once said that there were more kinds of damned things than there were things living. Some you could argue with. Others you could bargain with. A select few weren't even all that bad. Things that you could theoretically call 'necessary' evils.

"By will and by order and by strength of the Goddess of Lovers, Matrons, and Mothers, I cast you from here, away from here, back to your place of torment and pain!"

Then there were those, that, well, didn't give a shit about any of that. It snarled at him, fangs out, sulfuric spittle flying from its mouth. "I said *I cast you away from here!*" It dropped to the ground and gave a second, louder snarl, embers popping out of its eyes in response.

Negotiation? Reasoning? Or possibly being a *necessary* evil?

No, abyssian hounds do *not* give a shit about *any* of that.

It was big enough that the head could come up to your midriff. Muscles rippled under its thick, charred-black hide with every movement. Bone spurs and outcroppings of jagged scales dotted the beast from its head to the tips of its twin tails.

If all of that wasn't enough of a sign that something awful was staring at you, the frothing tar that poured over far-too-many rows of needle-like teeth should be. Or if not them, then the furiously glowing orange eyes. Or maybe the sulfuric stench that rolled out of its throat each time it exhaled.

It answered his attempted banishment with a loud, furious growl.

"I don't suppose you blame me for trying, do you?"

The hound gave a short huff of a twisted laugh and dug its nails into the dirt as it paced between shimmers in the air. The wards were barely strong enough to stop it from advancing on him and they were just enough to keep it from running away. How long they would last – or at least, how long they would keep it tangled up – was a really good question.

Akaran held Rmaci's sword up, keeping the pointy end leveled right at the beast. The dog? He had no idea if this particular breed even had much in the way of coherent thoughts. If it did, he was pretty damn sure it didn't believe or wouldn't so much care that it was trapped in the midst of the ward charged by the font of mana.

He wasn't wrong. It didn't care. Not in the least.

Hirshma recognized it for what it had been, and she just couldn't come to terms with what it meant. "Zenifer... no... oh Kora'thi, no..." Terrified, she grabbed the first person she could reach and yelled at them, trying to get them to run away. Her efforts worked – it didn't take more than a couple of shouts from her to get people to haul ass back towards the village proper.

The exorcist's shouts of "What in the *fisk* did you people *do?!*" helped.

She was joined by another idiot a moment later. Hobbling, battered and bruised from yesterday's rough treatment, Tornias picked that moment – the worst possible moment - to grow a spine. He then confirmed everything that Akaran had already figured out.

"That's the thing! That's the thing that tore up my husbands!" Tornias screamed. *Somehow*, the idiot had found a woodcutter's axe and had it brandished over his head, righteous anger overtaking the nearly non-existent common sense he'd been born with.

He almost got within ten feet of its eager jaws when Akaran

managed to circle between the twit and the demon. The hound snarled loudly at him as the exorcist stole another easy meal. As the medic protested, his savior continued to chant spells at the demonic mongrel. "You are *NOT* to be in this world you foul fisking little pit-spawned beast and so help me by the Love of all that is Holy I will see you brought to judgment and sent back to where you belong!"

Blinded by vengeful rage, the idiot tried to push past the priest. The younger man simply wouldn't let him. "Vengeance is mine by right! Move aside and let a real man take this thing to task! I'm no coward! I'll show you I can −!"

"Tornias you idiot, It's ABYSSIAN! *Stand down!*" That actually worked for a minute as the soldier finally sized up the threat before them. It was a little too late, but he did eventually manage to size up the beast and realize what it was.

"That... that thing is...! Demon! I wasn't a coward! It's a demon!"

"*No fisking shit, you **idiot!**"* Akaran snapped. He broke eye contact from the beast to look at the crowd one stupid soul after another. That was stupid, and his accusations could have waited until later. He gave Hirshma a look so foul that it could have come from the dog. "What did you people fisking *DO?!*" he shouted. "Walking dead?! Wraiths? Endless winter? Demons?!"

Progressively angrier by the moment, the hound (*Zenifer, she said?*) did **not** like to be ignored. And abyssian hounds almost never, *ever* traveled in anything less than in pairs. If he hadn't been so concerned with Tornias, he might have remembered that.

He heard the other one growl before he saw it. It had somehow climbed up on top of a two-storied abandoned house behind him. Bloody froth flew everywhere as Zenifer shook its head, deliberately trying to mock the priest.

"HUNSRI! NO!"

Hirshma's scream barely gave Akaran any warning or time to dive out of the way before the second hound jumped off of the roof and landed where he had just been standing. Tornias wasn't so lucky and didn't move away fast enough. The exorcist slammed to the ground shoulder first and rolled away fast enough to watch the hound do what it was bred for.

It was a quicker death than being sent to Maiden Piata, at least.

The presence of actual, honest-to-Goddess demons put his wards into overtime. The magic that made them work against the damned was also making them light up all around the village. It made the air crackle, almost glow, with a faint white fog. Even if it didn't get rid of them, it wasn't going to make their stay a comfortable one. Anyone with even a hint of magic in them could have felt it if they were anywhere near the village.

Someone did, and that was a fact that would come into play very soon.

The dogs howled their displeasure as they started to pace in a semi-circle in front of him. Little sparks of blue and white magic snapped against the monstrous hounds. They flinched whenever those magical embers would flash against their eyes. It wasn't much but it made him feel a little better about everything.

Hunsri and Zenifer suffered no illusions as to the source of their discomfort. As all four eyes locked onto him with an unblemished hatred. They began to howl and a feeling of dread and doom erupted from everywhere. With a surge of befouled ripples in the ether, the wards flared to their maximum.

Then they began to fail, popping like bubbles all around him. Akaran's face went white as they lost the restraints holding them at bay. Continuing to howl, they split away from each other and started to encircle him. Little chants of *Oh shit oh shit oh shit* in the back of his mind tried to overwhelm any other thought he could come up with.

Hunsri went on the offense first. Tearing Tornias's ribs out had given it a taste for priest, but Akaran was less than happy to oblige. He twisted at the last possible moment and raked his left hand across its flank as it skidded past. Purple flames jetted off of its skin and cowed the beast for a moment with a whimpering cry.

Zenifer charged head on and jumped at him. There wasn't time to pull away from it, so he used its weight against it. The move cost him his sword but it left the blade sunk halfway into the hound's ribs. When it swiped a heavy paw at him in retaliation, he wondered if it was worth it.

The raking claws left a gash as long as his forearm from his nipple to his hip. The pain wasn't blinding but *damn* was it close. He grabbed that mammoth foot with both hands and shouted a Word with enough force to shred demonic flesh and muscle down to yellow bone in a flurry of purplish starbursts.

The other dog lunged in and nearly bit his head off of his shoulders while Zenifer tore free and rolled away from him. He was able to get one hand on its throat, and the same spell sent blue flame spouting out of Hunsri's mouth. The hound whipped about and howled, ash, embers, and teeth all filling the air.

For a moment, he thought he had them beat. He even welcomed the sight of Vestranis running into the fray with some kind of single-headed pick held in his burly arms. Akaran felt a single fleeting moment of exuberance before he saw who else was joining the fight.

Shards of vile ice lanced through the air, cutting the blacksmith to shreds. His arm and the pick landed near the ruins of the fountain while Makolichi lumbered into the battle. "**DESTROY HIM! THE ARIN-GOLIATH MUST BE LEFT UNDISTURBED!**"

Hunsri whipped about and took another hard lunge at Akaran while acrid smoke billowed out from its mouth. Akaran was able to use its momentum against it to send it careening into the house behind him. The dog had enough force behind it that it crashed through the wall, shattering boards and destroying a window in the process. The other hound thrashed on the ground and broke his sword in half in the process.

The arin-goliath? What is... OH! "I know what that is! I know what Daringol is! It's a nesting wraith! You've got a nesting wraith!" he shouted, a sudden rush of delight momentarily eclipsing the fact that he didn't expect to live another five minutes. "Oh. You... have a nesting... wraith. Fisk."

If Makolichi cared about his epiphany, the demon didn't show it (and if anyone watching knew what he meant, they didn't show it either). A lance of ice half as long as a horse shot out from his arm and just barely missed cutting the exorcist's cheek in half. Behind him, Hunsri wasn't so lucky – a yelp of pain and a growl of anger blared out of the wrecked house.

"**DEAD MAN! RED STAIN!**"

Akaran scrambled out of the way from the next barb of ice, diving into the hole Hunsri had left behind. A third furry of frozen shards peppered the wreckage as he went, eliciting a fresh round of swearing when one of the missiles split open his left arm above his elbow. The hound lunged at him from the ground but Makolichi's ice spear had it pinned firmly to the opposite wall through its ribs.

He had just enough time to grab an errant iron fireplace poker before the demon tore the front of the house off. "**DEAD MAN, RED STAIN!**"

His mammoth hand came within inches of catching Akaran's head as he tried to barge his way into the building. The exorcist reeled back then lunged forward, thrusting the iron at Makolichi's face. The armored Abyssian flinched back slightly as Akaran's makeshift weapon skidded across the ice that entombed him from head to toe.

The iron wasn't going to do any good, but making the demon think it would was enough. A shouted Word rocked his opponent back outside, a flare of light blinding everyone looking anywhere near them. Mako grabbed at his shoulder and caught him for a moment, searing Akaran's skin before the priest returned the favor. Unlike their last encounter, he was ready for the touch this time.

He had stood out in the cold for almost a full candlemark last night preparing for this fight. Much to Mariah's half-conscious delight and (Hirshma's derision), he'd been nearly naked the entire time. Their thoughts aside, standing in the slowly-growing pool of wild magic let him cast a ward that was going to stick around for quite a while.

Carving it into his own stomach let him weaponize it.

The Abyssian recoiled back, his hand covered in steam and pale embers. "I'm clad in my faith, *asshole,* and it may not save my life but I *promise* it's going to make you *hurt* as you try choking me down," he seethed. Makolichi looked down at him with those giant sickly yellow eyes and didn't move away when Akaran threw a solid punch at the crystal barrier covering its face. Even backed by the Goddess it still felt like he punched a stone wall – but it made Makolichi hurt worse.

Ice cracked as streamers of light and wisps of holy fire streamed down its chest. Howling in wordless rage, the demon swung to backhand the priest away. All he met was a wall of ultra-thick brambles and vines that sprung up between them in the blink of an eye. The plantlife scooped Makolichi up and flung him across the snow-strewn clearing.

He had just enough time to notice that Hirshma was standing with her feet in the center of the fountain when Zenifer rejoined the fray, charging between them and skidding to a stop. It roared at the top of its lungs and launched a charge at the priest – and failed to learn from its first lesson. Akaran dropped his shoulders, planted his feet, and thrust his arms forward as the dog sailed through the air at him.

This time he didn't let go until he was sure his weapon went where he wanted.

The iron poker went into Zenifer's mouth and out the back of its head. Crowing in triumph, Akaran shouted a Word at the beast before its weight could knock over and pin him down. *"EXPULSE!"* The spell ripped down the length of iron and slammed into Zenifer's twitching face. The dog lost its head in a shower of black blood and purple flame.

There wasn't any time to relish the victory. Abandoning the

weapon, his mad dash towards the fountain got him to what was left of Vestranis's arm and the pick as Makolichi tore himself free of Hirshma's bramble-wall. *Please be Mariah's pick, please Goddess please please-!!*

It was. He felt the magic in it the moment his hands touched it. Goddess only knew where it came from, or Whom exactly had imbued it, but there it was: another divine-blessed item in a place that should have been bereft of them. *Oh, I'm gonna **enjoy** using this.*

Seething with pure hatred, Makolichi dripped caustic brine out of the crack that Akaran's spellwork had left behind. Hunsri came up beside it, a gaping wound through its side where it had ripped itself off of the ice-lance. If the two wounded beasts thought they were going to phase him at this point, he didn't show it. If anything, it empowered him.

"COME ON, YOU SON OF A BITCH! COME TO JUDGMENT!"

Hunsri charged first, eager to repay Akaran for the fate of its mate. It would have to wait. A new wall went up in its path. This time it wasn't of brambles, but of crystal. Pure white crystal. It bounced off of the barrier and flopped about on the ground while Eos'eno pulled herself through the immaculate ice like she was stepping through a door.

She didn't have time to do anything else before the Abyssian grabbed her by her throat and tossed her down at Akaran's feet. That one act, that one dismissive temper-tantrum, told the priest absolutely everything he needed to know about her nature and their relationship.

Water splashed around the girl and soaked her on impact. The water that was full of wild magic... wild magic that was feeding the purification magic flowing freely out of the bust of Niasmis. The purification spell that would have made anything Abyssian bubble and boil away. The water, the magic, the purification spell that now covered the frost-born waif head to toe.

The magic that didn't hurt her in any way shape or form.

While she stood up, Akaran shot a glance towards Hirshma and barked a fast order. "When I say it, pull up more brambles. Put them right in front of me!" Then he did the unexpected – and stepped between the two remaining demons and in front of Eos'eno.

"RED STAIN! PROTECTING THE WORTHLESS? SHE WILL SHARE YOUR FATE!"

The exorcist just smiled at him, blood coursing down his chest. "I can *only* hope, you *prick*. Step forward asshole – *my* Goddess would like a word with you!"

Makolichi took the bait. Hunsri regained its footing and circled off to the side. Time slowed to a crawl as so many things happened at once. Makolichi's arm sprouted no less than eight jagged spikes, turning into a bristled club as he watched. Eos'eno forced herself to the side of the exorcist and pulled a gnarled wooden staff out of thin air. A fog full of frost poured off of it as her body began to shift and change.

Her skin went from pale to nearly pure white. Her eyes started to enlarge, a glowing blue hue spilling freely forth. Her hair went from brown to a pale caramel laced with streaks of light gold. Her ratty robe fell away, showing her body in its naked and true, nearly-perfect form. Nearly perfect, because in all of her glory, there was a horrible scar on her shoulder – about the size and shape of a dog's bite.

There was a moment, just a moment, where Hirshma's world came to a grinding halt as she recognized the scar, and realized who the waif was... or rather, whom she had been. "WHAT?! **NO!!**"

Eos'eno stood her ground and shouted defiantly at the demon that had tormented her so. "*No! You will not take the protector of the Ice! You will not take the Guardian of Winters!*"

Then the dog charged – but not at Akaran. It went right for the alchemist behind him, right where he thought it might. Mako rushed towards them at the same time. Akaran snapped his plan into place as they both lunged. "EOS! BLOCK THE BASTARD – HIRSHMA, WALL NOW!"

Blessedly, the two women did exactly as ordered. Hunsri jumped for the elder as a wall of brambles erupted inches away from Akaran's feet. Eos'eno shot forward with her staff outstretched, her entire body half a foot off of the ground. The move took Makolichi by surprise even if not for long. The real surprise he had for them were the chains that neither of the demons had seen him use before.

The Bonds took form mid-whip, silvery chains that sliced through the air and wrapped themselves around the dog. Extending almost a full seven yards, they caught the demon around its throat as it tangled up its legs. He snapped the chains forward and pulled as the ethereal steel easily burned into the dog's flesh.

Hunsri didn't stand a chance.

The force of Akaran's jerk pulled the hound off course and forced it to fly right towards the exorcist. Before it could crash into him Hirshma's brambles finished sprouting at his feet and shot up another yard over his head. With a rage and pain filled howl, the hound slammed into the vines and lost both of its eyes to the thorns as the vines caught it and held it in place.

Behind him, Eos'eno forced Makolichi back and away from the

'Guardian of Winters,' using her staff to fight off furious blows and her touch to push him back foot by foot. She wasn't going to be able to keep it up for long – and didn't. The demon swung at her and hit her side hard enough that it tore a gouge out of her ribs half the size of Akaran's head. Not a single drop of blood burst from her wound, but a fountain of silver slush erupted from her side from just below her left breast down to her hip. She screamed so loud that it almost brought Akaran to his knees.

Unfortunately for Hunsri, it didn't.

Akaran swung the pick down and drove the hook into the top of the hound's head. A blazing gold light exploded through Hunsri's maw and burned through its body like someone had dropped a torch into a barrel of tar. Power once more surged through his hand as he said a Word that ripped down through it. The first muttered Word broke down the rest of its strength; said twice, "*EXPEL!*" sent the pit-born beast back to its kennel in the Abyss.

The hound's body buckled as if it had been hit by a boulder and erupted in flames. It jerked and shuddered as bones baked and tendons shriveled. It sizzled as fat melted and blood boiled. The dog cooked to bits of black bone and rank ash in the blaze in a matter of heartbeats.

That just left Makolichi. At least, that's what he thought.

Then his plan fell apart.

Vestranis's corpse provided the distraction that the demon needed. The body lunged up as Daringol's tentacles sprung to life and thrashed out through the gaping hole where the blacksmith's jaw had been and more had sprouted out of the stump where his arm used to be. White fire engulfed his feet from Akaran's purification spell, but that did little to slow it down. It latched onto Hirshma, and in her panic to fight it off, she fell onto the ruins of the fountain...

...and knocked the idol of Niasmis out of the rubble, sending it rolling away from the infused water. Akaran had time to curse and direct a ball of light from his palm into Vestranis's face, blasting the corpse away from the alchemist. Part of Daringol's essence boiled away into black steam at the impact, taking it back out of the fight for the moment.

That moment was all the time that Makolichi needed to press the attack. His arm came down over Eos'eno and nearly bashed her head in. In return, she forced a burst of wind out of her battered body with enough force to push the Abyssian back away.

It gave the exorcist enough time, barely enough, to cast his chains around her arm and *pull* her back to him and to safety. He met her halfway through the tug and shielded her body with his just fast enough to protect her for the trio of heartbeats it took for Makolichi to flung another spike of ice at the girl.

The shard hit him almost dead center.

It pierced all the way through his gut and out his back in a fountain of blood. He made a strangled cry of pain as bloody froth spouted out of his mouth and he went to his knees. The pick fell from his hands as Akaran stared up at the Abyssian. Everything hit him at once as he realized he had been right all along: Makolichi was going to kill him.

He just wasn't strong enough.

He just didn't have the skill.

He just wasn't able to protect the village.

He just didn't have any choice but to accept the inevitable. Hirshma screamed out his name. Eos'eno joined in the cry. Makolichi crowed in victory. As the world started to go black around the edges of his vision, there was one other thing that he knew wasn't able to do.

He just wasn't able to quit.

Akaran *made* himself stand up. He *made* himself charge forward. He *made* himself ignore the pain, ignore the blood, ignore the shock that was spreading through him. He *made* himself lunge across the spell-ravaged courtyard and he *made* himself grab the Abyssian with both hands. "*LUMINOSO – BONDS – EXPEL!*"

The light evaporated half of the cracked shell protecting Makolichi's face. The chains punched through the rest of it and tore into the bones around the demon's collarbone and ribs. The expulsion spell coursed through the silver-steel and *ripped* bastard out of his armor. The impact sent him flying across the field.

He didn't have the strength to finish the job. As the awful shell of ice fell backwards, Akaran fell onto it. He couldn't even register the pain as the toxic armor burned into his naked chest as he landed. He didn't need to finish Makolichi off – Eos'eno helped with that.

Piles of her own crystalline ice peppered Makolichi's exposed body. Bones broke and brine-soaked flesh was flayed off of him. While Akaran's vision blacked out, he saw the Abyssian roar and thrust itself upright. His head hit the ground as he heard a voice shouting out at him. He didn't hear what the Abyssian said, or see that someone else had just entered the fray.

Nor did he see what Daringol tried to do.

What he realized was that his own life was forfeit. His last thought before darkness took him was that at least, he had bought time for everyone to run to safety. He was wrong; they weren't going to run. They were going to stay, and they were going to fight.

Eos'eno pushed herself between the demon and the exorcist and willed a spiral of crystal out of the ground to wrap around Makolichi's legs. It caught him and held him fast even while he tried to batter the pure ice away with his only arm. It burned at his bones as badly as his ice had burned everyone else. Behind her though, another of the Daringol wraiths manifested out of thin air.

It was the biggest one that had made any kind of appearance thus far – at least the size and a half of the ones that had tried to siphon magic out of the broken fountain yesterday. It completely ignored Akaran and Hirshma, and went right for Makolichi's armor. Desperately eager tentacles lashed themselves to the construct as the monstrosity thrust itself inside.

It didn't make it. Someone else entered the fight – and took Daringol out of it.

"By Love's call, **I CONDEMN**!"

His voice cut across the field as the Word left his lips. The shout that followed served to punctuate his meaning. "By Her command, *I BANISH YOU!* BY HER WILL, I RETURN YOUR SOUL TO THE CONSTERNATION THAT GAVE YOU BIRTH!"

The second that the sentence left his lips, Daringol froze in mid-air. It didn't get time to try to shake the effects of the spell off before the heavily-armored man finished the job in a single move. With a thrust of his halberd as smooth and measured as only a master armsman could make it, the newest arrival to the battlefield cored the wraith straight through the center and out the other side.

"**EXPUNGE**!" At the Word, the spirit caught flame and boiled away in a cloud of black ash and pale lavender light on impact. The second thrust of his wrought-iron quarterstaff pierced the crumbling wreckage of the abyssian armor and gave it the same fate.

Nobody (conscious) knew who he was, but Makolichi realized that he had lost this fight. Openly frightened, the skeletal creature forced a fresh round of dagger-sharp brine shards to tear into his own legs above Eos'eno's glacial bonds and ripped them off at his knees. The second that it was free he sent the jagged blades at everyone else still standing.

The attack peppered the waif the worse and the man with the staff took a few shards to his chest as he shielded his fallen comrade. A lone blade scraped across Hirshma's eyebrow and nearly blinded her. It knocked Eos down, and kept the alchemist pinned. Akaran's ally shook the attack off with a furious gleam to his pure-white eyes and charged after the demon.

It was too late. While everyone was distracted, Makolichi vanished – where, and how, was anyone's guess. Fear of the newcomer's power was absolutely the only thing that kept it from being banished on the spot, and it knew it.

Akaran was also wrong about one other thing:

He wasn't going to die. Not here, not like this. Not today.

His friend rushed to him and dropped to his knees. A fog of white magic rolled off of his leather gloves and into the black spear of ice lodged in his stomach. "You bloody idiot, DON'T YOU DARE DIE ON ME!" The exorcist didn't respond. He didn't move, didn't twitch, and didn't breathe. He was going to be dead in a few more brief and struggling heartbeats if someone didn't do something drastic.

Eos'eno did.

The waif grabbed their newest ally and flung him back, shouting at the top of her lungs. Silvery blood spilled out of the wounds that covered her head to toe and seeped out of the corner of her mouth. She possessed enough strength to shove the paladin a few feet away and laid her own hands the exorcist. "No! No time no time, move, he has no time!"

Eos'eno grabbed Akaran by his shoulder, screamed his name, and they both vanished in a flurry of snowflakes that blanketed the bloody, muddy battlefield. All they left behind were victims and bodies, with no shortage of suffering in their wake. Two more damned souls had been ignored and left unaccounted for in the final minutes of the war; though they weren't discounted for long – and lasted for less than that.

Mariah-Anne picked up her grandfather's pick and used it to bash in the head of hounds' first victim, then drove it into Tornias's chest. Both of the zombies collapsed without further incident, ending what would be called the first *Battle of the Coldstone's Summit* as the wraiths that had taken over their corpses were forcibly returned to the pit. She looked around while her mentor crawled battered and bloody out of the fountain's wreckage and took in how much wanton destruction the fight had left behind.

If Akaran had heard her remark, he probably would have fallen in love with her right there and then.

"Shit."

Kneeling and fuming on the ground, their savior assessed the sorry state of everyone left alive and unleashed a curse that would have done the younger exorcist proud. Hirshma spoke up and offered a nervous, raspy challenge. "Don't... don't know who you are but if you mean us ill... we will fight, we will!"

He unleashed a second curse and stood up. He was clad in a steel plate cuirass with pale silver-steel chainmail under it and a matching set of greaves. He dropped his ruined cloak to the ground and slipped off a shining silver helmet that had only shown off his eyes. He struck an utterly intimidating figure to behold.

His eyes weren't just pale, they were completely white with no iris to be seen. He had dark hair that was graying in spots and a slight scar on his upper lip. It was the sigil that he pulled out from under his armor that hung on a gold chain down his neck that announced where he was from but it was the gravitas in his voice that demanded their full attention.

"My name is Paladin-Commander Steelhom, assigned to the Grand Temple of Love." Seething, he gave them a look so disgusted it could have churned milk. "*What* did that *idiot* boy do, and *where* did that elemental-kin take him?"

Nobody knew the answer to that question but a lot of people were soon to find out. None of them would like it. But finally, *finally*, someone had at least *one* last useful thing to say. "I... I don't... it can't be," Hirshma whispered, looking at where Eos'eno and Akaran had been.

"Miss? What can't be?"

"I... I know that scar, that bite. She... Eos'eno is my daughter! She's Mayabille!"

The paladin fixed both of them with a livid stare. "Should I care who that is?"

Mariah looked at the wreckage, looked at her mentor, and looked at Steelhom while he stood there waiting for someone to explain themselves. "Oh."

"Oh, shit."

End: Snowflakes in Summer
Book I of the Snowflakes Series
& The Battles of Coldstone's Summit

Akaran's adventure will continue (or will it?) in Book II of the Snowflakes

Series/The Battles of Coldstone's Summit! But before you pick up the next one in line, can you take a moment to leave a review on Amazon, Goodreads, or other? Your reviews matter – they tell me what I got right, what I didn't, and they even help me do a better job marketing. Love it or hate it, your thoughts and your opinions DO matter, and they help me become a better author down the line.

With that said, Steelhom needs to find his student, and Makolichi is still very much a threat. If they can't be stopped… then Makolichi's victims are just the first Dead Men in Winter.

Next: Dead Men In Winter
Book II of the Snowflakes Series
& The Battles of Coldstone's Summit

https://www.amazon.com/dp/B079VX7289

Joshua E. B. Smith

COMPENDIUM OF THE DAMNED
THE DIVINE
AND ALL THINGS IN-BETWEEN

Abyss/Abyssian Canyons/Abyssians
The pit. The last stop for the damned. A place of darkness and flame; of madness and pain. The Abyss is overseen by the Great Dragon-God Gormith, otherwise known as The Warden. The Abyss mirrors the Mount of Heaven and is otherwise ruled by the Fallen Gods, who rule over their own regions – the individual Abyssal Canyons. Abyssians are creatures – be they damned souls twisted through eons of torture, or things born of the Abyss itself – that call the unholy realm their home. Or at least, call it their prison.

Agromah
A fallen continental-kingdom to the North of Civa, Dawnfire, and more, across the Nightmare Sea. It is believed by most that the armies of the Order of Love abandoned the Order of Flames in the face of a demonic army lead by Archduke Belizal and his son. It's this belief (false as it is) that lead to Niasmis being exiled from the Upper Pantheon, and her followers to suffer the Hardening.

Akaran DeHawk, Exorcist
A neophyte exorcist in the Order of Love. Holds several minor exorcisms under his belt before being dispatched to Toniki, including a full-blooded demon. Has an... interesting... past that he doesn't talk much about. Specifically, he doesn't remember most of it.

Alchemist/Alchemy
A method of using the Laws of Normality to enhance mundane items throughout the world. Alchemists are also well known for their vast knowledge of potions, poultices, medicine, and poisons.

Bolintop Mine
North-east of Toniki, the mine was one of the few sources of sylverine ore in the eastern side of the Kingdom. When the roof collapsed and destroyed the pumping station in the middle of it, the mine was abandoned and nearly forgotten.

Charf Rats
Don't ask. Don't EVER ask.

Civan Empire
On the northern edge of the continental mainland, the Civan Empire boasts the largest concentration of followers of the Goddess of Flame in all of Kora. The Empire has been in a steady on-again-off-again series of wars with the Kingdom of Dawnfire for generations.

Demons/Daemons
*Demons are powerful beasts that roam the pit. Most have some degree of sentience, but not all. It's a catch-all phrase for the pitborn. Daemons, on the other hand, are demons of **immense** power and ability. These creatures represent massive threats to the world of the living, and even the Mount of Heaven.*

Equalin Mountains
The Equalin Mountain Range is a massive length of mountains that stretches across the middle of the continental mainland. It serves as a natural barrier between the Kingdom of Dawnfire, the Civan Empire, and the Free Cities of Ameressa. It is also home to the ever-warring tribes of barbarians and 'uncivilized' bands of nomads of the Midland Wastes.

Fellowship of the Alchemetic
Located in the city of Ameressa, in the Free Cities region on the continental mainland, the Fellowship of the Alchemetic is the ruling authority on all things alchemy. They are the true masters of their craft, and are sought after everywhere in the world.

(The) Free Cities of Ameressa

The Free Cities of Ameressa are a small kingdom in and of themselves, though they refuse to be acknowledged as such. They stand at the far east of the Equalin Mountains, the south-east of the Civan Empire, and well to the north-east of the Kingdom of Dawnfire. Home to the Fellowship of the Alchemetic, the Free Cities have forsaken the Gods in favor of the Laws of Normality – and they've forsaken rule by Kings, Queens, and Emperors in favor of an odd system of government called "democracy," which most of the rest of the developed world feels is a terrible idea that is destined to fail. Their feelings towards the rest of the world is just about as heart-felt and equal in derision and irritation.

Still, one can't fault them for how successful their systems of education, health care, and trade are...

Frosel
The Lower Elemental Plane of Ice. It is a freezing sea of saltwater and filled with glaciers that slice through the suffering souls condemned to it. All manner of monsters hide beneath the ever-churning currents to torment and terrorize.

Gonta
The sub-capital of Waschali Province. It's a three-day ride (under the best of circumstances, which haven't existed for a few years) away from Toniki, and at least a day's ride from the 13th Garrison.

Granalchi Academy
*Home of the Granalchi – masters of the arcane. They bow to no God as a whole, but simply seek to control and use elemental magic in any and all forms. While commune with the Gods to access upper and lower planes of magic is frowned upon, it is not verbosely forbidden. That being said, anyone that seeks to explore the vast power held in the Abyss is **strongly** encouraged to do so off of campus grounds. They'll also deny any knowledge of any student caught using forbidden arts – not that they aggressively seek to punish anyone that does.*

(The) Hardening
The Hardening is a direct punishment handed down by the Gods and Goddess on the Heavenly Mount against the Goddess of Love. Not only was She cast from Her rightful place on the Mount, every follower of every member of the Pantheon of Heaven turned hateful, spiteful, and antagonistic towards Niasmis and all of Her people. This lead to

immense persecution aimed at Her followers all across the world, and still persists two centuries later. The only place to offer Her people refuge was the Kingdom of Dawnfire... although the reasons behind that story is for another time.

Hunter's Guild (otherwise known as 'The Guild')
The Hunter's Guild is an organization filled to the brim with mercenaries, assassins, battlemages, and anyone else willing to make a quick bag of coin hunting people or things down. They get paid handsomely for their efforts, at that. They aren't to be confused with the more 'noble' exorcists and paladins, but they can do a wonderful job cleaning up any mess that the priestly Orders leave behind.

Kingdom of Dawnfire
Situated on the southern side of the mainland, the Kingdom of Dawnfire is home to one of the most diverse populations in the world. Followers of nearly all of the Orders of Light are welcome, and it is the only place in the known world where followers of the Goddess of Love are not (directly) persecuted. The Kingdom is comprised of six major provinces, each overseen by a provincial Maiden and her Consort.

Kora
The mortal world.

Laws of Normality
The laws that govern and declare what is 'natural' and what is 'magical,' as written by a combined effort of the Granalchi Academy, the Fellowship of the Alchemetic, the Handmaiden-Priestess of Purity, and the begrudging assistance (under threat of being boiled in a vat of oil) of a Harbinger of Plague (whom was summarily boiled in oil after the Laws were compiled... as a matter of course). The Laws of Normality cover everything from how mortal beings age to how living creatures must draw air and consume food, to how gravity works and the simple fact that the world is a globe. The Laws of Normality cover everything in every discipline of study – except anything remotely involving magic, which is treated as both abnormal and irritatingly ever-changing.

Lador
Capital of Waschali Province.

Order of Love

The followers of the Goddess of Love call the Order of Love home. It's divided into three separate branches: the Lovers, who spread the Word of Niasmis; the Templars, who use the boons of Love to heal the sick and injured; and the Paladins, the holy warriors and exorcists who use the powers granted by the Goddess to hunt and banish the dead and damned. The Order of Love is perceived to be chaotic, as the nature of Love is often unpredictable, and the Order itself is the most aggressive of all of the Heavenly Orders in seeking to expunge the unholy from the world.

Despite being despised by most of the planet, the Order of Love holds a special place in the Kingdom of Dawnfire, and has direct authority over the Grand Army of the Dawn. This authority has been granted by the Queen of Dawnfire herself, and as such, is incontestable (regardless of how much others may wish it otherwise).

Orders of Light
The Orders of Light are comprised of the various Gods and Goddess of the Mount of Heaven, with the exception of the Goddess of Love. The primary Order is the Order of Purity, and Her followers typically direct the other Orders in all manner of interactions in the Kingdom of Dawnfire and beyond.

Preternatural Beasts, Creatures, and Oddly-Animated Beings
Preternatural beasts are creatures that do not use magic as spells or incantations, but were simply gifted with it as a matter of creation or evolution. They are 'magical,' but they are not able to use magic outside of their immediate nature. There are creatures that can fly without having wings, and others that can phase through solid ground without disturbing a spec of dust. Pure "Elementals" fall under this classification, as they are a sentient manifestation of a specific element, but are otherwise alien in their rationality, sentience, and actions compared to 'normal' creatures.

Sisters of Love
Believed to be the only people that can hear the Word of Niasmis directly, they are the strongest members of the Order of Love, and they direct the actions of all three branches. They are able to engage in far-sight and, at times, a measure of future-sight; their ability to discern true evil from afar is matched by none. Their edicts are passed down directly to the Holy General, Johasta Fire-Eyes.

(The) Stewards of Blizzards
Priests of Istalla that dedicate their lives to preserving artifacts, antiques, and other works of art or amazement, to safeguard them against the ravages of time.

Sylverine Ore
An oft-sought-out amber-colored metal that can be used to either temper steel to resist magics or to provide a base for magical enchantments to take hold (depending on your school of study and ability), sylverine ore is only found in two of Dawnfire's provinces.

Teboria Lake
A large lake to the north of Toniki, nestled firmly in the mountains. The yearly thaw frequently causes the lake to overflow its shores, and send torrents of water down the streams that trickle down from it, serving to give Gonta the yearly nickname of 'The City of Mud'.

Tenants of Love
The Holy Scriptures of the Order of Love. It also doubles as a spell tome, and many a priest, paladin, and exorcist have added pages to the back of their copies to serve as their own personal testaments.

Toniki
A moderately-small village north of Gonta, and the northernmost town in the Kingdom of Dawnfire. Relatively unimportant, it boasted reasonable trade through both the efforts of the town alchemist, the blacksmith and the old Bolintop Mine – and it's steady supply of sylverine ore. When the mine collapsed, trade slowed to a crawl.

Treifragur
Often confused as the provincial capital of Waschali, even by scribes and authors of such tales who have to go back and correct their work in future revisions of the same tome... embarrassingly enough, it's one of those mistakes that always gets missed until after the scribe in question has already submitted it for the kingdom at large to read (and question).

Tundrala
The Upper Elemental Plane of Ice. Depicted in lore as filled with gentle mountains and snowy plains that stretch into eternity. Reportedly, the cold feels comfortable and invigorating, and the landscape pristine no matter how many times a peaceful soul strolls through.

Wards

Wards are divine Words placed on the ground (or another surface) that act to either dissuade unpleasant entities from approaching an area, to warn when one approaches, to help provide a measure of immunity against the effects that hostile magic may present. Some can even trap a befouled being.

Waschali Province

The easternmost provincial region of the Kingdom of Dawnfire. It holds immense strategic value to the Kingdom, as the primary passageway through the Equalin Mountains between the Kingdom of Dawnfire and the Civan Empire. Among other villages and cities, it encompasses Anthor's Pass, Triefragur, Gonta, and Toniki. It is under the direct oversight of Maiden Piata and her Consort.

Words

'Words,' as used by the magically-inclined members of the Order of Love, are specific spells used for a variety of effects. Some, such as 'Expulse,' 'Purge' and 'Expel' are used to banish the dead and defiled. Others, such as 'Luminoso,' are used to summon balls or flares of light that last an indeterminate period of time. 'Bonds' summon tendrils of magic (or in a specific case, silvery chains) that can act as a restraint (or in the case of said person, a weapon). There are far more Words than just these, and all of them hold power in one form or another.

Defiled

The 'defiled' are mortal/natural creatures that have been exposed to or twisted by Abyssian magic/auras to the point that they have become monsters in their own right. Corpses that have arisen from the dead on their own volition are lumped into this category, as are animals (or even people) that have been corrupted past the point of the Laws of Normality. Creatures, and even inanimate objects, that have been turned pose as much of a threat to the living world as demons... and some demons have been known to start out this way.

The Defiled can also be considered a broad category for various breeds of creatures that can fit on either side of the 'formerly alive' and 'entirely demonic' spectrum. Wraiths, for example, are often purely the souls of the dearly departed; dogs and wolves, given the right nudging, can grow into Abyssian hounds.

At the Battles of Coldstone's Summit, the notable Defiled included:

Abyssian Hounds
Nothing good can be said about these beasts. They are physically strong, fast, and violent. There is no way to reason with one, although they can be controlled (to an extent) by whomever or whatever summons them into being. They universally have thick black skin and rows of far-too-sharp teeth. They reek of sulfur and slaughter, hunt in packs, and should never be approached without caution.

Wraiths
Lost souls and malevolent spirits. They do not have a truly 'physical' form, though the concentration of foul magic and Abyssian energy that allows them to manifest on the mortal plane often allow them to interact with physical objects. Their numbers are legion and their powers varied from spirit to spirit. Some hold power and strength, others are barely shadows that still walk the world. They are the most common of the undead that haunt the living. Typically, they are relatively easy to dispatch, although non-enchanted or otherwise mundane weapons are rarely able to do any damage.

Zombies
Animated corpses. Through all sorts of twisted magic, bodies are able to rise from their resting places – be it by possession by a wraith, or by the direct actions of a necromancer or demon. At times, zombies will rise on their own if an area has been the site of terrible death and carnage. 'Zombie' is a catch-all phrase that includes shambling dead that can barely move to the fully-sentient and magically powerful Litches, or the horribly mutated and physically strong Zenorats. They are the second-most common form of the dead that roam the world.

Gods and Godlings
The World beyond the World is full of an infinite number of creatures and beings of immense power that dwarf anything mortal men can use. Some of those things are easier to cope with than others, and others still... are a different story entirely.

Illiya, the Goddess of Flame
Ruler of the Upper Elemental Plane of Fire, She has an ongoing rivalry with Her sister, Melia, the Goddess of Destruction. It should be noted that while Illiya is the Matron Goddess of Civa, Her sister is the Matron Goddess of Dawnfire. It is also worth noting that the followers of Illiya despise the Goddess Niasmis so strongly and fiercely that they persecute and kill anyone that bears allegiance to the Goddess of Love given any and all opportunities.

Istalla
The Queen of the Pure Ice, and ruler of Tundrala – the Upper Elemental Plane of Ice. Generally left alone, Her Stewards act as archivists and historians, as Ice preserves and protects all things in silent and peaceful cold.

Kora'thi
Goddess of Nature. She controls all-things Growth, and is the mother of the elemental Gods and Goddess. Her followers respect the lesser Gods of Nature, and have been known to work with them in the past.

Makaral
The Berzerker God, the God of War.

Neph'kor
God of Plague and Disease. Universally loathed and despised, even among the other Fallen. May well be the most hated Godling in all of creation. Despite that, He has followers everywhere – even if they're actively hunted by the priests of the Goddess of Purity, and openly challenged by the druids of Nature.

Niasmis, the Goddess of Love
Banished from Her rightful place next to the top of the Mount of Heaven by the other Gods and Goddess for an infraction against the Goddess of Flame that She truthfully is not guilty of, the Goddess of Love is considered by nearly everyone to be the least of the Divine, and as such, holds power only in the lowest regions of the Heavens, and... well... ...She has a bit of a chip on Her shoulder because of it...

Solinal
The God of Peace.

Uoom
The God of Death. Uoom's Ledger is the only record in all of creation of every man, woman, child, animal, angel and demon that was ever born or made – coupled with an ever-growing list of souls that have been and will be sent to everlasting eternity in one form or another.

Zell, the Brineblood
The Fallen God of Elemental Ice, and ruler of the plane of Frosel – the Lower Elemental Plane of Ice.

Joshua E. B. Smith

THE SAGA OF THE DEAD MEN WALKING

Year 512 of the Queen's Rule
The Snowflakes Trilogy
Book I: Snowflakes in Summer
Freshly minted by the Order of Love, a young exorcist is sent to the edge of the Kingdom of Dawnfire to deal with a 'small, simple haunting.' Between a winter that won't end, a girl that doesn't belong, and people being eaten in the woods, only one thing is for sure: he's over his head, and utterly out of luck.

Book II: Dead Men in Winter
As the search for the Coldstone continues, new allies enter the fray in the mountains around Toniki, and in the streets of the City of Mud. But new blood only means new bodies, and Makolichi seeks to provide those in excess...

Book III: Favorite Things
It's time for Usaic's Tower to ascend. Truths will be revealed, blood shall be spilled, and suffering shall become legendary. But it's not just the living who should fear the Coldstone being set loose. For though the dead will rise, the damned had best be ready for Who comes next...

Year 513 of the Queen's Rule
The Auramancer's Exorcism
Book I: Insanity's Respite
Beaten, broken, and battered, Akaran is sent to the Safest City in the Kingdom to recover from his battle against Makolichi, Daringol, Rmaci, and the rest. What he expects is peace and time to heal. What he finds instead is that insanity knows no bounds and offers no respite...

Book II: Insanity's Rapture
In life, the woman in his dreams had been a spy – a murderess, a liar, a fraud, and a thief. Sentenced to burn for her crimes, her screams have haunted his sleep since the moment she was set aflame. As both the city and Akaran's mind descend into chaos, only insanity offers rapture.

Book III: Insanity's Reckoning
The most dangerous man in the city is about to get his magic back – and he's got a murder on his mind. As he prepares to hunt a sadistic vampire, his past is about to come back to haunt him in a way he never could have imagined.

Book IV: Insanity's Requiem (Summer 2021)
It's time for the madness to end, but the insane have no desire to find peace –

and peace will only come when Basion City is turned into an open grave.

Origins of the Dead Men Walking
Year 510 of the Queen's Rule
Blind shot (Release date: TBA)
A self-professed Merchant of Secrets enlists the help of the Northern Hunter's Guild to trek to the Cursed Continent of Agromah to recover a relic lost to time. In this land of the dead, what chance does a blind man have against a demon king?

Year 512 of the Queen's Rule
Slag Harbor (An Interruption in the Snowflakes Trilogy)
After battling Makolichi in Gonta – and before facing him down for the final time in Toniki – Akaran decides to leave Private Galagrin behind in the City of Mud to make sure that nothing got missed in his sweep. What he finds is more than just stray shiriak; it's an answer to an unasked question...

Year 513 of the Queen's Rule
Lady Claw I: Claw Unsheathed
Who's to blame when a young girl is accused of murder? Did she do it, or did her father? And when she's cornered and the claws come out... does it matter?

Year 516 of the Queen's Rule
Fearmonger
Years after Toniki, a grizzled Akaran serves as a peacekeeper to the Queen – and nothing wants the peace to be kept.

Year 517 of the Queen's Rule
Blindsided
Stannoth and Elrok couldn't be any more different. Trained mercenaries in the Hunter's Guild, they absolutely hate each other – but they don't have a choice but to work together.

WELCOME TO A WORLD WHERE GOOD THINGS HAPPEN TO BAD PEOPLE AND THE GOOD PEOPLE ARE QUESTIONABLE... ...AT BEST.

Good things come to those who wait, but I'm impatient as the fires in the Abyss are hot (or cold, depending on Frosel). I'm working on the next book as fast as I can (I promise!) and I've got some stuff for you.

Please be sure to follow me on social media to find out where I'm going, what I'm doing, how I'm doing it, and the occasional stupid meme just to laugh. Plus, get some random business insights on the self-published side of the coin AND see what I'm doing when I dress up for charity purposes.

You can expect free stories, character information, special promotions, extra information about the World of the Saga, and more from the Dead Men Emailing Newsletter! Be sure to visit and subscribe (it'd mean a lot to me if you did)!

Amazon.com:
https://www.amazon.com/author/sdmw

Facebook.com:
https://www.facebook.com/sagadmw

Website:
http://www.sagadmw.com

Twitter:
https://www.twitter.com/sagadmw

Dead Men Emailing Newsletter
http://www.sagadmw.com/email.html

ALSO!
Please don't forget to leave a review. Your opinion on the story (and the series!) MATTERS. Loved it or hated it, thought it was amazing or thought it was garbage, your feedback helps me be a better author and helps me provide the best experience that I can for not just you, but other readers in the future. Let me know on any media platform – just be sure to tag me if you can, but a review anywhere is awesome!

Made in the USA
Middletown, DE
21 October 2021